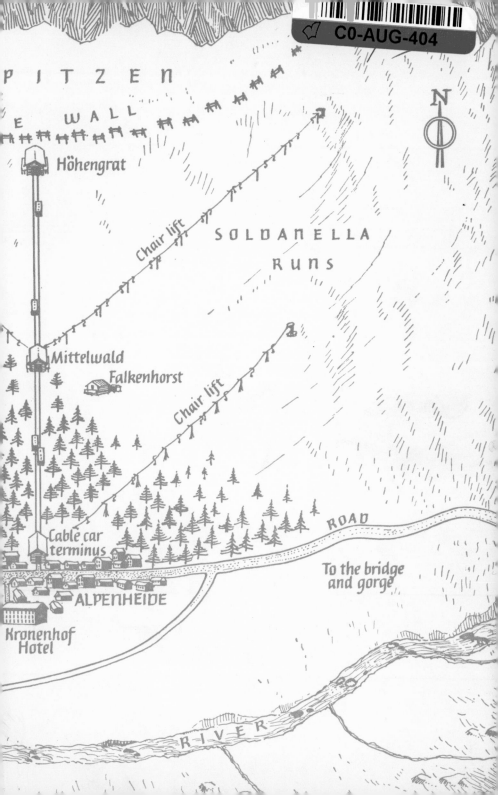

PITZEN

E WALL

Höhengrat

Chair lift

SOLDANELLA

RUNS

Mittelwald

Falkenhorst

Chair lift

N

Cable car
terminus

ROAD

To the bridge
and gorge

ALPENHEIDE

Kronenhof
Hotel

RIVER

CAB-INTERSEC

by David Walker

cab-intersec

BY DAVID WALKER

HOUGHTON MIFFLIN COMPANY

BOSTON 1968

To Mark Bonham Carter

CAB-INTERSEC

ONE

The month was February, and it happened to be my forty-second birthday. At eleven o'clock or thereabouts I was still wearing silk pajamas and a dressing gown in my flat at the foot of St. James's Street where traffic whined uphill through slush. On a footstool in front of me was that labyrinthine game with the two knobs, a metal ball and fifty pitfall holes you have to survive to the winning post. The board floated in gimbals, like a compass. My watch handy to the eye, I timed myself, reducing it to nineteen seconds, seventeen, and then a cool fifteen, not too bad for a chap who reached home at 4 A.M. Hermione had taken me out to dinner and the rounds, slipping crisp tenners tactfully below the table. Harry Ambler, gigolo. I groaned at that and got up to inspect myself.

The eyes were clear as white china, the features gravely handsome. In deciding to write this account, I have taken a vow to tell the truth and nothing but the truth, omitting the whole truth on occasion. So I admired my image, which hardly deserved to be so prepossessing, and went back to break all records with that game. My ambition was to get up and down in thirty seconds. Playing one knob with utmost delicacy and verve against the counterbalance of the other, I positively shot past every hazard to my goal and was starting back when the telephone rang. Hermione probably, she could wait. Home again — I had nearly clipped the thirty seconds. That thing still rang.

"Sorry," I said. "I was playing a game."

A moment's silence at the other end, certainly not Hermione. "Is that Mr. Ambler?"

"Yes, him. Harry Ambler speaking." Some creditor, I supposed.

"This is Brock Enterprises . . ."

"Sorry. I didn't get the Enterprises."

"*Brock* Enterprises — Sir Conrad Brock Enterprises."

The name clicked somewhere vaguely. "Yes?"

"Would you be able to come to our offices in Dover Street this morning?"

"What about — I mean, why?"

"It might be greatly to your advantage, Mr. Ambler." The woman's voice was cool and quiet.

Anything to my advantage would be a change greatly for the better. It was coming up to eleven-thirty. Shave, dress, five minutes' walk. "I can drop in about twelve," I said. "Who do I ask for?"

"Ask for the General Manager," she said. "At twelve, then, Mr. Ambler."

Being a quick mover in most physical respects, I was ready for the road by a quarter to. A man from Ballard's was due about the silver at three-thirty. My mother's Queen Anne desk had already gone, and so had the six Hepplewhite chairs, the two Stubbs, the Canaletto. The flat was a half-empty shambles, soon to be vacated. I could tidy it a bit after lunch. And lunch was with Hermione, more sponging, more passionate monologues about good works as she edged me back to the bedroom wall.

I walked up St. James's Street. It was rain now, pattering on bowler hat and waterproof. My umbrella stayed furled. I went into the club, said hello to Parsons, got myself a glass of sherry, and looked at *Who's Who* in the reading room.

Brock, Sir Conrad Angus . . . K.B.E. . . . Born 1903, educated Geelong Grammar; Jesus College, Cambridge. Chairman, Brock Enterprises etc.; AIE 1939-45. D.S.O., Crete. No recreations mentioned. *Addresses: Wirrawarra, Victoria; Halcombe Manor, Kent. Clubs: Melbourne; Travellers; Tavern; Royal and Ancient.*

It occupied about an inch and a half. There is mild amusement to be had from *Who's Who* — the simple vain who list their nothings in a whole column; the common run who stick to essential highlights more or less; the inverted snobs with much to state and nothing stated.

Outside again to this miserable day. Everyone else was hurrying, but I strolled wetly, crossed St. James's Street and continued to Piccadilly, passing those pavement grilles where down-and-outs huddle on winter nights to warm their backsides with plutocratic vapors, and I would soon be one of them. As it was, a penniless capitalist to the manner born, I crossed Piccadilly and walked along Dover Street to Brock Enterprises near the shoe shop, third floor up.

I knocked and went in. The receptionist was squeezed into a black silk dress amid leather armchairs and wall-to-wall. "Hang them up," she said, nodding toward a coat rack. I did so. "He's here," she said into an intercom.

I followed the ample woman through an office where two

girls were typing X hundred words a minute on electric ma-
chines; a ticker machine ticked too. On the glass half of the
door was: *General Manager,* and below it: *Miss M. Dunn.*

Miss M. Dunn, General Manager, did not move. "Do sit
down," she said, reading something.

The outside office had been plush-rich, but this was all right
— a big Shiraz carpet or imitation, waxed floor, a walnut tall-
boy in the corner, a couple of abstracts, an Australian Aborig-
inal painting — ghost gums, red rock, blue mountains and distance, the unbelievable country until you have seen it. It was a
hodgepodge, quite soothing to the eye.

The practicals of action and beauty I am fairly good at, but
in the humdrum middle ground a flop. Which meant at that
moment a bankrupt flop, being accorded a flop's reception.

There were three doors from this room: one through which
I had come, another to the corridor, a third wide and paneled
beyond the General Manager, presumably yielding access to
Sir Conrad. The only office indications were on her flat desk or
table: two file-boxes, the intercom and three telephones, black,
red and white. Two mean an outside line. Three mean something more. I noticed this, and then I observed Miss Dunn —
a pale face with a long long nose tipped at the end, black hair,
not just dark but gleaming black as the Iroquois's. She wore a
tweed coat and skirt, or so one supposed from the visible jacket,
a darker color than Colman's Mustard. Now she looked up at
me and said quietly, "Can you drive down to Kent with me,
Mr. Ambler? Sir Conrad would like to see you."

"When?"

"We should leave in five minutes."

"Today isn't on," I said. "I'm lunching with someone; and
then a chap's coming to my flat at half past three on business." The business was my Georgian silver.

"I think Sir Conrad's business might be worth your while, much better value than lunch and half past three."

And what would Miss Dunn know about the values of lunch and half past three? "Please," she said. "I do mean it." She smiled a little, her mouth going widely opposite to the nose. It was an odd face, something new to me.

"What excuse can I make for lunch, no good at excuses?"

She did not hesitate. "Say the solicitor called from Chelmsford — some final papers in the winding-up of Lady Emma's estate which absolutely must be signed today, so you have to catch the 12.47."

"But she'll want to drive me there. Sure as fate she will."

"Say; *No, thank you very much,*" said Miss Dunn tartly. "You can use the telephone in the outer office."

How come she knew about my late Aunt Emma? I didn't like it, not one little bit, but . . . I passed the two typing girls again, their keys rat-tatting at machine-gun speed, not even glances for me, it was surprising; and, using the fat receptionist's telephone (she must have taken off for lunch), I carried out my orders, even to *No, thank you very much* about the lift to Chelmsford. Hermione took a dim view.

"Let's go," said Miss Dunn in her mustard tweeds, plastic raincoat on the arm. I followed her to the lift, noting configuration, which was excellent. I was trying to remember the expression. *"Jolie laide,"* I said. "That's it."

"What?"

"H'mm," I said.

The lift stopped at B, and we emerged to a garage, which held several gleaming cars.

"The Bentley," she said. "Hop in."

I obeyed. One could not imagine oneself doing otherwise. A door slid up with equally automatic obedience at the top of a ramp, and we followed the lane or mews to Berkeley Street.

Twenty minutes later, London was thinning on the way to Maidstone. As one might have expected — somehow it was inevitable — she drove well, almost as well as I do myself.

"I'm thirsty and peckish. Let's stop for lunch."

"There's a picnic basket on the floor behind you. That's sherry in the flask. Would you mind eating as we go along?"

"What about you?"

"I never have lunch."

The rain had stopped. Patches of open sky came and went, and Diesel lorries threw wet dirt at us. She kept washing the windscreen while I drank Oloroso and smoked a cigarette. Then I tucked into a warm garlic *pain* with butter and lashings of pâté de foie gras, genuine Strasbourg, and a bottle of strong ale. It was some picnic lunch, ending with that marvelous fruit that tastes like a good grape, only better. "Litchis," I said. "I haven't had 'em since where was it?"

She did not help me. "Miss Dunn," I said. "What does the M stand for?"

"Mary, Mr. Ambler."

"What part of Australia are you from?"

"Victoria originally. How . . . ?" but she stopped.

"The way you say Mary. Slightly as in Litch*ee*."

"Oh," she said, taking a red sports job at ninety or so and back into line.

"Miss Dunn!"

"Yes, Mr. Ambler?"

"You kidnap me in a manner of speaking, virtually. Not only that, you seem to know about me, personal affairs and all that. How come?"

"Sir Conrad will explain. There's coffee, if you want."

It was espresso in a thermos, delicious with a gob of cream.

"Thanks for my wizard lunch, thanks to you or Brock or both."

"I am employed by Brock Enterprises. Thank them for your wizard lunch."

We were round Maidstone, hotwheeling it for Ashford in drizzle again. "This Brock," I said. "I looked him up at the club. He doesn't give much about himself in *Who's Who,* in fact downright cryptic."

"Sir Conrad wouldn't," she said. "Damn your impertinent little eyes," she added to a souped-up Mini nipping and tucking itself in front of us.

"What's he do?"

"What does Sir Conrad do?"

"That's what I asked. For his bread and butter, got it?"

"Got it," she said. "I wish I had." Miss Dunn emitted quite a human chuckle; and then she told me a bit about Sir Conrad Brock, Australian grazier, financier and industrialist. The Enterprises aspect was the holding company, below its tentacles (not her expression, mine) International Beef, Wirrawarra Wool, Queensland Sugar, Brock Publishing Company . . .

"What sort of publishing?"

"First, Bibles and school textbooks, they're the surefire gravy, as Sir Conrad says."

"H'mm."

"And natural history too — incidentally, Sir Conrad is an ornithologist of some repute."

"H'mm."

"And a small trade department — novels and that kind of thing. Sir Conrad writes those losses off to culture."

"H'mm."

"But Brock Electronics, with subsidiaries and affiliates in Japan, the United States, West Germany and the United Kingdom — that has become Sir Conrad's major interest."

"What kind of electronics?"

"Space systems," she said. "Communication media."

We had left the main road and were piling it on between high hedges. "What's electronics, anyway?" I asked, to occupy my mind, now nervous.

"Lord, you're dumb," said Miss Dunn, moderating for a tractor, and on we sped.

"Dumb I may be, but you define it."

"Don't you know what an electron is?"

"Something negative that moves, if I've got it right."

"Got it right," she said.

We idled through a village, and on beside a high wall for a mile or so to wrought-iron gates and a lodge adjoining them.

The man came through a side gate and to her window, touching his fore-and-aft gamekeeper's hat. "Good afternoon, Miss Dunn."

"Hi, Maddox," she said. "This is Mr. Ambler."

"How d'you do, sir."

"How do," I said. Dumb I may be, but I can tell a working gamekeeper when I see one. This chap was too tidy, too polished as to boots, too interested in cataloging me — a good keeper's eye wanders shiftily from human beings in the open air. But Maddox took my measure as casually and professionally as any cop, and went to unlock the big gates. "Dirty day, Miss Dunn," he said as we passed him.

The locked gates were unusual. Bare wires and insulators near the top of the inner side of the wall were more so. We rolled slowly along an avenue of lime trees from which jackdaws flew and called. I opened my window, listening to them. "I had a pet jackdaw once," I said.

"Did it steal things?"

"Died too young for much stealing. Well, actually . . ."

But I did not feel like telling her that actually my jackdaw took ill and I killed not cured it with too much kindness in the shape of brandy. How true of me, child, father, man. The window hummed up, obedient to my button. But even my button was junior to her master set. The left-hand window came down an inch again to put me in my place.

The house now hove in sight, rectangular, of reddish stone, early nineteenth century, quite pleasing of aspect, with a broad sweep of steps rising to a black front door.

"Look!" I said. "Can't you give me a clue? I mean, what *is* all this in aid of?"

"Don't worry. Sir Conrad will explain."

The Bentley hissed on wet tarmac, swished onto a gravel circle, stopped. "Well, here we are," she said. "Hop out." *Hop in*, she said in London. *Hop out*, she said in Kent.

TWO

The front door opened at our approach. "Hi!" she said again. "McVitie, this is Mr. Ambler."

"A guid day to ye," McVitie said. He wore a butler's dark clothes and a bouncer's physique, looked me over and said to her, "Sir Conrad's awa' doon playin' wee games tae hissel by yon burrn fornent the rhodies. He says for to tell ye tae pu' on boots. Whit size?" the man demanded of me.

"Tens or so," I said. I am an easygoing chap, but I can do without rude Scotsmen at the best of times, which this was not. Wellingtons were produced for me from a cloakroom, and Newmarket boots for Miss Dunn — her own, perhaps, from the excellent fit; and we sallied out to steady drizzle. The Yale lock clicked; I heard a chain go on. So much for open house at Halcombe Manor.

"It's too bad about the day. Halcombe is such a lovely place, with the parks and the swans in the lake. I wonder where McVitie meant. But he gets rather cross if you don't understand his funny language. Do you know Scotch well, Mr. Ambler?"

"Used to," I said. "Every summer holidays. He may

have meant that Brock is having little games to himself by the brook beside the rhododendrons or the Rhode Island Reds; shrubs or poultry, you can take your pick."

"Now I know exactly where he is. Sir Conrad is having fun with ditches, his wet-weather hobby." Soon we came to a swollen brook. It ran through a low-lying dell, with rhododendrons along high banks above. The man wore thigh boots and waterproof top. He was working with a square-ended spade.

"Hi, Sir Conrad!"

"Hold it — nearly through." He cut a last divot, lifted it, and water gushed down his personal ditch to join the brook. "Now watch her empty, satisfies ya, eh?"

Her was a big puddle, thirty foot or so across, and she emptied with a satisfying rush. Brock walked over. Australians come in two shapes roughly — the beanpole and the barrel. Brock came in the former — elongated, face scored and chapped old leather, eyes bloodshot, hands like muttons. "Mary!" he said. He put an arm across Miss Dunn's shoulders and gave her a hearty kiss just off or nearly on the lips which she returned with interest. "You speak to Pandex?"

"I told him to reduce inventories by half, get rid of Daddy Smith and Junior, scrap Mini-TV, cancel all stock options, and we might consider."

"Who'd you speak to?"

"Daddy Smith."

"Good." Brock chuckled, presumably about his ruthless employee telling an old man to get rid of himself, and she gazed at him as softly as any female slave. Brock turned to me. "She feed you properly?"

"Been fed worse in my time," I said. I was browned-off at their bad manners.

Brock laughed, great unbridled guffaws as he watched his

handiwork. "Diggin' ditches," he said. "Biggest ploy in Pommy Land."

"A nice change from Aussie Land." That hit home. I had hurt the tender feelings of these Down Under toughs.

"But Aour Country's rainfall . . ." protested Brock.

"Just consider Aour Country's Snowy Mountain Scheme."

"Look," I said, grasping the initiative. "You shanghaied me here. Now let's have the whys and wherefores."

"Fair enough," Brock said, and we turned for Halcombe Manor. "Max Vyan mean anything to you?"

"Max Vyan," I said. *Max Vyan.* Long ago, how long? Twenty-one years now, half my lifetime ago. But a lot of memories about Max Vyan whipped past as new as yesterday. "Yes," I said. "If it's the same one, I escaped from Germany with Vyan."

"Have you seen him since?"

I shook my head. "The last time I saw Max was at Patton's HQ in March, 1945."

"Have you heard of him?"

"Lately, yes — in the past year or two. I saw photographs of him in the *Queen,* at Gstaad and some other place. He made a fortune in the Argentine, I read somewhere. Once or twice I thought of writing Max a letter, but as usual nothing came of it. What's the name of that other place they said he heli-coptered over from?"

"Alpenheide," Brock said. "Were you cobbers, real close mates?"

Real close mates? Close partners, yes, walking by night across the wreck of Germany, closer than real mates anywhere. But Max was the boss; he called every tune. *You realize that if we were recaptured it would mean a bullet each for certain?* he said the first time he spoke to me. *So we go on those terms.*

And those terms meant a couple of quiet killings on the way, both done by Max Vyan with Harry Ambler as accomplice stooge. But I had my uses. I glided him out of Heifetz Castle. I flew him across the lines in a Fieseler Storch. Max contrived to short its ignition. I contrived to fly it, never having seen one before, but a hedgehopper thing like that was a piece of cake, and we made it, Superman and I made it, thanks to one another. How vivid that seemed now again. "Not real close mates," I said. "Vyan was not what you'd call a real close cobber-maker." Supermen ain't, I thought.

We squelched on in silence. There were ewes and lambs in this park in Pommy Land. "We have to fence off the greens just now," Brock said. "You play golf, Mr. Ambler?"

"At it," I said. "I see you're a member of the R. and A. Now it's time you explained this prying into my affairs, and hijacking to Kent and all the rest of it."

"You must have looked *me* up," Brock said mildly.

"In *Who's Who*," I said. "And apart from the little she told me in the car, and perhaps reading your name Down Under, I don't know a thing about you from old Adam. And now all this Max Vyan. It's time you came clean."

"It certainly is," Brock said. "And I will. But first let me say that there is nothing out of order or out of the usual in making inquiries about a man's circumstances and his doings. How else, for instance, can credit be established?"

"Disestablished in my case," I said, and Brock laughed. It struck me that under the hard shell there might be a likable type. "So you found out that I flopped first with an air outfit in Australia, and then I lost a packet with an air outfit in the Canadian North, and after blowing the rest of my parents' cash, I lost Aunt Emma's little lot and more on those bloody broilers. So here I am on my uppers. Well?"

"Those bloody broilers," he said in a kindly way, "too little working capital and most of it squandered before you even got production rolling, and that crook who fleeced you and the kitty. Anyone could have told you."

"Yes, anyone," put in Miss Dunn.

"Why the hell didn't you, then?"

"But you didn't ask us," they said together.

The idea of Brock Enterprises taking time off International Beef and Wool and Sugar and Bibles and Communication Media to put my now defunct broilers in the black seemed not unfunny vaguely somehow, but we walked on in grave silence until she said, "Oh, the poor thing!"

"Go on ahead, Mary."

It was a rabbit in the late stages of that disgusting myxomatosis. Brock killed it efficiently with his spade. "One more dead bastard," he said. "Soft-hearted, is our Mary. Wouldn't hurt a fly out of business hours."

Brock leaned the spade against a stone lion at the foot of the steps. The front door opened as before at our approach. "Yer tea's in the liberry," announced that butler, locking up again. Then he took Miss Dunn's Newmarket boots, his employer's waterproof clothing, mine with a sniff but no comment. He had a barrel chest, but the left side looked even more barrelish near the shoulder of his black jacket — a gun, I thought. McVitie went away, and I glanced at the locked and chained front door.

"Surprising as it may seem, there have been two armed robberies in this part of Kent in recent weeks," said Brock. "Hence we have to be a little careful." His manner was now quite smooth, noticeably different from his ditch-digging manner. The whole set-up had me suspicious and uneasy, so I decided to play it cool, take nothing amiss.

"Good tea," I said. It was a proper Australian brew, black as coffee in monstrous cups. Also Patum Peperium and cress sandwiches galore, and a delicious shortbread cake with strawberries between the layers. "Right good scoff," I said, looking round the library — books on art and birds in lower shelves, leather-bound tomes above, the complete Oxford. It was a lived-in room, not a tycoon's showpiece.

Miss Dunn also tucked into the food, making up for no luncheon, and soon was on her second quart of tea. Sir Conrad Brock toyed with both; then went to look out, silhouetted against late sun. Her eyes kept stealing to her lord and master, and mine to that Cyrano nose. I closed my left eye and held out my right forefinger to cover up the tip, what would she look like with a common member? She turned and caught me at it.

"We owe you an explanation," Brock said at the window. "In fact we owe you several. But first I must ask for your word that what is said in this room remains confidential — entirely confidential as between us three."

"You spill the beans," I said. "If no crookery's involved, I'll keep my mouth shut."

Brock turned, and they both stared at me. The feeling was uncomfortable. For the first time it was deliberately revealed to me that this interview was no confidential game of tiddlywinks. Without saying a single word, they warned me. The message came in loud and clear.

"More tea?" she said, perhaps to gild the poison pill.

"Just a halfie," I said.

"No crookery," said Brock, his back to me again. "Let me see, one afternoon, three years ago, no four, I was at the farm, late February, this time of year, our hottest weather. I remember very well — I had killed a tiger snake at the garden wall, came to look at the thermometer, a hundred and three, went to move the sprinklers on the lawn — that's a blessing, plenty of water on the farm — we're close to the Grampians, you know 'em in the Western District, gotta lovely water table?"

"Yes," I said. "I used to fly over that country."

"I was going back into the house when I heard a clank of someone crossing the cattle grill — it was an old Abo, something out of the ordinary because you don't see many Abos down our way. So I asked him in and gave him a slake of beer, no words spoken, you know how it is. Then he wandered to the porch where he had left his swag, his blanket roll y'know, and he brought in two things. The first was a cardboard cylinder, in it a rolled painting, a landscape, not of our district but a thousand miles away — the Centre, perhaps round Alice, ghost gums and red rocks and sand you couldn't credit unless you knew they were true. *You do this?* I said, and the old Abo nodded. Did you happen to notice it in Mary's office?"

"Yes," I said. "I liked it too. Go on."

"The other thing he produced was a leather bag, like the bag for a salmon reel you sometimes see. He undid it and poured out some semi-precious — the usual, like garnets, and a few colored pebbles. Well, to make a long story short, I bought his picture for ten quid, and the stones for a tenner too, far more than they were worth, and I offered him a lift along the way wherever he was going, or a bunk if he wanted.

"But he nodded his gray pate towards the Grampians, and the last I ever saw of him was shambling along beside the hot black bitumen; and then the Southern Doctor blew up and I opened windows to let the cool in. That's worth all the heat, that Southern Doctor compared with this god-forsaken climate. So I picked up the old chap's treasures to store them in a drawer — I was listening for the plane, the wife due back from Melbourne — and one of those pebbles seemed greasy in my hand, egg-shaped it was, the biggest of the lot, about the size of a pullet's egg, and I put it under the kitchen tap; still felt greasy, like a big drop of bluish gum. Well then, something hit me — ridiculous but just let's see — so I got a pointed awl, hard steel and sharp, but I could make no impression, not a sign, not a mark on it."

He paused in telling his story, back to me, whipped binoculars from the windowsill, said: "A goldcrest in the cedar of Lebanon, thought as much," put them down, and continued: "Next morning I sent a dozen men to look for that old Abo just in case the unbelievable might be true, and myself I flew to Melbourne to a jeweler who had done a few jobs for me before, bloke I could trust. True enough, it was a diamond, four hundred and eighty-three carats, by far the biggest ever found in Our Country. But no trace of the Abo, I didn't even know his name — and the painting unsigned too; I suppose he couldn't write.

"I know this story sounds like the original cock 'n' bull, but it's true." He looked round at me. I nodded. I believed him. Miss Dunn sighed faintly about something or other.

"It happened that I had to go to the States and then Europe soon after that, to be away all our winter. So I took the stone to Amsterdam, and they cut it for me, what's called an emerald cut. Show him the photo, Mary.

"Actual size," he said, "set in platinum with its own baguettes for the necklace, pretty, eh?"

"Pretty!" I said. "It's fabulous." The size was fabulous, but more fabulous than that was the blue-white luster, the extraordinary living sparkle even in a colored photograph. "It was to be a surprise present for the wife," Brock said. "I'm away a lot and she's worth ten farm managers to me. Won't travel herself, not out of Our Country. So I took my Koala Diamond with me that October, by America again — I called it the Koala to meself, first great diamond from Our Country, good name too. Well, I caught the afternoon Pan Am from London Airport, first class nearly empty, and I asked the stewardess for a whisky and soda, *one,* and the next thing I knew we were coming into Idlewild, must have passed out cold, and the next time I opened my locked briefcase was at the Waldorf Towers." He paused. "No Koala."

"What about the Customs?"

"I was in transit," he said, a touch lamely.

"Sir Conrad has virtually worldwide customs clearance," said Miss Dunn. "I should hope so too."

"But you hadn't declared it, so you couldn't even mention, eh?"

"That's the size of it," Sir Conrad said.

It was a funny thing, but I had believed all his story until about after the point where his wife was worth ten farm managers to him; then the rest was cock 'n' bull. Don't ask how I knew it, but I did. I am a simple chap, with sometimes that little extra hunch less simple chaps do not have. "H'mm," I said. "Bad luck. What next?"

"What next is that we have reason to believe my Koala is in the possession of Max Vyan."

"What reason?"

"A reliable tip-off," Brock said. "We hear that his . . . er female companion has been seen wearing it."

Miss Dunn frowned. It was that faint involuntary frown of virtuous disapproval, or it was that small frown of envy the good girls feel about the bad, or it was a bit of both?

"H'mm," I said. "You mean Vyan's secretary, or something different?"

Brock turned. He had a thatch of hoary eyebrows, and they twitched at me, perhaps suspiciously.

"Where do I come into it?"

"That depends. May I ask you one more question?"

"Go ahead." The sound of a plane grew rapidly — twin-engined turbo-prop, I thought. It swung in from the west, and I heard the change of pitch, coming in for a landing not far away. Miss Dunn looked down at her bare knees again, or nyloned knees beyond her short skirt. I liked her legs, no chap could help it. That nose bothered me.

"Did you part from Vyan on good terms in 1945?"

"I think so. Fact, I know so. We were never close buddies, I told you that. For one thing, he was ten years older. But age was not the point. People Max had no use for, he ignored or pulverized. People he could use, he used. He used me, for instance, treated me always the same — as a kind of joke, surprisingly enough." Miss Dunn snorted slightly. Yes, it was a turbo-prop, I heard the taxiing whistle. "As far as I know, we parted on the best of terms."

"Then I have a proposition to make," said Brock. "I have had a diamond necklace stolen from me, worth at a conservative estimate a million sterling plus. I cannot be sure, but I think Vyan has it, and no doubt from his point of view legitimately acquired. All I ask of you is to go to Alpenheide, meet Vyan casually again, or let him meet you on your skiing holiday. You ski very well, we understand?"

"So-so. You mean you want *me* to pinch your diamond back?"

"No," he said. "Most emphatically not." Brock paced the room, quite agitated. "I want you to do *nothing more* than find out whether Vyan has my Koala; and if our source is right, it would in all probability be on the person of, of — is Tanya the name, Mary?"

"Ugh-hugh."

"I remember now," I said, "from the photograph — Tanya Von something or other, and a smasher. That doesn't sound like too much hardship. But snooping on Max Vyan? I've got nothing against old Max. In fact, in most ways I admired him."

Brock gave me his full attention. For the second time I felt a mite uneasy. "You are penniless," he said. "And not only penniless but quite heavily in debt. You lose your flat in ten days' time. I am not asking you to undertake anything in the smallest degree dishonorable. You get on good terms with him. You ask no questions. You simply have to be yourself as you are when in funds, and we will see that you *are* in funds. You must not try to be clever — above all not that."

"Just be yourself," said Miss Dunn.

"And what do I get out of it?"

"Your debts paid off, a car, five thousand pounds — one thousand down, and the balance on completion of your mission, all tax free. There's no catch in it," Brock said.

I was pretty sure there was, but did not bat. "Okay," I said. "Sounds fair enough."

"Mary will arrange the details. You will follow her orders and injunctions to the letter. Clear?"

"Clear," I said.

Brock came over. "Let's shake on it," he said. We did. He was an old scoundrel, but I liked him.

"And now I must speed you and Mary on your way. Other guests are arriving." There were sounds beyond the oak door of the library. Brock stood before it, one hand casually on top of one of those big globes, the kind on which you can trace orbits if you have the ability and inclination. But he was barring the door. "Our people from West Germany, and a fine lot of blokes they are. I tell you what, Ambler — how about a game of golf when you get back from your travels?"

"I'd like to," I said.

"It's only nine holes, a typical park course, but reasonably bunkered . . ." A door closed outside, and Brock stopped stalling for time. He followed us into the hall where McVitie was en route to the cloakroom with an armful of navy blue raincoats; but he put them down on a bench and went to manipulate the chain and lock for us. Those dark standard waterproofs — from dressy West Germany? — it seemed unlikely.

"Good-bye," Brock said to me. "And the best of luck." He exchanged a kiss with his General Manager that was certainly not less than friendly. "Tomorrow, then, Mary child."

Yes, Sir Conrad." And we were going down the graceful steps of Halcombe Manor, before us the lake with a pair of swans, the park beyond it, all as peaceful and English as could be. The Bentley stood across, English as good solid streamlined English; and the colossal black Mercedes, if not English, was certainly solid plutocratic, now rolling round a corner of the house, presumably to its stable quarters.

"A Six Hundred," she said. "Sir Conrad's Number One car. Hop into Number Two."

THREE

Down at the gates the man named Maddox responded to her toot. "Evening's clearing away nicely, Miss Dunn," he said, his glance sliding over me to con the empty back compartment. "Traffic's heavy, so the wireless says."

We were on the London road by lighting-up time. She drove more slowly going back, keeping at the speed of traffic.

"This farm Brock speaks of in Victoria — a small place?"

"It's one of the biggest stations in the Western District, twenty-five thousand acres, all prime grazing land."

"Why call it a farm, then?"

"A good grazier like Sir Conrad doesn't put on dog."

"To call twenty-five thousand top-quality acres a farm in Australia is putting on arsey-tarsey dingo dog."

"God, you're annoying."

"Well, thanks," I said. "You're employing me. You asked for it."

"I know," she said. "It's only that Sir Conrad is such a super bloke that to suggest he puts on dog is just absurd. He may seem a bit rough-and-ready sometimes, even hard-bitten on the surface, but that's not the real Sir Conrad we adore so much."

"Who? His harem?"

"Sex," she said. "You're obsessed with it."

"First time I've even hinted at the subject."

"Your record more than hints at it," she said. "And you keep staring, Ambler. Sex is for juveniles in my opinion."

"Hear, hear," I said. "Now suppose you get down to the details of this job. Five thousand tax-free smackers and my debts paid off for locating a rock seems just a bit too easy and too much, to put it mildly."

"I know," she said. "I saw you thinking that in the library, and I don't wonder. But if you realize that the five thousand is not much more than a thousandth part of the value of that rock, does it seem so absurd?"

"Good point. The whole thing's out of my league. Well, let's have the details, Dunn."

It was fully dark now. She drove with her headlights dipped, keeping well back from the car in front. Dunn gave me the details while I sat away in my corner absorbing them; the cash in bank, the travelers' checks, the Silver City flight, the booking at the Kronenhof in Alpenheide; and then special instructions about communicating — only these last seemed in the least to sound like cloak-and-dagger. "That's the routine stuff, Ambler. Now two things: The first one is that you've got to be the genuine article — genuine rich Ambler as you used to be before you spivved it all."

"I was never genuine rich, just so-so twice. And what's spivvin' it, for instance, about that prang in the Barren Lands, the plane a write-off and two hundred miles through muskeg on my lonesome? You call that spivving it?"

"Not on your lonesome, I wouldn't," she said. Which was a crack about the Eskimo girl who happened to be along. Was there anything these people did not know?

"As I was saying when you interrupted me, it is necessary that your wealth should seem to be your own, and should bear investigation too. Accordingly, we have taken steps to obliterate your broiler fiasco; and we have taken care of that crook who took you for a ride."

"Bumped the b . . . , bumped him off? Well, I'm glad to hear it."

"That wasn't necessary. We have engaged him as a salesman with our American subsidiary. So he's out of the way pro tem, and he had better watch his step. In other words, we have sewed matters up in such a manner with all concerned that the legacy from your late aunt, Lady Emma, has only just come to you. Okay?"

"You mean I get the whole seventy thousand-odd again?"

"I do not, Ambler. I mean that it seems you have."

"Well, beggars can't be choosers. But no hanky-panky, Dunn, I warn you."

We were in a thirty-mile limit, and as we passed a lamp I saw the danger flare of Dunn's near nostril, quite remarkable. "The warning is on the other foot," she said. "And if it had been my choice, I would have had no part of you. But Sir Conrad seems to think that your relationship with Max Vyan must have been quite special and unique. Hence this risk."

We were in open country again. She put on speed to pass a line of cars, six or seven of them, the needle over eighty. "Why the sudden spurt? Have I annoyed you?"

"You've done nothing else all afternoon. But I wondered. Yes, I'm sure now that car is tailing us. Get down, Ambler, under the dashboard, quick!"

So urgent was her tone and, as I have indicated, so commanding a character was Miss Dunn, that I found myself crouching while a glow of light grew in the car, was intensely bright shining in from her side, was gone with a dwindling roar ahead. I don't mind admitting that my heart hammered hard.

"Okay to come up."

"What was that all about?"

"I was expecting it," she said. "You see, strictly in confidence, Sir Conrad has this big merger on the *tapis,* and certain interests are hotching to know who's in on it, so they spot-photograph us as routine. It happens all the time."

"Why hide me, though? I'm not involved in any merger, not that I know of."

"Nor do I," she said. "But you're leaving tomorrow on a mission for Sir Conrad. Or have you forgotten that?"

"Not forgotten," I said. "You said there were two other things. What's the second?"

"A car," she said. "We have various — an XK-E, a Cooper S, a Maserati — Sir Conrad likes fast automobiles for diversion, usually with me at the controls. But those are all registered, I mean already licensed, which might make for complications. So I think it had better be the Buick."

"A Buick! As big as a medium bungalow. On Alpine roads?"

"Not the Caramba. It's smaller than the Bentley. It's a custom job. It's hot. Take my word for it, Ambler."

"What sort of power?"

"About five hundred BHP, I think."

We were in Woolwich now. Nobody took undue notice of us — one more Bentley slipping past the common people. The feeling was cozy beside Mary Dunn. She drove without gloves, her hands at ten minutes to two o'clock in the classic position.

"You have any hobbies — games or sports, I mean?"

"No time for anything but work. I used to ride a lot, especially when I jillarooed one year in Queensland. And I liked surfing too. But that's all in the past. Not that I regret it. A sixteen-hour day may be exhausting but it's always electric with Sir Conrad. One never knows what may come up. Like you, for instance." She chuckled, quite a human chuckle. "Any questions, Ambler, about the job?"

"I don't quite get the idea of making me so obvious. That car, for instance, won't it stand out a mile?"

"Yes, and it puts you straight into Max Vyan's world — the jet set. I mean, unless you're a personality in your own right with the trimmings, a sort of enlargement from the boy-wonder pilot Vyan knew, you won't stand a chance of getting on the inner track. That's the reason you're going de luxe. From what we gather, Vyan spurns the common herd."

"That sounds like him. Ignored people, or was damned rude to them — not to me, though, oddly enough."

"Why do you think we're sending you, idiot? Sorry, Ambler, no offense intended."

"None taken, Dunn." I do not recollect how or why we had slipped into that plain *Dunn* and *Ambler* mode of address, except that Dunn was the one who started it. No other woman had ever been a surname to me.

"Okay, I see the point about being slap-up, and very well it suits me. But now this Tanya woman — suppose Max asks me to his chalet, and there she is first time off wearing Brock's Koala — job's over, isn't it?"

"Our source tells us that the woman wears it — visibly at least — only on the more intimate occasions."

"So you mean I might have to be involved in some more intimate occasion with this Tanya woman?"

"It's possible. The job will be no safe sinecure, let me tell you. There may be danger."

"H'mm," I said. "I can think of more healthy occupations

than playing fast and loose with any possession of Max Vyan's."

"Too right, Ambler."

"Does he ski?"

"Yes," she said. "Quite adequately. But the woman is brilliant, so our source informs us. Perhaps you could do it brilliantly together."

"Do you ski, Dunn?"

"Not any more. I hate the guts of skiing."

"Why?"

"Sliding downhill on planks is for juveniles in my opinion, is one reason."

"H'mm. Any other reason?"

"I suppose, to be honest, Ambler, because I'm no good at it. I hate the guts of what I'm no good at."

"Odd," I said. "Nerve and balance, you've got them both, I can tell from the way you drive a car."

"Thank you."

"Not at all. And you're well enough coupled too, I mean put together, I would say."

"Would you, Ambler?"

"Do you like dancing?"

"I adore it."

"Which means you're a good dancer, Dunn?"

"Quite," she said. "Yes, I think I am."

"Come and dance tonight, then. Have a farewell fling."

"I most certainly will not. For one thing I have at least four hours' work ahead of me to get you on the road. For another, I can't think of anything I would want less to do than take you out dancing and pay the bill."

"That's a dirty crack," I said. I felt the prickle of my temper coming. "You can have your Buick and your . . ."

"It was the truth," she broke in. "But I didn't mean to be insulting. I meant that this is business. Sir Conrad is the big-shot boss, but I'm your case-manager, and I don't go dancing with my employees unless it happens to be on the job. And I know you've done terrific things, so don't get me wrong on that one, Ambler. Strictly business is what I mean. Okay?"

"Well, okay," I said, mollified. "How old are you, Dunn?"

"I was five when you were flying Spitfires." Which made her about twenty-six, my tough boss, my case-manager. We had reached Pall Mall.

"Just one more question."

We were nearly there. She drew into the curb. "Make it snappy, Ambler."

"You've forgotten something. Supposin' I do get a look at this Koala, how do I know it's the real potato, not some fake?"

"I hadn't forgotten. I had it in my notes as a final bit of gen for tomorrow. But I'll tell you now. If you look square into the Koala from point-blank range — now remember this — in the very top left-hand corner you will see . . ."

"You mean in the very top left-hand corner as I would see it facing your neck, for example, Dunn?"

"Precisely, Ambler. In that corner is the faintest blush of pink; you can't mistake it at close scrutiny even in artificial light. It's not a flaw, in fact far from that, but what they call a diamantine bloom. Top left-hand corner, got it?"

"Got it," and she drove on. "What about tomorrow?"

"I'll call you at nine. Can you deal with the club porter before then?"

"Can do," I said. "Can do this evening."

"Here's some money," she said, sliding an envelope along. "I don't need it tonight."

"Please, Ambler," she said. "Strictly business, we agreed."

So I took it. Our parting was friendly, Goodnight to Dunn and Ambler. Thus began an unusual relationship and, as things have turned out, a new career for one named Harry Ambler. I was pretty sure that the job was phony; but equally sure somehow or other that Dunn and Brock were basically on the up and up; which made prospects interesting.

I let myself into the flat. My good furniture was gone, sold outright. But the paintings had not yet been auctioned. I could get them back. Then I telephoned my landlord to renew the lease. He sounded dubious, but I assured him all was well. People usually believed me because, although my record was thoroughly unsound in some respects, I was not much given to telling whoppers. In fact it was often blurted truth that let me down.

But now a troublesome thought occurred — a new life would begin for me tomorrow, and for the first time I would be living lies. Was I up to it?

FOUR

Two evenings later I lay in a bath at the Hotel Kronenhof in Alpenheide. From my sybaritic soak I saw far back to Miss M. Dunn, Chief Dispatcher. She had me equipped and on the road by 11 A.M., her last words: *Keep out of trouble, Ambler.* The Buick had the punch of a D.B. Five and the suaveness of a Bentley. One treated the right-hand pedal with respect. And so to our private flight by Silver City.

I got used to the car — although not licensed before, it had been run in, she assured me — and we soon were cruising the Route Nationale at a hundred on the clock with a big punch of power to spare. We went by St. Omer, Reims and Chalons; and then drove on late to spend the night at Besançon.

This second morning I had come through the Jura by Pontarlier and into Switzerland at Vallorbe. It was on the long climb that a black Porsche latched in behind. He could not pass me, but I could not shake him until we were over the top and a straight stretch enabled me to draw away. But that road is none too wide, so I settled back and he kept his distance. I stopped at Vallorbe for high-octane fuel, likewise the Porsche. He had French plates.

"What a superb machine, Monsieur," he said as the Buick drank in *essence*, which she could drink. "American — but I did not know that such a thoroughbred existed. It is a special *marque*, then, surely?"

"Yes," I said. It was somewhat special, even to the HA-1 license plates, which Mary Dunn had obtained by some miracle. H. Ambler's super-ostentatious secret mission.

"Please excuse that I mention it, but your left ski seemed to be loose a little, I observed at speed."

"Many thanks," I said. That side of the roof-rack did need tightening over my White Star. He was a slim chap in a green corduroy jacket, dark trousers, pointed shoes, a cadaverous type with those charming manners. The skis on his Porsche were Allais. "I see you're going skiing too."

"To Alpenheide first," he said.

"I'm going there myself. À bientôt."

"À bientôt." He bowed a little, smiling, and got into his car to move up to the pump which I now vacated.

And so down to Lausanne and along the lake. It was a glorious day, spring flowers in bloom, not a ruffle on the water, the Dents du Midi perfect and remote there to the south. I stopped at Montreux for luncheon and had the car washed, which task was undertaken with awed admiration. Parked later in front of the hotel, it drew large crowds. To Europeans, not least the Swiss, one beautiful good car is worth several beautiful bad women. This is putting the buggy before the beast, in my opinion.

But I enjoyed reflected glory and answered questions about acceleration (phenomenal), maximum vitesse (as yet untried), the Caramba's nationality yet GB plates, horsepower (O, la-la!), disk brakes, and so on. Then I buttoned all four windows down simultaneously for parting display, and drove off.

Our HA-1 ensemble had certainly drawn the public eye on the shores of Lac Léman. I passed the Château de Chillon, standing lovely as ever from the lake, but bearing the trauma of Byron's appalling doggerel, and so on to Aigle where we took to the mountains, climbing on and on into the Oberland. As well as a limited-slip differential, the Buick was fitted with tungsten-studded tires, and ice was no problem in the last winding miles to Alpenheide.

This was a new part of Switzerland to me. I had done most of my skiing at Zermatt, Davos and Pontresina; and in Austria at Lech — all far from here, at least in road distance. But Alpenheide, although a village for centuries, was a late arrival in the ski world, having been developed only since the Second World War. The runs were said to be fabulous, and I would soon try them out, on business too. *Don't forget business, Ambler,* she said severely, sending me to it in one of the flashiest cars on the continent of Europe.

Flashy is the wrong word, I thought in my bath at the Kronenhof. There was no chromium except on the bumpers. The thing was a plainly luxurious streamlined bomb, with which I was slightly in love, if you know the feeling. It was also a shrewd publicity cover-device for my odd mission. There were no flies on Brock and Dunn, and my doubts about them grew apace. The number HA-1, for instance — how does one wangle that overnight? Might it not be that they had plotted the whole thing for months, plotted even my broiler fiasco?

The telephone rang in the sitting room — probably the ski

school calling. I had asked the concierge to get me an instructor to show me the better runs — always a sound idea if one
can afford it. I'm rich, I thought in the bath. Yes, I really am.
Let telephones ring.

Soon, however, there was knocking. *"Komme gleich,"* I
called fluently, dried myself with an outsize Kronenhof towel,
and went to open the sitting room door.

It was Dominic the concierge himself, frock coat and all. I
had been accorded impressive treatment on arrival by him and
his minions. *A lockup for your beautiful car, Mr. Ambler, it
is essential.* But a visit in person from such a dignitary? "Come
in," I said. During a few minutes in the lobby I had heard
him speak French, Italian, German, Spanish, English and something like Russian fluently; so his English would certainly be
better than what I could do.

"An old friend is inquiring for you, Mr. Ambler. He saw
your name in the registration, and asked me your appearance
. . ." Dominic seemed almost excited. "I described your fine
looks, and he said: *No doubt, no doubt at all.*"

"Who?" I said. But I had a hunch about it.

"Herr Vyan! Mr. *Max* Vyan, sir!"

"Max Vyan. I escaped from Germany with a chap called
Max Vyan."

"So he says. So Herr Vyan says, and I am to ask you to join
him in the Ski Keller at the soonest possible."

"That's amazing," I said. "I haven't seen old Max from that
day to this. Is he staying in the hotel?"

"Oh no, Mr. Ambler. Herr Vyan has his fine Schloss above
the village. But sometimes he honors us with his party here."

I said that I would not be long and went to dress. What a
stroke of luck on the very evening of my arrival. I had thought
that I would chance to chance upon Vyan skiing one day soon;

and I was fairly sure that he would be pleased or amused to see me. So we would meet, and I might or might not find out about this diamond.

Putting in the links, on the silk shirt, tie, trousers, socks, suede shoes and jacket, I was thinking that things looked suspicious both ways — first, a job that didn't ring true; then too neat a coincidence that my man should zero in on me at once. *Calm, Ambler!* I enjoined myself, applying CAR, brushing my hair to a gleaming gloss, but the face was ruddy pink from fog and steam, not ruddy brown from sun. A day or two would fix that.

Outwardly calm and presentable, I walked down two flights of stairs to get to grips with my assignment. Come to think of it, I thought, it's extraordinary to be forty-two years old and never to have been in this kind of racket.

The concierge handed me to a bowing headwaiter who led the way into the Ski Keller, which was no cellar but an ultra-smart bar with people dancing to an accordion wizard and champagne in the bucket and banquettes or sofa seats round the walls, and coming to meet me Max Vyan himself.

"Hello, Ambler," he said as casually as if it had been yesterday, which it well might have been. The dancing had stopped, and we had the small open floor to ourselves.

"Hello, Max." We did not shake hands. That he disliked or shrank from physical contact was one thing I remembered, one of many things from yesterday. He was shortish medium in size, half a head below me.

"I'm glad to see you," he said. "I do believe I am." Which seemed to surprise him. He gave me a pat, no more than a quick touch on the shoulder. "Come on!" And he added, "Fella that's with us, business, can't be helped."

I followed him to the far corner, not immediately noticing

the business fella because I was immediately noticing the most beautiful bad woman that any chap could well imagine.

"Tanya," he said. "This is Harry Ambler."

Now, so much later, so much water having flowed and stormed beneath my personal bridge, I will try to recapture a first impression of Tanya for you. The hair — blond but not very fair; the half-curtained brow; the face narrowing from high cheekbones; the lips full and passionate. It would have been another beautiful rather sulky face but for the eyes, which were green and hot and shameless. Her dress was black velvet with a high collar or halter round the neck, leaving arms and shoulders bare, such brown sleek arms and shoulders as you never saw, and she turned to me, her bosom moving, challenging the velvet, and crossed her legs, one golden shoe swinging from the other and down again. She wore no visible jewelry at all. She did not extend a hand. "So," she said. "The famous Harry Ambler of whom Max speaks."

"Me famous?" I said. "Since when?"

"Since one hour for me at least," she said, and dropped her eyes to consider potato chips.

The man's name was Korber, over-cholesteroled and wedding-ringed, just flown in from Ankara. He was on Scotch whisky, plenty of it by the looks of him. Tanya drank Heidsieck '59, and Vyan reddish stuff with a slice of lemon. "Campari and soda would do me fine," I said, sitting beside Max who then ignored my existence. I looked round the room, a crowded room of cheerful faces, many of which turned from time to time in this direction. Vyan's table was a focal point of interest. From the opposite end, at a table near the door, two men watched the room but never looked fully at us. Tanya gave Korber her smoldering attention.

"You look prosperous, Ambler." Max spoke from an eminence; he always had.

"Me ups and downs," I said. "I hear you're as rich as Croesus nowadays."

"Where did you hear?"

"Didn't hear, actually — I inferred it from this and that about Annual Meetings and helicopters at Gstaad and yachts and so on. No surprise to me."

He raised his left eyebrow. It was always the left one. Korber and the girl got up to dance. The back of her dress or the absence thereof made a different story. She draped the clothed part of herself along the pudgy length of Korber to some slow tune. "Tanya is her name, you said?"

"Tanya von Silberbach, my social secretary." Vyan looked at me again. "Why no surprise to you, Ambler?"

"You told me yourself. You said: *For a start I'm going to make a lot of money out of a lot of stupid suckers.*"

Max Vyan whickered, a brief whicker or whine, his laugh. He took a sip of Campari, and turned the long glass in his hand, perhaps watching the oily swirl. I was thinking of the night at the airfield when he killed the sentry, knifed him twenty paces from me, came back and whickered briefly to himself.

". . . Sorry. I was thinking."

Again the eyebrow. "Were you, Ambler? I said I read that book of yours."

It was just after the war when I was in the limelight — my record in fighters, and then the glider escape, and flying a German plane across. They serialized it in the *Express*.

"It wasn't too bad an effort," he said. "But you left out the meat."

I supposed that the sort of meat he meant was not only that airfield sentry on the final night, legitimate murder; but a farmer a few days earlier. I could not have done it in cold blood myself, but I could not question that if Max Vyan had not done it, we would have been caught within an hour — which at that stage of events meant to be shot out of hand. Max was nothing if not logical, so supremely logical that . . . But he was noticing me again. "What have you been up to since?"

I gave him a brief history of Harry Ambler. Australia and Canada, how far away they seemed from this.

"Small air outfits are too vulnerable. The best of business heads can't win with them within the law." He glanced mockingly and quite amiably at my business head. "You have to be big nowadays," he said. "Which goes for everything. Do you keep up your flying?"

"Not this past year. I was on the brink of bush-piloting again, but a late-lamented aunt of mine came through with a healthy bit of cash, which should last a while — after that, I suppose flying again if I'm not too old." I was surprised at myself, the half-lies slipping out so easily. "Flying is all I'm good for, or was."

"Yes," he said. "You're a red-hot pilot, or you was. Catch, Ambler!" I caught the matchbox which he had tossed across the table. "You've still got your reflexes," Vyan said. Why would he test my reflexes? He had always kept one guessing, like some wicked sardonic headmaster god. In those days Max had been thin to emaciation, as were we all. He was still spare, not particularly wrinkled at about fifty-two, but the lines from nose to chin were cut in deep. There was an immense calm authority about him.

Tanya's partner danced like an Arthur Murray graduate, amorous graduate. "This Korber chap — what's he in aid of?"

"He's in aid of buying steel from me."

The music stopped, and Korber and Tanya came back. His hand slid over her bottom as he followed her in behind the table. "What's your line?" he said to me, or shot at me.

"I'm in the skiing business at the moment. What's yours?"

"Hardware," he said, and winked at Vyan. "Sophisticated hardware, that's my line." The remark was loud, and some heads had turned. But the accordion began again.

"Ambler," said Max Vyan. "Why not give Tanya a romp?"

"Delighted," I said as her eyes came onto me.

"Sure he'd be d'lighted. But this baby's . . ."

"Be quiet," Vyan said. He shut up Mr. Korber softly.

Tanya and I went dancing. It was a carioca time, and she followed marvelously, our bodies apart, our feet linked in sympathetic rhythm. "God, you can dance," I remarked.

"God, you too, Mr. Harry Ambler. It is nice to be dancing far away, but your hand — I would like it on my skin."

My hand had been decorously on the velvet at the right side of her waist. Now I moved it as requested to a silken back. "Better," she said, looking up. "Better than duty hugs to be endured. You I can like very honestly at least."

"I like you too," I said. She was sin, and what chap does not like honest sin? My glance sidled down from her green eyes to the throat. Was that just possibly the outline of a necklace under black velvet?

"You are wondering: Am I real? Is it all my own self without assistance?" Tanya von Silberbach came close to me, against me from bosom to knee for perhaps a second to prove her reality, and away again as that carioca stopped. Then he played for our benefit, other couples having yielded to expertise.

We danced casually with private conversation. "Hardware, this Korber says. What is he then, an ironmonger?"

"I do not know. He is a loving husband and a daddy who travels everywhere on business and also for pleasure, just lately back from fifteen days up the Amazon with Mrs. Korber who does not accompany him on business trips. I love my wife, he says while hugging me all brown and blue. You do not hug me all brown and blue, so you have no wife to love, Mr. Harry Ambler, isn't it?"

"It is," I said. "I mean I never did embrace matrimony, never quite, did you?"

She shuddered. "The bawling babies — uugh! But to think of nice things — will you be here long, Mr. Harry Ambler?"

"A fortnight, perhaps," I said. "It depends on the skiing." And on getting to know you better on some more intimate occasion, I did not say. I was a natural at this shady business.

"Is skiing also another thing at which you excel?"

"So-so," I said. "I'm not too bad."

"Then we dance and we ski, two things at least. You will see the helicopter land at the Mittelwald, which is the halfway restaurant, or even in special calmness of weather condition to the very top, but usually I take the cable car from the Mittelwald to the Teufelsspitzen. Tomorrow it cannot be until afternoon when he is gone."

"Okay," I said. "When who is gone? Is Max going away?"

"No, no — that huggering man. Now we must return, Mr. Harry."

"Thank you, Fraülein Tanya."

"Gräfin," she said. "But how could you know?" I followed the Countess, a thoroughbred in every line, to the corner where Max toyed with Campari and soda, and Mr. Korber's new drink had the pallor and small bubbles of ginger ale. Tanya sat herself beside him, in friendly proximity, and she said, "Now tell me more about this climbing the wild River Amazon with cannibals and man-eating fishes on every side. Your wife, was she not afraid, then?"

"No," he said. "Mrs. Korber — bless her stout heart — she's game for anything." His stout hand slipped below the table, and the Countess Tanya stirred. She did not now seem hostile to the huggering man.

"On our way," Vyan said. He rose, and waiters came, and I noticed those two men slip out through the door. "Are they looking after you all right?"

"Yes," I said. "It seems a pretty fair hotel."

"It had better be. Let me know if anything goes wrong. I would ask you to dinner, Ambler, but Korber and I have business to discuss. Perhaps one evening soon; and bring that car of yours I hear about. But we'll see you skiing. Watch for the chopper." He rattled these comments off in that staccato and yet unhurried way of his. "Lead on," he said to Tanya. Which she did, without a glance or a word for me. "Good night, Ambler."

"Wizard to see you, Max."

He mouthed the word *wizard*, whickered faintly, and went. If I have given an impression of Max Vyan as the strutting small dictator, then I have misled you. There was nothing small or strutting about him.

FIVE

I went over to the bar for another drink before dinner. The drink did not interest me particularly, but I had spotted a chap with a Ski Club armband who could tell me snow conditions, which he did, after Skolling for his Martini. Well, *Skoll* was at least one better than *Cheers*. Now rich again, I could afford to indulge my U.

A three-foot base, new powder high up, and sugar snow on the lower *pistes*, one could not ask for more. And the open field skiing was the best in Switzerland, he said — yes, better than the Jakobshorn — as easy or difficult as you cared to make it or could take it. "Any big stuff?" I asked.

"Lots. Most notably the Devil's Plunge — much too big for me." He giggled. "The moguls are so vast by now that only the chosen few are even allowed to ski it, simply terrifying." He lowered his voice. "That female you were dancing with, Mr. Vyan's lady, is one. A friend of yours too?"

"No," I said. "I met her this evening. Only chanced upon him too. I knew Max Vyan in the war." I was casual about it, not knowing friend from foe, nor pansy flower from snake in the grass.

"Mr. Vyan is Herr Alpenheide, literally. He owns the place, lock, stock and barrel."

"This hotel, you mean?"

"This hotel, the cable cars, chairlifts, little button tows, the restaurants, the pubs, the whole valley from log to sawmill and top to toe. Or I'm not sure about owning, I mean controlling. If one visits the wrong loo, Mr. Vyan knows about it, is the *on dit*. But all is rumor. Herr Alpenheide never mixes with the common herd." He giggled again. "Only with the likes of you. But that floozy — she gives me the creeps on skis or off. I can't help it, can I, if female sex symbols give me the creeps?"

"Every man to his creeps," I said, seeing no reason to disclose what kind the Gräfin Tanya gave me. But this remark set my present companion into peals of alto merriment.

There were two other people near us at the bar, the Porsche Frenchman from this morning, no particular coincidence there; but he had leafed twice right through his newspaper, so he probably was listening. The other man had moved over from a table beside Vyan's. He looked like a retired Major of the Royal Army Service Corps, shaggy dog, and so lugubrious that he probably was listening. I could not but be aware that the Hotel Kronenhof was taking notice of me.

Now I declined a quick one from the ski-club man, exchanged cordial Bonsoirs with my chance acquaintance of the road, and went for dinner and half a bottle of a white wine of the Valais, which wines have a family flavor uniquely their own. The dining room was packed, and there was dancing to a five-man band. The atmosphere of the place seemed good — a cosmopolitan crowd of real skiing people having fun, lots of jollity but no loud jinks.

I enjoyed my dinner and my wine at my recherché table,

took notice of a few not unattractive women. While giving attention casually to the form, I thought as hard as I was able. So far, one thought, it seemed very good. One had met Vyan by sheer chance, or at least sheer chance on one's part. One had been oneself, asking no questions, not making up, unless perhaps to Countess Tanya. But *give Tanya a romp*, he had said it himself. And what were the relations of Max and Tanya? Not very cozy, it seemed to one. A business team, one might hazard a guess, arranging a deal with Mr. Korber.

I signed the bill, slipped ten francs to my waiter for interim encouragement, and went through the lobby to the lift.

My room had been tidied, the bed turned down. Why would Mary Dunn have booked me a double bed through Cook's? And why did my suite face the sunny south, away from the ski slopes and the Teufelsspitzen, the three peaks of the Devil? I would get all the sun I wanted, skiing. I am not a touchy chap — *I couldn't care less* being my general attitude — but Dunn in retrospect annoyed me.

I prowled the suite a bit, fiddling with this and that. The furniture was modern, the bowl for the daffodils by Jensen, the oils were abstracts, bold and colorful. The general prospect pleased, so different from Swiss taste, no ruddy chamois on the ruddy alp, no leviathan dog bearing keg of cognac, no long puce vase with a single pink carnation and one sprig of maidenhair.

I put on my sheepskin coat, locked the door and went down. "A short stroll before bed," I told the concierge.

"If you would care for dancing, Mr. Ambler, I can reserve a table at Whisky à Go-Go. It is just up the village street."

"No, thanks, Dominic."

"A ski pole, sir? The walking is icy." He conjured one from

behind his desk. The concierge, a remarkable breed, untiring and unflappable, sixteen hours a day or something, from postage stamps to corpses smuggled out at dawn.

The night was clear and cold, but so alpine dry that one hardly needed gloves. I walked toward the main street — very sensibly they had built their modern hotel away from the old village. Directly ahead of me and far up there the three peaks of the Teufelsspitzen were in moonlight, not devilish at all, no black precipices, all three of them snow-covered to the summits.

But the northern sides (I had gleaned from a guidebook provided by Dunn) were another story — seven thousand feet of sheer drop and overhang, unclimbable, as if old Mephistopheles had decided to build himself a lean-to shelter — one long side sloping up from ground or valley level to meet the vertical wall, and crawling space for old Mephistopheles inside. It was a ridiculous simile about a magnificent freak of nature. All the works of nature are freaks, I thought, including even Harry Ambler.

I burst out laughing at myself sometimes, and this was a time. Alone now in Alpenheide in the moonlight my laughter echoed merrily all round. It is spontaneous, a kind of eruption, as surprising to me as to others, but no one else was there to be surprised.

One person was. The shaggy Major lurched at me from the shadows of a camera shop. He looked a good deal shaggier than before, with flying boots and baggy bags and very British reefer coat and walrus moustache and white-knitted headpiece topped by what the Scotch call a toorie. "Hello, old boy," he said. "Good joke? Mind if I join you?"

He suited the action to the question, and we walked up the cobbled street, which was icy, as Dominic had said. A few shops had lights in the back of them, but all were closed, and no glimmer showed through shutters overhead. There was music further on, but here Alpenheide seemed to be asleep, or playing secret possum, only visitors still abroad. We met two young couples from the hotel. Then a cow mooed nearby.

"Extraordinary, these hillmen natives, bedding down with cattle beasts underfoot. Can you imagine our health people standing for that, I ask you, old boy, now can you?"

"The valleys are jam-packed in winter. Cattle beasts keep the house warm. You get used to the smell. Better underfoot than overhead, I would say."

"A very good point," he said. "No one's explained it properly before."

We approached Whisky à Go-Go, accordion music and yodeling within. "Like to stop for a noggin?"

"I think I'll stroll a bit. On the way back perhaps."

"What I usually do, and no success with those bints so far. But the touch is gone, let's face it. In my heyday . . ." Mumble, mumble, then loud and clear: "Name's Moffett," he said. "With an E and two T's, not the common way. Major, actually. I gather you're Ambler." He stopped to pump my hand.

"How did you gather?"

"From Dominic. There's nothing that chap doesn't have at his fingertips. I asked about you because of, oh, you know . . ." He lurched against me. The Major had a rolling action. "You're a new boy, aren't you?"

"Well, yes," I said guardedly. "First time here."

"I thought as much. Take my tip, old chap, and start lessons at once. Of course, with that posh car of yours, and a suite and all that, you'll rate a private instructor. But to learn properly is the only way. Now after two months of it my stems are beginning to shape up nicely."

We had passed the shops, the pubs, the boarding houses,

and came now to open space between chalets, weathered wood almost black in moonlight, meadows steep above us to the right, below us to the left, all glistening under snow. It was a miraculous night of sound in stillness. "Two months," I said, letting it pass about my stembogens. "That's a long skiing holiday."

"Since Boxing Day . . ." But the Major's voice tailed off to a mutter. Mutter, mutter into his moustache.

Was that . . . ? My eyesight is fairly sharp. Had I seen movement above us, at the edge of the woods where a great pile of logs awaited transport, not transport of the wheeled variety, as I now saw, but by ice-chute, a sort of shallow Cresta run for logs, down the steep meadow to jump this road and speed on by chute to the valley bottom, to a saw mill probably, an ingenious use of gravity. Had I seen . . . ? But nothing moved up there.

The road swung round a shoulder. One blast of a whistle sounded in the distance, and echoed many times to nothing. "Same every night," the Major rumbled behind his gauntlet. "On the dot of eleven."

The whistle must have come from up the valley, from a hillock that rose quite alone within the valley. It was a flat-topped hill, and on the plateau one saw roofs, a few lighted windows. The curving hillside in itself was pretty, with some kind of hidden source of illumination on the wooded slopes.

"Whirly-bird's coming," the Major rumbled behind his gauntlet. The noise grew rapidly from somewhere in the direction of the Teufelsspitzen, navigation lights now blinking. Then I could see the helicopter, a big-bodied machine. It sank beyond the roofs atop the plateau, and the sound faded, but the Major mumbled on.

"Sorry," I said. "I can't hear very well when you talk behind your glove."

"It's bugging, old boy. They can bug you from a mile away with these beamed microphones; one has to observe a few precautions."

"Why precautions?" I said.

"Well, I'll tell you — I'll take the jump. The moment I saw you this evening I thought: This chap's true blue, the genuine rich playboy article. Honest — it stands out a mile, and the only tricks he's up to, well, the women beg him for it, what's wrong with that?"

"Many thanks," I said. "Shall we turn round now?"

"Fact is," the Major said, having turned, still talking into his gauntlet, "and absolutely between ourselves, Number One sent me out on Boxing Day. *Moffett*, he said. *There's a smell at Alpenheide. Go smell it, Moffett.* Which I have been doing, and a very tricky case I find it. I keep asking people about those lorries that come at night — not on this road, most of them, but along the one that loops round by the river and up to that Schloss. No one seems to know. And they say all the food supplies come up by night. Which is true, of course. But now you're here, and now at last I think I see the light. Would you mind turning round, and facing me directly?"

I did so.

"This way my bulk cuts their beam on you, and your bulk cuts their beam on me. So they can't bug us from either front or rear. It's an old trick in the trade."

"They might bugger us sideways, though," I said.

The Major's laughter boomed. "A difficulty there, old boy. But now to be serious: I've been making my reports faithfully every day."

"How?" I asked, out of professional interest.

"By phone to Staff — in code, of course."

"To Staff?"

"Number One's Chief of Staff. Number One himself doesn't speak to me much, not since he said: *I'm miffed with you, Moffett.* And why? Because I begged, I pleaded for one weekend at home. I haven't seen Mildred since early on Boxing Day, and here we are at the first of March, and Mildred herself is fit to be tied."

"Couldn't Mildred come here?"

"No wives on the job — Standing Orders are explicit on that point. But look, old chap, that's my personal . . . er headache, not for you to be bothered with."

We still stood face to face in the moonlight, the Major barring my way home to bed. "What do you want?" I said, or whispered, his sibilant whisper was infectious.

"I simply want you to be my contact there, at that castle of mystery behind your back."

"Vyan's, you mean?"

"Yes, Vyan's. There's something going on, you mark my words, something global, I would put it at. That chap who was with them this evening at the Kronenhof — you know him?"

"Korber, isn't it?"

"Yes, Korber of General Mechanics."

"What's that?"

"Not *that*, old chap, but *they*. And *they* just happen to have the biggest government contracts in everything from rocketry to what fits in the business end. *Hardware*, they call it. You heard him yourself.

"Now another thing — what are these helicopter flights after dark? It starts in the Gstaad direction, climbing, and then swings north somewhere round the peaks of the Teufelsspitzen. Why? There are no villages in that direction. Sometimes an hour away, two hours or more. What gives up there beyond the mountains?"

"Look here," I said. "I came to ski."

"I know, I know — that's the point, old boy. It's all pure chance, and no one will suspect you. Nobody could, with that transparent honesty of yours." He paused and looked at me. Perhaps the Major was shrewder than he seemed. "Unless — unless, of course, you're the big league boy I've been expecting."

"I told you," I said. "I only came here to ski."

"Just what I thought. And the point is: you know Vyan, he's even keen to see you again — you're a natural for the job."

"But dammit all, I'm not a spy."

"I am," the Major said. "And sometimes I think they're on to me. Sometimes I think that one of these nights . . . Oh well, never mind. Come on," he said. "Let's see the form at Whisky à Go-Go. Perhaps with your influence behind me, one of those moppets might take pity on old Moffett."

We walked toward the village. Over to the right the Kronenhof was still ablaze with lights at 11.20 P.M. There was one street lamp down where the shops began. Not a soul in sight. Not a sound but the squeak of cold snow beneath us.

The Major jostled me. That rolling gait of his was tiresome, and I dropped back a pace. "Nine weeks," he said, lugubrious again. "It's cruelty to an . . ."

I heard a hiss, a trundle, a quickly growing hiss, and ducked. Reflex action ducked me in against the hill, and I looked up to see just ahead a succession of objects cut across the sky, across the very moon, pair by pair of long pointed objects moving at great speed. The first pair flew over unimpeded, and the second. "Do keep up with me, old b . . ." The impact was not loud — a thud, then a clatter, and with the clatter one long gurgling sigh as Major Moffett fell. Blood gushed from his neck to spread darkly on the snow. The poor Major bubbled and died as I knelt beside him. The point had struck his neck just below the jawbone, literally slicing the front of the throat in two. The missile lay on the road. It was a Head Vector ski. The others had shot on unhindered down the log-chute at perhaps a hundred miles an hour. I knew that there had been others — three pairs or four in line astern, too many to count. But I had seen them. I can see them now as I write this sentence.

Nothing moved at the pile of logs up there. The weapon was a metal ski of high quality with only a few unusual things about it — blood freezing stickily to the tip, the number erased, the Marker heel-binding removed — for silence probably. It was murder by Head. It was unquestionably murder, and I ran from it.

One does not tend to be proud of taking to one's heels, and I am not; but looking back on my first night at Alpenheide, I think that my instinctive skedaddle was the right action. Poor Moffett was beyond mortal aid. I was defenseless. A ski had taken him. Might a bullet not take me?

I therefore sprinted downhill to that single street lamp, no bullets cracking; and when the hard-packed snow changed to slippery ice, I walked again, past Whisky à Go-Go where Moffett had been wont to drop in hopefully for a noggin. The street was empty now, not a soul about. I looked up the mountain, seeing clearly the twin cables of the Luftseilbahn, sagging and rising to a first pylon against the sky. Then I walked down to the Kronenhof, not knowing what on earth to do. Report it? Sneak off to bed? But on the way up I had been seen with Moffett.

Dominic still stood behind his counter, dignified, frock-coated.

"Ah, Mr. Ambler," he said. "You are back quite early."

"And you're working late, Dominic."

"It is usual, sir," he said. "Our guests arrive at all hours, even a busload from Zermatt where conditions are abominable, they report." A small smug smile.

The lobby was empty. "I want a word with you."

He accepted the ski pole from me, locked two drawers and showed me into the office behind. "At your service, Mr. Ambler."

"You knew Major Moffett?"

"Yes, sir, the portly gentleman from England. *Knew* him, sir?" He was on to that nuance in a foreign tongue.

"Right," I said. "Major Moffett is dead. He was killed by a ski twenty minutes ago."

"By a ski, sir? Where?"

"At the log-chute above the village. You know the place?"

"Yes, Mr. Ambler. And the body?"

"It was there when I left. We were walking together."

"Excuse me, sir." He dialed a number. Someone answered soon. "*Hör mal an!*" said Dominic, and spoke quickly and calmly for about a minute in Schweizerdeutsch, unintelligible to me. Then he hung up. "The police," he said, unmoved and inscrutable. "A loose ski is like a, how do you say it, like a projectile. Someone could have left the ski carelessly near the chute — such terrible accidents can happen."

"Not one ski," I said. "At least half a dozen. I ducked and saw them flash overhead." I watched Dominic.

But he frowned now, and said with warmth: "Ach, Mein Gott, sir, what merciful deliverance."

"One ski might be an accident. But a battery of skis? Moffett was murdered as sure as I'm standing here."

Dominic shrugged. "The English Major . . ." He said no more.

"I was on the upper side and just behind him. If I hadn't ducked in right quick, it could have been me, not poor old Moffett. I think those skis were meant for me, which seems hardly fair on my first night in this place."

"For you, sir, Mr. Ambler, but that is quite impossible. Why, even our patron came specially down to the hotel to see you."

"Oh?" I said. "That isn't quite what you told me."

"Purely as routine interest, I telephone arrivals to the secretary. And Herr Vyan himself called me to ask about you, Mr. Ambler, as I said, I do assure you, sir."

"Okay, okay."

"Our patron is a man somewhat withdrawn, with few close friends possibly, but this evening for the first time I saw him happy, even excited to meet his gallant comrade-in-arms, yourself. I assure you, sir, that you are the last person in this valley whom anyone would wish to harm."

"*The last person,*" I said. "Why a first person, for God's sake, isn't this a peaceful ski resort?"

I watched that hit home, and Dominic said nothing. Then I had a thought, a quick inspiration. Try it out for effect: "Max Vyan told me to let him know if anything went wrong. Well, something has gone very wrong indeed. Late though it is, I think I'll just telephone him. What's the number, Dominic?"

The change in our concierge was remarkable. He barred my way to the telephone. His face had gone greenish. He held

his hands up, palms toward me, in abject supplication. "I beg
you, Mr. Ambler. For all our sakes, I beg you not. It would be
terrible."

"Well, time's drawing on," I said. "I'll sleep on it. You'd
better come and see me in the morning."

"Very good, sir, certainly. At what hour?"

"Eight-thirty would do. I came here to ski, you know,
Dominic," I said severely.

"I know indeed, sir. It is most regrettable." He had control of himself again. "You will not call Herr . . . ?"

"No," I said. "I'll sleep on it. I told you."

I bade Dominic good night and went to bed. *Keep out of
trouble, Ambler,* were Dunn's last words to me. And here I was
already in the thick of trouble.

I put out the light. The bed was comfortable, but a double
bed is too big a bed for a single chap; one gets lost in it. *There's
something going on, you mark my words, something global, I
would put it at,* said the poor old Major.

But I had been engaged at a handsome salary to come to
Alpenheide merely to find out whether a gem of enormous
worth dangled from a woman's neck. Had something dangled
there behind the velvet?

I'm wearing it, Ambler, want to see? I woke in the dead of
night with those words ringing loud. But which woman wore
what eluded me.

SIX

The sun was streaming across my quilt. The rays of the sun did literally stream for a first few moments; and then it had climbed to full-born warmth above the valley.

Last night. Had last night even happened? The reality did not strike until I was shaving my own whole throat and saw Major Moffett's sliced in two at about the Adam's apple. I had to wait for my hand to steady.

But I forgot again in the pleasure of squeezing myself into dark green stretchables on a first fine skiing morning. They still fitted, which was an encouragement, strapping my waist and midsection, tapering to tautened instep. As usual, I admired my looking glass image before moving to the sundeck where an Italian waiter had put breakfast — not of the continental variety, but a glass of blood-orange juice, two boiled eggs (a grave threat to the liver, the Swiss contend), rolls, marmalade and strong café-au-lait. You will think it unfeeling of me to put away the Moffett horror. But I could and did, reveling in the sun.

The chime of a village clock for half past eight was fading as the knock sounded, and I went in.

We exchanged Good Mornings, and I offered Dominic a chair. Parting the tails of his frock coat, he sat forward on the edge — not edgily, but with straight-backed episcopal calm. His glance wandered by the terrace door to the hotel radio. I shut the former and switched on the latter. It was organ music, to baffle ears such as might reside in Dominic's hotel walls. "Well?" I said.

He came straight to the point. Seven other metal skis had been found at the bottom of the ice-chute, impaled in the great snow bank which was used to stop logs. They had all been removed mysteriously after hours last evening from Zimmermann's ski shop, and all were deficient of heel bindings. There was no evidence of any kind at the top of the chute. "But since a week, sir, we have had no fresh snow in the valley; hence it is packed hard by many boots."

"No fingerprints on the skis?"

"None, Mr. Ambler, but there would not be. Gloves are necessary to handle sharp metal edges."

Right enough. "*How* the deed was done is clear," I said. I did not want to ask *why*, having heard enough from Moffett to have a fair idea why he had been so bizarrely murdered. But in my innocence and outrage I should ask: "*Why*, though?"

He looked me straight in the eye. "I do not know, sir," and he continued carefully: "The police are, of course, making rigorous investigation. But there are no clues, no evidences whatever. I do not think that any of us will ever know."

"Have you told the poor chap's relatives, if any?"

"The Major's only address was London, England. But there was a London telephone number I obtained for him most mornings. I have therefore called it to say that Major Moffett met with a fatal ski-accident, but a man's voice said immediately: *No Major Moffett is known here.*"

"H'mm."

"If no Major Moffett is known there, our one possible contact — then is it not best, sir, that no Major Moffett is known
here? Such an accident or such a crime could do much undeserved harm to the reputation of Alpenheide."

"Why undeserved? The man was murdered at Alpenheide."

Dominic stared at his patent-leather boots.

"I know about it, Dominic. So do the police, the hotel staff
and the murderer. Who else?"

"I telephoned Herr Vyan. All matters of hotel policy are
brought to our patron's notice. Herr Vyan was in agreement:
There has been no Major Moffett."

"What about maids and waiters and all the rest?"

"There has been no Major Moffett."

"And you mean that Vyan expects me to subscribe . . ."

"Herr Vyan does not know of your chance presence. I did
not dare to tell him. If I had told him — what is your expression — if I had told him, heads would roll. It is true, sir, that
I promise you." Dominic was neither abject nor agitated this
morning, but convincing in his calm anxiety. "My head is
in your hands, Mr. Ambler. My head, and the heads of others."

I looked at the Jensen bowl of stainless steel, modern and
pleasing, but my thoughts wandered off to think that murder
by ski would be just Max Vyan's notion of a practical joke to
put paid to inquisitive nitwits like the Major. And why was
Dominic so certain Vyan did not know that I had been with
Moffett? And what would be the chances of carrying out my
mission if Vyan did link me with him? "All right, Dominic.
I don't like it, but I'll keep my mouth shut for the moment."

"Thank you, sir," he said.

"But why would anyone want to kill old Moffett? He seemed a simple ordinary harmless chap."

"To seem simple, ordinary and harmless, sir, is not. . . ." Dominic stopped and looked at me. "I am but a servant here," he said, and rose, and would I now excuse him?

As the ski-club man had said, the open-field skiing was fabulous. It could be taken steeply or easily the whole way from the left shoulder of the Teufelsspitzen at ten thousand feet down to Alpenheide at four thousand.

My mentor for the morning was named Rudi Viereck, Rudi the Square, and it suited him, a short *montagnard,* looking as broad as he was long in the Alpenheide anorak of gentian blue. He was a wonderfully solid skier, not leading me a dance but sensing the speed that I was good for. We did a lower run first, from the Mittelwald to the village, and up again by cable car. Then, after coffee at the Mittelwald, we took chairlifts up to the east and back, and up to the west and back. These runs, and the numerous variations of them, were called the Soldanella and the Wintergreen.

"Not tired?" he said at twelve, when clocks were striking faintly in the valley. "To the Teufelsspitzen, then." There was a queue for the upper cable car, but having an instructor, I went to the head of that; and then he asked me if I would like to ride the roof with him.

I most certainly would. It was a special honor and against the rules, but with my complimentary pass (*Herr Vyan's instructions*), rules did not much apply to me.

So I rode the roof with Rudi and three other instructors. Looking back on it, I shudder at the recollection. But I had no fear of heights. In fact I loved to look down a thousand feet upon the dwarfs weaving back and forth. There was a hum.

There was talk here and below us in the car; then the change of pitch, the steeper climb, the trundling clank, the long swaying at another pylon.

Rudi pointed out runs we had already made. We could see the valley too, with low cliffs on the other side above the river and below the forest. "What's that?" I said about Max Vyan's Schloss or chalet, alone on its plateau within the valley.

He glanced quickly at me. "That is your friend, Herr Vyan's place, Schloss Alpenheide."

"It looks big. Have you been there?"

"No," he said. "We have not been there." *We*, he said. Not *I*. The others had been joking in their Schweizerdeutsch, but they were silent of a sudden.

I turned to face the Teufelsspitzen as the car steadied after a last pylon. We were nearly there, one final dip and rise to the Höhengrat terminus below the ridge which climbed to the three peaks of the Teufelsspitzen. They were gentle mountains, not an avalanche slope that I could see except perhaps at the very top. But they must be steeper than they looked, for there were stout avalanche fences all the way across.

Below them, skiers were taking the long easy way, the shorter steep way, and courses in between. How slowly they all seemed to move, crawling and checking, even tumbling in slow motion. "Where is the Teufelssturz, the Devil's Plunge?"

"On the other side," he said, pointing to the left or west. It was a narrow gully, snaking down steeply, and even from here the glistening moguls were visible. "It is still icy," Rudi said. "Perhaps by two o'clock — I myself am to test if the Teufelssturz can be run this afternoon."

"Too difficult for me?"

"When your legs are strong . . ." Rudi was not a gladhander. He had given no word of praise to my skiing, which for a first day was phenomenally good, I thought. "With the moguls now so high and the course so narrow, the Devil's Plunge must be skied very fast — there is no other way. It is dangerous, Herr Ambler. Except for ourselves, there is one regular skier only at Alpenheide who is good enough to run it at this time."

"Silberbach — ach, Silberbach — du Schönster Liebling von Silberbach." These mahogany fellows roared with laughter as we slowed for the concrete cavern of cable car terminus Höhengrat. And yet somehow all their laughter stopped short.

"Now we ski a little faster."

We skied much faster. There is nothing like it in the world for me — not a flat-out hunt; not a motor race; not even long ago the juddering squirt, locked in on a Focke-Wulff, poor sod — there is no such pure and perfect pleasure as at the brink of control when my skis are speaking. Rudi stopped once on the way to the Mittelwald. "To be tired is dangerous," he said, a bit of a pedant; they usually are. He had been hired to lead me, not to teach me. Few of them can teach. But most of them lead well, sensing uncannily when your legs begin to weaken. I followed Rudi's chunky figure. He was not graceful, but squat to the snow, totally untippable.

We had wine and lunch together on the crowded terrace. It was that perfect weather which settles on the Alps in spring — not a touch of wind; an occasional wisp of cloud come from nothing, soon gone to nothing; and in the deep sky, jet trails needling their silent way.

It was so peaceful that I snoozed until Rudi said, "If you will see me make the run; then take the Wintergreen chairlift and ski across to the foot of the Teufelssturz."

I did that. It looked much more formidable from below than from the cable car. The Devil's Plunge just about described it, and here the man came. His feet were not quite together in copybook style, but copybooks were not the object. That was to retain control in a narrow gully which could be skied only very fast through the pattern of moguls. Rudi made sixty miles an hour, or whatever speed, look safe and easy. He shot out past me, his skis chattering, and did a long sliding turn to wait for me.

"Each day they are bigger," he said in slow careful German, smiling. "Soon it may not be possible, Herr Ambler."

Which was my very thought. We skied down open slopes to the Mittelgrat, and here came Vyan's helicopter. It was the same vivid blue as Rudi's anorak. "Die Silberbach kommt," he muttered.

"She must be a good skier to run the Devil's Plunge."

"Good, yes," he said. "And without fear altogether. But not for enjoyment, as we ski."

"What for, then?"

Rudi shrugged his wide shoulders.

"I think I might try the Teufelssturz myself."

"The run is within your competence, Herr Ambler, when your legs are strong. Not today, I would advise." He was quite stuffy about it.

"Okay," and we parted, Rudi to take a class, I to ski with Die Silberbach if the helicopter should disgorge her.

It did. She emerged in a one-piece outfit of that same blue of the Alpenheide Ski School, a sort of tunic sheath from shoulder straps to boots with a high-necked white sweater under the tunic. She strolled to the chairlift, followed by a man with skis. She stopped, and the man knelt to buckle her skis while Tanya stared across the valley, ignoring him and the world about her. Putting on skis is always a chore, but one that most of us struggle with ourselves. Not so Tanya. Fitted to them by the lip-biting man, she poled away without a word or glance for him.

We had a date to ski together, but her air of arrogance was such that I held back. She looked once round, however, saw me, nodded, and led the way to the head of the queue. The double armbands of the ski instructor would entitle her to that, and me to be her pupil, I supposed; so I tagged along, and no one complained, all eyes gawking at her.

She said nothing on the long ride up. So forbidding was her smolder that I kept quiet also. "Go first," she said. "I will watch your form."

I did as I was told, skiing fast until about halfway down, but there I eased. If Countess Tanya wanted to see my skiing form, I also wanted to see hers. She was better even than I had expected — I think the most graceful skier I had ever seen, a born flyer as different from girt Rudi as the alpine swift is from the mallard drake. I kept up with her by stretching it, and we were at the cable car. The same man came to unbuckle her skis.

"Good," she said to me, expressionless, a different Tanya from my dancing partner of the green and hot and shameless eyes which now lurked behind dark glasses. She stood before me at the front window and did not move, did not even stir during our journey to the Höhengrat. Few women have figures good enough for skin-tight delineation, those hips like ocean-going tugs. But Tanya's bottom was excellent, hidden now from me in the press of humanity. And once again her neck was hidden. Were I to grasp it with my fingers, would I feel a necklace below the soft cashmere? Were I to try any such foolish thing, my eyes would be scratched out. A devil seethed in her — for me, for what, for whom?

"Bonjour, Monsieur." It was the Porsche Frenchman right behind me. "*Ça va bien?*"

"*Comme ci comme ça,*" I said. "*Ça gaze.*"

The cable car slowed, stopped, swaying a little. Then I followed her out to climb the steps. She carried only golden poles. Her servant, vaguely incongruous in lederhosen, bore the skis which were Alu Presidents.

One sign pointed right to the Soldanella, the last run that Rudi and I had made. Two signs pointed left, to the Devil's Plunge and the Wintergreen.

"Which run?" I said.

"But the Teufelssturz, but naturally."

"It's my first day. Rudi Viereck said I wasn't up to that, not yet."

"Rudi Viereck, who is Rudi Viereck? Bah! Are you afraid then, isn't it?" She removed her dark glasses and stared at me, the eyes hot and green but contemptuous.

"Okay," I said. "You can pick up the pieces." I laughed at her, and the glare was of hate as she turned her back.

We walked on past the bar, the café, the small shop for wax, badges, souvenirs and Toblerone, into the open air, along a wide path below the ridge that climbed past us to the peaks. A latticework fence was above our path, with signs in four languages about danger, no climbing beyond this point. The sheer cliffs must plunge from the ridge above; but on this side it was not steep at all until we saw the gully of the Devil's Plunge. That was so precipitous a cleft within the placid bosom of the mountain that other people averted their eyes and hastened on to the easy slopes of the Wintergreen.

There was a chilly breeze up here. It blew from the Alpenheide Glacier that began to the west of us. How familiar those high places would become. They haunt me yet and always will. But it was all strange that afternoon.

I put on my skis and stood straight again. Her servant was

not being very smart about his task. *Danger,* I read. *To be skied with special permission only.* But I had had permission from an honorary member of the Alpenheide Ski School, wearing her own version of the uniform. I felt mild trepidation about the run, not very much.

"*Dummkopf!*" she screamed, and raised her pole and did not quite strike the cringing man. He was sweating, poor chap, one of the two men who had sat near the door last evening, not quite looking at Vyan's table. "Mittelwald," she ordered him, and to me: "Wait one minute."

Then Tanya von Silberbach was off, leaning far forward in faultless style, swing at this mogul, streak to the next, dancing poetry on skis, it was superb — she had gone from sight.

I waited, counting to a slow sixty seconds in my head, my foolish head, it looked quite awful. The vertical drop was not so very much from here to the mouth of the Devil's Plunge where I saw her standing now. But a fall anywhere en route would not be a common fall — it would be a fall and then a thrashing tumble of body and skis and poles to the very bottom or some rock. *It is dangerous, Herr Ambler.* How right he was, and how fiercely the blond blue woman brandished her ski poles to command me down. *Are you afraid then, isn't it?*

"Here goes," I said, and I was on my way, qualms forgotten in the wonderful contest of speed and balance. Unweight, check left — unweight, check right — too high on that one, teetering, teetering, got it back. My legs were not strong enough to boss my skis in this tight-winding funnel. But marvelous, I was almost through, one last mogul to be judged correctly to do the work for me; then out and past her.

But she was moving to cross my path, and here raced up the mogul, not the inner slope but the steep face of it.

When I fall, I fall, and this one was a beauty. I lay a while a long way down, assessing damage, and my breath came back. Both skis were attached to me by safety straps; both big toes worked; both arms came up and with them, poles; ribs ached, but that was going away. The murderous bitch, I thought, wiping ice-cold snow from my eyes and neck.

"You are alive, then?" called Tanya von Silberbach.

"Why in God's name did you cross me?"

"When I saw you falling, I must move. See, there I stood — we would have had a double *Umsturz* all together, with death no doubt. Or if I had survived, what pleasure would you grant me, dead?" Countess Tanya smiled with something near affection. She skied to me. "It was a glorious fall, and you are not the worse? Put on skis, then, and I will brush your snowman, and we will *weiter machen.*"

I did as I was bidden while she brushed my snowman. Had I been falling before she moved? No, I had not. Did she try to kill me? Was it a blooding exercise? Was my fall a catalyst for her wicked mood? Whatever dark reason, the change in Tanya was very welcome and perhaps worthwhile. "You are a bold bad Harry man," she said indulgently, but her face hardened. "Now we ski until I purge myself."

"Not the Plunge again."

"Not today," she said. "For once that barrel-bodied bone-from-the-toes-up Rudi Viereck was correct. But you have won your bloody spurs. I lead you fast and easily now."

She was as good as her word for the rest of that afternoon on the Wintergreen and the Soldanella, ski runs that bore the names of alpine plants. "That was Max's own idea," she said at one of our brief halts, "and right for Alpenheide, which in itself is the name of a plant, the creeping Azalea, Azalea Procumbens of our mountains here."

"Are you an alpine botanist?"

"No," she said. "I am an alpine whore," and led me again at the rate of knots, but safely.

That wiry Frenchman was ahead of us. I had seen him off and on. He skied like a bomb, alone, stopping occasionally to draw a small pair of Japanese binoculars from his plum-colored anorak, to study the view, the choughs soaring overhead, or this or that. "*Ah, c'est merveilleux,*" he said now at the Mittelwald, and I agreed, but Tanya, who was having her skis removed, summoned me peremptorily.

"That frogman snake," she hissed. "Beware of him."

"Oh," I said. "I didn't know."

"You are too innocent in those many ways," she said, which I was glad to hear. "One last time only, would you like?"

I would. It was a strange web that Tanya wove that afternoon, a contentious thread of gossamer to bind me. "Now *wedeln,*" she said above a pitch of untouched powder — that was the marvel, so much of it, skiing unlimited. "Now follow closely, and we curve our wedels into one another, meeting and mating on and on."

We halted below to see the looped rhythm of our tracks. They met and mated perfectly, and there was not another soul in sight except a plum-colored figure standing far above. "Now I am purged at last. Now kiss me, Harry, damn you, man."

It was not expected, but not entirely un. We faced one another, skis interslid, and I kissed her cool salved lips that soon grew warm and gave as good or better. I stroked her back, right up to the neck, right down again. Yes, a hard necklace was certainly there. We soon stood apart, her eyes hot and green and shameless.

"Tell me, Tanya, what do you think of when you ski?" She must think of varied things.

"Of hate, but now of love. So now you chase me to the Mittelwald and Glühwein."

Rudi Viereck had said: *Not for enjoyment, as we ski.* But he could not have known her very well. She skied this last time for enjoyment, even yodeling, but was silent as we neared the Mittelwald. "*Schluss,* Hermann," she said, suffering him to remove her skis. He was a slab-faced bodyguard type, a thin-lipped Slav with a German name, scared palpitating of his mistress. He took skis and poles to Max Vyan's twin-turbined helicopter.

"No," she said to the restaurant woman about using Max's private bar. "It is better to be safe in public," she remarked, adding a dash of VSOP to her Glühwein. "No? You are like Max, not too heavy a tippling man."

"Makes me sleepy," I said. "Saps the energy, I find." But the unfortified Glühwein, hot and spicy, stole in to soothe some aches. I had been lucky to get away with that fall, that *glorious fall* as she described it. But twice lucky in less than twenty-four hours was stretching the odds a bit.

"You shiver, isn't it? About some recollections or some chills?"

"About some Devil's Plunge."

She laughed, but briefly. "You will not tell Max?"

"Nothing to tell him. But why not?"

"Because he would blame me. But now I am reminded of my duties — to ask you to dinner tomorrow night at eight, black tie, and come in your car, Max says."

"Many thanks. A party?"

"Tycoons and like that from Gstaad. But they will be choppered home quite early, leaving us to chat, perhaps, if Max suggests this, which he may in your case, being you."

A tête-à-tête, I rather hoped. Why deny that my appetite

for a tête-à-tête with Tanya was whetted? "That fella Korber
— he was going today, you said."

"Ach!" she snarled. "Will you not remind me of such
beasts?"

"Sorry." I changed the subject: "Does Max ski much?"

"For exercise, and with some caution due to middle years.
As social secretary it is my one personal service, to ski with
him. This afternoon he has been working in the wildflower
garden, just now clear of snow. The birds and flowers — these
are his love and relaxation from the *Untermenschen,* submen
he despises. One more Glühwein, and we go down."

I ordered that, but it was on the house, like my Alpenheide
pass, even my fair skiing companion. Odd of me, I agree, to
accept all that when I was being paid very handsomely to
spy on the social secretary's neck. But I had not asked for any
favors. To decline them would seem churlish, and perhaps
suspicious.

"If he still loves the natural world and despises people, Max
hasn't changed so much."

"You only are an exception. *Harry Ambler,* he said when he
heard that you were here. *Now there's a chap who was something different.*"

"Was is the word," I said. "In those days perhaps I did have
something, possibly. Not now, by God."

"Yes now, by God," said Tanya von Silberbach. "And because of it now, we may be closer friends, so, Harry?"

"So, Tanya, but no more falls like that one."

"It was my devil at the Devil's Plunge. When you see my
devil, flee from me." With what innocence she confessed her
guilt. "Sometime, if a night is quiet, I will tell you the horrors
of my life, and you may understand. Now let me chopper
you to the Kronenhof."

The turbocopter's cabin was comfortably furnished, and the machine less noisy than most of them; a luxury helicopter but quickly convertible to freight-carrying, I observed. In two or three minutes we were settling on the square near the hotel. "Won't you come in for a while?"

"Max did not suggest it. Always the suggestion must come from Max. I am not free as air, but subject to his whim. If Max says: *Ski with Harry*, so I do. If Max says: *Pay a little call on Harry*, so I do with utmost pleasure. Not until, however, Harry man, except for stolen kisses here and there, which Max would say are fair enough. He is quite human about the nicer urgings of the *Untermenschen*."

I waved Good-bye to Tanya.

SEVEN

The aura of mystery, of *what goes on in there and why?* that surrounded Schloss Alpenheide had led me to expect that Vyan's dinner would be something different. I could not have been more wrong, at least as to the party itself.

Max was an excellent host, drawing people out, a benign referee at the head of the table. A misanthrope? Ridiculous. Tanya was a paragon hostess at the foot, talking well enough about Italian art to command respect from Harry Z. Gilpin, the famous collector; discussing climbs in the Himalayas with the Belgian princeling on her other side. The climber, the chatelaine, two more Tanyas to add to the list. She wore maroon that evening, with the high collar that seemed to be her uniform as social secretary. Her outer form or shell remained the same, but a chameleon dwelt therein.

I do not remember the Belgian couple's name, and it does not matter — they came and went that once, young people sure of their world, as much at home in a Ruritanian Schloss as at Buckingham Palace or in the high Himalaya.

But Harry Z. Gilpin — sharing one name with me, the sec-

ond with Zanzibar of all places, the third with the horseman —
stayed in mind, not only for nominal reasons. He was a spare
man in his sixties, eyes small and infinitely shrewd, a hint of
Aztec about the cheekbones. He had the air too, a member of
another team in the same league as Max and the Bel-
gians. And if one had not already heard of him as copper king,
collector and philanthropist, one might guess at the state of
Gilpin's pocketbook by the emeralds and rubies that embroi-
dered Mrs. Gilpin, upon whom he clearly doted. Gloria Gilpin
was too sugar-sweet a cup of tea to be my cup, but I took to
him.

After a glass of port we joined the women in the big drawing
room with curtains all along a southern wall. The fat butler
bore liqueurs, two maids the coffee. A slim man in a dark suit,
an unobtrusive secretary type, had brought a note to Max during dinner, and taken it away at his employer's nod. Now he
came into the drawing room with another, which Max glanced
at and dropped into the fire behind him. "So sorry," he said.
"That's Washington. I won't be long."

These were the only glimpses of international tycoonery.
It happened that both times I noticed Harry Gilpin's quick
speculative glance at Max.

"Is the chalet new, Countess Tanya?"

"It is both old and new, Mr. Ambler, in two senses. The
first Schloss Alpenheide dated from the early fourteen hun-
dreds — it withstood bloody assault at the hands of Charles
the Bold of Burgundy in 1476, and down through the warring
centuries was never stormed. It still stood, a neglected ruin,
when Max came to Alpenheide eleven years ago. It was his
inspiration to take down the old castle stone by stone, and to
build Schloss Alpenheide totally anew, or as I might say, with
the old wine pour new bottles, Mr. Ambler, isn't it?"

She spoke earnestly, now historian and archaeologist. "How very interesting," I said.

"But much of the surroundings have been preserved in toto, modernized, of course — as, for example, the moat and drawbridge . . ."

Max had come back. "Tanya, you sound like that guide at the Acropolis." Was it said indulgently or irritably? His left eye twitched, and he put up a finger to it.

"Now, Max, I rather think that we should board that superb machine of yours and be whisked over to Gstaad. My mounting decrepitude imposes early hours." All decrepitude must mount, but Harry Gilpin looked spry and fit, a measured comment, a social gambit by a man completely self-assured; and yet he could also mock himself at times, which was endearing. I wondered whether Max could mock himself. "If you are in New York next week, why not have luncheon with me, Max? Simply telephone or cable."

"I'd like to do that, Harry. Many thanks." It had transpired at dinner that each of them kept his Jet Galaxy at Geneva Airport for little trips across the world.

"It's been such a pleasure meeting you, Mr. Ambler, and hearing of your legendary flying feats from Max."

"Horse-and-buggy flying. Good-bye, Mrs. Gilpin."

"Good-bye. Do look us up at the Palace if you come to Gstaad."

"Yes, I wish you would," said Harry Z. Gilpin with enthusiasm.

We stood at a window to watch the helicopter take off, and then walked by one corridor and another to the drawing room. "Well, that's that," Max said. "Don't hurry, Ambler. I have one or two trivialities to cope with, but Tanya will entertain you until I get back."

"My dress, it is *so* tight, I stifle."

He raised that left eyebrow. "Unstifle then, for Ambler's benefit," and he went out.

"Make yourself comfortable, Harry, while I do the same — a drink or anything. I will not be two jiffies."

Alone now, I prowled the room, as is my habit. It was exquisite — the furniture, the tapestries, the carpets, the great window curtained in green brocade, the great sofa in gold, the tall plants and the flower arrangements, everything in giant scale. Was that what bothered me? Even the flower painting over the mantelpiece was about ten feet by eight. I went to inspect it — not the kind of painting I like, but marvelously fine with only the reservation of too much.

And then I looked down at six-foot logs of apple wood — cigar smoke, apple smoke, jasmine, heady smells — and saw a small piece of paper close beside the ashes.

Although alone, I did not feel entirely sure of being alone, turning now to warm my back, taking out a cigarette, slapping my pockets vainly for a match. I turned again, stooped to use the paper for a spill and lit my cigarette.

CAB-INTERSEC were the words in what is called cursive script, I think, not quite printing, not quite writing, ornate with curlicues. A cab at an intersection, a taxi where streets meet. *That's Washington,* he had said after glancing at the paper. It was not very interesting, and again I warmed my back. "Too much fresh air," I yawned to myself as Tanya came in.

"You are sleepy, no?"

"No," I said. I had felt drowsy in the heavy-scented room, but was now very wide awake.

She wore a white satin gown — or robe might be the word,

or toga — a Roman effect drawn in by a black sash at the waist, black sandals on bare feet, and from her neck there hung a diamond. Its sparkle was not colorless but distinctly washed with blue against the white robe, the rich brown skin. It was the same size and octagonal shape — at least an inch and a half on the longer side — as the photograph I had seen; and the baguettes which formed the necklace looked the same.

I should not permit myself to stare too obviously at Tanya's throat. I therefore glanced once, and looked down to her gilded toes and up again, a glance en passant, until my eyes met hers. "You look smashing," I said sincerely.

"Shall we dance a little, would you like it?"

I said I would, and so we did, to some slow tune. "Do you not notice anything around my neck?"

Thus invited, I could stare. *In that corner is the faintest blush of pink . . . What they call a diamantine bloom.* I saw it, no possible doubt, blue shading into pink against the brown of Tanya's skin, all brown into a vale of bosom.

"Do you not like what you see, then, Harry Man?"

"Very much," I said, and danced on more primly than one might feel inclined, but one was a guest of her employer, after all. "What is it, that stone?"

"It is a diamond — a necklace of smaller cuttings, and the one."

"Incredible," I said. "The value must be beyond belief."

"A million pounds, Max paid for it. But the true worth, who can tell, the market being rather limited. It might be three times so much, Max says."

"And he gave it to you?" The music had stopped.

"It is mine for safekeeping, to be worn at all times day and night but never shown in public." Tanya said that slowly —

parrotwise, one might think — and she continued: "But at the end of this calendar year, if I have been good, it is to be mine absolutely — lock, stock and barrel, as you say."

"*If,*" Max Vyan said. I had not seen him gumshoe in. "Well, Ambler, what do you think of the bauble?"

"Fabulous," I said. "I've never seen anything to approach it. And you think too risky to show it in public?"

"No," he said. "We have adequate protection. Besides, the thing is insured for what I paid. Risk isn't it, to hell with risk. The point is that if you flaunt your bauble, then you've lost it. Hide it, and you've got it. That applies to everything."

Possibly so, but there was a slight wrongness somewhere about the theory. "I bet Mrs. Gilpin would give her eyeteeth for even a look."

"Ach! That dolly puss!"

"She has already needled Harry Zee into making delicate inquiries of my bland ignorance. The word goes round, it always does, eh, Tanya?"

"Not from me, Max. Not one tiny whisper, I promise you."

He ignored her protestations, and whickered once, like a single neigh from a distant horse. "One-upmanship on little Gloria, see the point?"

"H'mm," I said. "Have you had it long?"

"Two years. Is it about that, Tanya?"

"Yes, Max — it was the month after I had come to be your social secretary."

"I heard about this diamond being cut in Amsterdam. Found in Australia, reputedly — hence called the Koala, although why call a diamond after a cuddlesome creature chewing eucalyptus leaves, I would not know — only the Diggers would think that one up."

"I like 'em," I said. "Good bluff types."

"Uncouth sentimentalists. Anyway, I had inquiries made about the owner. There are ways and means of finding out such items, in fact one has to for obvious reasons. But I failed. Schuurman and Decker, the diamond people, were inflexibly mum. They vouched that the stone was legitimately owned, and said that the necklace could be obtained for a million pounds. So I sent for it, liked it, and that was that."

It was a funny thing, but just as I had not believed Brock about the theft, now I did not believe Vyan about the buying. He was watching me. *"And that was that,"* I mimicked his clipped tones for something to say. "And very nice too at a million smackers."

Max frowned. *You're a well-bred vulgarian, Ambler,* he used to say. He had been a snob then too; and now a super-snob, one might deduce from his recherché dinner party. "And you wear it always, even skiing?"

"Even skiing always, and in secret — except now this special once that Max lets me gratify my woman's pride and show its sparkle on me to his old friend, Harry Ambler. It is a rare occasion, Mr. Harry."

"Safe enough to show it to me, I suppose, and thank you for the compliment. But if word has got round, surely a frightful risk out skiing — I mean to Tanya's life and limb with all the crooks there are about?"

She was close to me, and smiling, a damnably seductive woman. "Gently does it," Vyan said.

My hands were caught, my forearms crossed, my knee buckled somehow, and I flew over the fulcrum of Tanya's hip to recline in comfort on the sofa. "I see what you mean," I said, standing up.

"You can go now, Tanya."

"Yes, Max." She gave me her hand. "No little tricks this

time. So good night, Mr. Harry. I hope I do not hurt your body or your feelings?"

"Neither," I said. "Good night." I kissed the hand for another whiff of that insidious, doubtless million-dollar scent, and Tanya left.

"Quite a girl," I said, when the door had closed.

"She has her uses. Now show me this car of yours."

He inspected it in the courtyard, fiddling like a schoolboy at the window buttons, aerial, six-way seat and so on — all of which must have been old hat to him. Then he went round it, peering, tapping glass and mudguards. "Solid," he said.

"Virtually crash-proof, so they claim. As long as you have your shoulder belt on, you can hit head-on, or roll it, anything except jump a cliff."

"A special order job?"

"Yes," I said.

"It must have set you back a trifle, Ambler."

"Not too bad, considering. Some racehorse owner in Paris ordered it, but he went broke, so I made a dicker at half price."

"One of your better dickers, Ambler. Take me down the valley a bit, it isn't midnight yet. Hermann!"

Tanya's ski attendant stepped out of a shadow cast by the moon, and Max spoke fluent German to him, too fast for me to get more than the drift about half an hour, and to tell someone else. We rumbled across the drawbridge, water twenty or thirty feet below us. "Does this thing open?"

"Of course, Ambler. What do you take me for?"

"You must have to pump a lot of water into that moat."

"We don't pump it. I made a catchment lake up the mountain a bit, and we siphon from that. A moat and a drawbridge to keep out the plebs. I cherish my privacy, Ambler."

"A man's house is his castle, so they say."

Vyan grunted at my plebeian chestnut, and I drove down the winding road between high walls to the foot of his hill, and then beside a fence this side of the floodlit slope. A dog barked deeply in there. "That's Pluto," Vyan said. "I'll introduce you on our way back."

It was another moonlit night, just past the full, only forty-eight hours since I had walked with Major Moffett. We had taken the upper road, the one that climbed through the village and came on here to its intersection with the river road which by-passed Alpenheide. Now we passed that intersection or T-junction. CAB-INTERSEC — what went on in his mind, sitting motionless beside me? "Warm enough, Max?"

"Fine. But give us more heat, and I'll open my window. I like to listen." Our tire studs hummed faintly on the tarmac, crackled on patches of ice that had formed since dusk. The rushing of the river grew.

"Spring speaking," Max said as we turned downstream, headlights swinging across icicles on the cliffs beyond the river. We passed the sawmill, and a pile of snow in which some skis had buried themselves.

To the left and above us were the lights of Alpenheide. Between here and there were dark patches in the glistening white. And nothing moved; no wind stirred the needles of a fir — nothing moved except the river and ourselves. "A week or two," he said, "and all the snow will be gone down here."

"Are the wildflowers good?"

"That's why I came to Alpenheide — or one sound reason."

"And now you own the place, wildflowers included."

"Crass comment," he said.

I remembered his delight, his devout pleasure as if God were with us when we came on a patch of yellow jonquils in a clearing of the forest. He had knifed a man that day. "It's twenty-one years ago this month," I said.

"I was thinking of that."

"What did you do after the war — how did you get started, I mean?"

"Simple," he said. "Supply and demand. Very short supply, very great demand. I went into the smuggling business."

We had passed the village. Now Max Vyan's bypass joined the other road. "What kind of smuggling, Max?"

"The most obvious. I acquired a boat — it was child's play after five years' training in the bag — nylons, a drug or two. I promoted vanity and health at vast profit between England, North Africa and Europe until even those stupid clots became suspicious; at which point I eased off to South America."

"What kind of drugs?"

"Mostly sulfa and penicillin by arrangement with the U.S. Army for the benefit of the human race. I might have used you, Ambler, had you not been flying Vampires for His Majesty. None of the sods I worked with could be trusted. Ah, listen to that!" It was a high thin yap from the woods above us. "The fox is hunting," Vyan said. He closed his window.

"Drugs on the black market, I'm not too keen on that idea."

"The wages of sin is death, I'll say it for you, Ambler. Incidentally, this conversation tends to be confidential."

"Confidential it is. And in South America?"

"I went bigger there, satisfying a brisk demand for war-surplus ironmongery. As you would say, Ambler, the shekels rolled in. Then I had my nest-egg and could turn respectable, which did not stop me outwitting suckers. I've been doing it ever since." He paused; then added: "Money for money's sake does ultimately pall."

The road wound down the left side of the valley, which was

narrow now and steep. We met a few cars, all going fast. The headlamps gave some warning, but we were on the outer side, with no parapet, vulnerable to climbing jehus. Some little nipper — a Simca Mille — swung his tail at me on ice, corrected it and screeched on past. "Maniac," I said.

There had been none too much to spare, but Vyan seemed unruffled. "After the bridge we get the inner track. Then you can use your armored plate to push the pipsqueaks off."

The valley narrowed to a gorge, and the road crossed over. "Dip your lights twice," he said on the bridge. I did so, and a torch flashed back from the other side. "Not a bad bridge," Max Vyan said.

"Did you build it?"

"No. I told the Canton that if they would build a new one and improve the road, I would finance the ski development. The old bridge was a one-way bottleneck on wooden trestles — hence no skiing except of the langlauf-skins variety. This gorge, this bridge, is the key to Alpenheide." He stirred. He was a still and quiet man but now he seemed restless in his bucket seat beside me. "Keys turn two ways," Max said. "Two keys to the wildflower book."

I did not understand his cryptic comment, but stored it for later consideration. Now I pushed on soberly down the right side of the valley. There were still cliffs above us and below.

Headlights were swinging up to meet us, coming fast. "Here's your chance now, Ambler, judge it right. Swing in close and judge it. Now clobber the bastard in the guts!"

I did no such thing to the black Porsche, the face of that Frenchman flashing by. "Do you want me to go killing people?"

"I don't have much fun," Max Vyan said. "You can turn round here."

It was a deep recess on the inner side, a stone quarry. "Joke over, Ambler. Let's talk a minute. Then you can show me what this thing will do."

I was still alarmed, hence annoyed, about his idea of a joke. But I switched off. "Well?" I said.

"Well, well," he said. "Tell me, Ambler, why are you here?"

"Because you asked me to take you for a drive."

"I mean at Alpenheide."

"To ski, of course. I'm in funds for once." My limited intelligence warned me to play it equal with the postwar plutocrat, Max Vyan, who did not have much fun. "And that reminds me, thank you for my skiing pass."

"Not at all, Ambler. I hear from Tanya that you're worth every brass centime of it. What I'm getting at is only that lately there has been undue and increasing interest in my doings, not always healthy for those concerned."

"Anyone who shuts himself off behind a drawbridge in a mountain valley of which he appears to all and sundry to be the total owner, tends to become intriguing news, or doesn't he?"

"Intriguing news to you, Ambler?"

"We escaped together once. Or have you forgotten that?"

"No," he said. "I have not forgotten that. Nor have I forgotten that the world knows that. So you weren't sent here to join the throng of spies?"

"For Christ's sake, come off it, Max." Had I judged the tone right, just right?

"Sorry," he said. And he was, I am sure, I am afraid. "You have to understand, Harry, that when one reaches my position, and into the bargain has my built-in loathing for homo sapiens, so-called, one tends to be suspicious."

"I don't wonder, cloistered behind those walls. It would drive me dotty, not to say suspicious."

"You forget, or you may not know, that I can take the chopper to Geneva and be in New York in seven hours."

"But why Switzerland, why all this seclusion?"

"I told you, Ambler. As to Switzerland — that is largely financial, but you might not understand."

"Might not," I agreed. "Shall I take you home now to seclusion?"

"You're the sanest annoying halfwit I ever met," he said.

We crossed the bridge high above the river. Then I put the gun to her up the valley until Max said: "That'll do, Ambler, I get the point." The lights of Alpenheide came into view, and I turned left by the river, dawdling again.

"Back there when you told me to push that car off . . ."

"My little joke. Go on."

"Did you happen to notice the chap in the Porsche?"

"Yes. If I had known it was him, I would have been in earnest."

"Tanya warned me against him. Who is he, one of the spies you mention?"

"They come in various categories," Vyan said. "He's after the diamond, so I understand."

"I still don't see why you let her go skiing with that thing round her neck."

"I have explained once, Ambler. As for his taking on Tanya, let him try."

"She can't do jujitsu on a ski slope."

Vyan whickered. "You can appoint yourself her guardian in my absence."

"When are you going?"

"Tomorrow afternoon, I think — some items in New York to settle. So, go skiing with Tanya, have her down to the Kronenhof for a quiet drink. Just two things I should warn you about in your own interest."

"All ears," I said.

"First, don't get between Tanya and the enemy. Second, do not annoy her. She fancies you, Ambler. And there are moments of danger for those whom Tanya fancies."

"I'll bear it in mind." It was already well-etched in mind. "What's her history, Max?"

"Let's say I know enough of it to wield the whip hand, to put her talents to their proper uses. My other advantage is that sex left me cold and passed me by — neither women nor pretty boys, nor — in case you misunderstand my whip hand — flagellation, no esoteric lusts of the flesh."

"Nor of the spirit?"

"Ah," he said. "That's another story. You interest me, Ambler, such a simple dolt with glimmerings of intelligence, I might even say aesthetic feeling."

"Well, thanks."

"Your more boring aspects are a positive genius for the trite phrase, and a very vulgar yen for women."

"What's vulgar about what makes the world go round?"

"What could be more vulgar, Ambler?"

"Money," I said. "Money, money, not that I don't lust for the stuff when I ain't got it. You said yourself that money for money's sake does ultimately pall. You ought to know."

"I do," he said. We neared the bottom of his hill. There was some form of lighting all along and up the slope, but I could not see the source that lit the bare trunks of spruce trees, yet left the ground invisible.

"Stop by that gate," Max said. "I'd like you to meet Pluto. Lights off, Ambler." The casual staccato orders of one who is obeyed. "Wait here," he said, and went over. A dog barked once along the hill, a St. Bernard or something of that deep-voiced order. "Pluto, boy!" he said, unlocking the gate and going in. He bent his head.

It was a soft sound, the small soft whine of love that children and dogs make, as sweet a sound as there may be. But I could not see either man or dog until Vyan said: "Come and meet old Harry Ambler," and they emerged from the shadow, Vyan holding Pluto's collar. It was a colossal beast, pale in the moon with a dark square muzzle, and it rumbled. There was lethal menace in that rumble.

"This is Ambler, Pluto. Harry Ambler — *he's your friend.* Go and say hello to Harry Ambler — *he's your friend.*"

The rumbling stopped. Pluto cocked his head, and literally smiled, and wagged his tail, coming to say hello as amiably as any spaniel. "Now you're pals for life," Max Vyan said. "Or good behavior." Pluto put his chin on my right hand, and I put my left hand on his head, and again he rumbled, this time for friendship. "Good boy," Vyan said. There was true kindness in his voice and face, a simplicity of truth, strange man. "Okay, Pluto, say *Auf wiedersehen.*"

Pluto wowfed at me and went back through the gate in the high fence that bordered his patroling ground.

I drove on. "Super-dog," I said. "What breed is he?"

"A blue-blooded mixture. Tibetan Mastiff bred back to St. Bernard — that linked great strength, good nose and intelligence with a killing watchdog strain — and then Great Dane for height and speed. We've been breeding from separate bloodlines in all three, and now I think the type is holding true. But they would hardly do for household pets in suburbia, Ambler. Or stated otherwise: Anyone who is not Pluto's friend is there to be chopped up."

Once again size, an obsession with ultimates. There was a word for that . . . "Sorry. I didn't hear?"

"I said: Look after Tanya with the precautions aforemen-
tioned. How long are you staying, Ambler?"

"A fortnight or so, but that depends. Well, actually . . ."

"Well, actually what?"

"A girl I used to know in Australia is flying through — I
might pop down to Geneva to intercept her on the way to London."

"Why not bring the lady to Alpenheide? Twang, twang —
two strings to Ambler's insatiable bow."

"A bit less of that," I said.

He stiffened beside me. I could feel Max Vyan grow taut,
and I saw his left hand clench. He was rather mad, I knew.
But then he slapped his knee. "Harry Ambler," he said. "It's
good to have you about the place."

I drove up between the walls. "Let me off before the
bridge," he said. "I'll cross. Then you can watch her open up."

"Many thanks," I said. "I enjoyed all that." I got out to
watch his pet drawbridge open to insure his privacy.

"By the way," he called from over there, "if you're going to
Geneva, you might take something to the bank for me. Call
Sim, and he'll produce it."

"Who's Sim?"

"My secretary. Well, good night," and he added two syl-
lables quietly. Did he add: "Old friend?"

"Good night."

The bridge opened from the middle. The two halves rose
slowly with no sound that I could hear, climbing up the man
in his dinner jacket, in the moon, cutting him off, as it were, by
trousers, waist, and black bow tie and head.

I drove back to the Kronenhof. Harry Ambler, *he's your
friend.*

EIGHT

I made out a telegram to Parsons, the porter at my club: UNTIL FURTHER INSTRUCTIONS PLEASE FORWARD LETTERS NOT BILLS HOTEL KRONENHOF ALPENHEIDE HARRY AMBLER, and gave it to Dominic. There was a lull at his desk, the early skiers gone, the mid-morning brigade not yet afoot.

His pencil moved word by word and fast along my wire; his left hand tapped the bell for a messenger; and it was on its way, dispatched with the smooth efficiency of one's doctor charging a hypodermic.

"Thank you, Dominic."

"It is my pleasure, sir, and to have you with us longer." He consulted a registration list. "The day after tomorrow, Mr. Ambler, it will be possible to move you to a corner suite, as you requested — facing the ski slopes and the village."

"So much sun all day — one doesn't want it at breakfast time."

"Quite, sir, quite."

"By the way, Dominic, an Australian friend of mine may be stopping off at Geneva for an hour or two tomorrow. She said she would telephone from Rome this evening. If that eventuates, could the hotel produce a picnic lunch — I mean something better than the skiing variety in a paper bag?"

His hand protested such a notion. "Indeed, sir. I shall personally supervise. A white wine, Mr. Ambler, possibly a Riesling? I understand the Australian Rieslings are quite notable but do not travel. So a good Riesling for your friend's comparison?"

"Fine, Dominic. It's not definite yet, of course."

"Indeed, indeed." He was making notes. "Now, the weather will assuredly be fine, yet with perhaps a slight chill at this season — therefore hot soup in a vacuum flask — Lobster Bisque, might I suggest? And then to follow . . ."

"May I leave it all to you?" No doubt Dominic had been ordered to give me the gilded treatment, but he went about it with a will.

It was half past ten when I took the cable car. Two hours in the morning, an hour after lunch would be enough skiing today. There was a lot to think about before reporting to Miss Mary Dunn, my case manager. She had said that when she received the message via Parsons, she would immediately fly to Rome and telephone from there. It seemed a roundabout procedure, but not for her employee to reason why. There were other basic whys to bother me. Why pay princely wages for this ludicrous assignment, completed successfully, and without my lifting a finger, in about three days? And why did Tanya wear the diamond always?

But the riddles bothered me less than something else. Looking back at it all now, I see that my qualms of conscience were, to say the least, unwarranted. On that morning, however, I was none too happy about my behavior toward Max Vyan. After twenty years, he still held me in a special compartment of esteem. He had even told me the shady beginnings of his great success. He was on like a flash to the idea that I might have been sent to Alpenheide to spy on him. But when I protested that, he apologized, and meant it. It was all very awkward. I had never thought of the man as a friend of mine. He seemed to cherish me as his one true friend.

I took the second cable car from the Mittelwald to the top. The man in charge of it was a likable fellow with a mobile face, reminiscent of the French comedian. Everyone called him Fernandel.

"You ski alone, Herr Ambler?"

"For my sins, alone."

"For sins or for safety." He grinned widely, looking down at the Devil's Plunge, on which he must have seen me take an epic fall.

As it turned out, I did not ski alone that morning. Still not much pleased with myself, I meandered gloomily down the Soldanella and came on a family of three — testy father, anxious mother, small boy in a tearful rage. He was lying on quite a steep pitch with one ski off. "I'll hit you if you try," he sobbed, brandishing a wooden pole at his father.

"Jeremy!"

"You little devil."

"Hit away," I said, and put on his ski and shepherded him to an easier slope.

He had been ill, his mother said, and still tired easily. "Our fault," she said. "It's too steep for him, and we're only beginners." She was quite an appealing girl, which tends ever to encourage the good Samaritan.

So I took him for a while, a relief from those whys and nags of conscience. Being childish myself, I get on with them, and we had fun together. "Now we dance a bit."

"Now we *what* a bit?"

"We dance a bit. Skiing isn't all this trying all the time. It's dance, dance, dance, from one to the other. Watch now, and you do the same."

"Gosh, that was super," he said at the Mittelwald after our second run. "Could we ski again sometime?"

"Just give me a shout. Good-bye then, Jeremy."

"Good-bye. I don't know your name to shout it."

"Harry Ambler," I said.

"It's like dancing, Mummy, he says, and so it is."

"I thought you said dancing was for girls."

"Not with Harry Ambler, ski-dancing isn't."

She laughed. "Come on then, darling, down for lunch."

"Thank you so much," said the father. Their name was Grayson. "You made his day."

"I enjoyed myself," I said, feeling cheerful again, a bonus for my ego, which is more tender than you may imagine.

I got a bowl of powerful brown soup, more stew than soup, a couple of rolls, bananas, a big bottle of Hellesbier, and found an empty table on the Mittelwald terrace. No sooner was I tucking in than that Frenchman arrived with bows, and might he join me? We introduced ourselves — Gilles Dorion.

"Is this your first time at Alpenheide, Mr. Ambler?"

I nodded. "Not my last, I hope. And you, Monsieur?"

"Once before — a week in this January to whet the appetite." He spoke good English, much better than my French, so English it was, with a few French expressions to flaunt my culture. I find foreign languages exhausting.

"The snow will soon be gone in the valley. How long will the skiing last, do you think?"

He shrugged. "With so much sunshine, perhaps a week on the lower slopes. But there are large snowfalls still to come, they say. Will you stay the whole month, Monsieur, if the skiing lasts?"

"My plans are vague. And you?"

"It is the same. We are perhaps both gentlemen of leisure for this moment."

The atmosphere was cordial. I ate my bananas, two of those small ones, only bananas worth the name. Gilles Dorion was suave and easy in his manner, but surely it was not the smoothness of a crook. That simply did not fit. The eye was cool and steady. A soldier's watchful face? What was he? That air, that compact measured way of skiing — I had one of my hunches. "Are you a Chasseur Alpin?" I asked.

My blunt question caught him by surprise. "Why, Monsieur?" he said politely, looking into his vin rouge.

"You ski like one. It might be control, I suppose, from carrying heavy equipment. And you look like a montagnard."

"You are observant," he said. "Yes, my army service was with the Chasseurs Alpins. And you, Mr. Ambler, I might have guessed it too — that you are a pilot."

"How might you guess that?"

"It is the eyes, perhaps. But more, it is a similar thing of control, of being balanced — yes."

"How did you hear, though?"

"There is much talk in the hotel. That you were the pilot who flew Monsieur Vyan from captivity. It is — how do you say it? — the glamour story to end all glamour."

"Ancient glamour," I said. But once again I thought of what I was doing to Max Vyan. And about this Dorion — was it coincidence that he had followed me through the Jura to Vallorbe? "Shall we do a run together?"

"With pleasure," he said.

We rode in Fernandel's cable car, eight minutes up the Teufelsspitzen. They were gentle mountains to be linked by name with old Nick himself. But this was the southern view. On the other side were the tremendous cliffs that I had not seen. One of these days I must climb up to have a look.

"See," said Dorion. "The helicopter!" It rose from Schloss Alpenheide and turned the other way, climbing to the west and out of the valley, a blue and white machine blending into snow and sky, up over the curving glacier from which the river stemmed. "So Monsieur Vyan makes some trip away," he said casually, a question without the interrogative.

"To New York, he told me last night. Max keeps his private jet at Geneva, you know, seven hours from here to Park Avenue."

"It is not speed alone. It is the change, as from secluded cloister to teeming city across the ocean, just like that." He snapped his fingers. "It would not be bearable to me."

"Hear, hear," I said. "But a penthouse in New York can be a cloister too."

"Philosopher, Mr. Ambler," he said by the window of the packed cable car. "Also, with so charming a companion, the penthouse would be a cushioned cloister, so to say."

"H'mm," I said. Unless Dorion was dangling red herrings to draw me out, he did not know much about Max's relations with his social secretary. "I don't think she's gone with him actually," I said, and watched his eyes flicker to that. But then the car slowed at the Höhengrat.

We put on our skis and headed for the Wintergreen, passing the top of the Devil's Plunge. *Vollkommen Gesperrt.* Totally closed, the signs said today. "Have you been down that?"

"In January," he said, "when it was easier. And you?"

"Once," I said. "I was skiing with Tanya von Silberbach. I took a beauty of a fall."

"To take a beauty of a fall with such a beauty is at least some compensation," said Gilles Dorion.

We were of about even quality as skiers, and chose our own ways to part and meet on the Wintergreen which, as I have said, was on the western side of the spine that ran up from Alpenheide to the Höhengrat. We crossed over just below the Mittelwald, the halfway house. It was a slightly tricky place, requiring caution because of slower skiers. The path was narrow, with posts and a rope railing on the outer side. It ran around the shoulder, above one of the only avalanche slopes, cutting a bare swath through forest right down into the valley. Then we ran the lower half of the Soldanella to the east. Already patches of grass were showing near the foot.

"Will you ski tomorrow?" We had run nearly six thousand vertical feet in a few minutes, but his breathing was slow.

"I may be away tomorrow. The day after, though."

"The Pilot and the Chasseur Alpin, we could make good company together. Au revoir, Monsieur." He took the cable car again.

I walked to the hotel, considering this Gilles Dorion, too casual a guider of the conversation. *We could make good company together.* Was that a proposal? I had not told him about Vyan's departure, Tanya's presence, my absence tomorrow in order to dissimulate bluff honesty. I had told him on the spur of the moment because that is what I am like. I cannot pretend unless I have forewarning, as, for example, with Max last night. One of these hours or days I was going to put my blundering foot in it.

I left my boots in the *ski-raum* and went upstairs to ask

Dominic whether a telephone call had come. He stood at his desk, being besieged by a distraught woman, refined cockney, middle-aged. ". . . But I assure you, Madam, I do assure you that no Major Moffett has been our guest."

"He was. I know he was, even writing to me on the paper, Hotel Kronenhof, Alpenheide, it said as large as life, but I burned them, I always do. Please help me. Why pretend?"

"Mrs. Moffett," he said, leaning toward her, so genuinely kind and sympathetic. "It is some most unfortunate mistake. Please check our books. Please ask our staff. But, Madam, there are other Hotels Kronenhof in Switzerland — there is, for example, the distinguished Hotel Kronenhof of Pontresina. May I call them, please?"

She nodded, poor woman, her eyes brimming, and her name was Mildred. I had heard all this on my way from the basement stairs across the lobby. "This gentleman!" she cried. "You, sir! Didn't you know a Major Moffett?"

I had had that moment to think. Poor woman, poor wife of poor old Moffett, and what could I do to help either of them? "I'm afraid not," I said.

"Could he be here under another name? Could he be . . ." She stopped herself. "A big roly-poly man with a wide moustache." She stared at me in supplication.

I shook my head. "I am most awfully sorry."

"Friedrich? It is Dominic at Alpenheide. Yes, good. *Vortrefflich*. But we have here a worrying thing, and must ask your help. This English lady seeks her husband, a Major Moffett . . ."

"M O F F E T T," she spelled it out. "With an E and two T's, not the common way."

". . . Yes, thus. We have had no such gentleman with us in

this season. But it is possible that at your Kronenhof . . . You will check?"

"But I *know* George was here."

"We are at your service, Madam, I assure you. Ja, Fried-rich? You have had no such registration? Danke, Danke, auf wiederschauen." Dominic looked down at his glass-topped desk, and then at Mrs. Moffett. "I am sorry, Madam." And then he added carefully and kindly: "There are other Hotels Kronenhof that I would gladly ask, but it is time now for you to see the police. Only they can at once make countrywide in-quiries, and your husband will be safe and sound."

"Oh no, he won't." Mrs. Moffett stood straighter. She was plump, wore a woolen coat with a muskrat collar, a bronze tur-ban hat. She had some dumpy dignity. "I'll go to the police," she said. "But first I want a room here."

"But, Madam, this is high spring season. Every room at our hotel is taken, every lodging house, every garret even, in Alpen-heide."

I had been hovering at the picture postcard stand. Curiosity and guilt, and because Mrs. Moffett cast imploring glances at a fellow countryman.

"This gentleman will confirm that our situation, it is entirely hopeless, Madam, to my infinite regret."

The people had almost all changed over this weekend, but not quite — not Gilles Dorion, nor the ski-club man, nor a few others since the Major's day. There might be visitors who would remember the unmemorable Moffett. Their mouths could not be shut as could the mouths of every employee, every inhabitant of Alpenheide. If these dangers were cross-ing Dominic's mind, and they certainly were, he gave no ink-ling of that anxiety, only of his distress at not being able to help her.

"I'm afraid Alpenheide is literally jam-packed," I said. "You see, the skiing is still superb. I do hope you find your husband, Mrs. Moffett; and I'm sure the quickest way is to go to the police, as the concierge suggests."

"Thank you," she said. "George was . . . no, I mustn't say that. George is . . ." She picked up her suitcase.

"Let me get a boy to carry it for you, Madam."

"I'll carry it myself," she said, and went out, crying.

Dominic looked after her, and so did I. "Damn you," I said. "Ach," he said softly, even sadly, in his throat. I walked across the lobby and to the lift. It was a sordid bloody other world for me, and already I was up to my neck in it.

The call came through about six o'clock.

"Oh, Harry, is it really you?"

"Me," I confirmed. "Where are you? Rome?"

"I got in from Beirut this morning early. It's been such a heavenly day here, darling."

"Been a fine day here too," I said. "If you have nothing on, tomorrow could be even better at Geneva."

There was a pause. I had put Dunn off her stroke. Then she chuckled warmly down there in Rome. "Nothing better on," she said. "So you'll meet me, Harry?"

"Can do. What time?"

"Just before noon, I think. I can't quite remember the ETA. A quarter to would cover it, Ducks." She sounded more friendly and more Australian on this telephone than in real life.

"Any sheila oughto remember ETA's. Well, I'm bringing a picnic lunch, okay?"

"Good on ya, Harry boy."

"A real slap-up job. Like the treats you gave me in the Grampians, remember?"

Dunn giggled.

"Be good till I see you."

"What else would I be?" The tone was very warm.

"Cheerio, then, old Cobber."

"See you soon, then, Mite."

I paced my sitting room. She could act the lover girl by telephone, but tomorrow would be cold business. *Now report. Make it short and snappy, Ambler.* My efficient case manager. But I did look forward to seeing Mary Dunn, excursion to sanity from cloud-cuckoo land, play truant from the miasma of this Alpenheide. I sang a snatch from *My Fair Lady*, it was probably "The Rain in Spain," been singing it for years. That longnosed, shapely, annoying Dunn. . . .

Dominic would already have confirmation of my picnic, but etiquette required that I should tell him.

There was one other telephone call to make. "This is Sim, Mr. Ambler."

"Good evening. I told Max Vyan that I might be going to Geneva tomorrow, and he asked me to take something down."

"Oh, yes, Mr. Ambler. I have it here."

"I could come now — or later this evening." Later this evening might mean the chance of a more leisurely chat with Tanya. "After dinner would suit me best, Mr. Sim."

"But I can run down with it at once . . . No, not the least trouble, I assure you."

"Okay, then. I'll expect you in half an hour." No doubt the secretary leaped at a chance to escape that place — prison or secluded cloister.

I had a quick bath, dressed, and mooched from room to room, uneasy about Moffett's widow. And in denying knowledge of him, had I not made myself an accessory to his murder?

You should understand that, despite what might be called an adventurous life and a few brushes with the law for beating it up and this and that, I had up to then never personally known the scents of wickedness and murder. True, I had lurked nearby while Max Vyan killed a couple of Germans, but that was semi-legitimized homicide. And from my Spitfire I had squirted give-or-take thirty of the enemy to perdition. But I was still the innocent at large. Now sullied a mite, I could feel the insidious appetites to conspiracy and violence.

I switched on the piped radio. The music was Beethoven; the symphony the Sixth; the movement the one where birdies call, very sylvan and peaceful.

"Mr. Sim is here to see you, sir."

"Ask him to come up."

Sim carried a crocodile briefcase, one of those slim and highly expensive items. He shook hands with me, laid it on the sofa and unlocked a chain round his wrist. It retracted into the handle of the case.

"Neat dodge," I said.

"This key is for the padlock, Mr. Ambler, this for the briefcase." He laid padlock and key ring on top of the case, spacing them precisely. His hands were as sleek and supple as a woman's. Sim emitted a gusty sigh.

"Won't you take off your coat and have a drink?"

"A quick one, may I, a very quick one?"

Last evening Sim had worn a plain dark suit, a self-effacing air, one hardly noticed him. Now, sheepskin removed, the impression was different, in fact foppish in that way which raises eyebrows and little questions — black suede shoes, a four-button suit slightly lighter than navy blue, pipestem trousers with no turn-ups, double cuffs at the wrists, a red tie and flowing silk handkerchief to match, a chaste velvet waistcoat with silver buttons. He helped himself to a couple of inches of whisky, a dash of soda water, ice. He swigged down half of it and sighed again. All in all, Mr. Sim the Secretary was another of life's surprises.

"Take a pew," I said bluffly. He did. His yellow socks and mine were things in common, even dangerously so. "Max Vyan got off all right?"

"Yes, Mr. Ambler." He lit a cigarette with a gold lighter, a little awkward about meeting the flame. He drank again. The man was in a tizzy, something up.

"So you and Tanya are holding the fort?"

"No," he said. "Mr. Vyan decided at the last moment to take her with him. Thank God," he said and shuddered.

"Have a top-up, won't you?" They were his thanks to the Deity, not mine.

He took less this time. I gave myself a Campari and soda. "So you would rather be alone?"

Sim exploded: "I would rather be anywhere away from that disgusting beastly cruel — that vicious strumpet."

"She seems all right to me," I provoked him.

"Yes, to you! That she-devil incarnate!" His eyes were wide and woozy, I now observed.

"What did she do to you?"

"Last night my Theodore, my Siamese, wandered into her bedroom, her boudoir, she calls it, dirty harlot. It was while you were out with Mr. Vyan. I heard screams, terrible screams, and I ran." Sim put his head in his hands. "There was a noose round Theodore's neck and he was dangling from the candelabra and she was singeing him with a taper, burning his fur all over, screaming, oh dear God."

"What did you do?"

"What could I do? She would kill me."

"And then?"

"Then she let go the cord and Theodore fell down, moaning pitifully, and she said: *That will teach the beastly brute to upset bottles on my dressing table. Get out!*"

"Did you tell Max Vyan?"

Sim shook his head. "You don't know . . ." he said.

"And how is the cat?"

"He was so sore, poor little thing. But I rubbed Tan-gel all over. Theo is better this evening, resting quietly, I could leave him." Sim stood. He smiled wanly. "Now I won't bother you any more." He touched the briefcase, his long fingers spread, flexing them, flexing them. Then he took a breath and said, the words precisely enunciated: "The instructions for delivery are inside. Please insure that the briefcase is securely locked and hidden tonight. And, Mr. Ambler — you will stay on the Swiss side of the Lake? On no account enter France? Ah, thank you. Then may I come back tomorrow evening for the case and the bank receipt? Now, good night, and thank you so much. What a charming room, it is all Mr. Vyan's own taste, you know. I did help a tiny bit too. Oh dear, I can't forget, I simply cannot, that dreadful fiend, escape it somehow." He picked up his sheepskin coat and went, swaying a little, willowy walk.

All of which had taken a bit of taking in. I locked the door, and the door to my bedroom. Then I did what Sim had mutely asked me to do — opened the briefcase with its complicated key. Inside was an envelope, the usual quarto size, and a stick of sealing wax. The envelope was addressed to M. Jean-Claude Vaillancourt, Banque de la Fédération, Rue du Mont Blanc-Genève, and marked: *For Safe Keeping*. Attached to it by paper clip was a form of receipt: "Received by the courtesy and hand of Harry Ambler, Esq., one sealed envelope."

The envelope was not sealed, not even closed. I drew from it a piece of cardboard and a photograph. I will not titillate the appetites of some, nor offend the delicacy of others. I therefore can say only that the print was a bird's-eye view of Tanya von Silberbach in a state of nature but for the Koala Diamond, and of Mr. Korber in the buff. The photograph was decidedly blue, blue enough to shock even me a bit.

I acted quickly. To give me my due, I can get a move on. I took three flash pictures with my Minox (Mary Dunn equipment), put the photograph back and licked the envelope.

On the ring that held both keys was also a seal with a falcon's head — presumably Max Vyan's crest. I heated the wax, and applied a seal to each of the three seams of the envelope. Then I locked the briefcase. But where to hide it? I had to find a place where it could be chained securely, yet not be seen. I found such a place — the cold water pipe behind the bath. The maid never tidied the bathroom at night. The briefcase was heavy, a steel box encased by crocodile skin, and the retractable chain was hard steel — I tried a link with my ski file, and could not even scratch it.

And that was that done. To be still on the safer side, I pocketed my Minox which contained three negatives. They would blow up less sharp than the original enlargement, but sharp enough. And what were they worth? What would they be worth to Mr. Korber, for example?

I took a stool at the ski-keller bar and had not yet ordered a drink when Grayson, father of my small skiing friend, came over and asked me to join them at their table. They were nice people of the stockbroker-Sunningdale persuasion, safe ordinary people with no vice in them, one would bet, or would one?

"Look at that pair of roaring queens," he said. "Revolting."

"S'ssh, darling." She watched them too, with some amusement.

Sim in his elegant suit and the ski-club fellow in a high-necked sweater of Cambridge blue, pretty color, were talking animatedly. There was that fever, that absorption, that eagerness which so offends the likes of Grayson and me. And yet I can see the same feverish glow in a pair of lesbians and be fascinated, not offended. Like women so much, might be the reason. Like men so much, might be Mrs. Grayson's reason.

The secrets that Sim was sharing now were certainly not those of his employer. But did Max know about this? *She has her uses*, he had said. *Put her talents to their proper uses*, he had said. Did Sim also have his uses? Or was Sim forced, driven to break out tonight? Seek forgetfulness of tortured pussy cat? Seek catharsis with the bottle and the boy?

"Homo sapiens," I said. "A totally closed book to me."

"Not quite," said Mrs. Grayson. "Not if you know it is, it can't be."

NINE

The commissionaire came across the sidewalk and saluted. "Mr. Ambler? I will watch your car, sir."

I took the briefcase from under my seat and went in, to be shown to Monsieur Vaillancourt, who lived up to one's expectations of a Swiss banking panjandrum.

It was only as he was glancing casually at each seal in turn that I realized — the seal itself was still on the key ring which I had just used to open the briefcase. A foolish small error, but he had not noticed it. He signed my receipt as coffee and liqueur brandy arrived.

We discussed the skiing, and how was Monsieur Vyan, once my brother in arms, he understood. Then Vaillancourt disclosed a personal bond with Max of which he seemed proud — a love of wildflowers. That gave me a thought.

"I'm meeting rather a special friend at the airport. I suppose you wouldn't know a place where we could picnic, not far away. She has to catch a plane this afternoon."

He did indeed know such a place, less than ten miles from the city. He produced a map. "It is a paradise just now," he said. "The jonquils in the meadow make a cloth of gold — now please take this map, I do insist."

"Many thanks," I said. "But I've memorized it."

"Ah," he said. "The aviator's gift." Vaillancourt came with me to the door. "How I envy you, Mr. Ambler — to picnic with an especial friend on such a day of spring. Good-bye." He even stood watching while the commissionaire held up Geneva to let me drive away.

I might be acquiring shady habits, but I was also acquiring a taste for the VIP treatment, thanks to Max Vyan. And my Buick Caramba with the compliments of Sir Conrad Brock might help a little. A few days ago I had been straphanging with mundane slaves to bread and butter.

Geneva airport is five minutes or so from the center of the city, the only convenient large airport that I know. I was there by a quarter past eleven, parked the car, and paid my centimes to go up to the observation deck. By that time I had logged about twelve thousand hours, of which a thousand or so had been in Air Force jets soon after the war. Since then almost all my flying had been with internal combustion engines — Stinsons, Beavers, Cessnas, Otters, slow old Ansons, bush-pilots' workhorses all round the world.

It was over six months since I had piloted a plane, and I was not keen to start again. The less one does, the less one wants to, one shrinks from it, one is a little scared of it, to be quite honest, even if one has been airborne for literally a year and a half of one's forty-two.

There were a few propeller aircraft, but almost all were jets, parked or moving — the DC 8's and the 707's, the Caravelles, a VC 10, a Comet, the DC 9's and the 727's. I could not have flown any of them without instruction, and did not want to, and anyway, airline chauffeur was not my kind of flying. But the thrill of watching them was just as fresh as it had ever been — the Tiger Moths long ago on grass, these thunderous screaming monsters now. How clumsily they lumbered out, how reluctantly they gathered speed, clinging to earth, still clinging to earth at twice a Tiger Moth's top speed, off at last, the legs tucked in, and then that marvelous steep-backed surge to their element.

I would have watched longer, but duty called. I left the lovely monsters of the jet age and went down to meet my case manager.

One does not usually stand long at Geneva Airport in the skiing season without meeting some acquaintance. But that morning I saw nobody I knew, unless I knew every one of them — on the way to it or coming from it, an eager world on pleasure's run. Crime and cruelty seemed far from here.

Then Mary Dunn came through the arrival door, her black hair sleek as a Labrador's coat, not a pretty simile, but Dunn was not pretty. She wore a yellow coat, at her neck a scarf, in one hand an umbrella, in the other a handbag, all olive green. The General Manager of Brock Enterprises was unquestionably chic.

She came up to me and stood very close and stared, and went on staring. "Old Cobber's act," she muttered, smiling now.

An act or not, it was agreeable and flustering. "Got'ny bags?" I demanded.

"I sent them right through to London, Harry."

"Gotto confirma flight or anything?"

"That's all done, Harry. We have until four." She gave me the full fond mocking treatment with those blue eyes, and all for the public benefit, I knew. "Four solid hours together."

"Cm'on, then."

I headed west from the airport, into country lanes. "Where are you going?" The tone was not cozy any longer, a business-like inquiry.

"Chap at the bank told me a good picnic place — before Chancy, near the French border. Suit you, Dunn?"

No answer. I drove slowly, the road being not much wider than the Buick, left here, first right at the contour in a mile, first left again, and this was it, a small open valley between pine forest, a stream at the foot, the meadow golden with jonquils. I parked the car at a passing point of the road. "It is lovely," she said.

"Where shall we go?"

"By the brook?"

"The noise of water robs your ears. Never lie up near run-ning water, Dunn."

"This is a picnic luncheon, Ambler."

"Figure of speech. Max Vyan and I nearly got caught that way by a forest guard — never heard him coming."

"Oh, I see." She could be curiously respectful. "Would up the field be better?"

She carried the rug and I the picnic basket, and soon we were sitting among wild gold trumpets, sipping Punt è Mes. It was wonderfully warm, a light wind rippling on the meadow.

"Okay, Ambler, shoot. Tell me chronologically. Miss noth-ing out, but make it snappy, stick to the point."

I talked for half an hour, not missing much out, but not telling quite all. She listened in silence, her hands clasped at her knees, the tip of her long nose touching her hands. I went pretty faithfully, with minor omissions, up to and including a visit by Sim. But I held back the outcome of that visit, and my trump cards, which were in the Minox in my pocket. ". . . That's about it. Now let's start on lunch."

"I have a few questions." She asked them as we had our lobster bisque from cups — "Delicious soup. This Gilles Dorion — does he have a small nick in the lobe of his right ear?" — "Come to think of it, he does." On to the cold roast partridge, which she tore lustily apart with hands and teeth. "I thought you never had lunch." — "Not when I eat a hearty breakfast, Ambler. I denied myself to feast with you. Now this Korber man — *sophisticated hardware, that's my line.* Did you hear anything more specific about him?"

"Moffett said he was with General Mechanics."

This had quite an effect on Dunn. She rounded on me. "You missed that out."

"Why not? What's General Mechanics to the Koala Diamond?"

"A cut stone has many reflections." She laughed quite merrily. "Now I sound like Confucius or Sir Conrad." She was serious again. "But it must be confusing for you. Just tell me a few more things; then I'll explain a little."

Did that woman always wear the diamond? Tanya said so, and it seemed so. Did Max Vyan say where he obtained the necklace? He said he heard about it in Amsterdam and bought it for a million quid. Who from? He could not find out who the previous owner was. "That's all for the moment, Ambler. By the way, keep an eye open up in my direction, and I'll keep an eye open down past you."

"Surely nobody could follow us here."

"You never know." We shared the last of the white wine. "It's good. Not quite up to the Rieslings in our country."

"Is anything up to your Aussie hooch?"

"You rose to that one." She smiled at me, not a simple sheila, this. "Now say what's on your mind."

"What's on my mind is that sending me to find the diamond was a put-up job. That wasn't what you and Brock sent me for."

"Not quite true, not all true by any means."

"And Brock's story about the thing being stolen from him was a lie. Max Vyan bought it in good faith."

"Yes, that's true."

"So you sent me under false pretenses."

"We had to put you to the test. How could we know you wouldn't blurt out anything we told you?"

"Well, all right. And on my very first evening at Alpenheide, you as near as dammit got me killed."

"I told you it might be dangerous."

"Dangerous to go for an innocent walk?"

"You chose the wrong company."

"I didn't choose Moffett. He chose me. Who and what was Moffett? Did you send him?"

"We didn't send him. But Major Moffett was sent. As Sir Conrad always says: *The clumsy foil can lure the eye from the stealthy dagger.*"

"What a ponderous bore Brock is. So the poor chap was sent to Alpenheide to be murdered."

Dunn lay on her side on the tartan rug, her chin propped on her hand, it was a cozy picnic to the casual eye. "There was that possibility. It's a dirty business, Ambler."

"I don't even know what the business is. But I've done mine. I've fulfilled my contract, and now I'm through."

"Except for spilling the beans cluelessly — for instance, telling Dorion you would be away today — except for that, I think you've done wonderfully well, and so will Sir Conrad."

"I don't care a damn what Sir Conrad thinks."

She was looking full at me. "And you're bothered about prying into Max Vyan's affairs. Isn't that it, Ambler?"

"Max never did me down. He never told me any lies that I know of. You did, though. Well, I'm through, finished with your dirty business."

"I know we lied." She sighed, and her nostrils quivered. "Ambler!"

"Well?"

"Please trust me, Ambler."

"Why should I?" But the trouble was that I could not help trusting Mary Dunn. "Just come clean, and I might try."

"I can't come clean. And for your own sake, I wouldn't, if I could. And it isn't true that we were sending you on a false trail after the diamond. We were trying you out; but the Koala diamond *is* important for various reasons. All I can say is that we know that something very important and very dangerous may be brewing at Schloss Alpenheide."

"What kind of dangerous?"

"A conspiracy to power by a man whose mental stability is deteriorating, according to reliable reports. I'm saying no more. I don't know much more. We squared your debts; we gave you the car and a thousand down, the remaining four thousand to be paid on completion of your task. That goes to your credit at Coutts tomorrow. Now I'm offering you a new contract. You keep tabs on the diamond. You keep your eyes and ears open. You seem to ask no questions. You simply are available to your old friend, Mr. Vyan. Sir Conrad was right — that was a brilliant hunch of his."

"And Vyan was on to the possibility like a flash. He asked whether I had been sent to spy on him."

"Why didn't you tell me, idiot?"

"Calm, Dunn. He gave me some warning of the question. I laughed it off indignantly, and he apologized. But I felt a bit of a four-letter man, still do."

"There is every reason in the world why you shouldn't. If you'll take it on, you get another five on the first of April."

"Another five when I'm dead and buried, or incinerated — that's probably what they did to poor old Moffett, crisped him."

"Oh, shut up, Ambler."

"Make it ten, and I might consider."

She did not hesitate one second: "Ten it is."

All this time I had been keeping watch on the crest where the road came over and into the valley, a couple of hundred yards away. Now I saw a gleam in the sun, a black distinctive Porsche nose. It had stopped. I yawned and put up my hand. "Company there. Could be Dorion. How the hell?"

"Never mind how. He may be beaming a microphone at us. Sweet nothings, Ambler."

I picked a long old blade of grass and tickled Dunn's nose. "I dig you, black-maned filly."

Dunn giggled, and her arms reached for me. We embraced for the public eye. I myself am not an actor, cannot play a part, can only live a part I like, and she kissed me with false passion. It was a strain. "That'll do. Now have a look."

I rolled her sideways to have a look. "Not there now."

"Lurking, for sure." Her whisper was urgent, but calm. "Break it up slowly; then consult your watch. Pack basket with soppy intervals. Pistol in my purse. Can you shoot?" — "Yes, out of practice." — "Pocket it. Let's get going."

I broke gradually from our clinch, then packed up the picnic while Dunn sprawled on the rug. "So lovely to be together again. Come here, darling Harry." She could act all right. She was a cool one, and I had cold prickles in my neck. "Pull me up, Ambler. Then one last maudlin clinch. Then languidly to the car. Shoot to kill, if you have to."

We strolled amorously through the golden jonquils, and Dunn quoted Wordsworth, and I felt the weight of that pistol in my pocket. Nothing moved in the beautiful afternoon except ourselves and the nodding jonquils. In the car she said: "Start slowly out of this valley. Then go like hell."

I did as I was told while Dunn searched the inside of the car, under the dashboard, the seats, all over the narrow compartment, twisting, supple eel. "What are you doing?"

"We're bugged, you fool. But where the hell? Make all the turns you can." Which was easy to do, the countryside being a maze of roads. I had one hair-raising shave past a farm wagon. The poor horse shied into the ditch, cart tilting over. "Stop round the next corner and open the boot."

In a matter of seconds Dunn found what she was looking for. Behind us I could hear the Porsche's piercing horn, balked by that cart. "Now shake him."

The thing was round, and it sounded like hard plastic under her fingernails, the size of a two-ounce tin of Player's. "Got you." Dunn lay back in the seat beside me. "Twist about a bit until we lose the bastard. Then stop somewhere quiet."

I found a track winding into forest. "How does it work?"

"It sends a beep. He homes on it. Don't you home on beacons, flying?"

"Yes, but . . ."

"I've got more to tell you, but we need some space. Come into the woods."

She led me through undergrowth. The woods opened to a stand of old trees. We listened. Nothing but birdsong. She took two things from her handbag: a tiny pillbox, a spectacle case. They were bifocals, with wide earpieces. "See this pill, Ambler?" It was the size of a small match head, resting in cotton wool. "Now this one is only for demonstration. Its mate is built invisibly into the setting of the Koala. Walk over there. Put on the glasses and come back slowly."

I did so, ever obedient to Dunn's command. As I walked, a vibration grew behind my right ear, not quite a buzz, but a crescendo of vibration. "So the Koala's bugged, you mean?"

"That's just what I mean. Now do you begin to see a little method in Sir Conrad's madness? From now on, without even having to angle for the more intimate occasions so dear to you, you can tell whether that . . . that woman is wearing it. Put on your specs, and you know the answer. Incidentally, the lower lenses magnify a little, a help at your age."

"Many thanks. But must you be impertinent?"

"Sorry," she said. "I get cross about some things. Well, that's all, I think, except about meeting or reporting. Oh, there is one item of importance — if Gilles Dorion is who I think he is, watch out for him."

"Who is he?"

"Just the top man with execution rating in the French Service, that's who."

"Why follow me, though? He ain't got nothin' on me, not that I know of."

"Please don't be facetious, Ambler. I am trying to say that the wheels within wheels in this business are endless."

"What business? Brock Enterprises, Beef, or Wool or Books or Sugar or Electronics, which? If I'm risking my life, and it stands out a mile I am, I have a right to know what kind of shenanigans outfit I'm working for."

"Yes, you have a right to know, and I can't tell you. But I swear there are no shenanigans. Do you believe me?"

"Oh, well." I looked away from her to the old dark trees. "You finished with me?"

"Yes. We'd better go."

"I haven't quite finished with you, though, Dunn." Then I completed the story of Sim last evening. Suspicion and annoyance changed to avid interest in her expressive face.

"What kind of a photograph?"

"Compromising."

"Compromising of who and what? I have to know."

"Korber and von Silberbach. There are three negatives." I took the Minox cartridge out. "Who develops for you?"

"We have a good department."

"Promise me one thing."

"As your case manager I can promise nothing."

"You don't get the film, then."

She snarled: "Oh, all right, promise." I gave it to her.

"The enlargements are to go direct to Brock; you're not to see them."

She laughed at me, but she was also laughing with me, for once. "You're so maddening, Ambler, but sometimes one does almost have to like you."

We drove back to Geneva Airport. If I had anything urgent, I was to drive down to Aigle and telephone from there.

"There's one person — only one — you can trust absolutely."

"Who's that?"

"You met him at dinner — Harry Z. Gilpin. If he asks you over to Gstaad, don't fail to go."

"He's in New York this week."

"We know that, Ambler." She took a small penknife from

her purse and worked on the car bug again. "I'm making a soldering break. It looks natural, a bad bump or something. Put this back before you get home tonight. You can see the place from the circle left by the rubber vacuum cup. Dorion will find it and fix it, won't suspect a thing."

"Then I'm bugged again."

"Slow up a little, look — you unscrew this connection. As Sir Conrad always says: *To be bugged with a bug you can unbug is better than not being bugged at all.*

Sir Conrad's pearls of wisdom were fast becoming red rags to me, but I shrank from angering Dunn again about her hero, and changed the subject. "Why draw attention to our meeting? Why at the airport? Why not some rendezvous?"

"As always, it was Sir Conrad's brain wave: He wished to establish for the world to see that ours was a bona fide romantic connection."

"You're my mistress, you mean?"

Dunn blushed. I took my eyes from the road to have one quick look at the animal glow of Dunn when blushing.

"That sort of thing. My telephone call from Rome, my apparent delight at seeing you — all carefully designed to pave the way for a visit to Alpenheide."

"When?"

"In a week or ten days. I may just roll up quite openly, and the spying world will know I'm Jiving Jane on amorous pleasure bent." Her tone changed now. "But you will know that's a lot of bull. Have you got it, Ambler?"

"Got it, Dunn. I could teach you to ski in the line of duty, no harm to that."

"I suppose I might have to once or twice, for the sake of the act. God, I hate skiing."

"Is dancing on, for the sake of the act?"

"Yes, that. If you're any good."

"I was thinking back there — I cannot play a part. I can only live a part I like. Do you see my problem, Dunn?"

"I'll help you in public, Ambler. In private, there will be no problem."

We were nearing the airport. No one followed us, so far as I could see. "Is there anything else you haven't told me?"

I had told her almost everything. It was much later that I discovered the importance of what I had not told her. "What bothers me is this chap Sim."

"Me too. He's compromised to you. And you're compromised to him."

"Unless Vyan told him to do just that."

"Tell you, tell anyone what he has on Korber? That's impossible. My guess is that Sim had a brainstorm. They do, you know."

"A closed book to me, that league."

"Yes, Ambler. Here's a spare magazine for the gun; I'm putting it in your pocket. Now Sim again — my guess is that what he said about that woman and his cat was true, and he went berserk, blew up, had the brainstorm. Do you realize the built-in hate that a homosexual has for a wicked amoral bitch like that? Add the cat to it, and there you are."

"I wonder how Vyan got him."

"We know. He was a chartered accountant, the most brilliant younger man in Post Merriman, they said, charged with soliciting, and afterwards Max Vyan took him on."

"*We know*. You know. What is your real job, Dunn?"

"One real job is the one you saw at the office in London, and I love it. I hate some things."

I drew up in the parking place before the airport.

"You realize that if my guess about Sim is right, then as of now you're a danger to him."

"He's gutless. I'm sure of it."

"But desperate. Please be careful." She put her hand lightly on my knee and took it away.

"Thank you, Dunn."

"You wouldn't be much use to me dead, now would you?"

We walked arm-in-arm. Inside, she said: "Don't wait for the plane. I couldn't bear it, Harry. Thank you for making me so happy." We kissed one another to the indulgent approval of the airport world. "Silly old Ambler," she murmured in private. "See you soon," she said louder, starry-eyed, and walked away.

TEN

Max Vyan and I had turned the car at a stone quarry not far below the bridge across the river. It had been dark since I entered the mountains. No lights had followed me, and I had met a few cars, but none were coming now. I turned into the quarry, switched off, opened the boot and listened. By some acoustical quirk one heard the river on two planes of sound — a muted rushing from the gorge below, a booming echo of it in the quarry. One heard now also the clatter, trickle, clatter of a stone coming down the quarry wall. It was a hollow-sounding spooky place, and I felt uncomfortable.

Using the big torch which had come with the Buick — one switch for a spotlight beam, one for a red warning flasher — I found the mark of the vacuum cup behind the cloth lining of the boot, wiped the bug carefully with a duster, wet the rubber and applied it, noting with care the exact angle and position of a scratch on the surface of the bug's container. I was beginning to fancy myself as Private Eye.

As I straightened from that and closed the boot, the back of my head prickled a warning in just the way it used to do in Spitfire days. I jumped round — nothing. Nothing moved between me and the white splash of the beam traversing rocks beyond the gorge. "You're windy, Ambler," I boomed in the quarry. It can be good medicine to rebuke oneself when windy, but a snapping stick, a louder rumble of falling rock spun me round to search the quarry's broken face. I got into the car and got out of there. A man? A roe deer moving on the hillside? My overworked imagination?

The lights of the village were pretty and peaceful. The bell of the Marienkirche tolled serenely for evening service. Carefree people strolled about their after-ski occasions — the same kind of people that I had seen at Geneva Airport. But I noticed again a wariness, a watchful reserve in the face of every working inhabitant of Alpenheide, the cloaked expression of those who keep their minds and mouths shut for good health. Or was that also my overworked imagination?

I put the Caramba in its not very private lockup below the hotel and went up to the lobby. "Many thanks, Dominic. We thought your picnic lunch was excellent."

"A small service, sir, my pleasure. Mr. Sim from Schloss Alpenheide was telephoning. Should I say that you are back?"

"Yes, do. I shall expect him in half an hour."

"If it would be convenient, Mr. Ambler, we could change your rooms while you ski tomorrow?"

"Okay, Dominic. Do I need to pack?"

"Oh no, sir. But to lock valuables would be wise."

Sim arrived in due course, in a dark suit and overcoat, no bird of paradise, but a distraught secretary mouse.

"I handed your sealed envelope to Vaillancourt. Here's the receipt, padlock, key ring, all complete."

He looked at the receipt, locked the briefcase again and pocketed the key ring. "Thank you so much," he said. "I . . ."

"Let me get you a drink." I got him what he so badly needed, but needed too much, gulped too deeply, choked, and managed to make it to the bathroom.

He came back, greenish, eyes puffy. "I do apol . . ."

"Sit down, Sim. Drink slowly, and you'll feel better." I went to turn up the radio, Mozart possibly. "What's that?"

"Haydn's Clock Symphony." He held his glass in both trembling hands. "You sealed it?"

"Oh, the envelope? In three places — the flap, the other end, the seam down the middle. It was very courteous of you to leave it open, like a letter of introduction, really, not good form to close the envelope. Many thanks for the compliment."

"And you didn't look at the contents?"

"Of course not. The contents were none of my business."

"Thank God. Oh, thank God." He stared at me with bleary eyes. Believe it or not, the poor man believed me. "If Mr. Vyan ever knew that I had handed you that open envelope . . ."

"He won't. Pull yourself together, Sim. If it matters so much, why the hell did you do it?"

"I wanted you to . . . It was a madness of revenge against that terrible woman. I was beside myself."

"Some provocation. How is the cat?"

"He is much better, poor little thing. But the shock to his nerves — Theodore trembles the whole time."

"You're trembling yourself. Now forget about it, Sim."

"I cannot. I cannot live in fear and forget about it."

I got him another drink. "What are you afraid of?"

"I am afraid of everything about that house."

"Why not leave it, then?"

"I cannot leave it, Mr. Ambler. Even to go out at all, I must have permission, as for last night and now."

"Were you late last night?"

"I was insane last night."

"Surely Max Vyan is a generous employer."

"Most generous, and kindly too, and merciless."

"He was always a pretty ruthless chap — stop at nothing more or less, but you could trust him not to let you down."

"But if *you* let *him* down, Mr. Ambler?" Sim shuddered. "And that is what I did. If he finds out . . ."

"He won't find out from me. Now stop worrying, Sim."

"I trust you, Mr. Ambler. But there are spies everywhere."

"Your friend the ski-club chap — is he a spy?"

"Good gracious, no. Mr. Vyan even allows me out to see him. Mr. Vyan understands some things which you, Mr. Ambler, could not understand."

"I daresay. Do you happen to know when Max will be back?"

"In a few days probably. But I do not handle Mr. Vyan's American affairs. He keeps us in our separate compartments. The man is a financial genius, beyond any question."

"Well, if you'll forgive me, I must change for dinner."

"Yes, indeed. You have been so very very kind. Anything I can ever do, any service I can render, anything." He clung to my hand, embarrassing.

"Don't worry, Sim," I said again. But my film would already be at Brock Enterprises. Sim had plenty to worry about.

They moved me to new rooms next day, on the fourth floor at the northwest corner of the hotel. One window of the bedroom faced the ski slopes and the Teufelsspitzen, the other westward up the valley. Mary Dunn had told me to keep my eyes open, and this I proceeded to do. There was little ground traffic to and from Schloss Alpenheide, but the helicopter came and went. Just before dawn each morning it took off and headed up the mountain. I could follow the navigation lights with my binoculars until, somewhere up there, they disappeared for about a minute and a half. Then they showed again, dropping off height to the Schloss, a round trip of nine or ten minutes. At eight on the dot my breakfast arrived, and the helicopter took off, this time heading out of the valley to the west. The duration of that flight varied, but usually it was less than an hour, probably to get the mail. Then each evening soon after dusk it made the same return flight up the mountain. What did it go there for? To drop a man, to pick up a man? And these morning and evening flights were so brief that they certainly terminated on this side of the mountain. But Moffett had spoken of flights beyond the Teufelsspitzen.

I skied hard. After three mornings with Viereck, I think I was stronger than I had ever been. He waited for me at the foot of the Devil's Plunge. "Now there is some rhythm and control," he said, a first and only grudging compliment.

Each day I had lunch with Hilda Grayson and young Jeremy at the Mittelwald and took them on a few runs afterwards. Grayson himself had gone back to England. Hilda and Jeremy were good companions for the bachelor — a very feminine woman and her spirited small son. Sometimes I almost caught myself regretting that I had not married, almost. It was a pleasant and peaceful interlude, and I was being paid fat sums for doing nothing. Idleness rests well enough with me, too well, but it has to be idleness with some measure of excitement. Running the Devil's Plunge was still a brief thrill, and I had mastered it, no longer thrill enough. I was getting bored and restive, increasingly convinced that one key, two keys to the riddles of Alpenheide lay on or beyond the Teufelsspitzen.

"Tell me, Fernandel — are there bad avalanches above the Höhengrat?" We were in a corner of Whisky à Go-Go. "The mountain doesn't seem so steep."

"There is a small avalanche each spring in the couloir that runs down from between the western peaks. But it divides or is divided above the Höhengrat. It is not dangerous."

"Why, then, the new avalanche wall?" It was evidently new, a structure of great logs set in concrete, and it ran clear across the face of the mountain.

"There are certain conditions of very deep snow and rising temperature when avalanches could threaten. Above the tree line no slope is always safe, however gradual. So there is that reason for Herr Vyan's new protection, and another: A year ago two skiers climbed the Teufelsspitzen, a man and a woman totally without experience, and a snow cornice broke. It was two thousand meters to their next halting place, Old Harry." Fernandel grinned widely, quite gleeful about it. "So the wall was built against such stupidity."

"Rather an expensive wall to build against stupidity."

"With Herr Vyan cost is not perhaps of great importance." In common with them all, he dropped his voice a little at *Herr Vyan*. Fernandel came from the Engadine. *These locals are yokels*, was one of his quips. He was a bachelor like me, a wanderer like me. He had been a waiter at the Ritz in Boston, a ski instructor in Colorado, a mountain guide in the New Zealand Alps, and now crewed a cable car at Alpenheide — as fruitful an occupation as any for an inveterate woman chaser.

"Two thousand meters — they must be formidable cliffs. Sheer all the way?"

"With overhang, unclimbable. Not even the German lunatics would try to climb them. The legend of these Alpenheiders is that long ago the whole of that side of the mountain collapsed upon an underground lake. And if one looks from the safe place at the head of the couloir, one can see that this is true, for the Grabestal, the Valley of the Grave, is even still a desert of rock."

"Beer, Fernandel?"

"Thank you, Old Harry. But I see over there a new friend who was afraid of heights in my *Luftseilbahn* this morning. I think that she does not fear a shorter fall, that is my hope."

I left him to his latest conquest, and went dancing with Hilda Grayson at the hotel, and early to bed. She was a little miffed with me.

I woke to the sound of the turbocopter. There was quite an agreeable chatter to it, not a sordid hammering like the old ones. It made the usual flight, and I went back to sleep. After breakfast I wrapped two items of ski-touring equipment round my middle, zipped my anorak, and went up the mountain.

There was no sign of an end to this extraordinary weather, no wind at all, an occasional white cloud drifting and vanishing in the deepness of the sky. The snow was melting fast on the lower slopes, almost all gone in the valley bottom. Even high up, the skiing was sticky that afternoon. "One more?" I said. I had noticed something, or someone, who gave me one of my brighter ideas.

"You and Jeremy go. I'll wait here for you, Harry."

"Oh, come on!" I said.

So Hilda came, a most complaisant person. We stood a yard away from Jeremy who was talking to the operator — not Fernandel, the other one. One can talk privately at short range in the crowded hubbub of a cable car. "See that chap with the same anorak as mine?"

"Yes, and green stretchies too. Your back-view double."

"Look, Hilda, when we reach the top, I'm going to do a vanishing act. Tell Jeremy they telephoned for me. Then just chance to latch on to my double, and follow him. He's skiing alone, only a fair skier, you can both keep up with him."

"Why the mystery?"

"No mystery, but mum's the word. I'll explain when we have our last dance tonight, Hilda."

"Our last dance tonight, Harry."

At the Höhengrat I was out first, parked my skis and poles and made haste to lock myself in a lavatory. Then I turned my anorak from red to khaki. When I am skiing well, I wear the red side out. I am the sort of red-skiing bomb whom people notice. I enjoy being noticed, another thing you do not like about me, I told you I would tell the truth. I waited a few minutes, put on my knitted Norwegian hat (I had been bare-headed) and sallied forth.

It was nearly five o'clock, at which time the last cable car carried paying passengers down. After that, there was one final trip with waitresses and empty bottles.

The restaurant was almost empty, nobody I knew. I put on my skis and set off along the path that led past the Devil's Plunge. I poled myself clumsily in tyro style. It was an amateurish disappearing act, but I thought that I had got away with it. Now I must hide until ten past five when two ski instructors ran the Wintergreen to clear this side of the mountain. The head of the Alpenheide Glacier would do very well.

I had not been down it yet, but I had looked at the start, a glorious gently-winding run for miles, all beginners' skiing except for the big serac or ice-fall where the glacier tumbled, with many crevasses. Thus, only guided parties were allowed on the glacier. The sun dipped behind the western mountains as I waited out of sight. The cables were humming again. That would be the last trip up. A dog barked deeply far away, not from Schloss Alpenheide, but further west where the glacier debouched into the valley. Max's kennels were up there, so Fernandel had told me. The air was cool and thin and clean, the mountains afire, another day slowing to its end.

The humming stopped, and soon I heard men's voices. I raised my head to watch them sweep the hill, inspecting it for late or disabled skiers. Now the cable hummed. I still must wait until that laden car had passed the other. Meanwhile I had taken skins from under my anorak and put them on my skis. Now I confirmed through Trinovid binoculars (Mary Dunn equipment) that the cable car was coming empty. I went back toward the Höhengrat. The only people there now would be the cable car controller, and his wife. No one else slept at the Höhengrat — a big concrete box set on the mountain, just under the avalanche fence, two or three hundred feet below the peaks.

There were no windows on this side, and the door to the restaurant corridor was closed. I climbed round behind the building — a blank wall. All the windows faced the valley.

I stood under the avalanche barrier. The logs were fifteen inches or more in diameter, set vertically and touching one another, like a garden fence in giant scale. Every tenth log projected higher than the others, presumably to take anchor supports. I unwound the nylon rope which I had worn round my waist all day, some fifty feet of cord. I made a noose in it. I had been a fair hand once at roping steers. But could I rope a log twenty-five feet above my head?

Four misses, but I got it on the fifth. I made a bundle of skis and poles with the free end of the rope. Then I climbed hand over hand and boot by boot. It was none too easy, but there were knot projections on the icy logs. I rested at the top. Dusk had come, but I could still see clearly up the couloir, a shallow gully with rocks showing here and there. The left side looked easier, not a real climb at all, a plod on skins to the cleft between the western peaks.

The bundle made a small clatter coming up. I put on my

skis, rewound the rope, and climbed. It was an unbreakable crust, as hard as Arctic snow. I had one minor obstacle to negotiate, the small avalanche barrier which formed an inverted V into the couloir, set there to divide and neutralize the avalanche of which Fernandel had spoken.

I sidestepped to the hump of drifted snow that concealed the wall, put my bottom on it and swung the skis over; simple enough, and so was the rest of the climb up the side of the couloir, into the head of it. There were cornices on either side — treacherous slabs of snow projecting — but none from the couloir. I took off my skis, lodged them safely, and then edged forward, testing rock, and inched my head on to have a look down into the abyss — dark nothing. I slid back.

A night wind soughed about the peaks, but here in my hollow I was sheltered. The lights of Alpenheide flickered, and through thin air at ten thousand feet the stars were intensely bright. The bell of the Marienkirche tolled. I could see headlamps of cars, intermittent glowworms crawling.

Now the helicopter came. I saw its blinking lights before I heard it. The machine passed swiftly across below me, at about the level of the Höhengrat. Then darkness. But I found it at once with my binoculars, a slowly descending shadow, no change of engine pitch as there would be with a fixed-wing aircraft. The helicopter landed where I had expected, on flat terrain, on a bluff above the far end of the avalanche wall. Almost immediately it rose and swung back. The navigation lights came on near the Höhengrat. It dropped into the valley.

Night had fallen, but it was not very dark. I searched the skyline to the east. A man's silhouette would show against that, but I saw nothing, nor anything on the snow between here and the bluff, nor anything along the avalanche wall. I could see no man, and if I could see no man, no man could see me in my hideyhole. Not unless he carried one of those infrared tele-scopes, a possibility that I had not thought of.

Was that movement at the fence? No, nothing moved from left to right. And yet a man must have been put off. What other explanation could there be for the two return trips every night? Perhaps he had a small dugout in the snow from which to watch unseen. Perhaps there was no one at all, some other perfectly simple explanation.

I would wait here for half an hour, until about seven thirty-five, and then go stealthily down, keeping in the couloir. I felt very much alone on top of a frigid mountainside. Not so clever to forget that the king of the castle is pinned to his eminence. If I could not resist satisfying curiosity — quite contrary to orders — I should have hidden against the avalanche wall, an escape route near at hand.

I felt for the pistol in the left pocket inside my anorak. It was a handy little gun, Italian, a nine-millimeter Beretta. The wind above was louder, and even probed in here. Could it be that I was smelling snow? All this dark time I had been watch-ing down and to the left. It stood to reason that anyone, if there was anyone, must come from there.

But then there was another sound, a faint scrabble to my *right*. The beast was silhouetted against the sky. It crouched on its belly across the couloir.

Instantly and terribly, fear punched me rigid, and the ani-mal lay still. Two animals lay still, the hunter and the hunted, the pinner and the pinned.

At first I could not think at all. I stared at the monster's head and chest, silhouetted against the sky. But my heart raced up to pump my blood again. In a brief interminable time my mind came back.

The head was the size of a half-grown tiger's, but it was

the head of a dog — less swift, perhaps, and far more dangerous. The dog had been taught by men to master men. The dog
was thinking now, not with a smallish wayward feline brain,
but with a totally disciplined intelligence. Its orders would be
explicit — to stand guard, to forbid movement, to attack movement. And behind intelligence lay instinct: If I kept still, it
would not attack me. Would the dog's name be Pluto?

"Pluto, my friend," I said. I saw the glimmer of the dog's
bared fangs. Either Pluto was not my friend at the moment, or
this was not Pluto.

Stars were no longer visible beyond my watchdog; the
wind had risen; a first flake of snow brushed my neck; I was
very cold. Already my movements would be clumsy.

My gloved hands were in my lap. With my left glove I
grasped the fingers of the right. The dog growled. There was
all menace in that growl in the high place in the wind. One
leap, one spring divided us across the gully.

As my bare hand thrust inside my anorak, the dog was coming. Six inches to grasp the automatic, six inches to draw it,
ten feet to attack. Hot breath was on me as I fired; and then
the dog piled in.

My head began to clear. I shook it. I could shake it, gasp-
ing to draw air into my lungs. The body rolled off, thrashing a
little, and was still.

I like dogs until they are my enemy. I was not sorry for that
dog, whose name had not been Pluto — a dead bitch of about
my own weight, I suppose, twelve and a half stone, a hundred and seventy-five pounds, less or more, before or after
supper.

I struggled with the body in the couloir — drag it, heave
it, swing it head for tail and inch by inch — until at last it lay
on the topmost rock. Funny thing, the dead dog had a leather

boot on one of the front paws, a cut on sharp ice, perhaps. I
used a ski to edge the body further, further. Then it slithered
quite slowly over, next stop two thousand meters down in the
Valley of the Grave.

It was snowing lightly as I followed the couloir. Would they
have heard the shot at the Höhengrat? They might or might
not. Sound may travel better up than down. Sound is whipped
away by wind. Probably they had not heard.

But I moved away from the couloir to the left, halfway across
the avalanche wall. Then I lowered my skis, and this time rap-
pelled myself down, took off the skins and ran for home, taking
the wide way of the beginners' run on the Soldanella.

I could not see much, but from time to time a marker flag
loomed up to assure me that my bearings were correct. I was
very tired. Of all the moments of fear in my life, there had
never been one so instantly terrible as that. On the other hand,
in retrospect, I was pleased with myself.

Why was a dog posted at night to keep men from the peaks
of the Teufelsspitzen? Because they were important to the
owner of the helicopter. And if I was seen now, arriving on skis
after 8 P.M.?

My mission and my skin depended upon getting there undetected. Foolhardy idiot, I thought — oh, bloody fool. But
it was somewhat late for self-recrimination.

There were no lights in the cable car terminus, which was
close to the village street. Should I leave my skis and poles in
one of the racks outside it? People sometimes did that to save
themselves trouble. But nobody in his senses would leave a
pair of White Stars to be stolen. It had started snowing in
earnest, big wet flakes. I took off my skis in the lee of the house
that fronted on the street, then walked under the lamp and
across to the road that led to the hotel.

Once here it was all right — I might have been getting my edges sharpened at Zimmermann's. But nobody noticed me. The few people about were hurrying for shelter. I went in the side door to the *ski-raum* and took the lift up. So far so good. All's well that ends well.

All, however, had not quite ended, for who should be walking along the fourth floor corridor but Gilles Dorion. "Oh, hello," I said. "Have you been away?"

"For three days, yes, at Verbier. It is good, Monsieur Ambler, but not for comparison with this."

He glanced at my wet clothes, a very casual-seeming man. "So our weather has broken. But there will be fresh powder on the mountain."

"Let's hope so," I said. "I got soaked on the way from Zimmermann's. Well, I must change. Shall we have a drink later on?"

"*Volontiers*." But there was no sign of him later on.

Never explain, my father used to say. But I had explained with a fib which Dorion could easily check at Zimmermann's. And Dorion's eyes had paused a moment on my right sleeve, a stain on the khaki cloth, a large dark splash of blood.

I gave myself a strong whisky and soda, washed out that sleeve, and soaked my aches. The dog had struck me full on the chest. A few inches higher it could have been a broken neck; a few inches down it might have been a ruptured liver. As it was, I had a saucer-sized bruise above the sternum, a general soreness in my ribs, but no localized pain when breathing. I was lucky to be intact. If I had missed . . . If my cold fingers had fumbled for half another second . . .

But enough of near postmortems in the bath.

"You said you'd explain when we danced tonight."

"There was something I wanted to find out."

"And did you, Harry?"

"In a limited way."

"For a limited explanation. I told Jeremy you'd been called down in a hurry. At which he glowered. But after I had contrived more or less to trail that man with the clothes like yours, and we were here, back in our room, he said: *I bet Harry's some secret agent on some secret mission.*"

"What about a mission to a drink upstairs?"

"I'll just look in to see he's all right."

Alone with our drinks and the music, the crouching dog forgotten, not quite forgotten. "It's been marvelous for one small boy, and for one grass widow too. Wanton, I know — it's making wantons of us all — not much worse mums and wives, perhaps."

"A bit of wantonness — what's wrong with that if no regrets and no harm done?"

"Poor old bachelor, that's all you can imagine, wantonness, or soon it will be."

"Oh, come on."

"No, I mean it, Harry. Because you have no firm base to see the beauty of, to wander from and to return. A very moralistic amoral point of view, but I don't care. To be a secret agent alias a glamour boy at forty-two is to be headed to being a double bore, or to esoteric sex, or to a lucky tumble just in time. Or sudden death, of course."

"You're being clever. I don't understand."

"Every year you trim life to less complication and more Harry Ambler, don't you?"

"Well, why not?"

"You could be right," she said. "If life is meaningless." She was a good woman, and she made me think again, amoral prig.

ELEVEN

It was a dark easy slope, I ran it beautifully in control, my skis just chattering; but then it steepened, bells of warning, oh my God, two thousand meters to the Grabestal.

I woke up sweating. That chatter was the helicopter, that bell the summons of my wrist alarm, 5.40 A.M., how punctual of us all.

The upward flight was the same as on other nights and mornings. The lights disappeared as usual. The sky was clear, but plumes growing pink with dawn told of wind at the peaks of the Teufelsspitzen. Down here eaves dripped, and new snow darkened in two car ruts on the street.

I sat back from the open window, watching through my glasses. It was nearly daylight when the helicopter flew along the avalanche wall to the Höhengrat, and then edged up the west side of the couloir, following the route that the dog must have taken. Tracking it visually? But there would be inches of new snow, no tracks to follow. The boot on the bitch's paw, it must be that, some sort of tracer. The helicopter sparkled above the peaks and disappeared, no doubt to search a desert of rocks in the Grabestal where no man lived.

It was after seven when the machine dropped down to Schloss Alpenheide, coming not from the Teufelsspitzen but from due north over the Alpenheide Glacier. If they had found the body of the dog, surely they would have sought evidence of the man who had shot it at the only place where it could have been shot.

I went to fetch the Caramba from its lockup, and checked on the exact position of the bug. It had been moved. By all means let him bug me on an innocent drive to Aigle.

"It's like a shark, the Caramba, prowling along."

"Yes, it is like a shark," she said from behind.

"Couldn't we go faster, Harry?"

"Not here," I said.

But they were both so keen for speed, and I was so relieved to be away from that place, and reluctant to lose them that I ended by driving on to Montreaux, the next stop for their Geneva train. She was rock-solid at a hundred and twenty, with a lot more where it came from — one spurt, and I idled.

"Good-bye, Harry. Thanks for absolutely everything."

"Same to you, Jeremy. Perhaps you'd like to fly with me sometime."

"Oh gosh, yes. Any time."

Hilda laughed. "Almost any time," shaking hands with me, and so we parted.

I was low in spirit, driving back along the lake, thinking of something she had said to me, my many sins, hypocrisies, stupidities, the long climb ahead to that valley and those lovely bloody mountains, trapped. It was peculiar, that terrified dream of mine — I had no fear at all of heights. I stopped at a viewpoint in the Alpenheide Gorge, got out, and to test myself, stood on the parapet with five hundred feet of sheer drop below. I did not have the slightest qualm. So much for the verity of dreams.

Water ran in the village street, and from every roof came, or had already come, its own small avalanche, sliding, plopping with a voice of spring. The sky was blue and the peaks were sharper after snow, more ethereal, more innocent. I parked the car and stood a moment, looking up to the Teufelsspitzen. What lay on them, in them or beyond them?

Dominic had a few letters for me, sent on from the club, and there was a telephone message: Would I call Mr. Harry Z. Gilpin at the Palace Hotel, Gstaad? Gilpin, the cultivated Croesus, one person to be absolutely trusted. "Anything else?"

"Only that Herr Vyan himself is home just now."

"That's good news."

"Indeed, sir. You are not skiing today, Mr. Ambler? They say that the new snow is excellent on the higher slopes."

"After lunch, perhaps. I've been seeing the Graysons off."

"One of our nicest English families," he said. "And such a charming youthful matron."

I agreed with him, thinking that the matron would be amused to hear herself thus described. Upstairs, I read the letters, which were not of much interest except for one from Jim Stokes, my ex-partner in Canada, saying that he was starting a new outfit, twin-engined turboprops from Edmonton to service oil exploration in the Arctic islands, a certain winner, and would I come in for fifty thousand bucks? I wished I could with fifty thousand bucks even if I doubted Jim's certain winner. I wished I could face the hazards I had known so well, escape these alien man-made dangers, weaving a web about me that I also wove myself.

I went to the larger of my suitcases, unlocked it and looked for the cardboard match that I had wedged between lid and body at the back, but the match had gone. In the case were my climbing rope and skins (both dried on the bathroom radiator last night), and, wrapped in a cardigan, the pistol and two magazines that Mary Dunn had given me. The contents were intact, but they had been inspected. Neither my garage nor my luggage was proof against Dorion, or Vyan's people, or someone else, Brock Enterprises even.

I dialed the Palace at Gstaad, and Gilpin came on himself. "This is Harry Gilpin. Good morning, Mr. Ambler, or should I say: Good afternoon."

"Howd'you do again, sir, so you're safely back."

"Yesterday, after New York and London. How one does skip about, quite ridiculous at my age. Well now, Gloria and I did so much enjoy meeting you the other evening, and I telephoned simply to ask whether you would please us by coming to luncheon? I would suggest dinner, but the night drive is arduous, not to say hazardous, when every staid Swiss *bürger* sees himself racing for the world's championship . . . You can on Friday? Oh, that will be delightful, in time for an aperitif. I think two hours should bring you here. So good-bye, namesake Harry, if an old fellow may be so familiar."

Harry Z. Gilpin had the diplomat's touch, also the fist within the glove. His suave invitation was a summons.

I was casing my rooms for bugs behind pictures, under tables, on telephones, but I was no bugman, to put it politely, inspecting wires without a clue. I jumped a bit when the thing sounded off beside my ear; it was as if the damned telephone had caught me out. "Yes?"

"You sound flustered, Ambler."

"Oh hello, Max. Flustered by the telephone beside **my** ear. Welcome back. Did you have a good time?"

"Not a good time in your terms. I got some business done."
There was a pause. The purpose of this call?

"When am I going to see you?"

"Drop over this afternoon, if you like. Say, about four."

"Okay, that's fine."

"Ring the bell at the bridge, and they'll let you through."

He hung up, and I went down to luncheon. My chest was sore, and I was glad to have a day off skiing, in fact nearing the point, which happens every year, of losing enthusiasm. The snow gets sticky, the hedonism palls, even for me.

Afterwards I slept for an hour, a thing I rarely do by day, but what with this and that I was a bit behind on sleep.

Feeling ghastly, I drove over to Schloss Alpenheide, not without some uneasiness about Max's prompt invitation. Last night's snow had melted. Indeed, there was none left now except a few north-facing drifts. The crocuses were already up, the humble soldanellas, the spring anemones that chase the snow. During the next six weeks that miraculous book of alpine spring would turn its pages.

I came to the T-junction and turned right. No dogs were on the hillside beyond the fence. The spruces on that hill were limbed to about head height, but I could not see the sources of illumination that lit the trees only above waist level. It occurred to me that, opposition being absent, one could quite easily scale the fence and crawl up that hill in darkness to the outer wall of the moat.

I rang the bell, and after a brief delay — no doubt for inspection of H. Ambler — the drawbridge came down as smoothly and silently as it had risen on that night, and I drove into the courtyard of Schloss Alpenheide. The drawbridge had opened again by the time I got out of the car. One tended to have a prisoner sensation, which one must conceal. *"Guten*

Tag," I said to the man who touched his tyrolean hat. He was a new man to me, with a different countenance but the same loaded impassive air as any pro in the bodyguard league.

He led the way to the front door where the fat butler met me, and I was taken into the drawing room. Beyond the great window was a terrace, and on it Max Vyan with a dog, an even bigger dog than the one I had recently encountered.

"Hullo, Ambler. Pluto, this is Ambler, remember him?"

The astonishing thing was that Pluto did remember me. He strolled over, tail wagging, and rumbled a greeting. His body was dark yellow or nine-carat golden, his muzzle and brow almost entirely black with a narrow white line up the middle of his forehead — the Mastiff, the Great Dane, the St. Bernard were the progenitors of this formidable beast.

"Have a seat," Vyan said.

I sat in a chair, and Pluto lay beside me. Max pottered in his rock garden, or in one of them, for there were two, curving out at the sides of the flagstone terrace.

My mother used to be an avid gardener, so I had an amateurish smattering, enough to know that his rockeries were fabulous, and I said so.

"All plants native to Alpenheide in this one," he said. "Exotics on the right."

"Gentians so early — aren't they far ahead?"

"It's a sun trap, but I cheat a little too. These Gentiana verna, for instance, have warmed soil. Others will come naturally later on."

"You mean the ground is wired for heat?"

He did not answer. The answer was too obviously yes for Vyan to bother with it. "Viola biflora, you violet of Mt. Cenis, what could be more exquisite?" He touched the small yellow flower. "And you, humble soldanella."

"That's what I was thinking, coming over."

He turned, raising his left eyebrow at me. "Really, Ambler?" From sentimental love to mockery. "Well, what have you been up to?"

"Oh, this and that." I wondered what was coming. "By the way, I took your envelope to that banker chap."

"So Sim told me. Mission accomplished, thank you, Ambler, a precaution taken." Did that eye twitch under stress, excitement, suspicion, what? Turning from me to his beloved flowers and quickly back, I sensed a load of steam.

"Vaillancourt is a wildflower fanatic like yourself."

"A fanatic?" He waved a hand at his rockeries. "What could be less fanatical? Listen to Goethe:

> *Im Schatten sah ich*
> *Ein Blümchen stehn,*
> *Wie Sterne leuchtend,*
> *Wie Aüglein schön.*
>
> *Ich wollt' es brechen,*
> *Da sagt es fein:*
> *Soll ich zum Welken*
> *Gebrochen sein?*
>
> *Ich grub's mit allen*
> *Den Würzlein aus,*
> *Zum Garten trug ich's*
> *Am hübschen Haus*
>
> *Und pflanzt' es wieder*
> *Am stillen Ort;*
> *Nun zweigt es immer*
> *Und blüht so fort.*

"Understand that, Ambler?"

"I get the gist. *Am stillen Ort.* In a peaceful place. Like this?"

"Yes, like this."

"Inside a drawbridge and a moat." He stood very still, looking over the valley, hands clenched, but I watched them gradually slacken. "Vaillancourt told me of a good picnic place, near Chancy. The jonquils were lovely, I admit."

"You admit that, Ambler. I went there with him once. He bored me. All bankers ultimately bore me."

"Why?"

"They grow fat and complacent on other people's risks. So you picnicked with your Australian lady. Was she enjoyable?"

"Yes, thank you very much."

"You sound touchy, Ambler." He had turned the tables to mock me now. The quickness of the changes in him was a different thing in him. "Don't you like the subject?"

"Not to go on about particularly."

Max Vyan whickered. "Not in the Mess, Ambler. Never women or politics in the Mess. But she didn't come here?"

"Went to London. Might be back."

"So you've been consoling yourself with the fair grass widow and her little one, uphill, down dale, and after bedtime."

My temper stirred to that. "I saw them off at Montreux this morning. No doubt your spies have kept you posted."

"*My* spies," he said coldly. Pluto growled. At me? No, it was at Sim. "What is it?"

"The kennelmaster, sir."

"Can't you see I'm busy?"

"I wouldn't disturb you, sir, but this is most important."

"Important!" Max Vyan's eyes were popping. "What importance?"

"Sir, the bitch Minerva has been found."

"Minerva found? How do you mean, *found?*" Max went in a hurry, followed by the palpitating Sim.

My hand was on Pluto's head, the size of an average bucket. "Come on, Pluto, let's look at the moat." He had growled unpleasantly at Sim's arrival, but he walked close beside me across the terrace, leaning his head against my hip.

The terrace was rimmed by a low stone wall, the inner wall of the moat, which was some thirty feet wide, the water about twenty feet below us, clear black water with no sign of ice. It must be warmed. The other wall was flush with the hillside. Twenty feet down and thirty across, an impassable obstacle, unless . . . The top course of the wall was made of thick flagstone set in concrete, wider than the lower courses. I put both hands under the lip and heaved, absolutely solid, interesting. Then Pluto and I walked round the garden. There were some miniature daffodils in the rockery of exotics, many different orchis, violets and primulas, other flowers. I bent to sniff the tiny daffodils, three inches high, pale yellow with full orange trumpets, a heady scent.

But Pluto was rumbling a greeting to his master, the rumble came from deeper than the growl. "What are they, these?"

"Narcissus microcosmus Ayachi, they grew at one place in the Atlas, only there, and now here. No one else's bulbs were viable, I saw to that." Vyan strode to and fro.

"Oh, did you, why?"

"*Why*, Ambler. You are always *whying*. Because they are mine alone. No others exist."

"Does this apply to all your exotics?"

"No, it does not. It applies only to Narcissus microcosmus, upon which you have unerringly put your stubby finger. And in fauna, it applies to Pluto's breed, eh Pluto?" Pluto wagged his tail. "There are no other Giant Alpenheide dogs but mine. You like this Harry Ambler, Pluto, why?"

"Now you're *whying*. Because Great Master told you to like me, Pluto, wasn't it, I guess?" Pluto wagged his tail.

"I never told him to like anyone else. I could untell him very easily." Vyan put his hand through Pluto's collar. "This Harry Ambler, Pluto, he is NOT your friend. He's your enemy, Pluto, sic on him."

Pluto wagged his tail, and my heart was hammering. "What . . . What's the trouble, Max?" I made myself say it quietly.

"I'll tell you what the trouble is. My best young bitch from the other line, Minerva, has been shot. She was two and a half, just fully trained, due in two weeks to come into season to be bred to Pluto. Shot!" There were tears in his eyes, for this moment not the sole proprietor of his universe.

"What a ghastly thing. But how?"

"She was out of the kennel compound at the time. Her body was found by the helicopter an hour ago, shot through the mouth at point-blank range. If I find the swine, he will not be shot through the mouth at point-blank range."

"I'm so sorry," said that swine. "Point-blank, and in the mouth — it sounds as if she must have been attacking."

"Of course," he said. "They stand guard, and brook no disobedience."

"Tea is served, sir." It was the butler at the door.

"Guard him, Pluto!" The dog shot across the terrace to stop ten feet from the man, head low, the shoulder and the quarter muscles bunched, feathered tail out straight, like a giant pointer. The man stood as still as he was able, white-faced, trembling. "Come back, Pluto! Thank you, Burton."

Max Vyan whickered as Pluto came back to lick my hand. What a madhouse. "I feel much honored by Pluto," I said. And so, in a madhouse way, I did.

"Let's have a cup of tea. You flew Vampires after the war.

But no jets since. Correct?"

"Correct."

"How long would it take you to convert to a Galaxy?"

"With a flight simulator — four or five weeks, I suppose."

But further conversation was drowned by the arrival of that helicopter beyond the house, and we went inside, where the sound was no more than a faint pulsation.

Behind the tea tray sat Tanya von Silberbach. Pluto grumbled, it was another note between the rumble and the growl; and for sheer delight there was a childlike whimper.

"Go and lie by the fire, there's a good boy, Pluto."

"Oh, hello," I said.

She nodded, and her lips moved, probably to say Hello. In a brief acquaintance I had seen her face reveal hostility, suspicion, rage, desire, enjoyment, cruelty, but now she was expressionless. "There is China and Indian tea," she said.

"Indian, please. With milk and two lumps and as strong as it comes."

"Your tastes are plebeian, Ambler."

"I like pork and beans, cold bully and spuds, oysters, caviar, and what are these sandwiches?"

"Patum Peperium, or Ambler's Relish." That amused me, like the quick caustic Max of long ago. When had I last had Gentleman's Relish sandwiches for tea? At a house belonging to Sir Conrad Brock.

"Did you enjoy New York?"

"No," she said.

"Yes," Max said.

"Yes, Max."

"Tanya has been rather naughty. But she's going to be good now, aren't you, Tanya?"

"Yes, Max." There was fear in her face.

The sound of the helicopter dwindled, taken off again. "That chopper of yours leads a busy life. I hear it coming and going all the time. Makes for a streamlined Shangri-la."

"Schloss Alpenheide is no ageless, timeless refuge, streamlined or otherwise, is it, Tanya?"

"No, Max." She wore a black silk dress with scarlet dragons — high at the neck, miniskirted, slit at the sides.

"The telephone rang beside Max's chair. "Yes?"

"New York on the scrambler, sir." I heard Sim's voice.

"All right." He went out of the room.

Tanya muttered, looking down: "He is terrible today."

"The dog, I suppose."

"Before he knew that also. More tea for you, Harry?"

"No, thanks. I like your dress. Chinese?"

"The silk material is Chinese. Yes, I like it on my body." She went to admire herself in a long mirror, and I to inspect the flower painting over the mantelpiece. I put on the glasses which Mary Dunn had given me. Sure enough, the vibration sounded above my right ear, Koala present. I put the glasses back in my pocket. Pluto's tail thumped the floor as I passed him. Tanya continued to admire herself. "My body, does it meet with your approval, Harry?"

"Very much so, Tanya." The side-slit in the dress went halfway up her bare thigh, most provocative, her red dragons undulating here and there.

"Stop preening yourself for Ambler's benefit."

"Yes, Max."

"Ever heard of a chap called Brock, Conrad Brock, Sir Conrad of that ilk?" He rapped it at me in his staccato way.

I was prepared. "Brock, let me see now, there are Brocks in Canada, a place called Brockville too."

"This one is Australian — beef, wool, sugar, electronics."

"I can't say as I have. Why, Max?"

"Because he was the first owner of the Koala Diamond."

And if the second owner knew that in my pocket a device from Brock Electronics was buzzing quietly to itself about that diamond, my situation would be less than healthy. Max Vyan was calm again, smiling almost amiably. "Well," I said. "He got his million quid. That's not to be sneezed at."

"Ambler, you used to ring true to me of yore. The question is do you ring true now?"

"My ringing true to you might depend on you ringing true to yourself."

Tanya hissed, a short involuntary hiss, and Max Vyan did not move a muscle, graven rigid, watching me. "No offense meant," I said. "But you asked for it, Max. Same law for both of us, Medes and Persians. Either that, or we ain't the buddies we was of yore."

He frowned, crisis over. "Must you mutilate the language in that infuriating fashion?"

"Sorry, Max. You make me nervous is my trouble." He did make me nervous. I was sure now that Max Vyan was more than slightly mad, a madman in the way of Adolf Hitler, cold calculating madman, turn it off and on. "You were asking me about a Jet Galaxy. Yours is a Galaxy, isn't it?"

"Yes," he said. "I have toyed with the idea of offering you employment, Ambler. Interested?"

One minute the man suspected me, the next he sounded me out about a job. "That's very kind of you, but actually . . ."

"But actually?"

"Well, actually, it's not my kind of flying. I'm too impatient, too slap-happy to cope with an airline type of job, which is what flying a Galaxy would be." As for being a member of your tortured entourage . . . I did not say.

"So I rather thought," he said, and waved a hand to dismiss the idea.

"It would be nicer much with Harry as our chief pilot."

"Which reminds me — are you free this evening, Ambler?"

"Free as air," I said.

"It would be good for Tanya to have a respite from her social duties. Why not take her out for a drink, a meal?"

"Delighted," I said. The beast in me jumped, I do not deny it, nor excuse it. She was all wickedness known about and not yet known, that magnet of repulsion.

"Should I change, or would you like me as I am?"

"As you are would be simply fine." Tanya went away, skipped away, actually.

"Why not come too, Max — let me return some hospitality?"

"I would be *de trop*, Ambler. Also, I need a respite from that tiresome female as much as she needs a respite from her social duties. Also, I have some things and people to attend to here, among them Sim. You met him?"

"Yes, a nervous type and . . . er slightly one of those, I thought."

"More than slightly. That was how I came to employ him. And a reason I employed him was that he is a wizard — what you would call a whizz — in financial matters. My private secretary is a neurotic pederast who hates my social secretary who reciprocates with ten-fold venom. Believe it or not, but Tanya has a positively schoolmarmish horror of homosexuality. Thus, I have minor problems enforcing the peace."

"Divide and rule, I suppose is the technique."

"Ambler, you are an infallible stater of the obvious."

"But wouldn't it be easier to get rid of one of them?"

Max Vyan did not look at one much — he talked to his hands or the window or the fire. But now he gave me his full speculative attention, opened his mouth once and closed it, touched the left eyebrow which had begun to twitch. I had a clear feeling that he wanted to talk, ask for my help, it might even be. How different this story would have been if he had done so. Well, there would have been no story. But all he said was: "If by *get rid of* you mean sack one of them — that, Ambler, isn't quite on the cards at the moment."

He went over to the window. "Sunset again. Last night I saw the sunset in New York. Tell me, Ambler, do you have a gun, a pistol?"

So it had come. So he had been playing with me all this time. "On me, you mean?" I asked his back.

"Not on you. That would have been detected in the courtyard. We have our little apparatus. I mean in your possession?"

My room had been searched. Someone knew I had a gun. "Yes, I do. Bushpiloting, I always carried one of those parabellum jobs with a detachable stock, best thing to kill game after a forced landing. Unwieldy, though. When I'm traveling, I take a small Italian thing, Beretta nine millimeter." The hardcased bullet had gone clean through the skull, I knew.

"Do the Customs not object?"

"The Customs don't know. I wasn't your prisoner pupil for nothing, Max."

"None of the locals could have; ergo, reductio ad absurdum: My prisoner pupil shot Minerva." His voice was not high. It was thoughtful and quiet.

"Why couldn't the locals? They all have weapons. You said the dog was on the loose. In self-defense, why not a local?"

"Because . . ." he began, but thought better of it. "Account for your movements last night."

"I was in the hotel. And I'm damned if I'll account for my

movements. I have a gun, and I told you so. Can't you trust anyone?"

"No," he said. "I can't trust anyone." He put his hand on his forehead, and turned to me, turned for the *first time* to me since this had begun. "Ambler, I feel confused."

"You have too much on your mind."

"Yes, I do."

"It's sad about the dog. If you think a local is out of the question, what about that Dorion, the Frenchman?"

"Yes, possibly. In any case, he should be dealt with."

Vyan switched on the lights, and went over to kneel beside Pluto. "Poor boy," he said. "We lost Minerva."

Poor Max, I thought, I really thought that for a moment, with his small loves and his great possessions.

Tanya arrived. "My new coat, is it not beautiful, Max's present?" It was mink, of a pale shade, what is called pastel.

"Off you go, then," he said benignly. "You'd better make hay because if things develop I may have to call Tanya back quite early."

Pluto wowfed: *Auf wiedersehen.*

TWELVE

There was an unreality about the valley. I think that plainsmen and sailors of the sea or sky always feel a hemmed-in unreality within the mountains; but at Alpenheide it was something more — the lovely prison and the prison keep, some deadly non-existent beast. Even the river, roaring now in spate, made booms and echoes of unreality.

"You shiver, Harry, are you cold?" Tanya at least was real enough — as real and capricious as nitroglycerin.

"Not cold. Tell me, Tanya, is Max all right? He seemed hepped up this afternoon, even confused, he said it himself. Max Vyan confused is something new."

"Yes, it is new. But big things are happening."

"Big things?"

"I do not know. I am one tool. *I have my uses*, as Max says often."

I slowed for half a dozen *ski-lehrers*, sauntering abreast; no need to hoot, they would hear us in a minute; but Tanya pressed her window button. "Rude louts!" she screamed in German, and the men jumped for the sidewalks, their faces averted. "Ach!" To feel unreality, one must feel absence.

"*Guten Abend, gnädiges Fräulein.*" Dominic bowed deeply. She nodded half an inch and walked past his desk.

"Your sitting room is nice." She gave me the mink but held on to her handbag, a large black crocodile purse, and strolled round looking at the pictures, including a good print of Manet's *Dejeuner sur l'Herbe.* "This naked girl in company of well-dressed gentlemen — and the handsomer rake is of your own type, Harry — this painting I have always liked so much to shock the hypocrites. Some day we should have such a picnic, you and I."

"Sure thing. Now what would you like to drink?"

"Vodka."

"I'll get some up. And tomato juice?"

"Bloody Marys are also for the hypocrites. Plain vodka is my mood."

That arrived, and we occupied the sofa. I dipped into my whisky, shy a bit of this flagrant woman. "You said you would tell me about your life sometime. To have crowded so much into so few years — it must be a fascinating story."

"Yes, fascinating, and you shall have a brief extraction. My father, nobleman of Württemberg and soldier, transferred into the Waffen SS at its formation. Then came war, and Father fought through every theater, to win the Knight's Cross with Oak Leaves, Crossed Swords and Diamonds, the bravest of the brave, SS Obergruppenführer Graf Kurt von Silberbach. He was a cruel man, or merciless in the way of Max. That is why I worship Max, reminding me as he does of Father."

"He was a Nazi, then, from the beginning?"

"Certainly. What nobler thing to be?" She fingered one side-slit of her dress, gravely studying red dragons, and then she flipped them over to reveal her knee, and studied that with equal gravity, brown flow of thigh and knee and leg.

"I was eight years when my father fought his way alone to Schloss Silberbach. That was 1945, the terrible spring of Germany's betrayal. When a battalion of Americans came, he inflicted heavy casualties by tommy gun. It was only a Yankee threat to burn down the castle including his wife and little one that forced him to surrender."

"Sounds a splendid chap. A little vodka?"

"Much. They hanged him."

"How appalling. Why?"

"Some treacherous village of the Maquis put to the sword in just reprisal, that and a few trifling similarities."

"Oh, I see."

"You do not see. You dropped your atom bomb on Hiroshima, isn't it?"

"No, it isn't. I mean I didn't, Tanya."

"Not you, I know that." She sipped vodka, considering her bare legs, now entwined on the sofa, restless legs. "My body," she said, glancing thence to me with hot green eyes. "You like it?"

"Marvelous." And so it was. "Do please go on."

"Our estates confiscated, our ancient name reviled — after two years of destitution my mother found employment in being housekeeper to a colonel of Americans in Baden-Baden. He was a kindly man of a common sort. Loading my mother with PX goodies, he took her swiftly into bed. And so the years went by until at about my thirteenth birthday this colonel of the occupation force, his kindness underwent some change, for even at that tender age I was showing rare promise of my beauty, and was frankly eager to explore a sensual world. Were you eager, Harry, when Eros beckoned first?"

"Sure was. And then?"

"My mother, a most jealous woman, one evening blundered on us in the colonel's study. Not yet ruined, I was ripe for

ruination, thanks to stealthy seduction by that older man. Always the older men seduce Lolitas, Harry, isn't it?"

"I don't hold with that sort of thing. Disgusts me. Vodka?"

"Yes. So my raging mother — I hated her then, as now —
packed me off at the colonel's expense to a finishing school at
Dampéry. There I learned to ski, and there I encountered boys
from a fraternal establishment. It was in my second winter that
the accident occurred. Playing, how do you say — skylarking
— on the platform high up at Chanaplaud while awaiting the
téléférique, another girl stumbled over the railing and fell
screaming to her death. I was glad because I hated her for
certain reasons, yet it was quite unfortunate, no more than an
accident, but under some cloud I was bundled back to Baden-
Baden. Naturally, I went not to my mother but to the colonel's
office, and was within one week in New York City where the
colonel soon followed me to his retirement."

"Shall we order dinner up here?"

"By all means, Harry. Let us drink, dine, dance, enjoy our
way to pleasure. But as I was saying I am now in New York at
sixteen years, the plaything of that aging colonel. Yes, you may
order now. I shall have twelve oysters, filet mignon extremely
rare, no vegetables, crème brulée and Heidsieck '59. My tastes
are basic, Harry, like your own as you would say.

"Now, as to this passing colonel, he was infatuated with me
to the point of madness, and soon the little heart attacks began,
and soon life with an insatiable old stager became most boring
— one never knew how he would last. So while the colonel
rested at times under doctor's orders, I would explore the won-
ders of New York. It was then that I came to know my extraordinary appeal to men of every age and sort. My need for them,
also, it grew in me. I do not deny this, nor make excuse. I am
female, female, do you understand?"

"Very well. Come here."

She came. ". . . See, I obeyed with pleasure in your case, being you, the rare one, like at age sixteen while wandering . . . Patience now, I break away because our first satisfaction should be dinner."

"*While wandering,* you said?"

"While wandering through the halls of the United Nations, I encountered this same strange animal demand. Within five minutes we were taxiing. Within one hour I was confessing my boredom with that dumb old colonel, to whom I owed so much, and whom I could not leave in, as you would say, the lurch. *Small heart attacks?* he said. He was an attractive devil. *Sounds easy. Throw tantrums, reconciliations, that should fix him. If not, we'll think up something else.*

"I tried a girl's best, but to no avail. Despite all angry passion scenes, the colonel's health improved. Nor could I run away because I was an illegal immigrant, smuggled in by MATS, and that colonel, whom I grew to hate, would inform on me, he threatened it.

"Coached by my new lover, I became all sweetness, chose a moment when at dusk on fine evenings it was the colonel's habit to take fresh air on our penthouse roof, and I elbowed him to fall to his death in a disused lot below. Falling, to see victims falling, is quite good fun, whether simply pushed or by more modern methods.

"I am telling you these rather confidential things, no squealing, please."

"Not on your life."

"Not on your death," she said thoughtfully. "Even you, if Max were to say: *Kill Ambler for me,* I would do it with regret, such is my loyalty and worship. But to continue — the other man, I shall call him X, for whom my desires were then consuming, had provided a forged suicide note in the colonel's hand on the colonel's writing paper. This I placed in the apartment. Free at last, I fled bag and baggage to the arms of X.

"Ah, here is our dinner. These Italians, what apologies for undersized grease-monkey men."

"Thank you, Benito. We'll serve ourselves."

"Such things as perfect forgeries — I should have suspected X, but so young and innocent, did not. After one week of education when I learned at last what is love with a man who is a man, X coldly and cruelly hoisted true colors — he was agent for the CIA, striking this bargain: In exchange for legal immigrant status, I was to infiltrate a certain Russian on the UN payroll. Either that, or else . . .

"What could I do but yield? With my official papers safe deposited, I went to work on the Russian, wheedling much valuable intelligence, which I relayed faithfully to X, who had me hooked as you would say. So strong remains my hate for him that to this day I will not utter X's name, but he taught me two things — first, the tortures and skills of concupiscence; second, this lesson: never again to be the cringing lover-slave to any man."

"H'mm. Oysters all right, Tanya?"

"Yes, they appetize me. What X surely could not know, and what perhaps I had not known myself — was that a devil lurks in me. You have glimpsed it, have you not?"

"Yes, Tanya." She ate a last oyster, folded her hands and sat quite primly.

"One afternoon at the modest apartment house which was our rendezvous the Russian beast spoke suspicion of me, and at once my devil rose. *Any sign of trouble, slip this in his drink,* were my instructions. A tasteless powder, and within no time the husky Red was a craven weakling to be bound up easily and soon forced to reveal every core of the plot — far more than had come to me by diplomatic means. Thus, at a tender age, I learned of cruelty's persuasion.

"But such a messy hulk would be bad evidence. I therefore had to set a little fire to burn with him also the apartment house in which some innocents were trapped." Tanya curved fingers, two sets of painted talons on her knees, and drew them up, and looked at me: "It pleases me to cause you horror. I cannot say you are a softy, but too innocent you seem of this real world."

"H'mm," I said, again that magnet of repulsion.

"Reporting to X, I feared his wrath, but not at all, he was delighted with my total low-down, spiking the whole abominable conspiracy. But, rewarding me handsomely, he said: *You're too hot a dish to handle. Now vanish, keep your mouth shut and behave yourself.* — *How behave myself?* I asked that devil. *All my behavior you have taught me.* — *That's what I mean,* he said. *Now take this note to Oliver, Bell Captain at the Avalon on Park. But I warn you* — *any trouble and your dossier goes to the FBI. If I want you, I shall send for you. Get out!*

"He never did send for me, the handsome swine-dog, fearing my devil, I expect, and with good reason.

"Thus it was, Harry, I became a call girl. In those five years I was the most sought-after girl in New York City and beyond, so far beyond — to Rio on some business trip, to Aspen skiing for some long weekend, and by no means only weekend stands — to Kanchenjunga, for example, as back-up climber and companion. But skiing was the best — to ski all day and love all night, what more blessed survival of the fittest? And no hatred, never once did my devil stir until . . . Can you not find a less oily wop to wait on us? I must speak to Max."

"You'll do no such thing. Okay, Benito, the coffee, please."

"It is your boldness that I like, but do not overstep."

"Right, Tanya. Your devil never stirred until?"

"Until one night. Now I should explain it that in those five years I had made my rule never to suffer a single Frenchman *pour ami*. I speak perfect French because of Dampéry, but they it was who plotted the murder of my father. Them I hate totally.

"Until one night a man with perfect English and credentials confided in me, as every stupid man will do at certain times, that he was French Minister of Cabinet on a delicate mission concerning war criminals still at large. Do you wonder that instantly my devil seized me, my hand the little knife I carry? I executed him then and there upon the spot.

"My danger was terrible. I had come through Oliver the Bell Captain's agency, and Oliver was safe. But there were clerks, doormen, maids — escape, I must escape.

"So I stole out and pressed the elevator button — self-service for optimum discretion. It came, and from it stepped a man. He considered me with those same saffron eyes, so wise and merciless, as had looked down when my father bade me a last farewell in saying: *Daughter, remember the motto of the von Silberbachs:* DIE RACHE IST MEIN. *The vengeance is mine.*

"*Trouble, I see,* he said. *Come inside.* And within two hours we were jet-borne for Switzerland. It was thus I met Max Vyan." Tanya stretched herself, sleek deadly pussycat. "It has amused me, as I said, to shock you with these few snippets of my life. To no other man have I told such things, except to Max who seems to know even more than I have made confession, as I keep finding . . ." She was silent, started to speak, and stopped. "Yes, Cordon Bleu if there is nothing better. Now I powder my nose. Have this Neapolitan Untermensch roll back the rug for dancing."

I helped the Untermensch roll back the rug and tipped him ten extra francs, a very decent little chap, Benito.

She returned scowling to swig her balloon of brandy like a chaser. "There has been another woman here. I sense it."

"The maids come twice a day, you know that."

"I do not refer to servant sluts. Who is this other woman?"

"There is no other woman, and mind your own damned business." I tend to take fearful risks when riled.

Her fingers moved to the hasp of her purse, but dwelt there. "Harry, one day you go too far. But Ach! I am starved for a man who is a man like you. Come dancing!"

It was a tango, which seemed to suit her vodka mood, a sensual mood, no room for doubt. "Is there some faintest vibration that I feel between us at about our middles joining?"

"It wouldn't entirely surprise me, Tanya."

"Ah, Harry, you are quite a witty chap. More of yourself you have yet to prove."

"Back in a mo," I said, and repaired to the bathroom where I hid those blasted buzzing specs from my jacket pocket.

Returning, I found her inspecting herself in a mirror which she restored to the purse, put that down, thrust both hands up from the nape of the neck and over her head and tossed her blond hair in considerable abandon.

"Harry, there was one little white fib I told you by mistake."

"Oh, what was that?"

"Saying I wear the Koala necklace at all times day and night. But I am without it for my sun worship hours, my bath times, and my daily massage under the skilled fingers of that Hermann bumpkin. Now would like it to re-enact the *Dejeuner sur l'Herbe* but for breakfast have dancing with Tanya von Silberbach and the Koala Diamond, our dancing picnic, would you like it?"

" 'D like it."

"Then feel the collar at my neck, and with one smooth thrust unzip me of this stupid dragon sheath."

"Oh, damn! . . . What is it?"

"Mr. Ambler — that . . . Miss . . . she is to return at once."

"That . . . Miss . . . She . . ." Tanya snatched the telephone. "It is I, Gräfin Tanya von Silberbach."

"Mr. Vyan's orders," come the alto, tortured voice of Sim.

She slammed it down. "That filthy little thief."

"Thief? Oh, come on."

"Does he not steal from every decent woman?"

"Fanny Hill's point of view was similar." But this remark was lost on Tanya, perhaps fortunately. She was in a tearing hurry, and I drove her home.

There was a large black car in the courtyard. "Some other time our picnic, Harry man. Now duty calls," and she ran.

I took a risk on the journey back, stopped near Pluto's fence and called him. The mammoth hound came galloping to say Hello through wires. "I love you, Pluto." One does tend to reciprocate the love of great ones.

The Caramba insecurely locked away, I made for bed, or first to tidy the sitting room. Our activities had rumpled the place a bit more than might be good for my reputation. Bending to pick up a cushion, I saw under the telephone table a small black box which had not been there during my inspection in the early afternoon. It also was held by a suction cup. One could suspect that Tanya's capacious purse might have yielded this bug while I paid a brief visit to the bathroom with my bug detector.

I retired to bed to be bugged by scarlet dragon dreams. I was beginning to dream a lot, no wonder really.

THIRTEEN

For the next two days there was a high overcast, so high that only the tips of the Teufelsspitzen were in cloud. The skiing was quite excellent on granulated snow, what is sometimes called sugar, formed by one day of hot spring sun, and unchanged since. It was muted weather, sounds muffled, or carrying far between the mountains.

Both afternoons the helicopter carried passengers to the Höhengrat, dropped down to wait for them at the Mittelwald, a de luxe shuttle service to the top station from the halfway house. Apart from slab-faced Hermann, the passengers were Max Vyan, Tanya and a big burly fellow who skied badly, fell often, and cursed cheerfully in indifferent German.

"Who is that with Herr Vyan, Fernandel?" I asked, watching the trio from his cable car. Tanya led the stranger, and Max, a competent safe skier, brought up the rear.

"I do not know, Harry. He has been here twice this winter, that I know. They speak German together, that I know, but he resembles more a Cossack from the steppes." Fernandel laughed. "Do you know the story of the garbage man in New York City?"

"No."

"Come closer, then — I must not shock my fair passengers — The garbage man I will tell you at some other time. Now I tell you: the Cossack is *verrückt*, is crazed for that woman." He looked at me. "And I must also tell you: that woman is most dangerous. Now laugh at my very funny garbage story."

I did, enough to draw attention from fellow passengers, including the smiling Gilles Dorion. I kept away from Max and Co., except once to call Hello when passing. Max waved, but Tanya, helping her fallen Cossack, did not notice me.

On the second morning, having seen Dorion take off to ski, I made a quick trip to Aigle in the Caramba. "Good point," said Mary Dunn from London. "I'll see what we can rustle up." End of conversation.

That afternoon the overcast had come a little lower, so the helicopter stayed below, and the trio rode the cable car. All the locals were forecasting a big snowstorm: "For days it may stay like this — still as the grave — until suddenly a northwest wind will strike at the Höhengrat — out of nothing, wind — and then the storm begins."

Riding up, I passed the time of day with Max, who was calm and affable. "Skiing good enough for you, Ambler?"

"First rate, but none too easy to see."

"You should wear goggles."

"I hardly ever do. But nothing much helps in what the Eskimos call *Hila Kapuk*, the white-out weather, tricky to fly in, incidentally."

"Easy to die in, incidentally. *Hila Kapuk*, Ambler speaking, little Eskimos."

"Very funny," I said, and he smiled his tight reluctant smile. Come to think of it, that was the last time I saw him do so. He went to join the Russian at the window, and now for a moment

I was face to face with Tanya. "It was such a pity we must take a rain check on our dancing."

"Certainly was. Tell me, who's your boyfriend?"

"Alexis." She came close and breathed: "A Crypto-Czarist."

"H'mm. Telephone me when you're free."

"Oh, no! That I may not do." She seemed startled; then menacing: "Sometime I just arrive to find you preferably alone."

At the other end of the cable car lurked Dorion. In the middle stood Hermann, the bodyguard. So that was two guns anyway, a third inside my anorak — any more among the forty passengers? And now, of a sudden, silence fell — it was like those silences at lunch at school, at twenty past or twenty to, at the thirds of the hour, we used to say, forty boys and a garrulous master speechless. Only the hum of wheels on the cable overhead. Then people talked again.

I was in bed by ten, and after reading Joyce Cary, my favorite author, I soon put the light out.

As must be apparent to you, I do not think well at any time in any place, but better in the dark in the ascetic bed. I tried to compose my mind to consider what big things might be happening at Schloss Alpenheide. Here was a man who had achieved great wealth, such wealth by now that it could not but increase. He had said as much himself, and he had said: *Money for money's sake does ultimately pall.* So you are Max Vyan: a misanthrope, a gambler, a seeker of power, a worshipper of size, a man suddenly confused; *a man whose mental stability is deteriorating, according to reliable reports,* said Mary Dunn.

And what were the origins of Max? He had been born in the West Indies — Barbados or Grenada, I could not remember which. He had gone to school in England, but had not disclosed where, at least to me. Therefore — he had always been a snob — a semi-public school. He had worked in the city before the war; he had had a commission in the St. Paul's Rifles, a good Territorial regiment, had been wounded at Dunkirk in 1940, had, in the next four years and ten months, been probably the best escaping brain in Germany. He had been fearless and an ice-cold killer. That he would still be fearless and a killer, I also knew. But I knew something else: He was now far from ice-cold in every circumstance.

I lay in bed, hearing accordion music from Whisky à Go-Go up the street. The day after tomorrow I would see Harry Gilpin, a shrewd old man, a richer man than Vyan, a man who had lived all his life with wealth and power and the dangers of them. Gilpin might have an insight which a humdrum mortal like myself could never have.

Just then I heard the helicopter. Since the demise of the bitch Minerva, there had been no morning and evening flights. Now it climbed from west to east with the quite pleasant pulsating chatter, lights blinking on and off, heading not for the Teufelsspitzen but further east, about in the Gstaad direction. It was out of sight now from my window.

There was one light on the mountain, at the Höhengrat. No stars were shining, so the overcast still hung up there. The helicopter should be miles off by now — and yet, it did seem odd, I thought I could still hear it far away, beyond, behind, above music from Whisky à Go-Go. The distant sound went on, rising and falling for some minutes, did I hear it or did I not? But then there was only music, quite certainly only music after another sound had mingled with it.

I got back into bed. It was past midnight, so much time lost in half-baked rumination. Music stopped at Whisky à Go-Go, and soon the murmur came again, this time beyond a silent village. It went on as before, rising and falling, nearer and further for several minutes — north, south, east or west, until the helicopter chatter grew positively from an easterly direction, down to Schloss Alpenheide.

I dialed the weather report at breakfast. It gave heavy snow warnings for all the Alps above fifteen hundred meters and extreme avalanche danger following the snow.

But the weather had not yet changed — as still, as gray, as muted. The hotel was three-quarters full, after an exodus yesterday. "No problem about a room now, Dominic, if a friend of mine should want to stay?"

"None, Mr. Ambler. So late a season, we have had luck this year. Now a storm is coming, and then, who knows?"

"When will the storm come, Dominic?"

He sniffed the centrally-heated air of the hotel like a bloodhound in a beauty parlor. "This afternoon, Herr Ambler. And as I am saying to all our guests, even to a great expert like yourself — at the first puff of wind come off the mountain."

"Do you ski yourself?" One knew so little about the omniscient Dominic.

"Ah yes, sir. I hie myself to Scheidegg for one month of high vacation before proceeding to my summer labors at the Hotel Giuseppe Garibaldi on Lake Como. But excuse me. *Si, Señora. Los aviones por Madrid? Es muy facil . . .*"

I went hard all morning, ran the Teufelssturz twice, and the steepest of the other runs. That annoying Mary Dunn kept popping into mind. Bamboozled, bugged all over the place, ripe to commit some fatal *bêtise*, I needed my case manager's hardheaded guidance.

"Fernandel, would you agree that skiing is for juveniles?"

"To this, Old Harry, as *philosophe*, I must with all respect agree, speaking of course in confidence, not wishing to sabotage my profession and my *après-ski*."

"Then would you agree that sex is for juveniles? She says that too."

"This is a terrible thought that assails me perhaps once annually as *philosophe*. But a question occurs, Old Harry, with respect: Is the lady's view of sex similar to sex's view of the lady?"

"Well, I wouldn't quite say that. The features are unusual, the will is strong yet womanly, the spirit is mocking but not unkind, the general conformation is, well, I mean, y'know."

"Such a female can stir riot in a seasoned campaigner's heart, averring yet disproving this terrible thought that assails him once annually as *philosophe*. For me such a female would be purest peril — for you too, possibly, Old Harry."

I was thinking of stopping after lunch, but the blue and white helicopter flew up to disgorge Max, Tanya and the Cossack. What did she call him — a Crypto-Czarist? I had not known of such a breed, except perhaps in Paris taxicabs. I stayed away from Vyan's party, taking alternate cable cars, as also did Dorion. If I stayed away, so did he, it seemed. If I moved near them, he appeared at once. Was it possible that Dorion was Max Vyan's employee? Perfectly possible.

I found myself beside him, going up. "The weather will change, I think."

"So the radio says — heavy snow warnings."

He glanced up at the Höhengrat, gray below gray cloud. "Not a healthy day to find oneself high up the mountain, Monsieur Ambler, even with a rope and skins." The cable car made its small lurch at a pylon. *"Pardon,"* he said, moving away from my left side where the pistol was. I had felt its hardness, and so had he. "The high Alps," he said. "They have their special charms and dangers too. They are not kind to the foolhardy trespasser, however well equipped and armed."

"I suppose you had a lot of mountain experience as a Chasseur Alpin."

"While you so gloriously shot down the Boche, I also fought
him at lesser heights." He paused. "We were allies then," he
said, staring at me. "In those times was an *Entente Cordiale.*"
In these times not, the implication came through loud and
clear. I nodded and turned my back. Thus are wars declared.

The weather still held, the same gray mantle, it was curiously foreboding. I saw the helicopter take off for Schloss Alpenheide, bearing Max presumably, for Tanya and the man
went into the cable car without him. I squeezed in beside
Fernandel.

We were passing the other car when Fernandel said: "It
comes," pointing to the Höhengrat where a wind was blowing,
plucking snow from roofs, from gullies, corners, from every
unpacked place — snow-devils twisting, a gathering scud, a
gray-white wall obliterating everything, it happened almost
instantly; and now wind buffeted the cable car. "At least one
hour ago I asked them to stop this *Luftseilbahn.* At least five
hours ago the weather office issued warning. Madness, madness," the jovial Fernandel muttered angrily to me. "Now I
decide whether to ride this bronco down alone, or to spend the
night with Hans and elephant wife, or to borrow skis."

He laughed for the benefit of passengers, who were afraid.
The cable car lurched, dangling from its bogie-wheels. The
sensation was thoroughly unpleasant, and the roar of the wind
was frightening. Rudi Viereck pushed through to Fernandel.
We slowed for the Höhengrat. The man at the controls — who
would be Hans — brought us slowly, twisting and hitting, into
the concrete box that was the terminal. It was a relief to be
held in there, the wind howling below the open box.

Fernandel issued instructions in French, English and German — to go with Rudi Viereck to the west end of the corridor, put on skis, and follow him down the Wintergreen, right of the ridge, and near the Mittelwald turn right again along the sheltered road that wound easily down to Alpenheide.

"*Achtung!*" It was Tanya, forcing a way imperiously through us sheep, followed by her pupil. Wedged beside Fernandel, I had to wait for the crush to go. Some hurried, and some hesitated timidly. Even I, a veteran of Arctic storms fiercer and far colder than this, felt qualms in the howl, the blatter of that open box with a few thousand feet of mountain below us. Fernandel had been on the telephone.

"What will you do, Fernandel?"

"It is not yet so bad. I shall bust this bronco down."

I took my skis from the rack and climbed the steps, hearing already an exchange of bell signals with the controller above us. Then the cables were running. I did not much envy Fernandel his lonely ride, but the safety factors in cables and mechanism were enormous.

As I pushed the swing door, a man thrust hard against it, and I let him out. "Car's gone, Dorion," I said in English. "What's the matter?"

"My heel binding, Marker, where is it gone?"

"They do come unscrewed quite easily. Try in the shop."

"They can *be* unscrewed quite easily, Englishman," he said unpleasantly; the world was mad this afternoon. Dorion ran for the ski shop.

I went along the corridor and pushed open the restaurant door a crack to see Tanya and the Crypto-Czarist, Tanya commanding double cognacs in her most arrogant manner.

"But, *Liebling*, we should make haste to go down with the others."

"Bah, they are beginners, and I am a better guide than any

Rudi Viereck. Cognac for warmth, and we ski safely through the storm. Are you afraid, then?"

Are you afraid then, isn't it? I remembered from my own experience at the Teufelssturz.

Rudi's flock were moving out. I strapped up and put on my yellow snow goggles. Here at the west end, the full force of the gale hit me, not only wind but solid grains of snow, as hard and painful as thrown pebbles in the face. I plodded against it. But the wind came now from the starboard bow, and, averting my head, I could steer by the railing on the left, past the Teufelssturz where a signboard snapped and flew away, and to the head of the Wintergreen. Here came girt Rudi. "You will follow them, Herr Ambler? I lead slowly, by the green flags all the way. It is very safe and simple." He laughed loudly, a dour little man exhilarated by the storm.

Rudi was right. All they had to do was to follow the green flags and the easy slopes which would lead them to that sheltered road winding all the way down to the valley.

One could see a short distance, perhaps fifty yards, and the snow came from behind, hammering at one's anorak. It must be a ground blizzard still, for the temperature was too high for small hard snow. The flakes when they came would be big and wet, would eddy round to one's goggles, cluttering them.

We must be near the Mittelwald. Yes, there were the two arrows, one to the right where Rudi was now standing, one to the left, pointing the trail that led across below the Mittelwald, round that shoulder, the tricky place above an avalanche slope, much trickier in this wind.

"Okay, Rudi. Don't wait for me." He waved and followed his flock, and just then the new snow arrived.

Dorion must still be behind me, and so were Tanya and the Russian. If Dorion had been waiting his chance, it might be here. I took shelter behind a rock to await developments if any, and then easily find the road the others had taken. It was a bloody awful blinding storm, but not cold.

I took off the goggles, had one of my brainwaves, and found those glasses provided by Mary Dunn. They were fairly useless, less useless than yellow goggles, giving a little eyeball protection, yet not fogging up. The wind was terrific, but did I feel or hear that buzz above my right ear?

I did, and it was growing, and here the darker shadows loomed. "Follow closely, Alexis, it is to the left we go now." To the *left* they go now?

They disappeared, ten feet, twenty feet away. Then another shadow came much faster, shot past me, edging right, and vanished. Gilles Dorion had missed the boat.

I now followed the direction of the left-hand arrow, going by buzz. I saw the dim outline of the man. I slowed, and he disappeared; went on, and he appeared again. Now he had stopped. "*Was macht's denn,* Tanya?"

"It is this accursed safety binding, always releasing to save me when I am already safe. And I cannot reach it. Oh, I am so tired with this wild tempest. Please help me now."

They were on the path running round that one steep place. I was close enough just barely to see him move forward on the outer side. Then there was a sharp brief spurting roar within the bluster of the storm, a stab of flame to the left, the inner side, and the man was flung the other way. I watched his thighs strike the rope safety railing, to topple him on, poles, body, skis, in an untidy thrash, and he was gone. The vibration above my right ear grew fainter, and still fainter. Then there was no buzz at all.

It had been a sensation more of touch than sound, but it had gone. I put away the glasses. Tanya still knelt along there, doing something with her waist satchel. Then she stood, planted both poles on her right to brace herself, and looked over the edge. It was a wild exultant laugh, and she cried: *"Die Rache ist mein,"* her motto of vengeance whipped away by the wind. Tanya von Silberbach went on round the shoulder.

Even if I had tried to turn back, I could not have done so. The wind was now so strong that I had to wedge myself against the inner wall, using both poles to hold me back. Then I let the wind hustle me round the narrow path. "Track!" I shouted. "Track!" — managing to keep in from the edge, but if I was met by whatever had shot that man . . . "Track!"

"Harry! Can it be you? What are you doing?"

"I missed that turn-off, and then the wind was so damned strong, I couldn't stop." We were in shelter beyond the shoulder, the wind thundering, the air in this still pocket thin, my ears were popping. "What about that chap you were with?"

"Him I sent down safely with the others, with Viereck, as I was troubled by this stupid binding. And then, like you, the wind embraced me."

"Is your binding all right now?"

"Yes yes, I tightened it."

Well, that was good news.

"My God, man, you are tough, no goggles even." She took off her own and stared at me. The light was dim, but enough to recognize that incandescent look. "Like two babes lost in wood," she said looking down; it was said demurely.

"We can't ski back the other way, and we'd never make it down this side. The Mittelwald is the only hope. Restaurant people live there, don't they?"

"Yes, but there is a much much better place. Oh, I am so happy. Trust yourself to me."

Tanya jump-turned gracefully, sure of my trust in her; and

after a few yards the full force of the storm battered us from the left. She was following the edge of trees, the east side of the wooded ridge that formed the lower backbone of the mountain. Then she turned in toward the ridge. I had never noticed the path when skiing. Fallen trees already barred the way but she led me round them, and on to a chalet in a clearing.

"The Falkenhorst," she said. "See Max's falcon carved there on the door. Now here is the key in its hiding place, and so inside. Now, Harry, light the lamps. Now the fire for warmth, you do that too."

The chalet was small, plain, adequately bunked, a solid oasis in the storm which thundered even more strongly now, and timbers creaked, and the chimney boomed. I felt safe from the storm if not from my companion. Logs soon blazed up in the wide stone fireplace.

"Max comes here in the spring, to be alone sometimes. The paintings, they are his, so exquisite, do you agree?"

They were oils, each of a single wildflower and its foliage in actual size, work of the highest delicacy. "I didn't know Max could paint."

"He can do anything, but anything — except only that love has passed him by. Now I must report to Max that I am safe. But I have been thinking, Harry, and my thought is better not to say that you are here, it not being Max's own suggestion. In such ways he can be sometimes difficult. So, be quiet, and I will use the secret telephone to Max's workroom, it is a buried line from here to there. If you see this, then you have not seen it, Harry?"

"Okay, not seen."

Tanya touched a knot in the paneling, and a telephone on a shelf swung out. She pressed a buzzer button. "Yes?"

"I am telling you, Max, in case you worry, that I am safe at the Falkenhorst. I was caught in the storm below the Mittel-wald, but somehow managed to struggle here."

"And Alexis?"

"Having some stupid trouble in my binding, him I sent down with the others."

"Good."

The panel clicked shut. "Max is not very talkative except rarely. Now I will fetch the grog."

It was a hatchway in the floor, and steps, down which Tanya went with an electric torch. What did this devilish chameleon have in store for me? Should I shut it down and trap her? Yet I was the lunatic who had forced this meeting. "Harry, there is everything in this frost-free cubbyhole. My mood is cognac because I am so happy." For once, Tanya's voice was disembodied, floating up. "Or there is dole to warm for Glühwein. What is your mood?"

"Glühwein, please."

"Now as to supper, we are somewhat limited by cans, such as Campbell's Soup of every kind, or stew, or pork and beans, these common things for healthy appetite, you mind?"

"Don't mind. Damned hungry, if you want to know."

"Most certainly I want to know, and want you ravenous. Now I will hand up food and drink. Also our record player. Put it near the fire, and soon the batteries will be strong with warmth. Harry, what a blaze you made. I was chilled in the very bones, but now I simply stifle."

I also was hot, took off my steaming anorak and hung it on a chair. In an inside pocket was the loaded gun. My sweater too. My ski boots. I turned to find that Tanya had done the same, if rather more as to her upper half, veiled nakedness.

"This thermal underwear in crimson lake, that such wide mesh should trap body heat, I do not understand, but yes it does, and not unbecoming, Harry, do you think?"

"Very much so."

"Very much so, unbecoming?"

"I mean the opposite, so much that is . . . er most becoming to take in at once."

"Ah, that is more like you, Harry Man. Cognac until your Glühwein warms?"

"Love some." I sipped brandy, then took the bugging glasses from my anorak to inspect Max's miniature oils. The great diamond and the small baguettes were sparkling at her neck, *no buzz.* "A man who can paint like this — why not content to be an artist? Why bother with tycoonery?"

"There are only these, the nine of them, no others Max has ever done, he told me. They are some tiniest expression of himself. He paints, and then for one whole day he sits and stares at it as in some trance — I saw this, it was April of last year; and then he is a man possessed in opposition by ferocious devils. But come, join me for more cognac, or your Glühwein now is hot, if you prefer such weaker stuff."

"Glühwein, please."

"*Listen, the Wind!* There was a book called that. It thunders still more loudly, and I am still more happy. It is in one sense peaceful here with you after all this jetting; this stress and strain with visitors, that Russian, the Professor, all the rest of it."

"The Professor?"

"Oh, it is some physics egghead that is come. Do not be restless, Harry, settle down closely with me here to stare into the fire, it is not eating you I want to do. You heard a few snippets from my life. Now let me hear from you — the flying exploits, braveries, the wickednesses too, the women you have plundered, and most of all the wickedness, while I drink laced Glühwein, and you your hot insipidness. Okay I'm listening . . .

". . . Such a tale of daring pluckiness. Good gracious, it is ten o'clock. We dance again. No, some slowness, like sweet music here that softer falls, that is your Tennyson. My criticism is only this, but it is a very vital thing: Your tale lacks cruelty, which is the spice of life — the joy of killing even, it is absent. When I torture or I kill — ah, that is bliss!"

"I enjoyed shooting down the Boche, I can't deny it."

"You enjoyed shooting down the . . . ?"

"Keep your hair on, Tanya."

"Oh, dear, you are so funny. My one complaint is of soft-sisterness, not worthy in the man I crave. Nor is it worthy of the man who is Max Vyan's only hero."

"Me, his hero. Why do you say that?"

"But it is true. It is why from you Max tolerates back talk that even frightens me to listen. Such talk from me would bring more weals like this. I turn for you to see."

"Holy Moses! Do you mean he beats you?"

"Not beats, but whips, and only in just punishment for being naughty: like last time I played hooky in New York."

"So he's a sadist too."

"Max is not anything *too,* and nor is he a sadist. He wields his slender whip in total disinterest for my anatomy. It is most strange, but true. It is also true that you are Max's hero. Only you in all the world he cannot help himself to trust some little bit, he told me so."

"Quite a compliment, really, even if I don't deserve it."

"You are too modest, and modesty annoys me."

"Don't want to annoy you."

"Be immodest, then, not for the hypocrites. Yes, that is better. Now I close this hero subject with a warning of your dangerous responsibility — never to show feet of clay betraying Max's trust, which would make from him a retribution the most terrible. My goodness what is this so awful bruise upon your chest?"

"At the Teufelssturz, remember, when you tried to kill me?"

"You are so funny, and a Spartan too, making no complaint. It was not killing quite, I meant, although my mood was dangerous. Now put on some logs that we may lie watching the firelight dance.

". . . A time to love and a time to kill, I read it somewhere. To kill, then love. To love, then kill."

"You talk a lot about loving and killing, don't you, Tanya?"

"Yes, I do. And I am thinking now at this peaceful moment while the storm roars on, of the Arachnida, or spiders, in which the female after consummation executes her mate. How proper thus to rub out the exhausted slave. Man, the master — Bah, I say, and Bah!"

"You're not thinking of executing me, I trust."

"No, no. It is some academic thoughts that I am having. Man Harry, how I love your grand physique. Are you fond of mine?"

"It's simply smashing."

"Your compliments are clumsy, but everything one cannot have. At least you are an honest oaf with attributes."

"Thanks very much."

"Why, not at all. Now, that Alexis — I in my innocence swallowing it that he was Crypto-Czarist until Max found out the truth about him — a Communist dyed-in-the-wool, he was."

"Was?"

"Was or is, what matter? Does not the grim reaper stalk from yesterday until tomorrow?"

"Well, I suppose so. I hadn't thought of that."

"Thinking is not your strong suit, Harry. Now shall I work off energies by dancing a bacchanalia for you alone?"

"I wish you would." The firelight flickered on that sinuous body, drew sparkles from that giant gem.

". . . There! Did I please the lazy Sultan?"

"You were terrific."

"Am I not worth my clothing of a million pounds, to put a conservative estimate on it?"

"Ten million, I would say, with or without that priceless bauble."

"A much more worthy compliment. Here, catch it! I shall dance this once for you without adornment."

In that corner is the faintest blush of pink . . . Yes, there.

". . . But you are not watching. While I dance with all abandon, you are staring at some necklace. This is mortal insult."

"Not insult, Tanya. I said that with or without, you were worth ten million, as you have amply proved. I was only a little startled when you threw the thing, I might have dropped it. But what is the necklace without the neck? Come here, and let me put it on."

The great wind was abating now, but snow still slapped at windows. I put on more logs and went to open the door a fraction — feet of snow outside and wet snow in the face. I went back to warmth but not to sleep, watching the flicker of the fire. And then two mice came out to nibble at our crumbs before the hearth. Hunger appeased, they played together, chased one another in a most endearing fashion. Then they stood up and began a dance.

"Reach for my skiing satchel, Harry."

This I did, and went on watching, fascinated by those tiny stately creatures.

There was a sharp brief spurting roar, a bright stab of flame, and the mice flew across the room to lie still against the further wall. "You may cremate them, Harry."

My ears ringing, slightly dazed, I went to do so. "Why bump off a pair of harmless mice?"

"They are not harmless mice, but vermin. And why should dirty vermin dance upon my dancing floor, you tell me that?"

"I don't know. What is that thing, anyway?"

"Here, you may inspect. This is my new toy, a recoilless weapon for point-blank range, firing a shock wave, nothing more, but up to four meters it shatters every internal organ, thus causing instant death, perhaps too instant to be interesting, but efficient."

"It's almost a dead-ringer for a hunting horn."

"That is the principle — a bell-like muzzle to spread the supersonic blast, and with this tiny electric trigger on the horn. One holds it outward, thus — to avoid the back flame. Give it to me, and I load again with this simple rocket cartridge, so! Ready for action in my satchel. Is it not a handy weapon against evildoers, whether mice or men?"

"Yes, indeed. But mightn't it blow you up — if you fell, or something, skiing?"

"I, Tanya von Silberbach, never fall. Besides, there is a safety lock. Now, Harry, this has been a long hard day, and even I feel just a little tired."

"Same here. I think I'd better set my wrist-alarm for dawn, and leave you to your beauty sleep. I mean if anyone saw us ski down together, Max might hear of it."

"Max would certainly hear of it. This is wise of you. One other thing — you would not ever forget yourself and say to Max that you had once seen me kill two mice somewhere? Max loves mice, and I would be the sufferer, and later you."

"Okay. Sleep well."

"*Hasta luego,* Harry Man."

FOURTEEN

The wind had dropped. The cabin was silent but for a stir of embers in the fire and minor scufflings as I dressed. Now only the boots, my Henkes to be buckled. Tanya slept across the room, at least seven meters from me.

I put on logs, a chivalrous gesture which brought the fire to life, but also Tanya. "Such a lovely sleep I had. Harry, you are indeed up before the lark. Come here!"

"G'bye, Tanya. Have another lovely sleep."

"It is early yet, no need for hurry."

"Now now, Tanya, I've got my boots on."

"Your boots on! What did your Herzog von Marlborough care about his boots on?"

"Dunno. But Max mustn't hear of this."

"Yes, true. Well, go now, before I change my sleepy mind."

The door opened inward; beyond was snow, three feet of it at least, compacted cleanly to the shape of the paneled door, which I shut behind me.

The snow floated down in flakes an inch across, no zephyr of wind. I skied round, under and through snow-laden trees. It was a difficult passage, with many down — not uprooted but snapped off jaggedly at the trunks. I held a general course toward the paleness that meant dawn.

At the edge of the wood I paused to plot my course. But that was simple — one stayed close to the wood on the left of the ridge and skied downhill. The question was how far? I inverted a pole and tested for depth, four feet of new snow.

It was so slow that, running the fall line, I had to pole myself to get any speed at all. I tried to match in my mind the run of the ridge and the run of the avalanche slope beyond it. I had looked down that avalanche slope once or twice, thinking of skiing it, then thinking better of a foolish notion. There was a first long pitch, then an easing of the slope, then a steepening again. It was the flatter stretch that I wanted to reach, and a picture in my mind told me that the easier slope was immediately below the spur, a rocky protuberance of the ridge that paralleled the avalanche slope.

The ridge was on my right, and now a spur jutted from it, like a Roman nose. The snow had changed to faster-falling sleet. I took to the woods again to skirt below the spur. Tree damage was worse here; many months of work ahead to clear the tangle and to salvage timber, so precious to these mountain people.

Now I was through, standing below the small cliffs and broken rock of the spur. This certainly was it. I moved from the safety of those cliffs towards the open loaded slope. The sleet had changed to rain, which fell heavily, pocking the surface of the snow. I unclipped the straps which would hold boots to skis in case of a safety binding release. I took my wrists from the loops of the poles.

I slid forward gingerly, looking up the avalanche slope, on the lee side below the wind where great drifts always accumulate. It had been my calculation that, once falling, a body must continue — topsy-turvy, head over skis, and topple on — to the foot of the first steep pitch, and would slow here on the easier slope, would probably stop before the hill steepened again below. I had come to this place, my heart somewhat in my mouth, because last evening a peculiar thing had happened. It might have been a coincidence of failure, or it might not. I looked up the pitch, where untold tons of heavy snow were teetering on top of a slippery crust.

Standing stock-still, I found and put on my pair of bifocals. There was a vibration behind my right ear, and it grew as I slid and slid stealthily and slid, towards a slight mound of snow. By the time I had arrived below that mound, the vibration had grown to a pitch indicating point-blank range. I reversed a ski pole and prodded the mound, below it, above it, delineating it. I looked up the hill. It was full daylight, and nothing moved except the rain which came down heavily to load the snow still more, to make of it a brimming sponge. No humans moved and no animals. No other animals would be so foolish as to set foot on this slope.

I planted my poles and went to work, digging down by hand, hampered by having to twist my body from the skis, which faced across the slope. If trouble came, those skis would be my only hope.

The man sprawled on his back, and he was dead. I had grubbed two feet down to reach his stomach, and then went for pockets — two in the ski pants, nothing — two in the ski jacket, nothing — two outside, nothing in any of them but handkerchief, matches, cigarettes, key ring, a bit of silver wax.

There was a sound from the hill above me, a sort of gravid grumph, and I saw that a crack-line now ran across the slope. From my own excavation a lump of snow broke off, and rolled and grew, snowball down the mountain, gathering size and speed and satellites. In a moment the whole slope would go. But it did not. All the snowballs ran away out of sight.

At the crack above, at the run from here, I had stopped working. It was coming soon, I knew. But where? If the wet avalanche broke off above me, I might outrun it. If it started here or below, my chances of escape were virtually nil.

I took off those glasses and used them now by hand, which I should have done from the beginning, like a mine detector — not a ping, a buzz. BUZZ at the neck. Now got it, put away the glasses. He looked quite peaceful, color gone, a handsome corpse. I drew the cord over his stiff neck, his head, and out came a small bag of chamois leather.

Another sound from above — the crack-line had closed, not widened. The snow below had moved to open it; the snow above had moved to close it. The rain had stopped. There was not even that soft pattering to break dead stillness.

What I now had to do was to grasp my poles again and make the most tender tentative kick-turn that man could execute. Left ski round and set as gently as a laundry iron on Elizabethan lace. One ski pointing left, the other right, a most vulnerable moment. Now the right ski, reverse direction, tiptoe to the safety of that rock spur.

My right ski was halfway turned when the same grunt or grumph sounded up the hill. But this time it did not stop. This time the first soft grunt of subsidence swelled to the roar of a mountainside in motion.

I jumped to run the fall-line of the lower pitch, skating for speed, but that started my own avalanches as I went — then poling for speed. The roar grew louder, hunting me down.

Wet avalanches are slow, I knew. Wet avalanches rarely send a shock wave ahead of them, I knew. But avalanches can do anything, I knew. It was gaining on me, and starting with me. I could throw away my poles, and, with luck, both safety bindings would trip, and I could swim in prescribed fashion in a tumbling sea of snow, if it was only snow.

There was a shock wave. I heard its wind coming through trees on either side, and crouched for it and kept my balance somehow as it hit me, passed me — and here was my escape route, the winding trail down which Rudi had shepherded his flock of skiers yesterday, an open stretch of road which this avalanche always crossed. I owed my life to a turn I had not used for many years — the archaic Telemark — right ski far forward, left ski back, knee to meet boot and swing, the elegant old Telemark, with all hell thundering about me, sideswiping the tail of my left ski. I fell and rolled.

The avalanche had roared across the road at its appointed place, and on to die in meadows. Snow, rocks, mud and splintered trees — a dirty aftermath of power expended.

I skied down the road until the snow petered out above the village. It was raining again, but less heavily in a valley loud with water. *A foot of snow is an inch of rain*, was my rule of thumb, probably inaccurate, but near enough.

The village was deserted, very odd types not to stir at the wrath of avalanches, some close-wrapped superstition probably. I heard a man talking to a cow, and that was all I heard or saw of humanity — into the *ski-raum*, up in the lift.

I locked the doors and inspected my booty, using the magnifiers of my bifocals, the buzz annoying at close range. This Koala necklace buzzed; the other Koala necklace did not. The Koala sold by Brock to Vyan had a built-in bug. It had been worn by Tanya, if a buzz could be called proof of that. The Koala worn last night by Tanya had no buzz.

I set my invaluable if infuriating wrist-alarm for nine-thirty, unlocked the living room, locked the communicating door, and took my Koala to bed with me. But whose Koala was it? Who had stolen whose Koala?

My standing arrangement with Benito was that he leave the breakfast tray at eight in my sitting room. So everything was cold this morning except coffee in a thermos jug. I ate standing up, taking a roll and marmalade through to my bedroom to look at that avalanche up the valley. It came down once or twice every winter, or usually was brought down by explosives, running a channeled and harmless course through the forest to peter out below. But this time it had burst its own bonds and trespassed into the forest too, taking a mass of detritus. Somewhere in that mess would be the body of the man they had called Alexis.

But a knock. "I tried to telephone you, Mr. Ambler."

"Oh yes, sorry, Dominic — I unplugged them yesterday." True. "What can I do for you?"

"Indeed nothing, sir. It was to tell you only that Herr Vyan called last evening, anxious that you had got down safely."

"If he calls again, say I was helping Viereck guide people down, got caught and took shelter in that covered hayrick, the one on the hill road. Slept like a top. Oh, and tell him I'm sorry to see so many trees blown down."

"Herr Vyan loves the forests, a sorrow to him."

"Yes, I know. Well now, Dominic, I'm pushed for time — lunching over at Gstaad with Mr. Gilpin. You'd better report that too." I gave him an old-fashioned look.

"Why, certainly, sir, yes, if you wish."

"I don't particularly wish. I wish, on the other hand, that all my movements — who I ski with, who I dance with and the rest of it were not reported faithfully to Schloss Alpenheide. I am used to calling my private life my own."

"Sir, there was no such intention. Our patron on his return asked with such affection as to your welfare, and so I did say that you seemed much to enjoy the cheerful company of Master Jeremy and Mrs. Grayson. Was this my indiscretion?"

"Mildly so. Don't worry about it, Dominic. And no one could have been more kind than you have been to me."

"It is a pleasure, sir, to serve a real gentleman of the real old school." He paused, and added carefully: "It is sad only that we have these troubles, growing always now behind the gaiety of Alpenheide."

"What troubles, Dominic? Like poor old Moffett?"

He shrugged, and then said or whispered so quietly that I barely heard him: "Herr Ambler, we are all afraid."

"What of?" He shrugged again, and bowed himself out.

Down at the lockup I checked the Caramba for oil and petrol, having closed the overhead door behind me. Then I opened the boot and deactivated. As always, she started perfectly for a *real gentleman of the real old school.* I could imagine my father's caustic comments about that, watching my recent behavior from Elysium.

It was cloudy and mild as I ran down the valley. Tree damage stopped below the village, and the only evidence of the storm was the torrent in the inner ditch, overflowing at many places to cross the road in pulsating waves. I reached the gorge, through which in recent days the river had run as a broken cascading tumble. Today the water was unbroken except where torrents joined it, silent in the main.

I slowed on the bridge to look upstream, not at cloudy greenish glacier water, but brown spate. And high above it, coming fast along the side of the valley, was that black beetle.

I went over the bridge at moderate speed, and then gave the Caramba about half throttle, all she could use on that slippery surface. Beyond the next corner was the quarry where Max and I had turned, and beyond that again a long series of curves, swinging right and further right as the river swung. A car even a quarter of a mile ahead would not be in view for several miles. I turned into the quarry and out of sight. Then I ran to crouch among the rocks. I seemed always to be crouching somewhere, Beretta in pocket or in hand. I had taken up pistol shooting when I was a fighter pilot, thinking it good for co-ordination — at my best I could hit two lobbed soup cans out of three in mid air; but that was long ago, before I had heard of Max Vyan.

The Porsche went by, drifting on the wet surface, centered again. Monsieur Dorion was an accomplished driver, snaking down the mountain road in smooth control. But he had missed the bus once more, if I was the particular bus this time.

I gave him five minutes, and then followed fast, knowing that I could never catch him if he was trying to catch me. But I did not see Dorion again that morning — he must have turned left for Aigle and Lac Léman, whither he had followed me before, not right for the Col du Pillon and Gstaad. There had been a heavy fall of snow at the Col, but they had plowed it, and I reached Gstaad at a quarter past twelve, by which time the day was sunny and warm. I went shopping for a large tin of cough lozenges, a suitable envelope, a stick of sealing wax; parked the Caramba at the Palace Hotel, repaired to a private closet in the gents downstairs, and by twelve-forty was knocking at the Gilpins' suite. So far it had been one of my busier days.

There were only the three of us for drinks and luncheon. One's first impressions of people *gang aft agley* on further acquaintance, but not mine of the Gilpins. Gloria, as she soon asked me to call her, was a little winner by Jacques Fath and Cartier, too sugar-sweet a cup of tea, as I have said. And yet so very feminine with the big strong men that one did enjoy it. It transpired that we had mutual friends in Scotland — the Duncattos of Duncatto, Tarquie and Lois, the Lord and the Lady — from whom Harry Z. Gilpin had rented an ancient castle two winters ago.

"Two *winters* ago?"

"Yes, Harry. And I confess that my memories of Baltigg are ambivalent. First, I fell deliriously in love — ridiculous at my age, you must think, I know."

"Why so ridiculous, Harry Man?"

That *Harry Man* gave me a fearful jolt.

"In the eye of the strapping young beholder only, sweet one. Love blossoms from the cradle to the grave. But all ended well, as Gloria is proof. It was also the Winter of my Madness, when *I* had my lust for power. But I got over it, thanks be to God, thanks also in no small measure to the sturdy wisdom of Tarquie Duncatto."

"Tarquie's such a pet."

"A robust sort of pet, my dear."

"That's what I mean."

There was some small edge in this exchange, urbane on his side, girlish on hers.

"Lois is great value too," I said. "The perfect wife, I always thought, for him."

"Yes, indeed — so amusing and decorative."

"And she bosses his kilt off," said Gloria Gilpin, which uncharacteristic remark reduced her husband to doting mirth.

Coffee came, and brandy, which I did not take.

"How are things at Alpenheide, the skiing still good?"

"It was marvelous until last night's storm. Will be again at the top, I would think."

"Max Vyan is back, I understand. How does he seem?"

"He asked me over the day he came home. One of those big dogs of his had been killed, which upset him, well, naturally. But he struck me as being steamed up about things in general, not at all like the way I remembered him."

"Yes. I thought that when we had luncheon in New York. Now, Gloria darling, time for your little rest."

"Ah, pooh!" she pouted.

"You know he said you must, every day and then our stroll at half past three. Now off you run, there's my dear girl."

"He treats me like finest Meissen, Harry. So good-bye, we never did hear about your wonderful flying exploits."

"Some other time," I said.

When the door had closed behind his wife, Harry Z. Gilpin divulged to me with coy pride that Gloria expected an infant in September. "Think!" he said. "First time a Daddy-oh at sixty-five. Is it not remarkable?"

"Good work," I said. "Congratulations."

"Thank you, thank you. When I think of the vain and ridiculous ambitions that have haunted my life, culminating in that Scottish episode chez Tarquie . . ."

"Oh, what happened?"

"I too sought power. Yes, I admit it. I sought in my madness to eliminate the labor problem by creating — thanks to a couple of moronic scientists with I.Q.'s at the genius level — by creating a human artifact, a robot if you will, and a damned nice chap he turned out to be, too nice for this wicked planet, we had to fix him. Suffice to say that I was cured finally of my lust for power, although, to be fair to myself, I should add that my purpose was creative.

"So here I am, as domesticated as all get-out, trying always to be a better guy, never sarcastic — a weakness of mine which upsets her — going for little walks, cosseting dear Gloria from morn to night, or twenty-four hours a day would be more accurate, in strict training for the great event. Indeed, I have been training assiduously these past two years."

"Sounds wonderful. What regimen do you follow?"

"That has changed. Initially it was:

> *Si les femmes savaient tout le bien*
> *Que le celeri fait aux hommes,*
> *Elles en planteraient*
> *De Paris à Rom.*

"No laughing matter, young Harry. But now that the wonder has been worked, I am simply trying to be a better chap."

He considered his cigar, tipped an inch of ash, and looked at me, his eyes gray and infinitely shrewd and rather small. The climate changed in that five seconds. "Well?" he said.

FIFTEEN

But the telephone rang. "Yes? . . . Did I not ask you to show the lady up? *You thought.* Be grateful to avoid thought, as you call it, when thinking has been already done for you, young man." Harry Z. Gilpin replaced the receiver. "A hopeless youth. But sarcasm, there I go again. Mary Dunn is here," he added. "I sent my chauffeur to Bern for her. You look dismayed, young Harry."

"Anything but," I hastened to say. "Just one thing, though. Can I see you for a minute alone before I leave?"

He nodded, and went to open the door. "Ah, Mary m'dear, you look enchanting. And how is Conrad, your lucky employer?"

"Sir Conrad is just fine." Mary Dunn arrived blushing. "Oh, hello," she said to me.

"Oh, hello," I said to her.

Foxy old Gilpin smiled. "Allow me," he said, taking her short Persian lamb coat, probably provided by her lucky employer. Mary Dunn was dressed for *après-ski*, Icelandic sweater, plum stretchables, fur boots. She seemed pale after the blush had receded, sitting down to brisk business as usual.

"What developments, Ambler? Talk freely before Mr. Gilpin. Miss out nothing, but make it snappy, stick to the point."

"You told me that last time."

"Yes, and you rambled on, with omissions and afterthoughts and data withheld. Now try to do better."

So I gave a play-by-play since last I had seen Miss Dunn — Sim — the helicopter — the bitch Minerva — Max at the Schloss, the change in him, his knowledge that Brock had owned the diamond, his suspicions of me yet his offer of a job, the admission that he was confused — my dinner party with Tanya, and her early summons back — a Russian named Alexis — yesterday's events, the storm, the execution, and the chalet, Tanya's mention of a Professor, the mice and the rocket horn, my departure as soon as the storm had eased, I said — my debugging of the Caramba, and my giving the slip to Dorion.

Mary Dunn had heard it all without expression, knees together and hands on knees, looking down at them. "Was that . . . was the Silberbach woman wearing the necklace last evening?"

"Had it on."

"How do you know?"

"Saw it."

"Hear it?"

"When I had the specs on, yes."

"When else? Any questions for Ambler, Mr. Gilpin?"

"Later I might have a few questions for Mr. Ambler," he said blandly. "Now I have one for you, Miss Dunn, knowing that you would require me to make it snappy. May I proceed?"

"I didn't mean . . ."

"One rarely does, my dear," said that champion sarcast. "How much have you explained to Harry Ambler?"

"Well, just the background, really — that we're worried about something big being up, and to keep his eyes open and not do anything to arouse suspicion — and look what he does, shooting that dog, and that woman in that chalet."

"I didn't shoot that woman in that chalet."

"You see what he can be like, Mr. Gilpin — quite infuriating. Well, for his own sake, we told him very little really, except about the Koala."

"At first they lied about that too."

"For his own sake we had to lie about the diamond."

"Might I suggest that we now leave the subject of this jewel, this precious gem set in demi-paradise with bugs; the subject in its present context bores me? Might I suggest to you also, my dear young lady, that every worthwhile clue we possess is thanks to the intrepid work of Harry Ambler, to whom in my opinion you pay scant respect?"

"Not really, I don't. But I never slept a wink all night, and now I'm just bone tired." Mary Dunn looked at her undeniably lovely hands, blink, blink of long eyelashes. She did look tired and pale. "Please don't be horrid, Mr. Gilpin."

"Oh, my dear child, I am so sorry, thoughtless boor." He sprang up to pat her shoulder and fuss about. "There, there, now. Try some of these muscat grapes. I have them flown in daily from Morocco. Gloria has a whim, a little appetite or yen for them at present. Try a muscat, do!"

Dunn popped one in and said: "Delicious. Could you explain to him, Mr. Gilpin? I always seem to just get cross, and be unfair, I know I am." Another grape.

Harry Zee smiled and turned to me. "Now, young Harry, I shall get down to cases. You have heard of Interpol?"

"Sort of International Police. Correct?"

"Correct. And an invaluable organization it has been in

combating crime across the world. Essentially, however, Interpol deals with the common criminal, however uncommon he may be.

"Now, as you will know, there has been since the end of the Second War a tremendous proliferation in weapons of destruction. I do not refer only to nuclear bombs and missiles and the like, but to a wide range, a whole disparate family of biocides, if I may coin a term — killers direct and indirect — by bang, by poison, by disease. Do you know, for instance, that there is a virus, all test-tubed and waiting on both sides of the Iron Curtain which, admitted in minute quantity to any water system would, with wildfire rapidity spread to the human race as myxomatosis spread to Mary's rabbits?"

"Oh, please don't," she said.

"Sorry, I was trying only to bring the true dimensions of these horrors home. Now, the two Great Powers — they and the potent also-rans, such as Britain — have become more and more concerned that the Fearful Family should be kept within the family, so to speak.

"In other words, they have been and are increasingly afraid of these weapons falling into the wrong hands — into those of small chauvinistic nations — or worse, into those of some criminal consortium — or, most dangerous of all, into the hands of a psychopathic individual.

"Perhaps I emphasize the obvious when I say that these fears do not concern the manufacture of such weapons — the cost and complexity thereof being astronomical — but the theft of them at one stage or another.

"Accordingly — it was soon after the Cuban affair — an international organization was set up. So Intersec came into being."

Intersec, I thought. *Intersec.* Now where did I hear that word before?

"It was clear from the beginning that if Intersec were to enjoy the confidence and trust of the great powers, it must be entirely separate from — indeed, alien to — their vast intelligence services, which continue as assiduously as ever to ferret out one another's plots and plans and latest gimmicks.

"Intersec had one purpose only — to prevent leakage to undesirables. Now, if I may use a homely simile, it soon became apparent that the danger lay not at the grain elevator but at the farm. Stated otherwise, the stockpiles of completed biocides are so well guarded that the danger of theft is virtually negligible. This applies right on from the stockpile to the silo and the bomb bay. Those few of us who are cursed with imagination have a recurrent horror image of the berserk bombardier. But so comprehensive are the safety checks that this is no longer a valid fear. Now I shall not keep you long — short and snappy is my motto." Mary Dunn winced, placed a plump oval grape between her lips, sucked it in, pop, one succulent squish inside, two chews, one swallow. She reached for another.

"But, as ever, the quality of a service depends upon the quality of the man who heads it. In the case of Intersec it was vital not only that the Chief should be a man of rare quality and all-round scientific know-how, but also a man who was *persona grata* to, and entirely trusted by all parties — in this case, three — the USSR, the USA and Great Britain. France, you will not be surprised to learn, declined to risk his virtue in that company.

"Now it chanced that Conrad Brock was such a man. Heading a Commonwealth Trade Mission to Moscow some five years ago, he fell into talk with Comrade K. Talk became argument, and argument became insult when Khrushchev referred to Brock's beloved country as a desert in the ocean fitted by God for beach boys and marsupials. This angered Brock who, in fluent Russian, gave back better than he got. They squared off to come to blows, yes literally, and were separated by none other than that cool customer, Kosygin. Whereupon, as so often happens with schoolboys, fury gave way to friendship — and this, incidentally, has insured a continuity of trust in Brock.

"So he became chief of that small, super-secret supranational body — Intersec. *Protect our wares*, they said to him. *Trust me and take yer orders*, he said in his roughshod way to them. Thus it was that Conrad Angus Brock became in one specialized field of International Security, the absolute dictator."

"Roughshod is only one side to him. Sir Conrad is a most cultivated man."

But now I had remembered: Conrad Angus Brock, C.A.B., *CAB-INTERSEC*. "May I ask a question, Harry?"

"Do, my dear fellow. Pray make it short and snappy."

"What's your connection with Intersec?"

"A limited one. I might be called both professor emeritus and liaison man. I have known the perils of financial power, and I have learned my lesson. I provide contact with American industry. Also, I do help to tone down Brock when Brock becomes too brockish, Mary, eh?"

"Sir Conrad can never be too Brockish." She ate a grape. "Not in my book, he can't."

"And a very elegant collector's piece in finest vellum is Mary Dunn's own book, as Harry would agree, I know."

"Well, she ain't no jumbo paperback," I said, which remark found more favor with Gilpin than with Dunn.

"Now, I have nearly finished. Mary will explain in detail our fears about Max Vyan. I shall simply sketch in the background. As he himself told you, Max made a killing in surplus arms. With a first couple of millions — pounds not dollars — he put his remarkable gifts to legitimate work: first, international finance, then into light and heavy industry — aluminum, steel, and the manufactured products thereof, creating with what I must call genius the large complex he now controls."

"How much is Max worth, would you think?"

"In ultimately realizable capital assets, I suppose a hundred million pounds, not very big — not so small, though."

"No, not so small, though."

"Soon after Intersec was formed, it came to Brock's notice that the Republic of Bargomba sought to possess itself of a common A-bomb and, having had dealings with Vyan in his less respectable days, had again made contact with him. Quite properly, he gave them the brush-off. Possibly, however, this ham-handed approach gave Max an idea, a strangely appealing idea to a man who was coming to realize that money for money's sake does ultimately pall — you see how much we owe to Harry? Vyan never said these things in such a way to other people."

"Yes, I know," she said, leaning forward, a grape poised for popping in. "I don't deny it."

"His idea perhaps was that a man who had in his possession any or a few of these varied weapons — not to use them, of course never to use them, never to sell them irresponsibly — would truly have wealth to end all wealth, truly have power to end all power.

"What kind of a man is this? He is, as we keep saying to the point of tedium, a ruthless man. He is a lonely man, with no soothing frailties such as the bottle and the bed. He is a misanthrope, with nothing but contempt for the run of his fellow men. He has an obsession with size and the absolute — look at his castle, look at his drawing room, consider his minute paintings which Harry has described to us — with the absolute, you see. But as one remembers from college physics, no absolute may be reached, be it large or small.

"Lastly, we know that Max Vyan is a man without scruple. Harry Ambler's greatest coup, the photograph of one Mr. Korber, is a prime example."

"I'm not even allowed to see the picture. How can I manage my case, kept always in the dark? Who do they think I am, some teen-ager?"

"They, we, one and all agree that you are a young lady of remarkable talents, a case-manager par excellence."

"Must you be sarcastic?" M. Dunn was on the grapes again. She was afraid of him.

"Not with you, my dear, I promise, never. Would I, Harry?"

"Certainly not. Sir Conrad wouldn't stand for it."

"Oh, shut up, Ambler."

"Be quiet, both of you, and heed the sage. So devoid of scruple is Max Vyan that he resorts not only to blackmail but to murder by the skilled hand of his social secretary: to wit, the Russian named Alexis, whoever he may be."

"That's why I was up all night. Sir Conrad wanted a line on him, and I got the line, and now he's dead."

"How did you know about him being at Alpenheide?"

"We have other agents besides our philanderer."

"Miss Dunn, unless you are prepared to behave with respect toward Mr. Ambler, I shall address a word to your employer."

"But I do respect him. It's the debit side I don't respect."

"If you seek total perfection to respect in your employees, I suggest that you become a five-star female general in the Salvation Army, eschew the seamy world of Intersec."

"Sir Conrad warned me again last night. He said: *Harry Zee*

Gilpin can bite with a meaner-hooked set of fangs than any-
thing this side of a tiger snake. Just remind yourself he's a
decent bloke. I'm beginning to wonder, Mr. Gilpin."

"I apologize, my dear — this dreadful tongue of mine. Let
me say that my admiration for you is boundless, and Harry
would agree, I know."

"H'mm," I said. "To get back to business, I have something
to pass on." I told them about the paper in the fireplace on the
night that we had gone to dinner. "*Cab-Intersec*, it looks as if
he could have been on to Brock and Intersec even then."

"Phew! It does indeed."

"Ambler, couldn't you have told . . . ?"

"I could, if I had thought of it. So could you have told me
about your other contacts in Alpenheide."

"As Sir Conrad always says: *One jackass can be a productive*
agent. Two agents produce like a pair of mules."

"May I interject a word? If you two splendid people are
to carry this most hazardous mission through to success, you
must arrive at some *modus vivendi*. Squabbling will never do."

"Don't worry, Mr. Gilpin. I can put a public face on it, if he
can."

"You mean she's coming to Alpenheide?"

"*I* do not mean," said Gilpin with asperity. "And may I suggest that you essay direct communication in the second person
plural unfamiliar? I am bored with the role of whipping-boy
interpreter." He rose. "Do try a muscat grape," he said to
Dunn, who had nearly polished off the bunch. "No? But I
assure you there are bushels of them in Morocco." He removed
the silver salver. "Now Mary, if you will forgive me for one moment, I have photographs of mutual Scottish friends to show to
Harry. Should you wish to prink a little, we have what some
circles call a powder room."

He led me along an inner corridor of the Gilpin suite, tip-toeing finger to lips, presumably past Gloria's bedroom, and into a small study. "You want a word before you leave?"

"Yes, Harry. I wondered if you could look after something for me. It isn't mine, but I think it needs safekeeping." I produced the envelope, sealed by my thumb.

"Valuable?" he said, regarding me with those beady eyes.

"Very, I think."

"Into the hotel safe, then. I fancy that the Palace safe has held a few king's ransoms in its time." He weighed the thing in his hand. "You say that this is valuable, and does not belong to you. But you are engaged in a mission that is hazardous, to say the least. What is my position in the event of your demise? Or indeed, your position in the event of mine? I do not wish to pry, young Harry, but . . ."

"I'd better explain." So I completed the story of the two Koalas, the odds pointing to this being the genuine one, and my recovery of it.

"Oh, I say, what a fearful risk! What a fearless adventurer you are! But what, why, how? I confess to bafflement."

"Max had a replica made. Then promised the necklace eventually to Tanya. Then substituted the imitation. Gave the original to Alexis for services rendered, and had her bump him off. Body now buried under X feet of snow. Recover the Koala in due course. That's the way I see it."

"And very shrewdly do you see it. But what about your employers? Should Mary at least not know of this?"

"They keep holding out on me, so why not ditto them? Besides, what purpose would it serve? The deed is done. The thing is in safe hands."

"An interesting point of law: Who *does* now own the Koala Diamond? Presumably the heirs and successors of the late

Alexis, if rightful ownership could be proved. But the question tends to be academic."

"You said earlier that the subject of the necklace bored you at present. I had a passing thought about that. Would you find it boring, say, in September?"

"In *September?* Oh, I say, by Jove, September!" His beady eyes were gleaming. "What a simple transparent chap you are."

"True enough. The only thinking I can do is straight to the point, and it has to be simple, if you understand."

"I fancy I do, simple chap as I am myself. But would Mephistopheles? Now, shall we skip those kilted photographs? It is nearly half past three, and I should be waking Gloria with grapes, but I simply cannot fly in more until tomorrow. Oh dear, I shall be in my darling's doghouse."

"Dunn fairly wolfed 'em, didn't she?"

"Dunn did, a compulsive aspect there. But she is tired out, poor girl. At such times, I have observed, their likes become obsessive, and . . . er their dislikes too."

"She can't stand me, you mean. Well, it's mutual, let me tell you."

"I have long observed such antipathies between the finest people. If I may proffer a token of advice, young Harry, it is this: Turn the other cheek. Our cause is worth it. Indeed," he added quietly. Harry Gilpin's measured ways in no way diminished his potency: "Indeed, to have a cause, one must remain extant. Come, then!"

The car was brought, and into its modest boot I personally stowed Mary Dunn's two suitcases, ". . . I will try to turn it," she was saying. "I'm only human, though, Mr. Gilpin."

SIXTEEN

"Why not tilt the seat back and have a sleep?"

"Thanks. Any aspects of business first?"

"One thing — you work for Brock. Vyan knows about Brock and Intersec. Won't they be on to you?"

"Not a chance that I can see. I have few known contacts with Intersec except for the occasional case like yours. I run the holding company on a tight rein from Sir Conrad. And I run Brock Electronics on the side. Give me a payroll of five thousand any time."

"H'mm."

"I must say I think you've done quite well."

"Thanks, Dunn. Due to your good management, I'm sure."

"Thank you, Ambler. Any more business?"

"Only a couple of things: What did you find out about Alexis? And where do we go from here?"

"Right into the Schloss is the first essential."

"How?"

"You must be invited there again, and place sundry items. I have brought along some equipment. I like, for instance, that telephone from the chalet where you whiled away last night."

"Not so. Storm over, I got off my marks. And may I say that I found out quite a lot last night?" More than you know, Mary Dunn, I thought. "What about the telephone?"

"Two minutes in Mr. Vyan's workroom, and we could have a perfect tap. Now about that Professor — there was a defection three days ago — applied physics, h'mm, I must check on the blower."

"What about that Alexis?"

"I may tell you later. Now I'm dizzy with *what about's.*" She stretched and yawned. "Sorry if I was rude."

"Don't mention it. I wasn't too polite myself."

"That Mr. Gilpin — Sir Conrad thinks the world of him. Well, for once I can't agree. He's a sarcastic old square."

"For once I'm with Sir Conrad. Now go to sleep."

On that rare occasion Mary Dunn obeyed me, sleeping peacefully over the Col, and down to green lands with yellow flowers — oxslips, cowslips, wild daffodils.

The rear-view mirror was so placed that my eye, without shifting, would tell me of a car behind. But no one followed, and no side track held a waiting car. I watched them all while considering the situation. On what excuse could I get access to Schloss Alpenheide, on what possible excuse into Max's workroom? Suppose Tanya had told him of last night? Suppose the body of Alexis had been thrown out by the avalanche?

But it is not my nature to dwell upon dire eventualities. Now I played a game, which was to drive the Caramba as fast as possible without stirring my recumbent passenger. This is the best test I know of rhythmed driving, and it can be done well only in a car so fast that passing is a smooth certainty. By then I had driven the Caramba about two thousand miles, far enough to be the boss of her immense acceleration, to be her partner in the driving seat. She was tight and true, as different from the soapy soft American sedan as a barracuda from a bulbous codfish.

I slowed for the turn up the Alpenheide road. Mary Dunn slept on. Seeing her indolence and innocence asleep, I wished that the sight of her did not rebuke me. As I turned, she said something, still asleep. "The Southern Doctor," said Mary Dunn, asleep.

I knew that Doctor. It was a wind which came at the end of hot Australian days, bringing coolness from the Southern Ocean, from a hundred degrees to sixty-five in an hour or less, a good name for a blessed wind.

I began the long climb, not hurrying. I had been driving with the windows shut, the floor ventilators a little open. Now, at slower speed, one needed more air, so I dropped my window a couple of inches. Tranquil weather had settled on the Alps.

The road wound on from shadow to sunlight and to shadow beside the river. Normally I run no risks in a car except those from the lunatic opposition, and those which cannot be avoided if one drives fast, however sound the tires and so on. But I also like to dawdle on occasion.

I took the left-hand bend with perfect positioning at forty miles an hour and heard in my left ear a few staccato sounds that could mean one thing only to anyone who had heard them in peace or war. It was the multiple crack of bullets a few feet from my head.

I had been cruising in high gear — now foot down to override that — stick shift back to hold her in 2. The Caramba leaped like a catapulted jet, and my passenger slept on.

In the mirror was that Porsche, and the cadaverous face of Gilles Dorion, Chasseur Alpin and the rest of it, God knows what rest of it, but he was hunting me. "Mary!"

"Yes, Sir Conrad? Oh, shucks, it's you, what is it?"

"Dorion on our tail. Hiding back there. Shot at us. Hold on. Lie down."

"We're armored, Ambler. Don't you know that?"

I did not know that. She had not told me that. I lined up the corner ahead, a long curve — went into it at eighty, drifting, drifting. She was watching back. "You're holding him. Tommy gun on swivel mounting outside his window, control from wheel, it looks like."

A straight stretch now, riding ninety, ninety-five, a hundred. There was a devil's rattle at our back. "Stupid bastard," said Mary Dunn. "He's wasting ammo. Better keep your horn . . ."

A turn to the left, a Volkswagen, front wheels within inches, hard over left, my tail slewing to the verge, hard right and left again, a glimpse of a fat girl with a sagging jaw.

"This is fun. Step on it, Ambler."

"Stepped." I took her advice, switched on the barrage horns, and we heralded our approach as loudly as a diesel locomotive. Peasants came out of occasional chalets, hands raised as in surrender. We met more cars, all stopped in the inner ditch.

"He's gaining, Ambler. He's got us on the corners. We've got him easily on the straight."

"You say we're armored?"

"Armor plate all round, ditto glass and bullet-proof tires, defensive only, proof against small arms, but . . ."

A fiery streak, a supersonic clap, explosive impact on rock ahead, muck flying and we flew through it. I understood about Dunn's *but*. "Where'd that come from?"

"Low left, horn aperture — his left, your left. There's another on the right — that'll be mine," remarked Dunn calmly.

"How far now?"

"Hundred yards, still gaining. Anywhere we can duck in?"

Better-duck-inn, I remembered. *Overnite cabins.* Better

duck in for TV, courtesy coffee, sanitized seat for your protection in a continent of butchered this and that. "Two places we could. One a quarry ten miles on before we cross the river. One just ahead, mile or so, a sawmill. Better soon."

"What's he chasing us for, I mean, actually?"

"Search me." Search in the Palace Hotel safe? But I was trying to see that mental map of mine — a quarter of a mile straight, bend left, immediately sharp right to cross bridge, left swing into head of gully the sawmill, could be done.

I came into that straight with the needle touching eighty in second gear, into manual high, and she jumped, she hit my back to a hundred and ten, horns bellowing past two damned great buses, brakes, second gear, corner coming, brakes, accelerator, go into it biting, sliding, too much, snake it, steady, hard left into sawmill lane. "He tried," said Dunn in a moment. "Couldn't make it left, took bridge. Now get after him."

It was a quagmire from the rain, but the limited-slip took us through and round and out of the yard where sawyers gaped, no Porsche in sight. The windscreen was dirty after buses and the rest of it. Dunn pressed the washer-wiper button once, twice, three times. "What now? Can he do the same trick on us?"

"At the quarry, but he won't. I'm going to ride him." The Porsche in view again, and ahead were the miles of winding road, not sharp turns — a bend, a short straight, a bend again, always edging left above the river.

"Gas?" she said. "Less than a quarter tank."

"Five gallons left, okay, I think."

"He may have rockets in his backside."

"Have to risk that." Inexorably we were gaining — five hundred brake horsepower in two tons, not even the Porsche Six could cope with that. He was good, Dorion, a goddam good French froggy fighter, than which they don't come better. The Tommy gun had swiveled a hundred and eighty degrees and sprayed us again. That Porsche squat on the road like Rudi Viereck squat on skis. Yes, he had rockets in his backside, blew a hole out of the tarmac dead ahead; ride over the gaping hole, and ride the fragments. Mary Dunn did not even flinch. "Neat steering job," she said. "What's your plan?"

"Put your seat half up and lock it. Tighten belt. Hands on head, head down as for aircraft ditching when I tell you."

"Okay."

I lined it up — ahead that corner to the left, a sharp corner, beyond it on the inner side, the quarry, beyond it another curve to the straight stretch to the bridge — all along now on the right, all below us now, five hundred feet of gorge to the river, no parapet. The sharp corner could be taken at thirty-five, or a little faster. Fifty yards, forty, and his brake lights were on, he had to brake. "Now," I said. I took to the left — two tons aimed for his port quarter at seventy miles an hour.

I clobbered the Frenchman. He did not have a chance, poor chap. But poor chap is not what one feels when the blood is up. I skidded, corrected, over-corrected, recovered, stopped her six inches from the brink.

I watched the Porsche roll, bounce, roll, a last lazy tumble end for end, wheels racing, and it splashed into the swollen river, black from here, unbroken again, a swirl of air or something, again unbroken. "You fixed him," said Dunn.

I backed and turned into the quarry, which was becoming a familiar place, and I stopped the engine, got out and went for a walk; I just went walking, back and forth, and then I sat down, and then I walked, no boom of the river in this hollow place today; only a blackbird singing, only the pure white peaceful mountains.

"It dries in ten minutes," said Mary Dunn. She was dabbing paint on bullet marks. "Twenty-six," she said, applying dark green paint. "That's counting the four stars on the windscreen. Nothing to do about them, but they don't show much. Ambler," she said, after stowing the can of spare paint and brush, "there are some aspects of you that I don't dig, but my golly, you're fair dinkum when the bullets fly."

"Thanks, Dunn. You're fair dinkum yourself. You're cool. You're the coolest goddam sheila I ever wrassled with."

She blushed and then she laughed. Her laughter echoed all about that hollow place. But business never stayed far from the mind of Dunn. "How far on is Alpenheide?"

"Four miles, about."

"The bus drivers, or that girl, or all those others, they're sure to report us. We'd better go quick."

The Caramba started instantly, and ticked over as smoothly as if she had come from a tune-up, not a road race. I drove past the small house in the trees and over the bridge.

"The key to Alpenheide, Mr. Vyan called it."

"You have a good memory, Dunn."

"I remember facts and figures and things said. You remember what you see. So we might get somewhere — that is, if you don't hold out on me."

"Same to you, agreed?"

"With reservations that I'm the boss."

"I couldn't be long in doubt of that."

"I was trying to be nice," she said. "Why spoil it?"

We had been a team in action, harmonious in the aftermath of it, and now we both wanted discord. I did not know why I wanted a carpy edge between us, but I did.

"Max said that Dorion should be dealt with. He will hear anyway — the watchman at the bridge may have passed it on already."

"We weren't in sight."

"In sound though, Dunn. It made a smashing racket. Why don't I telephone Max and say I have news to impart? You're sure Dorion wasn't working for him?"

"He was working for de Gaulle, I told you that long ago."

"Well, he ain't no longer — he's good and drownded. Shall I tell you something, Dunn?"

Her nostrils twitched, a sure sign in Mary Dunn that I had annoyed her again. "Pour it out," she said.

"A small thing to you, I know, but it makes me feel funny — that was my first peacetime murder, actually."

"Self-defense, I would call it," she said. "Yes, telephone Mr. Vyan."

We ran into Alpenheide. "Such a lovely old village," she said, and sighed.

She had a most feminine, defenseless sigh, the steel-trap mind, the sweet soft sigh. "What's up?"

"Only the prospect of that ghastly skiing."

Two policemen stood at the street junction leading down to the Kronenhof. Both moved, and I thought they were going to stop me, but they did not, watching the car approach, turning as we passed. "They'll know us again."

"I'd better put it in the lockup. You register. Tell Dominic you're the one I spoke about."

"Oh, all right," said Mary Dunn, quite petulant.

The hotel boys whisked her bags out, and I put the car away. The stars on the glass were nothing much. The new paint splodges were visible at close quarters, but there were no dents in metal. Perhaps sometime she would explain to me about an undentable armor-plated car that weighed two tons.

"You looked after Miss Dunn?" I said to Dominic.

"Indeed, sir. Luckily, Mr. Ambler, we had vacant one of our best rooms, with bath, of course. Room 403."

"Any messages?"

"No, sir. I telephoned Herr Vyan as per your instructions. He expressed pleasure at your safe return."

"Oh, good. What's the skiing like, Dominic?"

"Indifferent, sir. But after sun, and with frost tonight, it should be superb all the morning tomorrow."

By then I had little booby traps about my room — a hair from the Ambler head set delicately here, another there, a paper match, and so on. None touched, so far as I could see. I telephoned Schloss Alpenheide.

First the butler; then Sim, who said was it urgent as Mr. Vyan . . . Well, I said, perhaps I really had better speak to Mr. Vyan; and after a minute Max came on. "Yes?"

"I went over to lunch with the Gilpins at Gstaad today."

"I know that. What about it? I'm busy, Ambler."

"Coming back, near the quarry — I had a slight contretemps."

"Get to the point."

"I pushed a chap off. I thought I should tell you."

"Who?"

"That Frenchman, Dorion."

Silence. The start of a whicker. "You'd better come up. Wait! Your car damaged?"

"A bit of paint, nothing much."

"I'll send the chopper. Be ready in ten minutes."

"Room 403, please . . . It's Harry."

"It's Mary."

"Settled in all right?"

"Settling. Where are you?"

"Next door, actually. If we both unlock, we communicate."

"Oh yummy. Let's communicate."

There were two doors, through which she came. The radio was loud. "Did Mr. Vyan know about it?"

"Don't think so. The chopper's coming for me. Want me to take anything?"

She ran to her room and was back — a small phial in one hand, also a small black disk, size of a dime; in the other hand a book. "If you can locate that telephone, lift the receiver, brush this glue round both the circuit buttons — or the middle cradle, if it's that kind — hold off ten seconds while you apply this disk to the microphone, replace the receiver. See?"

"No."

"Dual purpose. It makes connection, closes the speech circuit — and the disk amplifies. Rudimentary but it works. Did you ever give him a copy of this?"

It was a book called *Orbit with Icarus,* my one and only literary work. "No," I said.

"Here you are, then. Don't forget to sign it."

"The bloody book is mostly about us escaping together. And here I am . . . No, I can't do that."

"Life and death, you can. You must, please, Ambler. I'll explain tonight."

"If I come back tonight."

"You think I like sending you into danger. But what can I do?"

"You can go to Zimmermann's and hire some skis and boots — get buckle boots. Get Standard Heads, soft ones, six inches short for your height."

"Oh well, I suppose. Ambler!"

"Yes, Dunn?"

"I know I have to ski, but if you just realized how much I loathe it."

"I do," I said. But I did not.

Now I heard the helicopter. "Good luck," she said.

It landed, as before, on the square in front of the hotel. The door opened. The steps came down. A crewman in helmet and overalls followed them, and I went aboard. He eyed me, passing. He did not have that impassive bodyguard's physiognomy, but a real wicked mobile face. I wondered where Max had collected this one. He sat opposite, motioned me to do up my belt, and ignored my existence.

We were up, tilting to skim the meadows, over the round hill, over the roofs of the Schloss, a chair on a flat sundeck, the moat ahead, now dropping to land. The engines slowed from scream to whine to high whistle, low whistle, stop. I never did like helicopters, afraid of them. "Thank you," I said to this chap, who gave me the creeps and no word for answer.

It was the usual gauntlet of bodyguard and butler. "Good evening, Burton."

"Good evening, sir. Mr. Vyan is in the workroom."

He was as fat as old Plum, a butler I knew once upon a time, who wobbled. He stopped at a door in the passage — I had been along it once before, when we saw the Gilpins off by helicopter. Beyond were the hall and the drawing room.

"By the day after tomorrow at this time — six o'clock." I heard Max faintly and distinctly.

"But, Mr. Vyan . . ." mumble mumble. Then another door closed and Burton knocked. "Mr. Ambler, sir."

"Sit down." He did not stand himself, which might indicate a change in my status, or that this was a place of business, or whatever. By then I had so many possibles on my slate, with

Sim, Tanya, the dog, the necklace that *whatever* could be anything. I sat on the straight-backed chair, one of six round the walls and his behind the table, a set of Hepplewhite, much like those of my own which I had recently recovered from the dealers. There were four rugs, all Bokharas on a parquet floor. The paneling was of some pale wood. There was a safe recessed into the wall. On his table were telephones, a gold pen set, a blank pad of paper. Those were the contents of Max Vyan's workroom, but for one photograph on one wall. "Well, I'll be damned," I said. A nonchalant look round had been my intention, and my practice too, until I saw that photograph. It was of the American General George Patton between two bedraggled thugs named Max Vyan and Harry Ambler. "Oh, Jesus!" I said, my belly knotted up.

"What is it, Ambler?" he said quietly.

"Nothing like it before or since. I don't mean Patton."

"I know," he said. "And nor did I." Nor *did* I. "What's this about Dorion?"

"When I left this morning, he followed me. So I turned into that quarry and let him pass. I didn't see him again until this afternoon as we turned up the Alpenheide road."

"We?"

"That Australian girl I told you about. Since London she's been visiting some cousins in Bern. So I made a date to meet her at Gstaad, after my lunch with the Gilpins. Mary Dunn by name, and a damned nice girl she is, brave too, didn't turn a hair when things got hot."

"What happened?"

"He latched on behind, and the next thing I knew was a flaming rocket past my head. To summarize, I shot off into that sawmill and got behind him. I don't take well to people shooting rockets at me, it's a nasty feeling, particularly the second one,

from his tail when I was following, a short in the middle of the
road, only splinters on the windscreen. So I really chased the
bugger and gave him a nudge at the quarry corner."

"And the car?"

"It went into the deep place. Well, it's all deep today, but
the deep pool, you know it."

"Thirty feet, anyway. Why, Ambler, if I may ask?"

"It's not as if it was the first time — I don't mean shooting,
but following me. Trailed me skiing. He even trailed me that
day I took your envelope to the bank, then met this girl — well,
I can't be sure, but a black Porsche appeared during our picnic.
Why? That's what I want to know."

Max Vyan started doodling with the golden pen on a sheet
of paper from the block. How could a man with taste like his
bear to use a gold fountain pen? "That's what *I* want to know,"
he said. He was drawing a bird with a thin hooked bill,
a chough. "A few things seem to be adding up, in fact rather
too many, Harry Ambler."

"What adds up might be that picture on the wall. Was
Dorion after the diamond, or was he after you? If after you,
and he thought I was in with you — couldn't that be an explanation?"

"Possibly," Max Vyan said.

"Why after you? What gives here, Max?"

One of the telephones rang. "Yes?"

"The lab, sir." Did I hear that?

"Okay, I'll come." He looked at me. "Make yourself at
home. I won't be long." The other day Max had blown his
top, or shown excitement at least three times. Today he was
entirely calm, but the eyebrow twitched. He went out by the
other door.

One telephone bore the letters Sc, large S small c; the second was a house exchange telephone; the third was marked F, with a single buzzer button. Sc might stand for Scrambler, F for Falkenhorst.

His table was diagonally across a corner of the room, on the left of it a big plate glass window, on the right the other door. I would be in view from the main hillside, but behind glass from a couple of hundred yards away — no danger surely there. An almost totally bare paneled room, no cupboards, no lamp brackets, no holes or corners to spy from that I could see. The telephone marked F had a central cradle which rose half an inch when I lifted the headset. I took out the phial, unscrewed the top with a brush in it, like that gum you buy. I applied a thin coating to the neck of the cradle, held the headset, slipped the black metal disk onto the diaphragm — magnetic — counted a few seconds, replaced the headset. The cradle stayed up. You would not notice unless you looked for it.

Taking the gold pen, I inscribed the title page of my opus: *To Max from Harry,* and signed it *Harry Ambler.* Then I crossed the room to look at that enlargement of me and my buddy with General Patton, who had tended to make pets of us. The same photograph was reproduced in *Orbit with Icarus.*

You will perhaps understand my compulsive urge to turn as the door opened and say: *Look, Max!* Tell it all. Instead, I swanned over to him at the table. "I rustled up a copy of that book of mine, long out of print, but they found one somewhere. A present, if you want it."

"Thank you," he said. "That's very civil of you, Ambler. If I remember aright, the book is better than the title, which would not be difficult. By the way, our people at the bridge did hear a loud crash, but saw nothing. And there were numerous complaints to the police about two cars racing. That is fixed. So Dorion will rest undisturbed. And you — what are your plans now?" He was doodling at the legs of his bird. "More murder most foul, or what?"

"If a chap shoots you up . . ."

"Yes, I know," he said soothingly, as to a child. "You're touchy, Ambler, aren't you? You used to be the least touchy clot imaginable. *The lady doth protest too much, methinks.*"

"You haven't been driving at a hundred plus on a road like that."

"No," he said, "nor battling with blizzards."

"Oh, that wasn't so bad. I acted as rear guard to Rudi Viereck and his flock. Waited in case there were stragglers, and when I did take the road, trees were falling all over the place, so I crawled into that covered hayrick and slept until this morning early. I crossed just in time — the avalanche came down like the wrath of God." *Never lie,* Father used to say, *but if you must, lie as near to truth as possible.* Someone must have seen me in the early morning.

"Tanya also was benighted, a pity you didn't get together. But now Tanya has a rival. That won't be very popular, Ambler." He drew in the claws of his bird, two rear ones on each foot spread out, two front claws curved down. The chough was perching, but it perched on nothing. "Your plans? I asked."

"I thought another week here; then hang the boards up. But I dunno. That shook me this afternoon. I killed a chap."

"What of it, Ambler? Killing chaps, as you call them, is enormous fun." What was he drawing now on his table in his workroom? "You've killed plenty and enjoyed it."

"In battle, yes. Well, that was like battle. But who wants war? I don't. Do you?"

"To want *war,* one must respect the species." What he had

drawn — with the paper slanted sideways — was a chough perched on a flat ledge of rock beneath an overhang above a cliff. The few bold lines suggested an immensity of depth. He crumpled the paper, and left it lying. "No, Ambler," he said. "You must stay your week, I do insist. Just give me two days, and I shall have this deal completed. After that, all sorts of lovely picnics and excursions. We could even give Tanya sabbatical leave to ease the Lothario situation. In the meanwhile I can't have you risking life and limb on mountain roads. Stay safe and have fun at Alpenheide." He looked at me, the eyebrow twitching, but he did not touch it. "I mean that, Ambler, my erstwhile friend. Now we must find you transport back. The chopper is busy, my chauffeur away. Perhaps Sim would oblige — another one of your admirers."

"In a nice way, I hope."

"In a very nice way. Like Dominic, he considers you to be a real gentleman. After you." He picked up my book.

"A bare room, this," I said. "Not even a dictionary."

"I think best in austere surroundings, not in the boudoir or the battlewagon like real gentlemen."

"For such a profound thinker you certainly talk a real lot of cock," I said, and preceded him with a sensitive back along the passage and into the drawing room where Tanya was listening to pop music at low volume, but she sprang to turn it off.

"Au revoir, then, Ambler. You will find Sim in the courtyard. Thanks for this." He put down the book and went out.

"Well, Tanya. None the worse, I hope."

"He suspects. I know he does. I should confess about last night, it would be better, less bad for me."

"Go ahead, then. But don't forget the mice."

Sleek green-eyed serpent uncoiling from the sofa — God, she was wicked and beautiful. "So you would make blackmail against me, isn't it?"

I headed for the door. "Not what you'd call blackmail it isn't. Just a word of advice. Well, bye-bye, Tanya."

"For less than that . . ." But I had closed the door behind me, and with four words, *Don't forget the mice*, another enemy behind me. It was some tightrope I was walking.

Sim was waiting in a Peugeot. "Good car. Your own?"

"No, Mr. Ambler. I would have no use for a car myself."

There were two men on duty now in the courtyard, another at the drawbridge, which rose at once behind us. "What's the extra security about?"

He turned on the radio. Did everyone in Alpenheide turn up radios? "I don't know, Mr. Ambler. It has been like this all week."

Sim clung to the wheel like a nervous woman. The gears were uncrashable, but we chugged. I liked poor Sim. Vanity, vanity, let's reciprocate. "Has that Russian chap gone?"

"Yes, Mr. Ambler."

"I can't quite visualize life in the Schloss. Do you have meals together?"

"I have mine alone. Mr. Vyan and that woman eat lunch and dinner in the dining room, and the guests, of course, but it depends. I do not understand how Mr. Vyan tolerates her."

"She worships him. That always helps."

"Not with Mr. Vyan. He is above such things as adulation. I know so little of him, Mr. Ambler. He is a secret, perhaps even to himself — a terrible man who never forgives, and yet his kindness in this village . . ." We were on the upper road, above us the dirty spew of that morning's avalanche.

"The Lord of the Manor — the Company Town — same old story," I said to encourage Sim.

"But it is not like that. He helps in secret so many people whose gratitude is worth nothing — the wastrels and the cretins — this inbred valley has plenty of them."

"Does anyone in Alpenheide stand up to him?"

"No, Mr. Ambler. Except you yourself. And each time after he has seen you, he seems much disturbed. Just now, for instance, when he asked me to drive you down, and I said *Certainly*, he screamed at me: *What do you mean, Certainly? Who and what is certain?*"

"Sounds a bit mad to me."

"If one comes to trust nobody, Mr. Ambler, not even one last single human soul . . . Well, here we are."

"I don't quite see what you mean," I said. But I did see exactly what Sim meant. "Thank you very much. Goodbye."

SEVENTEEN

Mary Dunn and I talked in my sitting room, and then we dined together, putting on a friendly act. But I enjoyed Dunn's company, and she was good value, off duty or on, whichever you care to call it, telling me about life at home — it is amazing how they love Our Country, and I sympathize, I understand, I do myself — about an institution called the Ghan, a narrow gauge railway that limps to Alice Springs — about jillaroo versus jackaroo in Queensland.

After dinner we danced downstairs. If one woman at Alpenheide was the best skier I had seen; then another was the best performer I had danced with. "You can shuffle O.K."

"You hoof it not too bad yourself."

"Dunn!"

"Yes, Ambler?"

"I wish you'd go away tomorrow morning."

"Why?"

"I wish you would."

"You mean dangerous."

"I mean it's dynamite."

She put her cheek against mine *pro bono publico,* or to com-municate. "Perhaps I would if it was only dynamite."

We went upstairs to our *arrangement,* so tactfully contrived by Dominic. We were not blatant. We had closed and locked communicating doors when we went out. We returned to our respective rooms. But a lipstick was on a table in my sitting room to spread the word.

She tapped a fingernail, and I let her in. "Are your doors double-locked?" I went to do that, and Dunn came back with some apparatus, like a moon antenna or similar monstrosity in miniature. Needless to say, the hotel radio was going. She led the way, telling me to leave the sitting room door ajar, and in semi-darkness opened the west window in my bedroom, moved the bedside table, set up her instrument, aimed it, tuned it, slipped one earphone out and gave that to me.

"What's it beamed on?"

"S'ssh!"

The voices came faintly, the man's louder than the other. "You're sure you got him?"

"No mistake, Max, could be possible. I was on the inside of the path, calling to him to help me with my binding, and when the dirty rascal came level with me, I fired up to the chest and belly. He was dead instantly, toppled over and gone, and no single scream did he emit, but naturally the storm was loud."

"And Ambler. You never saw him last night?"

"Max, you have asked me this three times. I never saw him, this I promise faithfully."

"Ambler seems to get around. Says he slept in a hayrick, and crossed just before the avalanche. Confirmed by Karl Semmler who saw him walk into the village. But I wonder."

"What do you wonder, Max?"

"Be quiet." There was a louder, rasping intermittent sound,

perhaps like pages being turned on television. And his voice again: "Listen to this from Ambler's book. 'I saw the end of a house, suddenly quite real with a window below the roof and a lamp shining through. I stopped. Was it a house? But then the picture faded, and I saw the two trees as they were, and the white stone which had been a lighted window. Next, it was a church, half seen from the corners of my eyes, with a fine steeple stretching up to the sky. Was that the church bell I heard ringing in the night?

" *'You're weaving like a drunk. Take a pull, Ambler, damn you.* And Max Vyan slapped my face in the moonlight in the forest. Max was strong. He was unconquerable. I never doubted it in all that time.' You know," the faint voice went on. "I could have said the same for Ambler. He writes quite graphically too, considering a limited intelligence."

"May I speak now, Max?"

"Go ahead."

"And you will not be angry?"

"Speak!"

"This Harry Ambler, Max — I too thought at first of limited intelligence, a jet-set Glamour Tom, some handsome witless beast such as I have experienced in scads. But there is more than that."

"There always was. Go on."

"He is not stupid, but most cunning with idle questions like, *Max seems hepped up. Is Max all right?* — and *Who's this Russian chap?* and so on. I know it is most precious, your old friendship, Max. But since this Harry Ambler came is trouble. And now some horse-faced paramour, so we are told. Some accomplice, I will bet, sharing bed and board and conspiracy. And with that Sim he is also in cahoots, I know this."

"How do you know this, you jealous bitch?"

"I suspect this, then. And you say *jealous bitch* to me. But I say only in return that I kill for you, and I die for you."

"Spare me the melodrama, and see you behave yourself tomorrow. She has rented skis. Keep away from them on the mountain. I am still not certain about Ambler."

"You still cannot bear that he is not worthy of your trust. And I, whom you can trust totally unto death, you do not trust one atom, isn't it?"

"Get out."

"Could I ask one favor only: To ride tonight in the helicopter?"

"No. The Professor's coming. Now go away."

There was a clap as of something shutting, and then a quieter sound, perhaps a door, and then he said: "I refuse to believe it quite."

We listened on, a door closing again, and that was all.

Dunn picked up the instrument and went back to the sitting room. "Horse-faced," she muttered en route. "True, I suppose."

"What did you beam on?"

"Your book, of course. All in a perfectly innocent binding."

"There are limits, Dunn," I said.

"There cannot be," said Mary Dunn. "Please listen to me."

I listened for some minutes . . . "However big, it makes no difference. It doesn't excuse a dirty trick like that."

"You are seeing it in your own image — from your own selfish honor. But how do I see it?"

"You mean no rules at all apply?"

"I mean just that — no rules at all apply."

"Which you feel has justified you in playing me for a sucker from the first go-off."

"Yes," she said, no equivocation, *Yes*. "Listen! There it goes. Put out the lights."

I opened a window in the sitting room. The helicopter climbed from west to east, the flight a repetition of the last that I had watched and listened to — fading to a distant protracted sound which might come from anywhere.

"I'll try with this," she said. "It might give direction if the building doesn't interfere." She put on both headphones. She traversed and stopped; traversed on, back and stopped; swung the instrument away. "You try."

For once, Dunn and I were in entire agreement. A louder sound came from the couloir between the two left peaks of the Teufelsspitzen, that couloir where I had killed the bitch Minerva. It was a night of stars, the mountains breaking them.

The noise grew again and became determinate. Soon the helicopter flew east to west and down to Schloss Alpenheide.

"Bed for me, if you have no more orders."

"None."

"The passage doors are all double-locked."

"Yes."

"May I make a suggestion?"

"Do."

"That we leave the inside doors a little open."

"Why?"

"In case you need help. I assure you that your honor is entirely safe."

"Thanks."

"One last thing: I couldn't care less about your ethics or the lack of them, but to make me do that with my own book to Max Vyan is something I don't forgive. Now go to bed."

"It wasn't my idea, Ambler. Sir Conrad said . . ."

"Spare me Sugar-uncle's sayings. Go to bed."

"You're horrible." She slammed her door with a resounding crash that shook the place.

I went to bed enraged. I had had grievances before, but now I had a whopping grudge, nursing which is not my form at all. But nurse it I did for an hour at least until an opposition whisper came, a grumble, an accusing growl: What about yourself? Did you not hold out too? Did you not yesterday slip a diamond necklace to another party? Misappropriation, Ambler. And worse than that, you gave it for safekeeping to the one man she had said that you could absolutely trust, a man rich beyond avarice, whose cute little wife just happens to be expecting an infant in September. Oh, you dirty dog. You hypocrite.

But I heard something, and was instantly alert. A door was being opened stealthily. An outside door? It could not be. An inside door? But then I heard a stumble, a muffled: "Oh, Hell's Bells," and silence.

Sleep closed about me. Sleep flowed kindly, very nice until I was tugged from dreamless sleep by my alarm, that annoying agent of another day. So I plugged in the jiffy-jug for tea, and went to close communicating doors. Benito would be here at half past eight.

I peeked at Mary Dunn asleep, and prone — not a neat sleeper, not at all, but sprawled across, the arms spread wide in sleep's surrender, the hands loose on the pillow, the head turned sideways on the pillow, the hair black as night, the shoulders pale, and Dunn asleep. Her nose was so long, so patrician delicate, so straight, so beautifully tipped in contradiction.

The jiffy-jug, that dangerous little beast, was clamoring with pant and gurgle. I shut her door and mine.

All ready for the road at nine, I grew impatient and tele-phoned. "M'mmm?" she said from sleep.

"Hello, Mary." It was a rule that we must use Christian names or warmer for the public benefit.

I heard her swallow. "Harry darling, are you up?"

"Yes, I'm up, and we're going skiing."

"Oh, shucks. Give me twenty minutes."

"That doesn't allow you time for breakfast."

"I never eat breakfast. Surely *you* know that."

"Yes, yes. Well, there's coffee if you want it." I hung up. Her tone was petulant, but so could love be petulant, doors slamming in the night. Dunn never ate lunch or never ate breakfast, according to which she happened never to eat that day. But I had resolved to turn the other cheek.

"How much skiing have you done?" I asked her in the first cable car.

"Done it 'n' done it," muttered Dunn, her head depressed, "ad loathsome nauseam."

At the Mittelwald, I carried her skis across. There was no queue, but a fair crowd of people, mostly strangers. *The top runs are fabulous,* was the word, and it would have gone be-yond this valley.

I led her by the longest way on the Soldanella — miles of practice slope, as easy as that. She had a copybook stem, and her turns were impeccable, the weight, the edges, everything except the one essential. "Try to loosen up. Relax!"

"Relax! You're all the same. As if I could."

"Now we'll traverse a little across this slope. Sideslip and straight." She traversed the infant slope quite well.

"Very good. Now from the traverse, make a turn downhill. Bring your skis together and take this short bit straight."

I waited for her. She achieved the turn; then her skis came

together, widened to railway tracks, and Dunn sat down.

"You must lean forward."

"If I lean forward, I'll fall on my nose."

"You won't. And anyway, what does it matter?"

"It doesn't to you."

As hinted above, the nose was all about Dunn that mattered to me — apart from business. And other business seemed far away that morning. My only business was to make her ski for fun. I had had success with similar cases, infinite patience and at last a breakthrough.

"Think of dancing," I suggested, often a successful tactic.

"Strapped to these bloody planks, how could I think of bloody dancing?"

"Moderate your language," I said with some severity. This was at the end of our first run to the Mittelwald. "Another?"

She did not answer, but kicked off her skis, entered Fernandel's cable car and went to brood alone.

"Old Harry, could this be the one of whom you spoke?"

"H'mm," I allowed.

He made a vast Oh with his mouth, bungled the bell signals, and was rebuked by telephone.

The pattern of our second run was similar, if worse. I came to see that she was a hopeless case.

"God, I hate it."

"You mean you're frightened of it."

"So what, I'm frightened of it."

We were alone, Dunn on her backside after the one hundredth sitzmark. "Look at you yesterday in the car with bullets flying — and look at you now, plain windy, you should be ashamed." To provoke courage by insult is a last resort.

It did not work with Dunn. "Oh, take a powder! Go and show off to everyone, you Glamour Tom."

"You'll get a wet bottom sitting on that sugar snow."

I left her to it, and skied badly in bad temper until lunchtime at the Mittelwald where I found her with Fernandel. They were sharing lunch on the terrace, a large carafe of wine, and much conviviality. I fetched a tray, my usual spartan midday meal. Dunn was tucking into piles of stew with chilis, to be followed by a slab of apple tart. "Too much lunch," I said, "puts your center of gravity too much amidships, like being pregnant in a way."

They greeted this entirely sensible remark with peals of merriment.

"Cable car broken down?"

"Yes, Harry. It is some mysterious fault that is to be cured when I have had my lunch."

"Gosh, you're funny," said Mary Dunn.

Fernandel departed in due course. "What shall we do now? Ski halfway down and walk the rest?"

"You can," she said. "I'm going up."

I thought that the wine might have emboldened her. So I went up gladly, not having quite abandoned hope. The girl had guts. She had marvelous balance on a dance floor. It made no sense at all. In the cable car she was drawn to Fernandel as the moth is to the lamp. I left them to it.

"What a lovely funny lovely man," she said at our destination. We skied again. She was no braver, hence no better. The helicopter landed by the Höhengrat, and Tanya von Silberbach shot past alone, was ferried up, and in what seemed no time came again, closer this time, but taking the steep slopes. The skiing was beyond compare, and I was footling with Dunn. "Look at Silberbach go," I said.

"Just look," she said.

Once more she and Fernandel had eyes and ears for one an-

other only. There was a blatancy about it, and on Dunn's part
a flagrant contravention of her role with me. I caught myself
wishing that Sir Conrad might be here to see her conduct.

We took the same dim old Soldanella by the long easy way,
swinging down and into a last pitch common to all the variations of that run. It was not steep, but steeper than the rest, to
be stemmed back and forth in grim rigidity by Dunn.

I never saw the flying figure come, heard only a German oath
as Tanya von Silberbach ran down Mary Dunn, or ran at high
speed across her skis between tips and toes, and was gone in a
wake of Teutonic vituperation, and Dunn fell forward, flat on
her face at last.

It was a slow fall of the most dangerous kind: one binding
out, I released the other, both boots moved, nothing broken
there, but Dunn lay prone. I lifted her. She had broken
through the sugar snow to be plastered overall. "Your nose!"
I said, taking off my glove to wipe the snow from it. "Oh,
your nose, it's bleeding."

"Forget my bleeding nose. Put on my skis."

Bewildered, I did, and watched Dunn go. She ran it straight,
leaning far forward, until far forward was too far, and she took
a fearful headlong toss, sprang up and laughed.

My arch enemy — and she was now avowedly that — had
done the trick. The helicopter flew away to Schloss Alpenheide.

"Your poor nose," I said, wiping reddened snow from it. "Oh
dear, oh dear."

"To hell with my nose."

"But I love it," I said.

She stared at me. "Have you gone crazy for a Bondi loop?
Come on! The cable car."

We made more runs. It was remarkable. I pleaded with

the intrepid girl. "I'll soon be dead anyway," she said. "So what the Hades does it matter?" And off she plunged.

"God, I love it," she said, no word of thanks to me. We were taking off our skis for the walk to the village.

"You were lucky. A cross like that usually means a broken leg at least. Head on, she could have killed you."

"I have made a little vow."

"Yes, Dunn?"

"If it is my last act on earth, I am going to kill that woman." Dunn's nostrils flared. "With my bare hands too."

"I ought to warn you that she's trained in close combat. She even threw me once."

"Only once?"

The sun slipped down beyond the mountains, and an hour of day remained. The light was soft and shadowless — gray stone, faded stucco, dark timbers of an ancient village, and one new hotel — but that was gabled too, it was in keeping.

She halted, unzipped a pocket and bowed to the new sliver of an ancient thing. Dunn bowed seven times, while jingling the pocket. "Go on," she commanded. "And don't divulge."

"But I ain't superstitious."

"Do as I tell you. You're going to need it."

So I made my bows to the crescent moon, wished my wish, did not divulge, and we continued to the village. "As Sir Conrad always says, a bloke without superstition is either a cow or a conceited bagga wind."

"Thanks."

"Don't mention it."

"Shall we order up some tea or have it in the lounge?"

"Suit yourself, Ambler. I'm having tea elsewhere."

"Oh?"

"Fernandel asked me to his chalet. We have many things in common to discuss. I'll see you later."

"But, Dunn, look here, I think I ought to mention, I mean, you know, Fernandel is a charmin' chap and all that, but his reputation, well, it steams a bit."

"Hot dog!" she said. "Here, you can take my skis."

Which I did, and repaired upstairs for a solitary cup of tea. There was a waywardness now, explicable perhaps in the light of a new-found nerve. That kind of euphoria reaction happened. But as Dunn had been the first to say and kept on saying — *Duty first,* and *Business is business.* She was in flagrant breach of Sir Conrad's instructions. Can't trust 'em, I thought. Can't ever trust 'em. With my case manager written off to Eros, things boded ill indeed.

EIGHTEEN

I had found *The African Witch* in the hotel library, and was renewing that particular acquaintance with my favorite author, how well he conveyed the plangent potency of woman; and as backdrop I was hearing the womanless tundra music of another favorite author, when fingernails played tattoo. I let the woman in.

"Turn it louder. I've got some vital dope."

"What vital dope?"

"About Schloss Alpenheide, idiot."

"Who from?"

"From Fernandel, of course. He knows the geography from A to Z."

"How come?"

"Because he has a friend at court — the domestic staff do get out, you know. Well actually, from A to Z is wrong, because the domestics are limited to the living quarters . . ."

"Who's his friend?"

"The second housemaid, actually." Dunn blushed, but slightly. She was already pink. "I tell you, Ambler, it's been the most rewarding thing for me to meet Fernandel at last."

"At last? You mean you knew about him?"

"I ought to know about our best Intersec man in Alpenheide. He's been on this job a year. You're only new potatoes, despite your importance and the trust we place in you."

"Thanks for the trust," I said. My gorge, whatever that may be, was on the rise. "Got vital dope, you say. Let's have it."

"Well, this girl — Trudi's actually her name — one of this Trudi's jobs is to keep the sundeck clean — it's the place on the roof where that woman sprawls all day and altogether."

"Saw it from the helicopter, yes. Not altogether, I don't mean."

"One morning Trudi was cleaning this place when a sudden gust blew up and her duster simply took to its heels across an intervening roof to lodge in the next flat place against some sort of cagework bars. Well, Trudi is a mountain girl, as nimble as any female chamois, so Trudi thinks: Why go all the way downstairs for another duster? So she scampers up the slope where two roofs meet, and down another to this next flat place where this duster now is clinging, and she recovers it.

"Inside this grille of bars there is an open skylight atop a shaft down which she looks forever to the bowels of Schloss Alpenheide, which rumor has it is the Lab, top secret and forbidden ground. It is a positive maze of pipes and certainly a lab, and up this shaft men's voices float in some outlandish tongue which Trudi does not understand, like English. So Trudi skips back, and her next evening off she tells this adventure story to her ole pal, Fernandel, quite innoshently."

"May I ask one question, Dunn?"

"You may."

"Have you been drinking?"

"This is strictly my own business. But yes, we had a couple of Fernandel's Double Bass, he calls it, like crass, please note,

as in Ambler, not in giant violin. It's Dunkelbier with a shot
of vodka. He says the English especially like it, reminding
them of stronger ale at home. Well, it reminds me of Our
Country's beer, not that insipid pommy stuff. Got'ny beer and
vodka, Ambler?"

"Not for you," I said. When driven to it, I can put the whip
into the voice, my father taught me. "Sober up," I whipped.
"Or by God I'll know the reason why."

She flinched, and sobered up at once. "Here is the thing,
then, Ambler, a fearful risk, and our only chance: We still don't
know what's cooking. We have some clues, but we still don't
know. One thing we know is that time is short — *the day after
tomorrow at six o'clock*, he said to that professor. *Give me two
days*, he said to you. That's tomorrow evening, Ambler, and
who said it? Mr. Vyan said it."

Mr. Vyan, she always called him respectfully. Sir Conrad,
Mr. Gilpin, Mr. Vyan.

"It's our last and final chance tonight. We know how we can
cross the moat — you told us, and I brought the gear.
We know that the castle wall beside Mr. Vyan's rock garden
terrace is as simple as a ladder with those jutting stones —
you told us. Then an easy scramble up between the roofs, that's
obvious — into the sundeck, which it stands to reason will be
empty — skip over to the skylight where we look and listen,
find out the gen, and back we come. It's just a gift."

"You omitted one thing — the high fence and the hillside."

"No, we thought of that."

"When do you start, then?"

"We had a long talk about it. And Fernandel and I, we
reached unanimous agreement, Ambler — that the you must
be *you* — it's inescapable."

"May I ask why?"

"You may, although the answer is self-evident: Pluto would tear us limb from limb. But Pluto happens to love you, Ambler, as you have told us with self-satisfaction. I'm afraid we simply can't escape it, much as we would like to."

"But it's a fearful risk, I mean, even compared with anything I've done."

"It *is* a risk, admittedly. But with the equipment you will carry . . ."

"I won't do it."

"In that case you have not only failed myself, Sir Conrad and Intersec, but probably mankind."

"To hell with 'em. Well, I don't mean you entirely."

"Fifteen thousand pounds tax-free and the Caramba, all for two weeks' work, that isn't peanuts to any bankrupt pilot."

Dunn was not aggressive. She bestowed on me that pleading gaze from dark blue eyes astride the nose which bore some scratches. "Oh, all right, damn you, I'll have a bash."

"Good on ya, Mite. Here's what we do. We dine at eight. After that, we stroll abroad. You carry a parcel, an Easter present in advance for Fernandel — gosh, he's funny, I adore him — and so to base camp, and on from there . . ."

"Change behind the curtain, Ambler."

The one-piece rubber suit fitted perfectly, so did the sneakers. I emerged from the sleeping end of Fernandel's cabin or log chalet.

"He looks good. Doesn't he, Fernandel?"

Fernandel nodded, avoiding my eye.

"Now I'll just put the black stuff on the face. It comes off easily, but not in water . . . There! Now we sling this satchel, and we tie it at the waist, no flopping, There! In this satchel are the two grapnels and the lines."

"Suppose Pluto doesn't like me black? Suppose he hates me, period?"

"If he loves you so much, period, what has blackness got to do with it?"

"Biscuits — I must have a biscuit or two for Pluto."

"They're in there too."

"I need a close-contact weapon. A rocket blaster like Tanya's would be fine."

"This is something much better than that woman's horn. See, this tube fits into this zipper pocket in the suit. All you do is press forward the safety catch and press this button."

"What is it?"

"Our new Laser — silent, no recoil or backlash, range up to thirty paces, drills a neat hole of penny size in anything, repeat anything. But a one-shot weapon, Ambler.

"Now the procedure is this: Fernandel and I take an evening constitutional along the path. We sound quite friendly and we seem quite innocent. You follow at a respectful distance. If we yodel once, that means danger, hide. When we yodel again, that means all clear, proceed. We shall lead you nearly to the fence. Then it's all yours — the baby is your very own. So the best of luck from both of us, eh Fernandel?"

He nodded, the shifty hangdog fellow.

I followed them. My rubber suit was lined outside with something soft, like wool, so it was silent. This path ran along the middle of the valley, between the roads. Ahead to my right were the lights of Schloss Alpenheide. Directly ahead, the indeterminate figures led me on. It was a quiet night as usual in the valley, but not quite as usual, for now an isolated puff of wind came from the west. A black rim of mountains hedged me in below the stars.

A dark chalet, a chink of light in an upper window, a stir

of cattle beasts within. Mary Dunn and Fernandel were singing. They sang a quiet lullaby, perhaps from Schubert. *Sleep,
Go to sleep, my little Prince.* In other circumstances it might
have sounded what is called "affecting." At that time it
affected me with irritation.

Another darkened chalet, no yodel yet. The fence was near,
and they stopped at the upper road.

"Go to it, Ambler."

"Best luck, Old Harry." He forced a strangled whisper.

"Where will you be?"

"We'll be around."

I went on toward the fence. The top of it stood out; the bottom was in darkness. Would Pluto be on duty, or some other
dog, or Pluto in a different frame of mind? The night was
deathly quiet now. A fox yapped somewhere. *The fox is hunting*, Max had said with pleasure at the fox's hunting. First
task: Find out about the dog. Friendly contact with a dog
named Pluto, or no climb for me.

There was a growl, a deep dark growl off to my right.
"Pluto," I said. "Is that you, Pluto?"

Yes, it was, whining: *Pleased to meet you.* I saw his muzzle,
fed him a biscuit through the wires. "S'ssh, Pluto! Coming
over."

The climb was not difficult, but the top of the fence was
tricky, being an inward sloping apron, brightly floodlit. I knew
it was not electrified, because there were no insulators, probably too dangerous for big dogs. I dropped to a hearty welcome from my friend, who licked my blackened face all over.

I crawled up the slope in darkness. Like all passive defenses,
it had the failings of its merit — neutralize the sentry, and you
are safe in black no-man's-land beneath the lights. But Pluto
was more than neutralized; he hampered my progress with

mammoth licks and loving cuffs and nudgings of affection. I remembered the seeking-out or hunting orders employed by Scottish gamekeepers. "Ha-*lawsst,* then, Pluto boy," I said. "Ha-*lawsst!* Go sikkim!" It works with any dog. It worked with Pluto, gone.

And here was the moat. I looked from darkness across to light. I took my time. This was the real starting point. Once I left here, I would be committed. From here, I could still turn back. But I saw no men; I heard no voices.

I planted one grapnel against the coping of the wall, which was nearly flush with the ground. The grapnels were similar to those four-pronged hooks that Eskimos put into seal holes in the ice. The luckless seal comes up for air, and hooks himself. The grapnel hooks the coping, and provided that is solid, it stays hooked. I had tested the coping beyond the moat. I tested this one — it was solid. I had a spike for this first grapnel, spiked into the earth to insure that it did not move before tension was applied.

Then I took out the other grapnel and its coil of black polypropylene, a quarter-inch diameter. I looked across to the terrace between Max's rock gardens, the only things in shadow — plants would not do well in constant light. No men in sight or sound.

I cast my grapnel, which was rubber-coated — they had thought of everything — and it landed with a thud beyond the moat. I drew it back, met resistance, tugged, tugged harder. It was lodged.

I tied the end of the other grapnel's rope to the waistband of my satchel. Now I was ready. Thirty feet across and twenty down. I could jump half the lateral distance to make a mighty splash.

Some people have said that I am a lucky chap. I would say

that when I call the heads, the tails turn up about fifty-fifty. But that time it was heads. A distant rumor, a gathering rush, an isolated squall of wind storming coldly down the valley from the glacier, to thrash the trees, a loud world all about, and gone.

But by then I was in the moat, now climbing with my padded gloves, shoes against wall, hands gripping rope, and I was lurking in the rock garden, stowing my expended grapnel, pegging the free end of rope that was my lifeline to retreat.

And no one was about. I chose a route close to the shadowed rocks. Then I ran for the junction of the two walls beside the terrace. It was not dark, but in penumbrous contrast to the floodlit castle. I climbed again, this time from course to course of two-foot blocks of stone, alternate courses sticking out, a gift to cat-burglars, and then I froze.

A man came round the corner of the building. He was in full sight, and he carried: slung from his right shoulder a tommy gun; slung from his left shoulder a rocket horn like Tanya's, a hand on the sling of each; and dangling from his neck a walkie-talkie.

He had only to glance up this way to see me in the partial shadow. Should I snatch out my Laser and drill Herr Hermann? *A one-shot weapon, Ambler.* Drops fell from my hair on the shoulders of my suit. Drip, drip, he must hear it. But he could not have looked, still could not have looked, was underneath, was gone. I climbed again, and soon was under the rone or gutter. I rested, clinging to the pipe which carried down water. Then I tested the gutter with one hand, as solid as every tangible thing at Schloss Alpenheide, chin myself up, leg over. I was on top, at the meeting point of two sloping roofs. I walked up the lead channel.

Now I heard a voice: "He snuggles there in the hotel with

some horse-faced paramour. *Don't forget the mice!* So he would blackmail me. So now I swear that I will slit his handsome throat. And with my own hands I will strangle her. *Die Rache ist mein.* Accchhh!" A door closed. Tanya von Silberbach had gone to nurse revenge.

I stood at the apex of those roofs, the night about me, the heavens above — the Milky Way, Orion's Belt and Sword, the Pleiades, Arcturus and Polaris, a million unknown worlds out there observing us, if worthy of attention — even, possibly, observing Harry Ambler on a castle roof.

My body was hot and sweaty; my head was cold. The only immediate light or glow was from an open grille, an accurate report by Trudi, second housemaid and friend of Fernandel.

I saw far down to an empty floor, a square delineated by the ventilation shaft. But not entirely empty — the top left-hand corner as I looked was crossed by something black, not quite a perfect square of floor downshaft.

"And what are your intentions with it, Mr. Vyan? I think I have a right to ask."

"You have a perfect right, Professor Ribling. And my answer is that I have no intentions, none at all. It will do no harm whatever, that I promise you."

Max's promise carried conviction to me up there upon his roof. As I have indicated once or twice, to spot lie from truth is a thing that I can sometimes and with some people do.

"Two hours' sleep these nights, Mr. Vyan, and I am utterly exhausted; but now I do feel sure that every system will be double-checked by 6 P.M. tomorrow. Yes, I feel almost sure."

"Almost is not enough, Professor Ribling. Are you *sure?*"

"Yes, yes, I do assure you. And at six o'clock tomorrow?"

"The helicopter will ferry you to Geneva. The Jet Galaxy will take you to Prague in an hour and a half or less. We have already obtained provisional clearance for the flight. You will be dining in Prague at half past eight, I promise you."

"Thank you. How can I thank you for this sanctuary? And no one will know that I have been here?"

"No one here knows even your name except myself. To the few in this castle who know of your existence you are The Professor, some anonymous professor. Now as final proof that my intentions are bona fide, here is a deposit receipt in your name from the Bohemian Peoples' Socialist Bank in Prague for one hundred thousand American dollars. All yours, Professor Ribling, for a *finished job*. Do I make myself clear?"

"Yes, Mr. Vyan. You are extremely generous."

"Get on with it, then. Good night." Max had moved into the framework of the shaft. I saw him touch and touch and touch the black object that cut across the corner — part of a long cylinder or pipe. Then Max walked away. My built-in truth detector promised less than all for the Professor.

I crossed the maze of roofs again, and down the lead channel to the gutter. It was quite a steep slope to a drop of forty feet or so, but heights never bothered me. I crouched there, watching again from darkness into light. I felt the urge to hurry, but I must not hurry. Nothing moved.

I put my right hand out to grasp the gutter, my left hand across and beyond it in preparation for sliding over, swinging down. Then a door opened and a man came forward. It was Max. He stood between his dark rock gardens, then turned left and walked below me. His evening shoes made a clip on flagstones. Round the next corner I heard his voice in German. *"Pass mal auf!"* he said sharply, hardly. *Keep awake. Watch out.* Soon I heard footsteps again, and Max went in by the door to the drawing room. He had been once round his castle.

I swung over and climbed down, very simple. I lurked in the

recessed corner. Did one run for it or sneak for it? One listened and one looked both ways, and then one ran for it.

I looked left first — the way Hermann had come before. Now I sneaked forward to look right, put one eye round the angle of the walls — and here on rubber shoes came Hermann. If he had seen me, a word into his walkie-talkie, and I and my one-shot weapon would be pinned from two directions. An owl hooted in the night beyond, oh melancholy owl.

The tube was in my hand, safety catch forward, my thumb on the button. It was a small tube, open at one end. Hermann came into view in profile. Aligning it, I pressed the button.

The green light of extraordinary brilliance hit him in the left upper arm. It drilled clean through and out the other side. Hermann slowly crumpled to a small clatter of his tommy gun. He moaned.

I crossed the terrace, snatched up my cord and jumped. There was no wind to drown the splash. I ran up the further wall — ran is not quite the word, but almost ran, so demoniacal was my hunted strength. Stuffing the evidence into the satchel, I looked back. The waters of the moat still tossed and swirled. Hermann still moaned across the way, drilled through the lungs and liver probably. I could have done a neater job. There was no alarm.

I scuttled downhill. "Pluto Boy!" Here came my vast ebullient friend to knock me down and smother me with canine kisses. "Have a nice biscuit. Steady, Pluto!"

That gave me a few seconds' respite while he downed his dividend, and then, hoarsely whispering, I sent him on a Ha-*lawss*ting sikkim mission. I climbed a last time, negotiated that awkward apron of barbed wire, and jogged across the empty meadows — no cattle yet, they never put them out to grass until after jonquil time. There were no humans either.

My colleagues, who should be around, were not. There was no company for me but the hooting of that melancholy owl.

I passed the first chalet and the second, made along the path for Fernandel's log cabin. And now, only now, were there shouts from the castle on the hill.

I stood a moment at the cabin door, looking back, saw nothing, heard far Teutonic screams, heard close behind me: "Fern'-del, we oughter go lookin' fer 'im, shouldn't we?"

"That Old Harry has the nine lives of a prowling Tom."

"Y'know, Mite, ya got the funniest nose I never saw, I love it dearly."

"These very sentiments are mine in opposite."

To state that I burst in is not to overstate. Dunn sat on a stool at the feet of Fernandel, who was taking his armchaired ease. Beside both of them were glasses of brown liquid, creamy-frothed. I boxed Dunn's ears for her, and who would blame me? They both stood up. Fernandel, who seemed entirely sober, showed signs of squaring off. "You try it," I said, "and I'll break your jaw." He changed his mind. "Old Harry . . ." he began.

"Now listen!" I said from behind the curtain. "I had to drill Hermann, but I got clean away. The balloon's gone up, half a minute ago. We must reach our rooms unseen before they call hotel. Have alibis, you understand?"

"Yes, Harry. I go immediately to hold attention of Dominic, divert him from telephone. You take this key, my skeleton. Go in by *ski-raum*. Leave equipped under bed. I will dispose somehow."

The door closed, and I was dressed, pushed satchel and wet suit under his bed. "Come on! Take my arm if you have to."

Dunn took my arm. "Oh, dear."

"See anyone, play giggling tipsy, damn you, Dunn."

She did not have to, but clung on, and we achieved our goal unseen, so far as one could tell. Into my sitting room where the radio played on. "Ambler!"

But the telephone. "Hello."

"Sir, it is Dominic — a small matter only." He sounded fussed. "But this morning your breakfast tray was at eight-thirty, and always before it has been at eight."

"Eight-thirty, thank you, Dominic."

"And, sir, the young lady — shall I call her room?"

"No, she's here. What time breakfast, Honey?"

"Coffee, Pet," she said. "Just coffee."

"Miss Dunn will share my coffee. Better send some extra, Dominic. Goodnight.

"Well?" I said.

"Please forgive me, Ambler. I was sick with worry, wanting to go out, but Fernandel said what could we do, we would only look suspicious, which was true, and then I had two more of those. Oh, dear." Dunn sobering up again. Dunn contrite. "It's the stress and strain. Everyone can't be without a single nerve in all their bodies, not like you. And Fernandel, he plied me."

"You're unreliable. You're on the water wagon from this moment, got it?"

"Got it, Ambler. What did you find out?"

"I'll tell you in the morning, if there is a morning. You have aspirins?" She shook her head. I went for four.

"*Four.* But won't four kill me?"

"Take 'em. Now go to bed, and lock your windows."

"But I always sleep with my windows wide."

"Close 'em and shut off the heat. I'm ashamed of you, Dunn."

"Me too," she said, and wiped at tears.

NINETEEN

Mary Dunn was shaking me. "What time is it?"

"After seven, Ambler. Please wake up. It's vital."

I was awake, my peace invaded, and I fought back: "Here, plug in the jiffy-jug. Extra cup in the bathroom." This she did and brought, and I turned on the radio. "Don't hang over me like a praying mantis. Have a seat."

"But there isn't one."

"Sit there." Dunn perched on the foot of my bed in her dressing gown with ships on it. She was a bit of a mess, hair tangled, salty cheeks, long parallel scratches like tribal markings on her tribal nose. "What's vital? Give!"

"On the blower, Ambler, I slept with one earphone, just came through, a top priority in verbal, here's text decoded: Carling Korber, senior executive vice president steel alloys division general mechanics arrested yesterday charges pending treason later suicide by poison pill press US UK hotching cannot withhold story beyond sixteen hundred Greenwich STOP Press also know certain photograph exists no fault of ours STOP Matter of time trace link to Alpenheide STOP Your positions potentially grave danger STOP If further intelligence impossible get out repeat get out Cab."

That jiffy-jug had long been on its blustering rampage. "Warm the pot. Three heaping spoons."

"Don't teach your granny to make a dish of char," she bit me, and put in four.

I sipped my tea and lit my cigarette. Dunn had retired to the foot of the bed, from which she attacked as follows: "I apologize, Ambler. I am very sorry. Got it?"

"Got it."

"That's not accepting it."

"Accepting it. Go and put cold water on your face."

". . . Less awful?"

"Yes. Now what?"

"What does he mean: *Get out?* Sir Conrad must have taken leave. Who does Sir Conrad think I am?"

"Dunno. All I know is that you and your precious pal pass the buck to me, and after I've shot my way out of that place, I find you dipped into the bottle because you can't stand the stress and strain. That's who I think you are."

"How typical. You accept my apology, and then you start in."

"I'm giving you what you deserve. And not only that — you put the blame on Fernandel."

"I wasn't myself. I don't exactly quite remember. Oh dear, what a beastly bitch I am."

"Stop the self-pity."

"I hate your guts," she said.

"Good. Now to business, but one thing first — you can be the strategic boss, for policy. In local tactics you take my orders, got it?"

"Yes, Ambler. Actual action, you decide. God, I feel crook. Now make your report."

". . . And you just saw a black segment, you say. How thick, how long?"

"A foot, eighteen inches thick, I don't know. The piece I saw could be four feet long, like part of an overgrown pipe, big oxygen cylinder, something like that."

"A cylinder." Dunn whistled. "That leaves the gate wide open. Did he call the man by name — besides Professor?"

"Ribling, it sounded like. Yes, Ribling."

"Ribling," she said. "Professor Amos Ribling of the Bundallochy Proving Ground in Sutherland. Well, I guess that sews the wallaby up, one way or another."

"Explain."

"Bundallochy is the place where they test everything new from tanks to telemetry. For that job, it doesn't initiate, it evaluates in a three-hundred-square-mile sealed paddock of the emptiest county in Britain. Which is top secret stuff but not *ab initio* secret, if you understand me, it originates elsewhere. What Bundallochy also is — cross your heart now, Ambler."

"My God, woman!"

But Dunn did not flinch. Her abundant self-assurance had returned. "Bundallochy also is the place where the ultimate aspects of weaponry are dealt with. The other stuff is not cover, but it *is* perfect camouflage for what really matters, which is the wedding of material to delivery device — nuclear, thermonuclear, chemical, bacillary. They even have their own scientists' juvenile bad *bon mot* about it — *Bundallochy's Baby Is Weaned at Woomera*. Ambler, would you happen to have a comb? Hair and brains all tangled up, no good."

"On the dressing table. Be a sport, and hurry, Dunn."

She gave brief hell to her hair, and came back, looking almost cool. "You're a patient old plug," she said. "Where was I? I was almost finished, told it badly. Well, a week ago tomorrow, Ribling flew to London for a pre-Woomera conference, attended it, and vanished. It was only the next evening when the Director at Bundallochy telephoned London to inquire about the non-return of his ultimate weaponry man that anyone missed him. The first we heard of it was that a man with another passport but possibly answering his description had flown to Geneva; and that was all anyone knew until you solved the mystery last night. We do know more now, actually, because it transpires that Ribling has been a card-holding Party member since '31, another tiny bo-bo by MI, they overlooked it. As Sir Conrad always says: *Take the eye from MI, and you have a sightless Marxist.* Not bad, eh, Ambler?"

"Appalling. Do you not realize that while you queen it, lolling on my bed . . ."

Dunn was off my bed, and stamping a bare foot. Even as I tried to remind her of the fearful dangers that now beset us, I did enjoy baiting Dunn, so passionate when baited. "Be calm. Sit down again. I get Ribling and his know-how. I get Korber and his hardware. What about the late Alexis?"

"Alexis was the Kommissar of a staging warehouse for refined super-lethal materials of every kind — not far north of Tomsk on the River Ob. Incidentally, that cynical old pedant Mr. Gilpin is for the birds about granaries — only the ultimate ones are secure."

"Get on with it, Dunn."

"I am. Alexis also was a Crypto-Czarist. He also was a defector, in reverse, one might say. He also had his features completely rebuilt at the Rivard Clinic in Lausanne. We knew a lot about Alexis — the Russians have been just as worried — we knew, I think, all about him except the type of goods he had absconded with, because all their store-sheets seemed to tally."

"Brock says if we can't do anything, get out. Well, what *can* we do? I wouldn't put my money on that Professor's chances once he's done the job, whatever it may be. But I would bet anything Max spoke the truth when he promised that the thing would not be used. So why not . . ."

"Why not skip, you mean? Thanks to your gallant work — and I mean it, Ambler — we know that this is D-Day, and zero hour is 6 P.M. Now if you work toward a crisis hour, you avoid trouble, avoid any action that might be suspicious until that hour arrives. So we are safe in thinking that Mr. Vyan will play it quiet until six o'clock. Agreed?"

"Agreed."

"Well, I don't agree," said Mary Dunn. She could be most annoying. "Because the crisis hour is not six, but *four,* when the Korber story breaks. Mr. Vyan still thinks he has got away with it. Hermann's death is just another incidental."

"We don't know Hermann's dead."

"If you multiply white-heat a thousand times or so, and then push the poker through by liver, lungs, etcetera, and out the other side, destroying bone, muscle, fat and every tissue absolutely, death tends to supervene. You look squeamish, Ambler, but those are the facts.

"Soon after four Mr. Vyan will learn of Korber's arrest and suicide, also hear that there are strong rumors of a certain photograph. Might that not change the situation? And is there not still one way whereby we *might* glean additional intelligence before we skip . . ."

"Good girl," I said.

She blushed, the animal glow of Dunn when blushing. "I'm a hopeless mess," she said, and continued briskly: "That's the general outline. Now the minor tactics, Ambler, your department. How do we pass an innocent day?"

The scratches on her nose were healing nicely, decoration not detraction. The perfect passage of a day for me would have been to gaze at her nose beyond the counterpane. But that would hardly do with Dunn. "Better pass it skiing," I said.

"I was afraid of that."

"You haven't lost your nerve again? Oh Lord, don't tell me."

"I wouldn't tell you anything." She flounced out. Little had I thought that I would ever see Miss Dunn flounce out.

And skiing was a nightmare repetition. I can say only that, as befitted a real gentleman of the real old school, I endured the rough edge of her tongue. And rough it was, the worst Limehouse or antipodean equivalent, Bloddy King's Four-letter Cross at every sitzmark. In the cable car she brooded, with sunken head. I felt quite sorry for Fernandel, cut dead by Dunn. "Why does she hate me now, Old Harry, this girl who is so marvelous? Last night she was as your poets would describe it, strictly dewy-eyed."

"Last night she was strictly pie-eyed, and is on a remorseful wagon now. See you keep her to it." I was not as severe as I might have been with him because all the merry cynic had left Fernandel. He was a club bore on the subject of Miss Dunn, proving something, disproving something. But I did not listen. In this brief respite from my case manager's cowardice on skis, I was planning business: "You have a car?"

"Indeed, Harry, my Karmann Ghia, in my shed it rests."

"Might need it. I don't think they'd ever let the Caramba through. Spare key?"

"On my chain. I will remove." He slipped it to me.

"Any news?"

"Only the rumor of Hermann is out. If we see the white smoke, it will be Hermann, not a new Papa. But naturally they could have cremated in the night. The last one was your Major Moffett."

"So you knew about him?"

"I launched the Heads on him, in my double role, you see, as cover."

"In your double role as cover? Oh, yes. I must say I think you were a bit unfair on Moffett."

"It is not nice, this game, Old Harry. But nice for you to have escaped by lightning reflex."

We lunched at the Mittelwald. I had one beer and Dunn two cranberry juices in the hot spring sun. By then I was as rich mahogany as any ski instructor. I wondered what dead rich mahogany would look like. "Well, I won't see, anyway," I said.

"You won't see what, my pet?"

"Dead rich mahogany. Dead poor olive, I would guess."

"Darling, that's your clever riddle-talk again," she said as lazy-sweet as honeyed bee. We were in public on the terrace. They seemed harmless, all our neighbors, but one never knew. I sweltered in my anorak, gun at armpit, looking down the ridge from the Mittelwald. Dunn's eyes were closed behind dark glasses. "Come on, love," I said. "Let's ski again before it gets too slow."

She came. "They have an air about them, haven't they?" A comment about us, as nobody else was moving.

"A petrified air," she muttered, putting on her skis. We took a chair-lift. "I'm scared of everything," Dunn said. "If that bloody bitch would only come, I mightn't be."

"It's going to be all right," I said, which I far from felt, and put my arm across to pat her other shoulder once.

"You can be nice," she said. "One side of you can be most awfully kind and nice."

The skiing was no good. "I'm soaked," she said, getting up. "Wet through and through, that's me."

"Look!" A white plume of smoke rose from Schloss Alpenheide. "There goes Hermann."

"*There goes Hermann.* What do you mean?"

"I mean they're crisping him."

"You're so cold-blooded and disgusting."

It was a trying afternoon, time to fill in somehow. We must stay on the mountain. Therefore I must pretend to be teaching Mary Dunn. At half past three we went back to the Mittelwald for soft drinks. Sunbathers still lounged about, but they were thinning too. Most took the cable car back. We skied down the left side of the ridge.

"You agree that this is the realm of tactics?"

"Yes," she said. "And you're the boss, I know."

"Right, then. We hide our skis, and we walk to the chalet. There, one of us keeps watch. If an alarm, we run for it. If we can't both get clean away at once, I'll play for time, lead them a dance while you beat it down, take Fernandel's car, and get out of the valley quick."

"Why me? Why not you?"

"Because I'm armed."

"So am I," she said, touching her waist satchel. "I've got a Laser."

"So much the better. Now is that clear?"

"No, it's not. You go."

There was nobody in sight, the Mittelwald over a rise above, Alpenheide under a rise below. We hid our skis, and then we walked through snow — a foot or less of it left in the woods. "Probably there will be no alarm, in which case we both walk down, forget the skis, get into Fernandel's car and go. If there is an alarm, you do what I say."

It will seem to you that I was laboring a point, belaboring it, but I knew enough about Miss Mary Dunn to know this: She would not run out on me. Keep her off skis and sober, and the girl was a tigress. I therefore told her that she would either yield, or we would both abandon ship now immediately.

"Then I'll go it myself."

"You couldn't find the key, and even if you did where would you look for the telephone? Obey my orders, damn you, Dunn."

There were no recent tracks round the chalet, no tracks at all except the raised railway lines of snow compressed by skis, tracks in reverse, as often happens. I entered. It was four-fifteen. "Stay near the door and listen."

I found the knot in the paneling. I supposed that if I had tampered with the right telephone in Max's workroom, and if it remained undetected, there would be a click at that end when I lifted the headset. Perhaps there was, but it would have gone unheard in the conversation to which I listened. I had noticed with Max that he held the receiver at some distance — he still had very sharp hearing. The Falkenhorst telephone would be two or three feet away from him at his table.

". . . Banner headlines, Mr. Vyan. PHOTO KEY TO KORBER SUICIDE? That's the *Star*."

"What photo?"

"I don't know, sir."

"You're paid to know."

"I only first heard ten minutes back, and Korber being a friend of yours, I called at once."

"Any news agency quoted on the photograph?"

"Global, sir,"

"What contacts there?"

"We have Timothy Keating good and hooked."

"Get on to him and call me back." Clonk of a telephone replaced. The slide thump of a door. I laid this telephone gingerly on my woolen hat, and went to Dunn and told her.

"Do you want to listen now?"

"You," she said. "I'd rather listen to the birdsong."

Than to that filthiness in there, she meant.

If Max had been out of his workroom, he was back again. "Yes?" he said, after the first ring.

"Keating says it's an incriminating picture of Korber and . . . of Korber and a woman."

"You're alone there?"

"Yessir."

"So am I. This is a scrambler line. What woman?"

"Tanya von Silberbach. He's seen it, looks like a blow-up with a mini-camera, but unmistakable. Mr. Vyan!"

"Yes?"

"Keating says her record is a mile long, and everyone knows where she lives — been glad to have her off their hands, the cops, the FBI."

"Meet Keating at once. Find out why Korber was arrested. Call me back. Then be available on the hour, every hour."

That talk ended. "Now, let me see — she might have met him in New York." Buzz. "Come here!"

Dunn was standing outside, not standing still, but turning slowly. I had a good sentry.

"Did you ever meet Korber anywhere but here?"

"No, Max, never." Sshwick! Sshwick! "Max, I promise."

"In New York?" Sshwick!

"No, Max, I swear it on my hands and knees. That brute, you know I hated him. Only for you . . . What is it, Max?"

"Korber is dead, and they've got the photograph."

"You know who took it, Max."

"Took it, developed it, enlarged it, sealed it, sent it by Ambler. That negative was in the safe." His voice faded. His speech was more clipped, as cold, as logical. "Still in the safe." Louder again. Buzz. "Come here!"

". . . Yes, Mr. Vyan?"

"That charming photograph you took of Tanya and Korber — how many copies did you make?"

"One, sir."

"What did you do with it?"

"I put it in the envelope, sir, sealed that in three places, gave it to Mr. Ambler in accordance with your instructions, and we have M. Vaillancourt's receipt, sir."

"He is lying, Max, I know it."

"Soften him up. Move the rug first."

The softening up of Sim, even by telephone, was more than I could easily stomach. I went to bring Dunn up to date.

"The robin is so tame," she said. "Look at him." The robin sang on a shrub nearby. She put her hand on my arm, her turn to be kind. "Some peace would be nice some time."

I went back. ". . . That'll do for the moment. Leave him alone, I told you."

"Sir, I have been true to you always, but that night she took my Theodore, my gentle Siamese and strung him from the chandelier and burned him, tortured him."

"Did you do that?"

"I singed it, Max, yes just a little on the fur."

"I'll deal with you later. Continue, Sim."

"I brooded and brooded, Mr. Vyan, this horrible disgusting beastly female thing — and I knew Mr. Ambler was like those other men, entrapped, and so I took the envelope to him open, unsealed, I was beside myself with hate and madness. But he never looked, that was the miracle, Mr. Ambler never looked."

"My seal?"

"I put it with the keys, and sealing wax too, and Mr. Ambler sealed it without a glance, good manners, like an open letter of introduction, Mr. Ambler said. This is the whole truth, Mr. Vyan, I promise you, and nothing but."

"So you believed Ambler?"

"Of course, Mr. Vyan, who could help it, oh no, please . . . !"

A buzz. "Be quiet! Yes?"

". . . Splendid, Professor, and a whole hour ahead of schedule. Just wait there. I'll call you in a minute."

A knock. *"Herein!"* he said. *"Wegnehmen."* Take it out.

"Oh, Mr. Vyan, you have been so good to me, I loved you always as a father, mother, sir, this one mistake . . . oh . . . oh . . ." Animal terror, no longer words.

"He's all yours. Now get out, and send Müller to clean that blood up."

He was alone again, talking to himself again. "So it was Ambler all the time," he mused, yes, mused was the word.

The buzz of the house exchange, as I now recognized. "Hello? I'm free, Professor, if you would like to come. Or would you rather see me down there?"

"The instructions, Mr. Vyan — I have listed them in detail — it would be better if you . . ."

"Okay, I'll come."

He went out, and I joined Mary Dunn. "The robin flew

away," she said. "He was within a few feet of me and coming nearer, singing on and on, to his mate, I suppose."

"To you, perhaps," I said.

"And then suddenly he flew away. No birds are singing now. Perhaps I frightened all the birds away."

"Or someone else did, or something else."

"I don't hear a sound," she said.

"He's on to me and the envelope. Sim confessed it."

"We ought to go now."

"Soon, Mary. As soon as he comes back." I went in again. On the walls were Max Vyan's oils in miniature. Over the telephone came Max Vyan's voice, growing louder as he reached his chair. *"Bleib draussen, Müller."* Stay outside, Müller. "Well, Professor, I cannot thank you enough for your quite excellent work. And let me assure you once again that it will never be put to harmful use." The first time Max Vyan had given this assurance, he had spoken the truth of his intention.

"How can I thank you, Mr. Vyan? For planning so long — for helping me to escape — for sanctuary here — and now for sending me on — now at last I shall be able to serve the cause of freedom — serve the mute masses . . ."

"Yes, yes, Professor. Before you go, I would like you to accept this gift. It is a hunting horn, such as is used to rally hounds, even to rally mute masses too." He whickered. "All your very own, Professor. Do you seriously imagine, you brainy little nincompoop, that I would allow you to go to Prague?" A brief spurting roar and crackle in my earphone. "Take it, Müller," he said in German. "Incinerate both at once. Send Fraülein von Silberbach."

". . . But I had not finished, Max. Five minutes more, I needed."

"So you tortured a dumb animal. Take this for that, and this, and this."

She did not scream. I did not hear her whimper. "Beat me to death, then. Let them, let anyone beat me to death, and I will not betray you. All the others will betray you. Your friend, look at him beside you on the wall, does he betray you? Yes, beat me, and then beat me more because I lied to you. I did see that wicked Ambler. He did come to the Falkenhorst. He blackmailed me not to confess it. In this only have I failed you, Max, my hero and my second father, Max . . ." The line went dead, alive, dead, alive, dead for some seconds.

Then it stayed alive, and he was talking to himself. "Funny thing about Harry Ambler. *Max was unconquerable. I never doubted it in all that time . . .*"

"Ambler! Quick!"

The panel clicked shut, I ran, pulled door shut, hid Yale key. "Yes?"

"Listen!"

It was that sound, on a still afternoon, that pulsating chatter, a white plume rising beyond the ridge, a white plume shattered, spread in smoke.

Tracks may be covered and false trails laid. Given time, you can even lay false trails in snow, but you cannot cover tracks in snow. We ran down through the woods. "He bumped Ribling after getting instructions for that thing. She told him I'd been at Falkenhorst. Line went dead. I should have known then. Made a mess of it, sorry."

The helicopter skimmed the ridge above, settled to the Falkenhorst. The snow was petering out down here, nearing that spur which had guided me to the body of Alexis. It was hellish going, over and round fallen trees.

"Into those rocks, Ambler — we can take them on."

"Do as I told you."

"I won't."

The chopper was coming. "Please, Dunn!" I said.

"You're crazy," she said, and kissed me on the lips and went, her tracks still showing in an inch of snow. I made for the rocks that formed the spur, an opening below, landing for a helicopter. Two men out — one this way, one after her.

I saw the intense green light, felt it warm on me, directly in line. Mary Dunn had drilled that man. The one who came for me was the wicked-faced little thug who had traveled with me in the chopper's cabin, yesterday, the day before. I shot him between the eyes. It was enjoyable, blood spreading on the snow.

And then I directed my Beretta with seven shots left at the curved perspex and two pilots, but the bullets bounced off — they ricocheted, I saw them. Then I put bullets into the twin-turbine orifices, and they bounced off — they ricocheted, I saw them. No one had followed Mary Dunn, I was sure of that.

We had reached a stalemate, with two bullets left in my automatic, so they had me pinned, but what could they do?

"Herr Ambler," she said.

I heard her say it above me, and I heard her grunt, Tanya von Silberbach grunted as my head blew up, exploded whitely.

Max Vyan sat on one of his Hepplewhite chairs, and I sat on
another, my ankles bound, my wrists handcuffed round the
back. I had a teeming headache. The curtains were drawn
across the window beyond him, but a chink showed a little
light — six-fifteen, six-thirty — only an hour since they had
clobbered me, Tanya had clobbered me, I seemed to think.
"What d'you say?"

"I said: *Intersec.*"

"You keep saying Intersec. What's Intersec?"

He picked up the long horse-breaking whip from the table
and hit me twice across the face with it. "You're lying."

"I came to ski, I tell you, tell you. Did I try to see you? You
even showed me that thing, Koala. Well then, I got ideas.
Why deny it?"

"Shake, heave, sluice, and bring him back," Max Vyan said.
They dragged me out.

It was a chair again, this time of metal, cold on the bottom.
They clamped me to it by ankles, wrists and upper arms. The
thing shook me, like the machine that shops use to do a thor-
ough mixing job on paint. It shook me tooth-loose screaming

blind and deaf. So the change was nice to a slow plunging, heaving, swooping, but not very nice, so dizzy then, I felt so sick. I puked all over the place, all over myself, my guts out retching, it was awful, retching awful. Then they sluiced me with cold water, put my long underwear over my wet naked-ness, handcuffed me and took me back to Vyan's workroom.

"So you got ideas?" He still sat at his table, a handkerchief now to fastidious nose. He waved the men from the room.

It was dark outside. Two hours — she should be down at Aigle by now, or had they caught her? My shots at the helicop-ter, my head exploding — then here in his room seemed to be the next thing. "Got ideas I might pinch diamond. Flop as usual."

"So you planned to steal from me."

"Didn't *plan*."

"Did I ever steal from you?"

I shook my head, meeting the whip left, meeting it right, but I did not feel that much, still trying to think — must gain Mary time. Now *Intersec* again. Yes, I had seen the photograph, copied it for a chap in London, not Intersec, didn't know In-tersec from Adam, chap who employed me to steal Koala, saw him once, named Brock.

"Brock is Intersec," he said. He was very patient.

"News to me. He owned the diamond. You said so too."

"And this woman Dunn was Intersec."

"No, quite innocent, I promise. Friend of mine."

"Take him out again." It was worse each time, the seasick electric chair — dried out, only blood to retch.

"Did I ever cheat you?"

"No. Can't speak. Water."

He called them in. "Give him water."

I drank, not neatly, and the man bashed my mouth with the

mug. The telephone, house telephone rang. Vyan listened, his ear close to it. Then he buzzed. "Bring his book from the drawing room."

Tanya von Silberbach arrived with it. "Go!" Vyan said. She went. He opened a pocketknife and slit the binding carefully round the edges, ripped it back. "Neat," he said.

"Apologize for that. Damned dirty trick, failed too."

"*Raus!*" Sometimes Vyan spoke German to them, sometimes English, and the two men who had tortured me went out. He brushed the book sideways off the table to fall spread-eagled on the floor, and took up that horn and toyed with it.

I wished that he would do the job. "Get it over with."

"Be quiet. Now tell me all you know."

The water had cleared my brains to try, to try, to try to tell him what he would expect me to know via the Falkenhorst telephone: About Korber and the photograph — about some Professor — about Sim — about Alexis? No, I knew nothing, had never succeeded in beaming with the book.

"Not with the receiver in her suitcase?"

"No good. A flop again, like everything. I hid stuff in her case. Innocent, you know — she's innocent."

"And the Laser she used?"

"I gave it to her then, just then, before."

"To kill Hermann?"

"No, no, today, the helicopter chap. Hermann was my job. Pluto let me up the hill, and I used grapnel across the moat, intended to pinch Koala, met Hermann, had to bump him, sorry."

"But you didn't have to bump Pluto?"

"Certainly not, friend of mine, old Pluto, welcomed me."

"A friend of yours, old Pluto. What about Minerva?"

"Her I killed, not a friend of mine. Got curious about the

chopper's visits. It was her or me, so it was Minerva, sorry. I've told you everything. Can I have it now, Max?"

The house telephone. "Ready? Good. One minute."

He turned the horn-shaped weapon full on to me, but put it down and went to the safe, back to his table, charging a hypodermic, I was going to get it that way.

"Not quite yet," he said. "You must be patient, Ambler." He came behind me, bared my shoulder, I felt the prick. Those men came in. "Put all his clothes on," said Max Vyan.

There was some light from two bulbs high up. The nearest thing to me above was a wooden bunk. I had been falling forever, down and down forever, but probably it was from the bunk. I shut my eyes again. "Hello!" I said, and no one answered. If I don't know where I am, I thought, I can't know who is me. There is no me. But there was a thirst, a thousand pains, some me.

I slept again. Through all this awful sleeping thirst there seemed to have been sounds — a drip, a hum always now — once, or was it twice, my wrist-alarm, I felt it churring; and sometimes a persistent call, *Ky-aa*, like my pet jackdaw I killed with brandy medicine, *Chuff*, it said too in conversation, but somehow that seemed to be before my fall.

I was on a matting, quite decidedly awake below the single bunk against the rocky wall. Along the wall was a wooden table, and on it a double electric ring, and on one ring a kettle. I crawled across, croaking a bit, one croaks a bit for water, hope eternal, and I reached its handle, slopped, so heavy, drank from the spout. I drank and drank, what pure and perfect bliss to soak it up, to be again water-seeped, but careful, do be careful.

There had been another time, one other time when I pranged

in the Macdonnell Ranges, also pranged my water cans. The Abos found me, kindly Abos very strict, with little sips at first. That time, heat and drinklessness had not dehydrated me as efficiently as Max Vyan's swooping chair.

I felt much better now until I had a bloody coughing spell and went to be sick decently in the old-fashioned convenience in a corner. But I was not very sick. My body had lapped most of that drink right up. Torture by vomit, torture by thirst, not a bone broken unless the skull was cracked which seemed unlikely when one could think quite clearly, all considered; not even the skin seemed broken on my face, some long upstanding weals, reminiscent of some tribe or something. It was all very civilized; less sanguinary, after all, than the fate of that secretary whose name I had forgotten.

The furnishings of my cave were rudimentary but not uncozy. It was like some troglodyte's hunting camp with some modern conveniences, such as electric heat, and some less modern, such as the thunder box in the corner opposite the intermittent drip. I was now unmistakably hungry, and with good reason if my judgment was correct — that I had been here a night, a day, a night again — my watch said three-fourteen.

In the cupboard — next along the wall from the table and the bunk — was food. I had a choice of Klim, Fraybentos, Huntley and Palmer, Farm-Fresh Butter, Domino, Instant Quaker, Chivers, Tobler, Nescafé, Spam, Tuttifrutti, Libby's Pears, Coffee-mate and even Romary. So I switched on an electric ring and soon had café au lait with a buttered biscuit, a frugal snack, my first or last, or both. After that choking fit I had a drink of watered Klim, delicious, but my throat was sore.

I had to face what, as strength increasingly returned, became an increasingly queer presence or companion. It was a black object with the general configuration of a Havana cigar, but longer, about nine feet long, three of my paces. It was more than a foot thick or wide. It sat on a cradle with rubber dolly-wheels, similar in principle to the carriage that conveys coffins until the pallbearers take over. Indeed, except that the shape was unconventional, it would have served very nicely as casket for an average basketball player.

It was this object that had hummed latterly through unconsciousness and thirst; too bright a light once or twice, it seemed; and other noises heard. The hum was of an Accutron watch in super scale. I touched the thing's cold smooth curving metal. It occupied the middle of my cave — its cave more properly — and this was certainly a cave of sorts, of dark rock faces and rough-hewn walls.

There was also a door to the cave. Unlike all the other interior surfaces, it was flat, and beyond it I thought I heard a stir of wind. Beyond that door were sentries, probably.

In some ways there had been other times — like being thirsty, for example. In some ways not — no one had tortured me before. I had begged too — *oh, for Christ's sake — oh, for Christ's sake, stop it.* And I had begged Max Vyan to kill me with that horn. But I had not squealed on her, could not be sure — I did not think so.

Those men were probably outside. I listened at the door, heard nothing. It was a sliding door, from right to left, it would be locked, or if not locked, they would be waiting.

The door moved easily, so easily I had to check it. Through the slit I felt fresh air and saw a star or two, no sign of the enemy but one could not tell.

I felt pretty awful, about as awful as one could feel and be on two legs, not revert to four. If they were there, they were, so what the hell, get it over with. I pushed the door hard left, and it rolled on smoothly, open wide.

Nobody and nothing, but garage doors lead somewhere, in and out. I took one step, another on flat rock or concrete, saw down to the stubby outline of my Henke boots — fully dressed for skiing, I remembered him saying something to them about clothes.

Now I looked ahead, straight away from the glimmer of the cave. It was too black a night to see the meeting of earth and sky, but a few stars were coming and going from left to right, and that meant cloud was drifting. The cloud drifted obligingly now to reveal star by star the most familiar of constellations, and then Polaris, quite definitely Polaris straight ahead up there for a brief time before the next cloud swallowed it.

To be orientated was to have a lifeline of direction, if of nothing else. The North Star was obscured, but I had stood between it and the rectangular opening of my cave. So, walking square away from the cave, I would walk due north across this rocky plain, was the idea.

Looking up, I saw nothing — looking right, I saw nothing — looking left, I saw nothing — looking ahead, I saw nothing — looking back, the cave, even the black nose in it — looking down I saw my blunt boots against a glisten that might mean wet rock. It seemed cold for wet rock. I bent down, one glove off, and verified the wetness, even slight warmth, I thought, how odd. The bending made me dizzy, so I sat a while with a coughing spell.

Sitting, half-lying, I turned to have a look at home, in the center of it that black-nosed thing, which I did not like, black-hearted hummer, so I stood and went exploring from. At that point I had a very clever thought, which was that the basic motive of exploration had always been more *from* than *to*. One could argue it.

I walked tentatively and carefully, checking back every few steps for contrary direction, counting — fifteen, sixteen . . . twenty-seven, twenty-eight, and counting — the fashionable way these days was down *and counting;* but mine was up.

I tested my footing at each step. Like wading for salmon, I thought, wading the Dee in heavy water. One has to be extremely careful, never commit one foot until the other is secure, and on the Dee one has a wading staff to test ahead. I could have used a wading staff — a ski pole would be excellent — . . . forty-eight, forty-nine and counting, as dark as hell itself might be, now my right boot's turn to probe again.

That boot met nothing, NOTHING, and my left foot, which was anchor, slipped, and I was turning, scrabbling, fingers, elbows, chest and stomach, slipping back, slipping to the void of nothing. But there was a crevice, a finger-hold, another — try. Try one last time, and my left foot did find something, lost it, found it, held it. I rested. Two clumsy glove-holds, one trembling foothold, my shoulders going, gone, worn out. What use to rest? That sapped me more.

Please try, Ambler. Some of my few friends, my enemies, they called me Ambler, plain.

I tried. Forever and still ever I was trying, weaker. I got the other knee, slipped off, got it again, the boot, the thigh, a heave. I was on top.

I crawled away from it, that hideous depth into the Valley of the Grave, of course I knew it now. I was the animal that crawled for home, the cave, my black-nosed humming friend. I put my arms round it and cried. I hugged it, crying.

In here: safety. Out there: terror, and it would not leave me, terror. But I could be safer from it, if I dared. I dared to crawl again, to shut the sliding door, how easily it rolled on Timken bearings. I followed it, protected by it until with my right hand I could cling to the cradle of my big black friend, and with my left hand push the door, to roll on, click shut.

I bunked down under the blankets provided by kind hosts and slept again peacefully, not even ever falling until my wrist-alarm woke me at eight o'clock, which could be night or morning, because it was an implacable self-winder self-alarmer at each full revolution of the hour hand. Seven-thirty was my usual time, changed to eight when Mary Dunn arrived.

But surely it was morning — and I remembered why, crouched on the bunk — cold sick with memory.

I had the courage to slide the door open a slit. There was sun on mountains to the north, between me and them a flat ledge, a platform across which I had walked at night. It was quite big, a hundred feet square or so, this cave in the middle of one side, the other three sides stopping short at nothing.

I had walked to that northern edge, slipped at it, over it. "Dear God," I said, and shut the door.

There was a wash basin, soap, a towel, even a comb, and a small mirror pitoned into the wall of the cave. My stubble surely confirmed two days, no razor provided by the management. The top of my head was not combable, being matted with blood and too painful to wash. The weals on my face were bluish through gray beard — funny thing, no gray hairs on the cranium. I looked like death warmed-up or chilling-down, not yet arrived.

The cave was dry everywhere — roof, walls, and floor — except in the corner with the drip which turned out to be a dripping tap, quite mundane. But the drip was explained by the water pressure when I filled the kettle — quite colossal, they should have put a notice up.

I decided on Instant Quaker since my stomach felt less stable than would accept bully beef. And biscuits I had to be careful of too, causing tickles in the throat, more coughing spells and beastly blood. But that was not so frequent now. The well-known healer was mending me. Mending me for what? An excellent question.

The hum was unceasing, the drip went on, the *Ky-aa* sounded now outside just after breakfast time. I slid the door open to see our visitor, a bird, importunate, a chough. It ran a bit and hopped a bit and cocked its tail while calling *Ky-aa*.

"Just a mo," I said. Every problem required careful thought, and I decided that one could not fail to please a garbage-loving chough with wholesome bully beef. So I opened that can with its own gadget, spooned off a piece of bully — knives and forks were not provided — mixed Klim and water in an enameled plate, and took along breakfast. That glossy bird, as glossy black as my humming friend, did not trust my friendship quite to the door, so I had to open further, and push the plate a yard or so. Then the chough loved its breakfast greedily.

When it had finished eating bully — first things first, or solids before liquids — it drank up its milk, wiped red bill clean on glossy shoulder, said "Chuff" to me, and walked slowly away in a northerly direction such as I had taken in the night. It was appalling to see the chough walk slowly to its doom. "Stop!" I called. But it paid no attention, perched on the very lip of nothing, and I could not look.

Bravely enough, I crawled out for the plate and back with it, shut the door almost, dared a glance — no chough.

"Morning, Ambler." His voice came from the roof. It was not surprising and not interesting, because I was over the edge where the poor bird had fallen. I was trying . . . I was slipping . . . But a bright light came on. "Have a better look at you. Good morning, Ambler, for the second time."

"Morning. Too bright, that thing." But actually it was nice because it shut the horrible outside away.

"Quite comfortable?"

"Very, thanks. What are you doing up there?"

"I am not up there. I am down in the bowels of home."

"Oh, I see, sort of magic eye, what bowels, your workroom?"

"Have you had any visitors?"

"Just one I can remember. A chough came for breakfast, but it won't be back. Dead, a pity."

"Dead? Did you kill it, Ambler?"

"No, fell off, poor chap. There one second, gone the next."

His whicker filled the cave from wall to wall. "Poor flightless chough. The Common Chough, not the Alpine Chough, which is interesting. Now, Ambler, it is time for a blow-through. Do you remember those blow-throughs in prison days, to expel the filthy stink of a hundred filthy lags?"

"Remember them."

"The purpose of this one is more limited — to expel the filthy stink of one lag's blood and vomit."

"Same thing," I said. "You end up with blood. That's the vomit you end up with."

"The door, I should explain — it shuts automatically at the approach of aircraft — a quite simple device linked to the emanations of an unshielded ignition system. But I should explain because when that door shuts, it shuts. One cannot thwart it, as one can thwart an elevator door."

"Thanks for telling me."

"Not at all. Now open it."

"I don't like it open. I like things cozy the way they are. I won't." The noise cut through my aching head. I held my ears, curled up in the smallest ball, but no escaping fiendish sound. It stopped.

"Simply a refinement of the torture one experiences from one's car horn if it runs amok. A useful disciplinary gadget. Open the door for your blow-through, Ambler."

I slid the door open, keeping it between the outside and myself until I reached my humming friend, to whom I clung and pushed the door on wide, one-handed. Then I retreated along my smooth black humming friend into security in the cave. "What is this thing? I like it very much, the way it hums, what is it?"

"Over by the tap you will find a bucket and a mop. Swab down your messes on the floor. We must have clean stables, Ambler."

"Tap leaks, not up to standard." I filled the bucket and swabbed the floor down. My messes he spoke of were inconsiderable outcomes of my coughing spells, poor me. "What is it?" I said, swabbing round about the wheels. "Will it run away?"

"The wheels are locked solid," he said patiently. "I can stop it humming now," he said. The humming stopped.

"You're the boss."

"Precisely, Ambler."

"You still haven't told me what it is."

"Rudimentary, Ambler. Have a guess."

"A guess. Well, my guess would be a sort of private H-bomb."

"Where are the tail fins, nincompoop?"

"I wouldn't think tail fins matter much. Not germane to the essential H."

"Much better, Ambler."

"It wasn't *what* so much I meant to ask as *why*." I had finished swabbing down the cave. So I swilled out mop and bucket, and took a seat at the breakfast table. "Anything else I can do?" I asked, looking up, his humble slave.

"Have a rest," he said. "Recoup your strength. As may be apparent to you, Ambler, I do not indulge in torture for my own amusement, but to get results. I got them. It was too bad about your little girl friend." He whickered. "No, turn your head, that's better, how woebegone you look. Now listen, and I will tell you *why*, inveterate whyer that you are or were."

I listened while he told me. It was in essence the story that Harry Z. Gilpin had hazarded to Mary Dunn and me at the Palace Hotel. The Republic of Bargomba first had the effrontery to approach him. But then . . . *As you would say, Ambler, one got ideas.* Or an interesting idea for the man who has everything, nothing more to own, the fun gone out of acquisition, unless there might still be something one could acquire that was not in the personal possession of any stupid —— alive. The word he used may not be written, at least by me.

That was the starting point from which the real fascination grew. What? Whence? Where? Who? It became an intensely complicated and delicate planning operation, not unlike, on a giant scale, our glider escape from Heifetz Castle.

I could see little similarity, but did not like to say so. Even now, he was harping back to us together.

"It's been a good blow-through. Could I close the door?"

"By all means." I closed the door by my usual method. "You seem quite fond of Excalibur."

"Fond of . . . ?"

"*Excalibur.* Surely even you know that one, Ambler."

"Yes, sorry, I didn't hear. Good name."

"Doesn't frighten you?"

"No, I like him, especially when he hums, keeps my mind off other things. Why sometimes hum and sometimes not?"

"The hum means Stage One Readiness. Excalibur is simplicity itself except for the radio control, which I confess I do not understand. Should I explain the rest of it?"

"Don't bother, thank you. I took an elementary course before I left the R.A.F. A quick shoot-together of Plutonium or U 235, and that warms up the D_2O or Tritium to fuse, and bob's your uncle, pretty simple, as you say. Is he . . . er dirty — you know, radioactive?"

"In this condition entirely clean. Postfusionwise, however, very very dirty, so I am assured. That wouldn't bother you much."

"No, of course not. How many megatons?"

"Forty-one was Ribling's calculation — that is, Ribling the Professor."

"The Professor bought it, I thought I heard."

"You heard aright."

"I think I understand most things now, except this comfortable cave, I mean where is it, or would that be classified?"

"Highly classified, Ambler, but you have earned Top Secret clearance. That cave is some hundred feet below the couloir where you killed Minerva. We discovered it by helicopter. And such is the overhang that from the couloir not even the ledge or heliport is visible. We worked on it inside and out, laid cable from the Höhengrat, all rather top secretly by night while the avalanche wall was being built last summer."

"So some workmen must have known, surely a risk in that?"

"Yes, they knew. Indeed, eventually they knew too much, even if they knew a small fraction of what you know, Ambler."

"The whole thing rather reminds me of what you said one night about the Koala Diamond. If you flaunt your bauble, then you lose it really. If you use Excalibur, then you lose him really, lose a lot more besides — that chough, for instance, and your flowers, all the things you love."

He gave me a shot of sound to curl me up, unbearable, I screamed against it. "I will not tolerate impertinence," he said, peace again. "I have told you a great deal, Ambler. Once before I almost told you, when I still thought you trustworthy."

"Yes, I remember that, after tea one day. I wish you had. Then it would never have come to this. I don't mind if you blow me up."

"I do not intend to blow you, or indeed even anything that matters up — that is, unless I am forced to it. And who, in that case, would bear the onus of forcing me to it?"

"I would, it's true, I'm sorry."

"There were some ticklish moments yesterday when Swiss security people arrived in force from Bern — that accounts for your favorite hum of Stage One Readiness. I threw the place open to them, and said: *What is this absurdity?* There were abundant witnesses to say that you and your lady friend had last been seen driving much too fast in a Karmann Ghia, meeting your fate, alas, at the self-same spot where you pushed Mr. Dorion in. The only inaccuracy was you, Ambler, and you were sleeping it off with Excalibur. Everything went well, and they were most apologetic. These Swiss are sticky about interference, you know. They cherish their sovereignty."

"But Korber and Tanya?"

"What Tanya did with Korber in New York is hardly my fault, although, for the sake of my reputation, I must soon face a change of social secretary. And Korber's act of treason was to sell specifications to the Republic of Bargomba, not the skeleton of Excalibur to Maximilian Vyan. I planted that evidence on him as insurance."

"Is your name Maximilian? I never knew."

"In our long true friendship you never knew."

"You never told me."

"You never asked me."

"About Mary Dunn . . ."

"Ah, there is a question that must be asked. Miss Dunn met with an accident at that corner. And salvage operations — you can imagine the problem in a precipitous gorge at high spring flood. No, don't look away. LOOK HERE! The trickle of manly tears, how very touching a tribute to your immediate boss in Intersec. You confessed that, you know."

"Go and fuck yourself," I said. I waited for it, and waited for it, and waited for it, but all I heard was Max Vyan's whicker. Then the bright light went out.

TWENTY-ONE

I did a number of things that day. There were the physical things, like eating several modest meals, and drinking small amounts, bringing my machine back into order. I was sick only twice, and the second time no blood. Then there was the chough to look after, voracious bird, but grateful, always saying *chuff* before it walked away to perch upon the lip of nothing. Eventually I absolutely made myself stay watching until it flew away.

One mental thing I tried to do was not to think about Mary Dunn dead in a Karmann Ghia, not think — *Non-think* did someone call it? — but that was different. So think, then — think: Did you confess about Intersec? Don't think so, but don't know. So think — with Mary dead, what do they know? What evidence do they have against Max Vyan? Plumb nothing, isn't it? Nothing from the United States about Korber except a dirty photograph, nothing from Russia about Alexis, nothing from Britain about Ribling. Bodies? Buried in snow or incinerated. No evidence.

And at Schloss Alpenheide, an affronted Herr Max Vyan,

only too willing to cooperate with our own authorities, *the Swiss, I said, not some foreign power,* one of Switzerland's most distinguished citizens, perhaps the most affluent, certainly the one who has contributed most to winter sport development, to their precious boring little pockets. And a major figure in world industry — accuse him of harboring an H-bomb? On what evidence? None. Not even that distinguished philanthropist, Harry Z. Gilpin, could produce more than a fairy tale about some unknown Russian being done to death for no known reason.

The fact was that the only people with evidence to support this ridiculous accusation would have been Mary Dunn or Harry Ambler — one dead in the gorge of the Alpenheide River (that had rung true, he had spoken truth), one awaiting death in a cave six thousand feet above the Valley of the Grave.

Excalibur (a vulgarly pretentious name on second thought) no longer hummed. I liked him better humming, but I still liked him well enough. If he blew the top off Europe, what the hell did I care? And if his radiation drifted downwind very dirtily to the Ural Mountains, that would be just too bad.

What I feared most terribly through all my tortured guts was the abyss — suppose Vyan drove me so mad with the piercing horn that I ran, holding ears, on and over and down, far screaming down. I was not dry-coated any more. I sweated cold.

A craven about that, but not a craven altogether yet. It may be that my hatred of Max Vyan came from that. No, it came from something else. I had not hated him before. I had admired him, liked the caustic in him, been sorry for him, been appalled by him, disliked him, but I had not hated him.

Whether I was to be allowed to starve to death (it would

take weeks and weeks with available supplies), or removed by
helicopter for execution, or disposed of otherwise, or THAT, he
had to do it somehow.

I did two other practical things that day. The first was an
examination of Excalibur. I slid open the door for better light,
and gave him a careful going-over. He was black and glossy
as that chough, but no red beak or legs. Or you could say that
his legs were the cradle on which he rested, wheels locked solid,
Max was right, of course, as usual. Excalibur had two visible
entrances, and they were closed. One was simply a seam on
the forward flank, with a keyhole in it, an oval seam almost perfectly smooth in Excalibur's rounded flank. The other was in
the blunt end, the burning end of the cigar. It was more complicated to operate than a common keyhole, consisting of a
circular hinged door with nuts of eccentric shape recessed. Not
square nuts or hexagons but nuts with excellent rhymeless reason (e.g. a crescent moon, a truncated pyramid, a common
question mark) which only box spanners of equally rhymeless
reason could provide any hope of fitting, damned ingenious.

I wrote off Excalibur and his radio control, beyond my ken.
But the power supply was another matter. The cave was lit
and heated. Even the heliport or landing pad was heated with
wires set in a coating of blackish concrete, hence its wetness.
Reasons — keep down snow and ice for landing, and possibly
another — I was thinking very well, perhaps for the first time
in all this chronicle — vertical cliffs and overhangs hold no
snow, so a flat ledge holding snow stands out against a colossal
cliff, a dark ledge one does not notice when flying by.

I sat on my bottom and slid out timorously backwards from
Excalibur to look for the source of electric power, for the route
of the two cables which entered the cave above the door. The

cliffs rose sheer, then swept out overhead in a fantastic arching overhang. Those cables, the thick one and the thin — the power and the closed-circuit TV, one might guess — had been dropped from the couloir and pitoned, secured, all the way in, under and down into the cave by the men Max Vyan had employed by night. They knew too much eventually, those men — bad luck, their ropes broke, one might imagine.

I was sitting outside, looking up, when the camouflaged door began to close. To be locked out on that ledge. *Oh, Jesus*, I thought and think piously. It closed quite fast, but I was faster, safe inside as an airplane flew past, not a chopper, I did not think, but a propeller job, my own kind of aircraft, flew along and away. It was not near. How I could have spent twelve thousand hours of my miserable life with all the voids of pinpoint death below me, I did not understand.

The plane had gone. I slid the door open again, needing daylight to trace the cables in the cave itself. The smaller one ran up out of sight into the roof, forget about it. The other, thick armored stuff to carry a potent load, must go to a contact breaker, main fuse-box or the like. You have to divide your load, you simply have to protect each circuit. Even an ignoramus like H. Ambler is aware of that one. The main cable goes into such a fuse-box — the others spread out from it.

The main junction box was on a recess in the wall out of sight above the door. I hauled over my single bunk and stood it on end and climbed on top, no good. A better idea, I dragged over the table, got onto it, struggled with the bunk, had a coughing fit, a bloody bad one, but Ambler, miserable acrophobic coward that he was, had not said die yet. I climbed up my bunk on top of the table and found what I was seeking — the main make and break before the fuse-box — you pull the handle, and two prongs spring free to break the circuit. Dare I try it? I did, and the roof lights went out. Handle in, a small succulent spark, the lights on again. Okay, down.

The cave was in shipshape order when the bright light dazzled me sometime after five. "A nice day, Ambler?"

"Lovely, thanks. I'm feeling better."

"Glad to hear it. Any visitors?"

"The chough comes often."

"Any other callers?"

"A plane flew past once, and the door popped shut."

He gave me the sound, into the core of my screaming head, and hands to ears I was crawling to the door. It stopped. "You know what that was for, Ambler, don't you?"

"Yes. Sorry I was rude. Won't occur again."

"All is peaceful on the Alpenheide front. Two apologetic calls from Bern. Oh, and Harry Gilpin telephoned — was it true about you and some young lady in a Karmann Ghia, so I said Yes, according to police reports, and confirmed by Fernandel that he lent it to her after skiing. Why didn't you lend her your Caramba? Gilpin sounded most cut-up, sympathized with me about your demise. Harry Zee used to be quite an operator before little Gloria hooked him for a domesticated poodle."

"She clings a bit, I quite agree."

"We have been skiing this afternoon. I thought it perhaps in questionable taste so soon after the death of my oldest friend. But one must put a brave face on things. I shall sign off now, with my compliments and those of your devoted admirer, Tanya."

"Thanks. Same here."

"The blackbird sings to him, 'Brother, brother,
If this be the last song you shall sing,
Sing well, for you may not sing another;
Brother, sing.'

"Sleep well, Ambler, for you may not sleep another."

A cheap twist of quotation, it seemed to me. The bright light went out. The small lamps in the roof were enough to see one's way about, and I went hunting. What I hunted was a piece of ferrous metal, a strip of it. Excalibur and his cradle — a ton at least of metal, but no strips. The food cupboard — all wood. The single bunk — all wood. The bench — all wood. The table — better, it had four bolted metal supports across the angles between tabletop and legs. But how to get one without a spanner, without any tool better than a dessert spoon?

I solved it though. I was pretty desperate or past caring much. Upending the table, I maneuvered the bunk until I could get one wooden leg inside one diagonal metal bar, stood on the table upside down and applied six-foot leverage with my sturdy bunk. Something had to give, and it was the wood through which the bar was bolted, broke one leg of the table and got a bar or strip of metal, common iron.

It had been a tiring job, and probably to no useful purpose. But I remembered very well — and it was thanks to Max Vyan that I remembered, because he had told me of a mass escape in which he had taken part in the year 1942 — long before I was shot down. By shorting a lead into the camp, a lead which came from *outside* the main camp fuse-box, stupid Germans, they had been able to blow right back to the town transformers, and had blitzed the wire in darkness; it had worked. Now if I could put my metal bar across the two main contacts, would

I not achieve a similar result, blow the whole thing at least as far as the Höhengrat?

What purpose this would serve beyond sparing me bright lights and probably that fiendish horn, I did not know. I was too slaphappy and disorganized a creature to have many sound rules in life, but one was: When you come to the helpless hopeless blank and seeming end, *do* something, anything, but *do*. That had got me into trouble too, but out of more than in.

After one more snack, I loosened my boots to the end of the buckles, stowed the bar underneath me out of sight and prepared for sleep. It was my third night in the cave, my first undrugged, although the remains of that injection still woozed about with everything else. *Sleep well, for you may not sleep another.* He did not torture without purpose. He did not threaten idly. He would bump me off tomorrow. I thought that he would have to kill me before his urge to use Excalibur on Harry Ambler got so much the better of him that he took the things he loved along with me. Taking a few million Europeans along for the ride would not bother him at all. It was *me*. It was what Tanya had said, and Sim had said, and the photograph on his wall had said. *Did I ever steal from you? Did I ever cheat you?*

Max Vyan had been first, last and all the time a pragmatist. Even his rubbing out of Mary Dunn had been pragmatical. The psychopath had been well served by pragmatism. But no longer. Not much longer. The human nuisances — ignore them, rub them out as necessary. The things you love — the jonquils and the snowflakes in the wood — but do they ultimately matter more than retribution?

I woke to the hum of Excalibur soon after 4 A.M. He hummed again at Stage One Readiness. I opened the door to listen, but there was not a sound. It should be surprising to me, I remember thinking, not to be afraid of it. I was not in the least. And yet the thought, the very notion of venturing out on that bare dark ledge made my heart race up, sweat sting my eyes.

I lay down again, and soon the light came on. "You're sweaty, Ambler. Are you panic-stricken?"

"What's the matter?"

"Oh, nothing. People telephone. I put Excalibur on Stage One again as much for fun as anything. I rather like playing with him. And I confess to being in two minds. It might be amusing to let Excalibur loose on you. On the other hand . . ."

"But wouldn't that be letting Excalibur loose on you?"

"Certainly not. I am entirely safe down here in the control room. I had it built ten years ago as a shelter against H-bombs, not unfunny. No, it would be other considerations."

"Yes, I understand." Then he gave me a shot of sound so long and terrible that I was at the door, heaving at the door, locked shut, I thrashed about all round Excalibur.

"Barbarian!" he said. "How dare you presume to understand. And do you imagine that I would let you take the easy way by jumping off?"

"No easy way," I said. "There never is, come to think of it."

"Some are harder, Ambler, though.

> "The Garden called Gethsemane,
>   It held a pretty lass,
>   But all the time she talked to me
>   I prayed my cup might pass.
>
> "It didn't pass — it didn't pass —
>   It didn't pass from me.
>   I drank it when we met the gas
>   Beyond Gethsemane!

"Would you be ready for your cup, Ambler?"

The light went out, and the hum went on. It was monotony, unchanging hum. I dozed again until five past five, wide awake at five past five. I went to check that door, safely locked. *The Garden called Gethsemane, it held a pretty lass.* Not pretty, though.

Not think about that. *Do.* Observe the rule, let's make a cup of coffee. One could hardly say that one's cave was not luxurious. One could say with some assurance that it was a great deal more luxurious than any living quarters occupied by Max Vyan in less affluent days, in four years and ten months' prison days. You might put the starting cause of it back there, I thought, the crowds, no end to them, humanity to be endured, most people sheep, don't mind it, love it really, safety, crowds and crowds, but not Max Vyan. A steaming cup of coffee, and a thought again, an urge again, it showed how ill I must have been — a cigarette. But I had none. I had, though. I found one crumpled Player's Mild in a pocket of my anorak, no matches, put on the electric ring to glow at High, very easily solved, a lovely cigarette, drunken dizzy-making, all too quickly gone.

Five twenty-six, I noted carefully on my watch, a PING to break the nice monotony of hum. Five twenty-seven, PING. Five twenty-eight, one minute on the dot, a PING. "Stage Two," he said. "Hear the difference, Ambler?"

"Yes," I said, looking up. I did not wish to give offence.

"Stage Two is readiness stepped up. Stage Three, were we ever to reach that Stage, would sound much the same to you at first." Light off.

The minutes pinged along by tuning fork, Accutron hum — five forty-one. A voice said: "Stop." Then: "Ambler!"

I said nothing, didn't hear it, imagined it in my head.

"Ambler!" It was not in my head, it was beyond the door.

"Yes?"

"Open up!"

I tried the door, locked against my taking Vyan's notion of the easy way. "I can't."

"You must."

"Hang on."

"I'm hanging, idiot." Dunn had returned in voice or spirit.

My table, now rickety on three legs. My bunk, I heaved it up, with coughing spell, that cigarette, with smoker's cough. My iron bar. An insulator? Who but H. Ambler would forget that one? But there was a rubber mat on the floor in front of my commode. I doubled it and wrapped it round the bar and climbed.

I had some reason, some atavistic unthought reason, for blowing everything, not simply breaking contact by a strong pull on the handle. Teetering on my pedestal of three-legged table and upended bunk, I pulled that handle; then I put the iron bar across copper contacts; then I ducked my head and pushed the handle forward. Everything blew up like gunfire, and I fell on Excalibur; humming away, he pinged in my ear, I hit my leg on him.

The door was free. The dawn was pink on mountains to the north. Mary Dunn hung a few feet above and beyond the ledge, between me and the mountains. She swayed about. "Come and catch this rope," she said.

I dithered in the open on the ledge. "It's the height. Fell off nearly, just can't stand it."

"Crawl, then! Look at you, talk about plain windy. Crawl!"

I crawled on hands and knees and finally on stomach to about ten feet from the edge where I had slipped — struggled, weakened, slipping, all would happen to me now again.

"Catch," she said, and threw a coil of rope. I spared one hand and missed it. The rope slid slowly back to her and over, hung down out of sight. Dunn coiled it. "Catch!" I caught it. "Now, crawl back!"

I crawled back for Excalibur, felt resistance, felt her swinging, kept on crawling. But now the drag was off it, and she stepped out of a cat's cradle of rope. "Tie it inside," she said. "Get this mess out of the way. Give me room to work."

I moved table and bunk. By then I was thinking straight again. "Lights and power fused, but not the closed-circuit TV. Small cable. Got a hatchet or anything?"

"I'm not here to chop kindling wood," she said quite rudely. "Where's the TV scanner?"

"Up there, I think."

"Better shut door. Stand above me. Hold this light."

It was a pencil torch. I stood above Mary Dunn, covering her and the stubby end of Excalibur from observation from up there. "Stage Two," I said. "Pings every minute."

"I know," she said. "I'm lining out the tools. When I hiss, shine it down on them." She hissed. I shone it on them, two dozen implements more or less. They were straight and very thin and delicate, each with a small cross-handle. "First these four, the crescents, must be one of them. Shine up."

"Ambler!"

"Yes, Max? It's all dark down here. What's happened? There was a sort of splutter and the lights went out."

"Open the door."

I put out the flashlight, moved along Excalibur, pretended at the door. "I can't, jammed solid." I moved back, felt for Dunn's head, stood over her and shone the light.

"Where are you, Ambler?"

"On my bunk. I'm listening to Stage Two. I rather like that

ping, relieves monotony. I like Stage Two." But I was standing over Mary Dunn, watching her fingers try one tool, discard
that to her left hand, try another, how exquisitely and absently
those fingers worked to fit the shaped point within the socket.
Then she turned to the left, an audible click, a sigh from Dunn.
There were six to do, and that was one.

"What is that noise I hear down there?"

"It isn't down here, Max, it's up. You're down there, you told
me so."

"What is that noise?"

"My hand on the floor, I'm frightened, Max. Couldn't you
please get the lights fixed somehow?"

"I know you, Ambler. It has taken me a long time to get to
know you — twenty-one years or more."

"Slightly off and on, though, Max. Six months would be
nearer the actual truth."

Dunn hissed for light. I pointed it down. The long slender
tools, the long thoughtful fingers, quick and unhurried.

"What?" His voice was high. "They want the drawbridge
lowered? Say that *I* am asleep. Say that I, Maximilian Vyan,
may not be disturbed." His voice dropped to speak quietly and
thoughtfully to me. "All night I have debated with myself
alone. But that is over. Stage Three, Ambler, listen for it."
PING.

"Time it, Ambler," whispered Dunn. Must I always be Ambler, even in Stage Three?

I watched my second hand. "What tools?"

"Bundallochy kit, match Ribling's. One ten-thousandth
tolerance. Asking a lot," she muttered.

PING, just under sixty seconds. I let another hum go round
to PING, another. Oh, excellent watch with luminous hands
and alarm and all the rest of it. PING. She had turned a sec-

ond key, click, it was two, and four to go. "It's dropping a second every time. Fifty-nine, eight, seven, six, five coming up."

"Let me see, in arithmetical progression, that would be thirty minutes and thirty seconds total. Twenty-five minutes left."

"Ambler!" He was back again.

"Yes, Max?"

"What is that light I see?"

"No light unless it's daylight filtering in."

"The daylight does not filter into Excalibur's cave."

"Soon will, though, if I've got this count-down right, or is Stage Three a false alarm?"

"Soon there will be no cave, no Alpenheide, not much Switzerland and very little Ambler."

"Good point," I said, and heard *Ky-aa* beyond the door. "There's my chough, do you hear him?"

"He is not *your* chough. He was mine long before you ever knew him."

"Not yours much longer, Max. You know, Max, I had you wrong — I always thought you loved the birds and flowers because they weren't your own, not your property, could not possess."

"True," he said. "That was the beauty I saw so well."

"But now you're going to destroy it, and the beauty you saw will all be gone, crisped up, to use what you would call an Amblerism. Why not stop it, Max, switch off Excalibur?"

"Stage Three marks a point of no return. Until then I controlled it."

"So now you control nothing."

"Oh yes, I do. I control your destruction, Ambler. *Max was unconquerable. I never doubted it in all that time.* You wrote that, Ambler."

"I wrote it about another man. He was not a megalomaniac Jehovah."

Vyan whickered from the ceiling.

"I've done four of them. What interval now?"

PING — HUM, PEACEFUL HUM, HUM — PING. "Twenty-two seconds."

"Four minutes and thirteen seconds left," she said. That amazing brain of Mary Dunn's, supposed to be dead in the Alpenheide gorge. "Now the rhomboid slot," she muttered.

"What is that other voice I hear down there? I hear a woman."

" 'The Garden called Gethsemane, it held a pretty lass, but all the time she talked to me, I prayed my cup might pass.' "

"You betrayed me, Ambler. Your cup didn't pass."

"Yes," I said. "And I'm very sorry. So was Judas."

Soft click, Mary Dunn hissed once more, and I shone the light. PING — HUM, PEACEFUL HUM, HUM — PING. "Fourteen seconds."

"Ninety to go. Still that question mark, the hardest one of all."

"Max!"

"I am here, and in a little more than one minute you will have paid the price for all of them."

"You mean for all the stupid suckers, Max?"

"Yes, only one of them I ever trusted, and you played me for a stupid sucker. But who is now the final sucker?"

"Me," I said. "But does it amuse you to know that I took the genuine Koala off the body of Alexis?"

He said nothing. Not one peep did he emit.

Click, a last soft click. "Move, Ambler. Open the door."

PING — HUM — slide open the door — PING. "Help me, quick!"

"Ambler!" Vyan did not scream at me. He said it quietly.

I helped her draw out the thing, which was a shell case for something like an eighty-eight, or the modern equivalent, high-velocity gun. It weighed a fair amount, and we carried it beyond Excalibur to the door. "Roll the bastard off," she said. "Get rid quick."

I rolled it half across that ghastly ledge; then sat and kicked it, and it rolled right off. "Hullo, Chough," I said. It was keeping a respectful distance, on the hopeful make for breakfast. From the cave I heard a solid *sonck* as of a striker hitting and soon from below there was a big boom bang as the shell exploded. The chough flew away. She carried the rope, nylon or that kind of thing. "Here, I'll put this on you. Stand up. Stand still."

"I can't do it, Dunn."

"He'll come in the chopper. We've got to get out of here."

I crouched. "I can't."

"Bloody coward," she said, and boxed my ears for me. "That's all square. Stand up."

I stood in the open while Dunn put the rope cradle on me. She drew a walkie-talkie from inside her anorak. "Okay up there?"

"Okay."

To me she said: "Hold the rope with your hands. I'll hang on to you." And into the walkie-talkie: "Haul away! Out to the edge now, Ambler, quick, or we'll pendulum. Coward!" She was cruel to me. "Shut your eyes, then. Shut them!"

This I did, and Dunn put her arms round my neck, her legs round my waist, riding me really, one has to say it. She was strong, as strong as anything, my eyes shut against the awful swaying, swinging, eyes tight shut. "You badly need a shave," she said. "Are you all right, Ambler?"

But I could not answer. "Tell me that poem you were saying."

> "The Garden called Gethsemane,
> It held a pretty lass,
> But all the time she talked to me
> I prayed my cup might pass.
>
> It didn't pass — it didn't pass —
> It didn't pass from me.
> I drank it when we met the gas
> Beyond Gethsemane!"

I said that off for Mary Dunn, and then we were safe, helped over and into the safety of that couloir where I had killed the bitch Minerva. It was Rudi Viereck, undoing my rope. "Run to the Höhengrat," he said in his bad hard German.

We ran, but I was not well trained for running now; I coughed and coughed, and each of them took an arm and hustled me. But here was the avalanche wall, built by Max Vyan to keep people from the Teufelsspitzen. "Jump!" I jumped into soft deep snow. "Inside, Ambler. I hear it coming." They chivied me round and into that side door which faced the west — to the Teufelssturz, the Wintergrün, the Alpenheide Glacier.

In the doorway were two soldiers with an automatic gun, tripod, self-loading cannon, shells in clips. Paratroopers, they looked like, not village call-ups. Mary Dunn ran past them and I followed her along the corridor. "Hans!" she was calling. "Hans! Get him back here." Then we were in the Höhengrat terminus, and the hawser was moving, drawing up the cable car, a thin rope looping down from it.

"What's the rope?"

"He lowered me and hauled us up, Fernandel, walkie-talkie relayed. Got it?"

"Got it," I said. "I thought you . . ." But I did not finish because of cannon fire: WHOOMP — WHOOMP — WHOOMP, two-shells-a-second sort of speed, then not one cannon, the roll of cannon-fire exchanged, blue and white helicopter in sight below us, below the open-ended concrete box of Terminus Höhengrat. The cable car windows disintegrated as it climbed toward us. Then I saw the draw-cable start to snake this way, and the cable car shot down its standing line, ran away, ran gravity-berserk, joyride to destruction. Did something fall out? "Oh, no!" said Mary Dunn. "Oh, no."

I got her out of there before the broken cable came writhing in to flay the place. WHOOMP — WHOOMP along the corridor, and then one blasted in, and the cannon was silent.

Run along here. Now run back there — this time I led, pushed away the bloody mess that had been a soldier, and was in behind that gun as the helicopter swung for another pass. "Feed 'em," I said to her, she was right there with me. Dunn fed the clips of eight as I watched my tracer through the open ring-sight, every second shell a tracer. The light ack-ack boys, airfield defense, used to let me have shoots for fun. Now I nursed the fiery needles of my tracer — what a lovely racket — up the thick-set body of the chopper and behind the pilot's cabin and to those turbine intakes, side by side. The helicopter belched smoke and swung away, its rotor spinning, losing height over the lip, the beginning of the Alpenheide Glacier.

"Good shooting," she said. "What next?"

"Max Vyan until he's good and dead, if not already."

"Me too, that bitch," said Mary Dunn. "Our skis are here. Fernandel got them last night when I arrived. Fernandel."

"I think he bought it, might have jumped. Why only one gun here?"

"They're storming Schloss Alpenheide. I tried to tell them more strength here. You ever tried to tell the blank stupid soldiery?"

There was nobody about, no Hans and elephant wife, no Rudi Viereck. But he was in the ski shop, having his leg bandaged by that wife — a flesh wound, he said, he would follow us. I took a tommy gun from one body, a pistol from the other. They were young to die, those boys, one with fuzzy cheeks.

It was just half past seven, a glorious morning at the Höhengrat, no sounds of guns, no sign of people, only the bell of the Marienkirche tolling in the green valley.

"You're unarmed, Dunn. Take this pistol."

"I've got my Laser and my knife."

"I thought you were drowned — so did Vyan."

"I got out," she said. "Opened window, equalized pressure, got out, hellish scramble along gorge for miles, got out."

The helicopter had pitched on its nose, which was crumpled in, a write-off. The sugar snow hissed underneath my skis, a peaceful hiss, tommy gun ready, both poles in left hand. The cabin door was open. "Come out!" I said. But nothing stirred.

"Tracks," she said. "Two pairs on foot. Watch it though, Ambler — the pilots." But the pilots were dead at their controls, one shot, the other's head lolling, whiplash, it looked like.

"His and hers," said Mary Dunn, "like that corny ad," the man's boots and the woman's, ribbed ski-boot tracks leading on down the glacier on hard snow. They would have fifteen minutes' start, but twenty miles an hour on skis, against seven on foot, dropping to six, to five, like Stage Three, arithmetical progression. But I must not think of that, nor of Mary Dunn riding free on that rope, simply hanging onto me above six thousand feet of nothing, nor of Fernandel on his hell-bent ride. So many nightmares, slow and quick.

The bed of the glacier was smooth, unbroken by crevasses. They said it was like that all along its length except at one place — the serac or icefall where it plunged a few hundred broken feet. But all the way now, rising on either side of this smooth winding white ribbon, were rocky slopes. There was shelter among those rocks for them to lie in wait for us.

The tracks still went down the middle. Ahead the glacier swung right. It swung at a single distinctive mark, a tall column or obelisk, familiar to me from picture postcards at the Hotel. *Die Kanzel,* it was named, *the Pulpit,* unlike any pulpit I had seen. The serac was just beyond.

I skied to the right to close the angle, be nearer cover. She followed me. Now I could not see the boot tracks. "We must be nearly up on them. Tracks?"

She shaded her eyes with both hands. The sun was very bright in here. "Can't see. Can't. Yes — to that tall rock."

Keep skis on, or get rid of them? A handicap now in rocky ground at the side of the glacier, but on the serac . . . I kept them on and went cautiously from rock to rock. I was nearing the Pulpit, less than a hundred yards, pole straps on my left wrist. The poles clattered on stone, and I saw movement, ducked. The bullets cracked above my head, a burst. "Okay?"

"Okay," she said.

I saw Max run. Only for an instant, but I saw his left side, green anorak. He ran on while bullets came this way. "Leap-frogging," she said. "If we let them play that game, they'll get us sure — sitting moving ducks. That woman is still at the rock. Keep her head down. Fire a burst or two. I'll go round."

She made a sweep of her hand by the rocks above us, skis off already, she was gone.

I gave the base of the Pulpit a short burst, skied to another rock, crouched again. My finger was closing for a second burst but I stopped it in the nick of time as I saw Dunn running in, and Tanya von Silberbach with the horn. But a slow, almost a lazy flick of Dunn's right hand, a flash, a spinning gleam, and the knife struck home, the horn was dropping, and Dunn piled in. She chopped the other woman twice, heel-handed, one chop across the throat and one chop back, quickest thing I ever saw. I ran in to cover her, to crouch at the Pulpit, inappropriately named. "Where'd you learn to throw a knife and chop like that?" To tell the strict truth, I was strictly shocked.

"In Harry Z. Gilpin's Salvation Army." A real woman, Dunn, still had it in for him. Tanya, dead, looked just as wicked, and no less beautiful once I had set her blond head straight on her broken neck. "Take that thing off the neck if it's there."

I removed the Koala that Tanya was wearing, and straightened her head again. Dunn cleaned her throwing knife in the snow.

"My turn," I said. "You keep out of this. Don't come down the serac until Rudi gets here. Got it?"

"Got it," she said. There was no more fight in Mary Dunn. She walked away, and sat, and cried. She had earned a good cry, I rather thought.

I lay down and edged to the lip of the serac. It was not quite vertical, but it was bad enough, great blocks of ice, colorless ice, green ice, white bridges over blue-green depths. No sign of Max. He must be somewhere in that icefall. But I must know where, or I would be what Dunn called a sitting moving duck. To pick a way down would be hard enough. "Max!" I called.

"Well, if it isn't Ambler." On the left, quite far down in a petrified tumble of ice.

"Come out with your hands up. I've got you covered." Hands up or shooting, I would drill him dead.

He laughed. It was not the whicker of a distant horse. It was a big common laugh.

But I saw a way. I could get down the right, take a long traverse, a diagonal, covered all the way across. And someone else had been, old ski tracks here and there, over this ice bridge, over the next. Skis spread a man's weight. Where other skis had been, there I should follow.

I made that first traverse. The crevasses were not nice at all; bridges a foot wide above green depths, and no one holding me on a rope. It was too broken to be terrifying quite like a cliff, but suddenly I felt myself again at that cliff, again at that cliff, must sit down, not endurable.

But I got over it, and kick-turned to make the traverse back. It was not difficult, with big ice, great blocks of ice below me, and each crevasse an immediate problem, now a corner to negotiate, and then, now, here, an open crevasse, no bridge, hole gaping at me. I fell to save myself from it, and that saved me from Max Vyan's burst of fire. He had moved. How soft was my head not to know that he would? He was not over on the left at all, but straight below me.

Then, while my ears still sang from a shower of bullets splintering ice above my head, I heard a quite different sound, a different small crack, a collapse of ice, and one call from him, a clatter; then one more call, much fainter. I did not hear the second call over the steep surface of the serac, but from down inside the open crevasse below me here.

It was very difficult. I could not turn round, so had to take off my skis, precious skis, climb back from that chasm in the ice, skis on again, so tired, try another way; and the other way brought me to Max Vyan's tommy gun beside the hole where he had fallen. "Max!"

"Here, Ambler." His voice was weak and a long way down. I shaded my eyes to see down there, green into darkness, and I saw him, wedged in ice, aiming a pistol at me. I moved my head just the fortunate half second soon enough.

I had a large account to square with him, perhaps larger than his account to square with me, I do not know, how would I ever know?

"Will you do me a favor, Ambler?"

"A favor? Christ!"

"Take old Pluto for a walk. Go for a walk with Pluto to the river. I don't think suburbia even with his old friend Ambler is quite the thing for him. Will you do that for us?"

"Yes," I said. "I will."

"Tanya dead?"

"Yes.'"

"Good riddance. Did your girl kill her?"

"Yes."

"And she disarmed Excalibur?"

"Yes."

"And got out of that car in the river?"

"Yes."

"Quite a versatile wench."

"Yes."

"And you took that bauble off Alexis?"

"Yes." I lay back from the hole and pushed the tommy gun in, about twenty left to spray Max Vyan. "Any other questions?"

But he laughed, a big common laugh again, and it boomed in there. "No," he said. "I think that sews things up."

The bullet did not come in this direction. I heard a drip, a drip, but that soon stopped; and when I peered down, I saw that he was dead, wedged not untidily, and dead. He was sane, you know, before he shot himself — tried to shoot me, patronized me, and then shot himself — in character.

I threw in the tommy guns and kept the pistol. Then I went down the rest of the serac. Rudi Viereck shouted to me from above to wait — he was bringing Mary on a rope. But I did not feel like waiting.

After the serac, it was the same smooth hissing on sugar snow, running tranquilly on and on until I reached the messy run-out of the glacier, the moraine. There I left my skis. I was finished with skiing for another year, I left them and I walked, thinking as predictably as usual, thinking about the bride's body, wasn't it, preserved in ice, coming out young to the dotard bridegroom, did Mason write that story? Certainly not about Tanya von Silberbach.

Soon the valley widened, and I passed the kennels of the Alpenheide dogs, no dogs in evidence.

And so to Schloss Alpenheide, which was buzzing with soldiers, police and security types. They tried to stop me, but that was the wrong morning to try to stop me. The household staff was corraled in the drawing room. The place buzzed particularly about one immediate problem, which was the ferocious dog, at present in Max Vyan's bedroom. "Ah, here is Mr. Ambler," said fat old butler Burton. "Pluto is very fond of Mr. Ambler."

I told them to get everyone out of sight; then Burton showed me the way to Max's bedroom, and wobbled off himself. The dog snarled in there, it kept on snarling. I did not expect Pluto to like me now, and if he did not, some lethal gas or some cool man with a tommy gun would be required.

"Pluto," I said. "Me, Pluto. Harry Ambler." He stopped snarling, but he growled, and growled again, and I went on talking to him until he rumbled a greeting, I thought it was his greeting rumble. "Want a walk, Pluto boy?" Now he whined.

Pluto and I walked together through Schloss Alpenheide, across the courtyard and the drawbridge, down the hill and along the road that led to the river. He was quiet, my hand on his collar, his head against me. When we got to the river, we sat for a while on a jutting rock, watching the milky river storm below us. I do not know whether Pluto knew. He had not spoken nor had I all the way from the house to here. He did not move, did not even turn his true great head when I stood and shot him. Pluto fell into the river. So that was that favor done, one thing in which I had not failed anyone but Pluto.

The valley had seemed unreal to me from the beginning. It still felt unreal, but so did I. "What about Fernandel?" I said to Dominic.

"Fernandel escaped with cuts and fractures." He did not look at me. "Herr Vyan, sir?"

"Max Vyan is dead."

Now Dominic looked once at me. "So you have completed your mission, Mr. Ambler." He turned away, and I went up to bed. *That isn't fair*, we used to say on rare occasions when we were young, a boy's ultimate plaint. But perhaps it was fair enough.

POST MORTEM

After a shave, a bath, a bite, I disconnected the telephone and went to sleep for untroubled hours. It was a nice change from recent experience to be wooed from slumber by modest knockings on the door; they came, they stopped, more humble knocks. "Come in."

"Shall I draw the curtains?"

"Do."

"Would you like a nice strong dish of tea?"

"Sure thing." While that was being prepared, I looked out of my bedroom windows at the three sunlit peaks, the Teufelsspitzen, kindly mountains — then along the valley by faded stucco and old dark wood over meadows to Schloss Alpenheide in the afternoon.

"Good tea." Australian quality, trust Dunn. "Have a seat."

"I'll get a chair." The end of my bed had been good enough before, but now she hauled in a chair. Dunn wore a splashy dress in all sorts of greens and reds and blues, vivid as Gauguin. "Here's a telegram from Sir Conrad."

AMBLER DUNN KRONENHOF ALPENHEIDE GOOD JOB EXPECT YOU

LATE LUNCHEON TOMORROW STOP SOME GOLF AFTERNOON IF FIT
CAB.

"We can't get there for lunch — impossible."

"But excuse me, Ambler, by air it's easy. I ordered a car
ferry from Geneva. Will you be fit for golf?"

"A few holes, perhaps. Will you?"

"I loathe the game. Golf is for juveniles in my opinion."

"Including Sir Conrad?"

"As a golfer, yes. But, Ambler, I don't really think
you should. You look so peaky and you've lost a lot of weight."

"What's a bit of weight? You're thinner too — I mean the
face mostly, is what I mean." The cheeks were hollower, the
tribal scratches were almost healed. "The rest of you looks
much the same." Dunn left the room. She seemed nervous,
and soon returned with a small bowl, cotton wool and hydro-
gen peroxide. "That cut on your head. May I try to wash it?"

"That's awfully nice of you, but please don't bother."

"No bother." The water was warm, the touch feather-light.
"Must just be patient."

"I am being patient, dammit."

"I meant me be patient. The hairs are so matted. One thing
Rudi and I were discussing. May I ask you now?"

"Go ahead."

"To get Mr. Vyan's body out would be difficult, and terribly
dangerous with the shifts of ice. So we wondered if you would
agree to that . . . that woman's corpse being heaved in too,
and then a few sticks of dynamite to seal the job, if you approve."

There was a far crrumph, a distant rumble. "What was
that?"

"The dynamite."

"I approve. Thanks for asking me."

"Not at all. Is your head very sore?"

"Medium aches. May I ask you something?"

"Oh, yes." Dunn drew in breath. "Ask anything."

"About the gorge — was it ghastly?"

"Yes, it was pretty much so, yes. They pushed me off like you pushed Dorion, but going the other way. I don't remember much except a whale of a splash, the window, seatbelt, out — gosh, it was cold — and then I stumbled and fumbled down forever until I climbed and hopped a lift to Aigle. Then I got through to Sir Conrad in the small hours, and Sir Conrad raised the skyscraper roof with Washington and Moscow who put absolutely Laser heat on Switzerland, and that's the story."

"But why did they let you disarm the thing and rescue me, not that I'm not most awfully grateful?"

"Because I know those ultimate precision tools — a sideline of ours — but really because I was your case-manager, as it were, I was, I mean I were, it was my duty, I considered."

"Well, thanks. Do you think you hit your head when you fell into the gorge — some slight concussion?"

"I don't think so. Why do you ask?"

"Oh, nothing."

"There now. That's every single hair all separated."

"Are you a trained nurse too as well as everything?"

"No, my only nursing was once being stand-in Nanny to another little boy, rich people, they were Pitt Street farmers. It's a huge big cut, but healing nicely. You must have a cranium like some rhino, Ambler."

"Well, thanks."

"I have super ointment in my room for bruises. Could I rub it on those awful whip marks on your cheeks? They'll be gone by morning, that I promise."

"Well, thanks."

That soothing salve applied, there were loud knocks on my bedroom door, not modest knocks as Dunn's had been, rattled handle and rude thumps.

"I locked your door while you were asleep." She went into the sitting room, some conversation, she came back. "It's the Press. They're here in shoals. I've been stalling them all day."

"Tell the Press to take a running jump. I won't see 'em, final, got it?"

"Got it . . ."

"That's the daily papers, Ambler, fixed; but there are still the world magazines."

"What magazines?"

"*Look, Life, Stern, Paris Match.*"

"Tell 'em to take a running jump."

"But, Ambler — I even checked this with Sir Conrad while you were asleep. My own lips are sealed, of course, but if you make no mention of Intersec, it's quite all right, Sir Conrad says."

"I don't care a damn what Sir Conrad says."

"I understand, but please don't be cross. Oh, I know you've been through more than any mortal man could bear. But there's a fortune in it, do you realize? They'll bid one another up to almost anything at all — a hundred thousand anyway."

"Tell 'em to take a running jump. Tell 'em in no uncertain terms." I was not making money out of Max Vyan, not that kind of bastard money, anyway. I heard Dunn tell them in no uncertain terms, but when she came back she was her new humble self, my handmaiden with a touch of faithful Nanny. "I like you in that dress. It suits your dusky locks, like Minnehaha."

"Thank you," she said, the animal glow of Dunn when blushing but never a smile, those full wide lips pressed together as in pain. I was sure she must have slight concussion.

"I think you're the one who should be lying here," I said, and Dunn shot out, so restless, no companion for a chap in my condition. Then it was the telephone next door.

"Hello. Oh yes, Mr. Gilpin, good afternoon. He's had a lovely sleep, but he does seem very tired and thin, and sometimes . . . well . . . Yes, if you must ask, I have. I've turned it until I'm blue in the bloody face. Certainly I'll ask him.

"Will you speak to that old snake?"

"Plug it in," I said. "Hello."

"Young Harry, my congratulations. A splendid job by a matchless team. Indeed, I fancy that together you have saved humanity for what it's worth, not much, but Gloria is at my elbow, chiding me for cynicism, and she sends her love."

"Same here," I said.

"Tell me, my boy, I do not wish to seem intrusive, but I have your welfare much at heart — are you achieving some modus vivendi with Mary Dunn — are you, despite every provocation, turning the patient other cheek?"

"Beat it, would you," I said to Dunn. "Shut the door. Hang up the telephone."

"Oh, I say, young Harry, you do sound rather strict."

The other telephone was hung. "Fact is, I'm worried. Dunn isn't like the real article at all, no bite in her, and makes no sense at times. What I'm afraid of is some slight concussion from her fall into that gorge. She's been through hell, you know. I wonder, should I get a doctor? What would you advise?"

"Pray calm yourself while I marshal thought. Now first, I would carefully observe the patient. As to calling a physician — most certainly if symptoms do not soon abate. But do give

Dame Nature the chance to be her own physician. I implore you to be kindly, indulge every whim. Under no circumstances use the rough edge of your tongue, as I heard just now."

"Okay, I'll do my best."

"By the way, although I had no inkling of concussion, it did occur to me that the poor girl might be a touch under the weather after the fearful strains and dangers of these days, and I have therefore taken the liberty of sending my chauffeur over with some grapes — I dispatched my Jet Galaxy to Morocco for an extra few this morning as soon as the wonderful news came through. They should be arriving any minute now."

"That's good of you. Dunn fairly dotes on 'em, or did."

"May I make a suggestion?"

"Do."

"Why not, as tentative concussion therapy, put Dunn to bed with grapes?"

"Well, I dunno. If I put Dunn to bed with grapes, she can't look after me. As good as a Nanny, she really is."

"Yes, a problem there. One cannot nurse one's Nanny and have one's Nanny too. But one last word — I am alone here now — do I have your private ear?"

"I can hear her talking, it's the grapes arriving, yes?"

"In that other matter, to which I have given long and earnest thought, it is my conviction that the eternal verities should be respected. I make this suggestion as practical politics, not from ethical grounds or such tommyrot. Make a clean breast of it is my advice. Then, who knows, we might work something out."

"Thanks, Harry. Well, I'll have to see. The truth is Dunn's got me so bothered, I haven't had much time to think."

"Bless you, my boy. Patience, remember, at all costs, patience."

"I say, Dunn, are you there?"

She came at a run, with golden grapes. "Yes, Ambler. Anything I can do? Want a grape?"

"No, thanks, I'll watch you eat 'em." This she was already doing. Pop — one succulent squish inside — two chews — one swallow. "Quite delicious." Pop and so on.

"He sent his Jet Galaxy to Morocco for them as soon as he heard the news that you were safe."

"That's the sort of thing that makes communists," she said, in popped a grape. "Don't you agree?"

"Yes, yes. A kindly thought, though, wasn't it?"

"Well, I suppose so, but Mr. Gilpin can certainly afford it; and I would never trust his motives."

I watched grapes disappear at the compulsive rate of knots, poor girl, she did look wan. "I've been meaning to ask you: What's the news of Fernandel?"

"He jumped clear — a miraculous escape from death. I was wondering, Ambler, if you could spare me for just half an hour, could I go and see poor Fernandel, laid up?"

Indulge every whim. "Why, certainly, of course, by all means, do. What are his injuries?"

"He broke his left leg once, and his right arm twice, and many cuts from broken glass."

Which should suffice to limit the activities of even Fernandel. "Well, I'm glad to hear it," I said heartily.

The last grape gone, she gazed at me with dark blue eyes in sorrowful reproach. "I know you have to be like that," she said. "All the real killers are. You have to be to do the things you do and say cold-bloodedly with ice-cold heart, I'm not complaining. May I get you a whisky and soda before I go?"

"No, thanks. Remember me to Fernandel."

"Try and have another little sleep."

"Try not to . . ."

"Try not to *what?* Tell me, Ambler, please."

"Oh, nothing." I closed my eyes. I had been going to say to her: *Try not to drink too much.* But that might be unkind, a reminder of her weakness. She was gone just as I remembered that drinking was the worst thing for concussion. This real killer lay and saw that Mary Dunn throw that knife with that lazy flick of wrist, and then pile in to do what she had sworn to do, with those bare hands kill Tanya von Silberbach — chop, heel-handed, chop. I wondered where Dunn had taken training, at some Intersec Academy, no doubt. You know, I thought . . . Why were my thoughts so alarming still? You know, that humility might well be but one facet of some slight concussion — gentle Nanny; then chop-chop. I dozed again. I was uneasy in my doze.

When I awoke, it was to darkness here, and to a monologue next door: ". . . That print — that painting, oh, it's good art, I quite agree, by Manet, *Dejeuner sur l'Herbe,* but to me it simply exemplifies poor woman at the hands of man. Look at them, a couple of dandies in frock coats — yes, Dominic, dressed for all the world like you — lolling in full fig with one poor girl entirely figless, and another beyond, well on the way to be . . ."

I put on my dressing gown. Dunn had been drinking.

"Ah but no, dear Mary, no, it is the very opposite — it is our most humble reverence for Eve in all her glory."

"Be quiet, Fernandel, I'm doing the talking here, and what I'm saying is, it's typical of man's contempt for us, you're all the same — licentious prigs and lecherous stuffed shirts. And you know the worst of all? Well, I'll tell you who, it's Harry . . ."

I went in.

"S'Harry," she said. "Harry Zee Gilpin, he's the worst."

The occupants of my sitting room were Fernandel in a wheel-chair, Dominic in his frock coat, and Dunn in her Gauguin dress. The last named shot to their feet. "I think you're unfair to old Harry Gilpin, a most moral chap. Surely there's nothing wrong in a touch of sex about a man's attitude toward his wife. I mean, how otherwise can our society survive?"

"I didn't quite mean it," she said. "I sort of got muddled again, again. It's a sort of ambivalence in my feelings." Dunn put some of my vodka into my dunkelbier and drank it down.

"That's the worst thing for concussion."

"But, Mary, do you have concussion?"

"He thinks I have, Fernandel. I don't know what's come over him." Dunn left my sitting room for her bedroom.

"Old Harry, you are sick?"

"Tired," I said. "Worn out, fast on the mend, and I wish you wouldn't ply that girl with drink."

"But I did not, Harry. This I promise you. I offered black currant juice and ginger ale, but she insisted on my Double Bass. I myself, so mummified with casts and bandages, am in no condition to contest her will or impose my own, indeed."

"Mr. Ambler, sir, my duties call me. But first I apologize for an unfortunate remark this morning. I was grieved at the death of our Patron, although a blessing, poor Herr Vyan. But I have since heard from Miss Dunn herself of your terrible sufferings, your matchless valor . . ."

"My matchless valor, my bloody foot. I was scared palpitating on that ledge, and well Dunn knows it."

"Oh dear, I can't just seem to say anything that's right." Poor humble Dunn was back in the doorway.

"And so, lady and gentleman, Miss Dunn and Fernandel, I

now ask you to join me in a toast to a real gentleman of the real old school — Mr. Harry Ambler."

They drank, but Dunn choked on it, she fled again.

Dominic took his leave. I gave myself a whisky and soda.

"This Mary Dunn, she is so marvelous, so passionate and so amusing, brave as a lioness and with such a figure, oh la! la! — and to you is all the luck, Old Harry, to be traveling to England with this Mary Dunn tomorrow."

"She worries me, not like herself at all. Well, perhaps a good night's rest will do the trick. I tell you what, Fernandel, why not have dinner with her? Dunn likes you very much, keeps saying so, in fact tends to be a crashing bore about it. Try to cheer her up. Where are you, Dunn?"

"Here, Ambler."

"Off you go now. I shall have some dinner in my room."

Dunn wheeled her admirer along the corridor. I peeked. It was true about her figure, mini-skirted, I dared to look. "A real gentleman," Dunn said. "Of the real old school," said Fernandel. They laughed quite wildly.

It was nearly eleven, and I was drifting yet again to sleep — my capacity for sleep seemed limitless — when I heard her in the sitting room, approach my door, heavy breathing, at it again, I feared, a slave to the bottle at age twenty-six. And the mood? Was it to be Nanny or chop-chop? "That you, Dunn?"

"Me, Ambler, yes." The mood was not aggressive, the speech a little slurred.

"What is it?"

"I was only just wondering if I could do anything, like bathe your head again, or tuck you in or anything at all."

"That's most awfully kind of you, but I am tucked. Now off you go and have a good night's sleep, that's what you need."

"But I'm not sleepy."

"There's a good girl, off you go."

"Not good," she muttered. "Bad through 'n' through 'n' simply achin' to be badder."

"Don't forget the aspirins."

"How many, Ambler?"

"Three should suffice, Dunn. Now, good night." I barked the *good night* a bit. If Dunn thought all men were licentious prigs and lecherous stuffed shirts, then Dunn could think again.

We got away by eight, farewell to Alpenheide, and I meant *adieu*. I drove to the gorge, but then I could not stand the heights.

"Poor Ambler," she said, taking over. "I know it's the most appalling thing — I've seen other people simply frozen with it. Shut your eyes, and I'll go slowly, you can trust me."

"I know," I said. "I could trust you with almost anything."

She sighed, it was that most feminine defenseless sigh. But she drove the Caramba like a man, as well as I drove it myself. "Would you like to take her now?" she asked when my eyes were open, no more precipices.

"You drive like a man. In fact, you're like a man all round. Keep on."

We were early at Geneva, so we parked at the Hotel de la Paix. Dunn went to look at shops, and I to see Monsieur Vaillancourt at the Banque de la Fédération. I was ushered immediately to the presence. He spoke of the tragedy of Max's death with Tanya von Silberbach — an accident on the Alpenheide Glacier was the press report so far. And then, rather diffidently, he raised the question of that envelope which, at Max Vyan's request, had been kept separate from his other papers, in Monsieur Vaillancourt's own safe. And as Mr. Vyan's old friend and comrade in arms . . . Vaillancourt knew somehow that there was something about that envelope.

"I suggest we burn it here and now if you'll let me take the responsibility."

"But certainly," he said, trusting me. By this time you might begin to ponder why some people seem to trust me. We burned that envelope in his office fireplace. "I have wondered . . ."

"Yes?"

"Forgive me, but I have wondered often — did you safely find the meadow with the jonquils for your picnic on that glorious day of early spring with your especial friend?"

"Yes, indeed. A perfect place, and thank you very much again. Actually, she is flying to England with me now this morning. I have just one little thing to do before I leave Geneva. Would you happen to know of a good jeweler — not a big shop, I mean, but a really reliable man in, for example, diamonds?"

"Ah, but most certainly there is such a man, perhaps the best in all Switzerland, a true artist and very moderate — Gustave Charbonneau, a mere stone's throw from us here. May it be my pleasure to telephone him?"

"You're very kind," I said, soon parted from Monsieur Vaillancourt, called upon Monsieur Charbonneau, and returned to the hotel to find Mademoiselle Dunn pacing the handsome foyer.

"I thought you were never coming. I thought you'd had a fainting spell or something. Are you sure you're quite all right?"

"Feel fine, thanks. What about yourself?"

"Oh, me." She was wearing the same mustardy-colored coat and skirt.

"You had that outfit on the day you shanghaied me down to Kent," I remarked en route to Geneva Airport. "Lotta things happened since then, eh, Dunn?"

"Yes, Ambler, and I wish they hadn't, none."

"This flying — gives me the willies, I must admit."

"I've been worrying about that — perhaps if you just close your eyes like in the mountains; or I could pick up tranquilizers at the airport, should I?"

"Never had one. Wouldn't dare."

But it transpired that flying did not frighten me. "You know, Dunn," I said when we had reached cruising height, the Caramba in its compartment, and us in ours, "you look a bit washed out to me, dark circles and pinched lines, I mean."

"I never slept a wink all night, not one, I just couldn't stop thinking, not at all."

"Sleep now, then. Have a lovely snooze."

"You're so good to me when all I deserve is plain abuse."

I patted the poor girl's shoulder. "You've got me plain baffled, Dunn. I can't make head nor tail of you."

"You pat me so kindly like as if I was some little bitch — and that's what I am, a proper female bastard."

"Oh, don't say that," I said. "Tut-tut."

I escaped Dunn to visit the pilots — decent chaps, like most of us. I stayed with them all the way over France, and we dropped off height across the Channel to those well-known cliffs, soon now to land at the private airfield of Sir Conrad Brock.

Mary Dunn was sleeping. She looked no happier, asleep. "Time to wake up," I said.

"Yes, Sir Conrad. Oh dear, how typical, I am so sorry."

"Dunn!"

"Yes, Ambler?"

"Couldn't you just blow off at me for once?"

"Shouldn't, wouldn't, simply couldn't."

Brock was there in person, with a tame Customs Officer, a mere formality, and we were through, being driven in the Number One Brock car, the black Mercedes, length of a medium house. Halcombe looked very fine, the swans on the lake, the golf course manicured, the spring flowers everywhere, that Scotch butler at the door, all ultra smart and perhaps slightly non-U except Sir Conrad Brock himself in a terrible tweed jacket and patched corduroys, face scored and chapped old leather, eyes bloodshot, hands like muttons, genuine article from down below.

There were the three of us at lunch, during which I reported my end of things, and Mary Dunn recounted hers in downcast monotone.

"A crackerjack job," said Brock. "Proud of both of you. But whassamatter, Mary, not feeling up to scratch?"

"She didn't sleep a wink last night."

"I got pie-eyed last night, Sir Conrad, if you want to know."

That seemed to surprise him, set him back, he hummed and hawed, knotted bushy brows, and then said: "So you blew off steam. Good on ya, Mary."

"Oh, do shut up, Sir Conrad."

"There, there," he said, looking mighty puzzled, and turned to me. "What about that game of golf? Sure you're fit for it?"

"Nine holes, okay?"

"Nine holes, it is. What's your handicap?"

"I'm four at the R and A. What's yours?"

"I'm four at the R and A. Play level?"

"Sure thing, if I can borrow decent clubs and spikes."

"Got all that, Spalding Elite, Arnie Palmer, Jack Nicklaus Autographed, take your pick, decent enough, would do?"

"Do fine. What we we going to play for?"

He considered me. "That four handicap — important point."

"They put me at it after the Spring Medal last year. Fair enough?"

"Mine after the Calcutta Cup last Autumn Meeting, fair enough. Funny we never met up at St. Andrews."

"I don't play much."

"Nor me, no time. You like a gamble?"

"Betcher life I do."

"Makes it worth a bloke's while to pull his finger out, that's what I like, meat and drink to me."

"Same here."

"Come on, then. Name the stakes, young fella."

"I tell you what. Give me some paper and an envelope. I'll write down the stakes, and Dunn can hold 'em."

"Fair enough, our Mary holds the stakes. You walkin' round with us, Beautiful?"

"Don't call me beautiful, Sir Conrad, please, goddammit, and you know my views on golf."

"Have a nice kip, then, Mary child." We went into the library where I wrote out the stakes, sealed them and handed the envelope to Dunn, who sighed. "The best of luck, Ambler," she said to me. "McVitie will fit you out."

I went to the cloakroom to choose a set of Spalding Elite, a pair of spikes. "Watch he doesna pu' the woo'"? Oh, pull the wool. "Sir Conrad's a fair bugger fer the gamesmanship. And the last hole's the worrst, I'm tellin' ye."

"Thanks for the tip," I said, warming to the bluff McVitie.

Equipped with golf carts, Sir Conrad Brock and I skirted

the lake. He explained the topography of the course, which ran down the big park, a short hole across, and back again. "Home hole's a real tester," he said. "Have to carry the lake." He threw some bread. "I like matey swans about the place," he said as we proceeded to the first tee.

It was soon evident that this man Brock would be hard to beat. With a wide stance and a half-swing, he hit the ball not far, but on the button, what McVitie might call a pawky gowfer. However, despite residual aches and pains, my eye was clear that afternoon. It had better be, which usually does the best clearing job on me. There was little conversation and no gamesmanship apparent. In fact, he was generous with short putts. "Can't get over our Mary," he muttered at the fourth. "Most respectful always, hangs on my every bloody stupid word. Bit my head off."

"I find it's just the opposite. No punch to her."

"When it start?"

"Just yesterday. Yes, in earnest yesterday when the job was done." I hit a lovely four iron, with a touch of draw, sank my putt for a birdie, three, all square.

"Been a tough case for her," he said at the sixth, and laid it stone-dead from a bunker, now one-up on me. "Hardest she was ever on, I think. Found you none to easy to manage at times. But I said to her: *Mary,* I said. *Gotta give a bloke like that his bleedin' head a bit. Ambler's a different jackass from the common run of agent.*"

"Well, thanks," I said. The seventh was four hundred and seventy. I got up with a drive and a three wood, down in two putts to square the match.

"Tired," he said at the eighth. "Plain tuckered-out is what she must be. And this drinking, it worries me. I never saw our Mary imbibe more than what you might call merry social."

"If you want to know, I think the fault is yours — you work her sixteen hours a day on your Brock Enterprises, Electronics Wool and Sugar and all the rest of it; then you take her slam-bang from that into mortal danger with Intersec. Can you wonder if the bottle beckons? And no holidays, she says."

"Goddammit," he said. "I try to make her take 'em, she won't."

I did not give him the short putt, and he missed it, growled, and that brought us to the ninth, all even. The tee was on a small promontory jutting into the lake, the distance a hundred and seventy yards, almost all over water, the green sloping this way, bunkered on all sides, a most testing golf hole.

I teed my ball. Brock threw a few morsels of bread to the swans nearby. I swung back true and easy as something hissing white loomed up. I hit the ball crisply, and was at once attacked by the Cob, the male mute swan. I routed it with my Number Six. My ball rolled round the green to come to rest beside the pin. Mary Dunn stood on the steps of Halcombe Manor.

"Cool bastard, ain't ya?" said Sir Conrad Brock with deep admiration, guffawed most heartily, and put his in a bunker.

Thus it was, with a birdie two and even fours, not too bad for a chap who had recently had the rough end of the stick — that I pipped old Brock.

"You cheated, Sir Conrad. I saw you deliberately entice that swan to the attack. He often does, and in my book it's a horrid dirty trick. Well done, Ambler. Congratulations!" Dunn entered the house.

"Just my bit of fun," he said. "I always give 'em another shot. Well, thanks for the game, a worthy winner." We shook hands. A splendid old scoundrel, Conrad Angus Brock, CAB-INTERSEC, at whose dictate both Washington and Moscow trembled.

"But our Mary, dunno what to make of her, no sense of humor, gives me hell. Come on in, Harry."

Tea awaited us in the library, dispensed by Dunn. There were Patum Peperium sandwiches, a real gentleman's favorite relish. "Where's that envelope?" said Brock. "Best man won, I'll pay my debts."

Dunn drew the envelope from her purse and opened it, withdrew the paper, stared.

"Read it to us, Mary."

"*I will play you for a half-share in the real Koala Diamond.* What real Koala Diamond?"

"Well, there's this one," I said, producing the necklace from my trouser pocket. "Had it checked this morning in Geneva. The baguettes are real, the big stone's a fake, a remarkable fake, he said, never seen anything like it, but the refractive index is wrong, two point one in sodium light, can't be a diamond."

"But what real Koala Diamond do you mean?"

"I mean the one I took off the body of Alexis, damned nearly got killed in that avalanche, gave it to Harry Gilpin for safe-keeping at the Palace in Gstaad."

Dunn glared at me, nostrils arching. "You bloody bludger," she said to me.

"Now, look, Mary, that won't do. That's the worst insult you can offer in Our Country. Take it back at once."

"You bloody bludger," she said to me.

"Call a bloke like Harry a bloody . . . I can't even say it — you take it back, young Mary."

"I won't take it back, Sir Conrad, shut your trap."

"Don't worry," I said to Conrad Brock. "It's music to my ears."

"Half-shares seem fair enough," the great man mused. "I

got my million, didn't I? Here, explain what happened, you old bastard Harry, and what you have in mind."

So I explained the matter while Dunn seethed behind the silver teapot. "I told you too," I said. "Or I told Max Vyan while you were working on that thing in the cave. I thought you knew. I thought that was one reason for your strange behavior. Half-shares is what I thought, between us, if okay with you."

"I wouldn't touch that Koala with the back end of a barge pole."

"Not asking you to. Harry Zee wants to give it to Gloria in September."

She laughed. It was quite a lovely thing for me. "You're hopeless, Ambler," said Mary Dunn.

"In future I am never Ambler, I am Harry, got it, Mary Love?"

"Yes, Harry Love."

"Our Mary's taking some holidays," said that splendid old rascal, Conrad Brock. "Back in Our Country. See to it, will you, Harry? Now I have Intersec business to attend to, a new job coming up."

He left us in the library. So my story ends with a beginning.

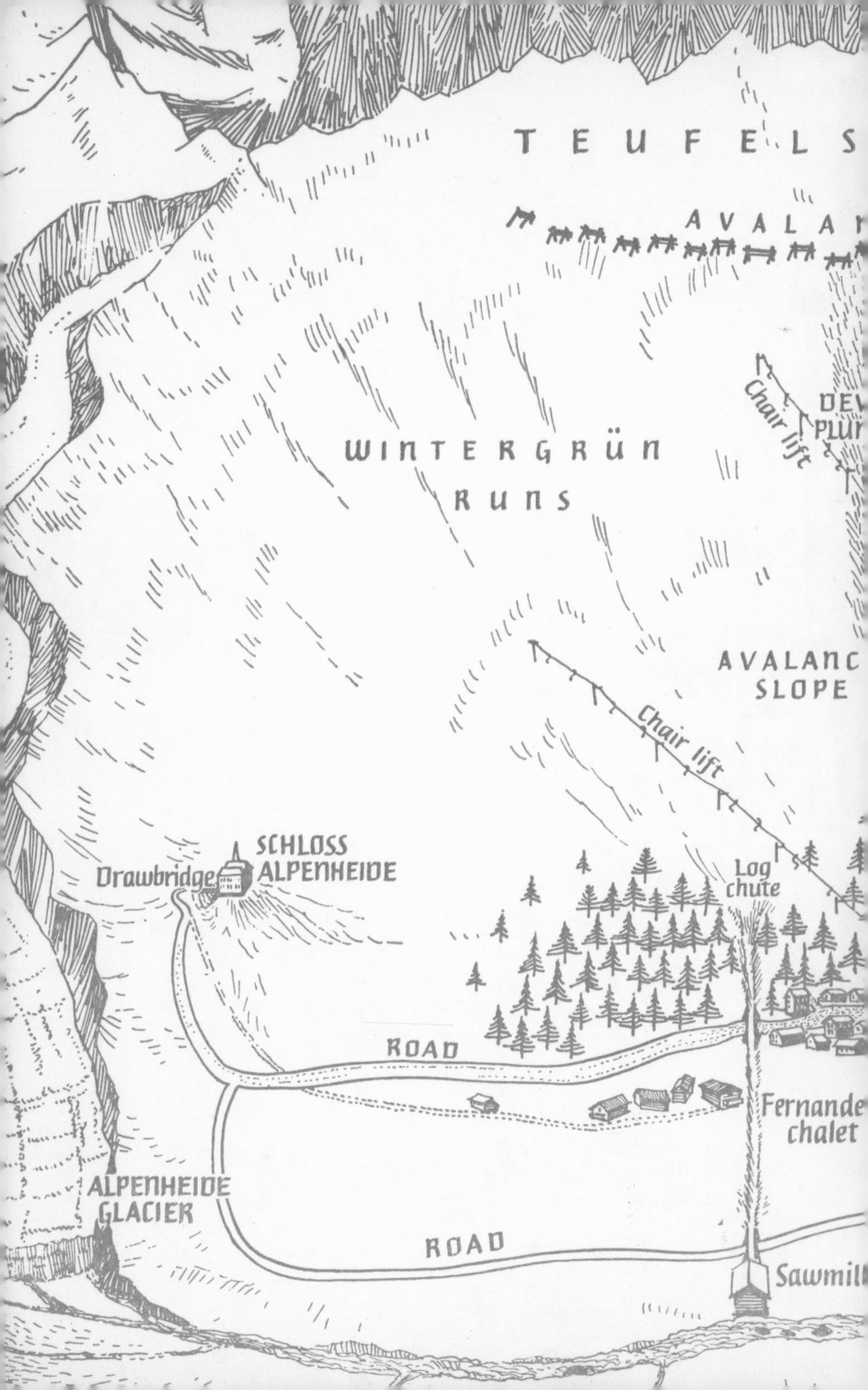
TEUFELS
AVALA
DEV
PLU
Chair lift
WINTERGRÜN
RUNS
AVALANC
SLOPE
Chair lift
SCHLOSS
ALPENHEIDE
Drawbridge
Log
chute
ROAD
Fernande
chalet
ALPENHEIDE
GLACIER
ROAD
Sawmill